B ̶ ̶ ̶MING
PATH

BOOK ONE

BLOSSOMING PATH

BOOK ONE

Carlos Calma

Podium

In loving memory of Max,
who taught me that there's nothing wrong with
enjoying a nap on a hot summer's day.
Or any day, really.

Cover design by Kongsi

ISBN: 978-1-0394-8856-4

Published in 2025 by Podium Publishing
www.podiumentertainment.com

Podium

BLOSSOMING PATH

BOOK ONE

CHAPTER ONE

Descent of the Heavenly Interface

People called it the Day of Awakening.

Cultivators of higher order said it was the Celestial Convergence, an event that brought the world as a whole closer to the heavens.

From the lowliest mortals living on the Tranquil Breeze Coast to the ancient Spirit Beasts of the Celestial Summit Plateau, everyone received the same message. All could see an array of words and understand their meaning and intent, regardless of their ability to perceive language.

WE ILLUMINATE THE PATH TO ASCENSION.

A mysterious magic that called itself the Heavenly Interface became a part of every entity's life from then on.

The system within the Heavenly Interface was both intuitive and comprehensive, presenting one's cultivation progress in a clear and organized manner. It tracked one's skills, techniques, and breakthroughs while also providing suggestions for improvements and new paths to explore in rare moments.

As for notifications, they were timely and informative, alerting one to crucial moments in their cultivation journey. Whether they were signifying the completion of a skill, the discovery of a technique, or the impending arrival of a breakthrough, the notifications alerted all who used the Heavenly Interface of their progress and potential pitfalls.

The Heavenly Interface served as both a compass and a chronicle, guiding everyone on their individual cultivation path while documenting their achievements and experiences.

From there, the continent underwent a seismic shift.

Atop the Pillar of Ascension, a stone column that pierced the heavens and towered above the Heaven's Pillar Sect, a man wearing simple white clothing opened his eyes, mild surprise coloring his face. The jade pendant around his neck glowed dimly as he awoke. Elder Li looked over the message box, stroking his beard and humming lightly.

Responding to his mental command, the Heavenly Interface showed him a variety of information, from the stage of cultivation he was at to the skills he had at his disposal. It only took a few seconds to adjust to the unique magic and its controls, but Elder Li still maintained a sense of caution and wonderment.

It wasn't often that the Sect Leader of the Heaven's Pillar Sect was caught off guard.

"How curious! Heavenly Interface, is it?" He searched his mind, going back centuries to try to recall anything like this magic to no avail. "Most frightening. It knows all about me, down to the last skill I possess."

Having his techniques, cultivation, and titles all displayed so prominently brought equal amounts worry and eagerness. Looking down three hundred li below to where the sect was, he could see commotion in the usually tranquil grounds. Even through the clouds and snow, the man saw with such clarity, it was as though he was right there by the gardens with the disciples and other elders. Elder Li guessed the events were interlinked in some way and decided to rise from his seated position.

"It's been terribly long since I last went down. I wonder what Junior Brother Huang has been up to these past few decades . . ." he mumbled to himself airily. The jade pendant glittered primly, unaffected by the harsh winds and below-freezing temperatures where the elder cultivated with ease.

In the same way, with the Heavenly Interface's appearance many old monsters rose from their slumber and began to move.

Elsewhere, in the depths of the Jade Mist Valley, a group huddled together in quiet astonishment at the message before them. They were dirty and haggard, and many of them possessed weapons of questionable quality. They had broken from their usual routine of raiding caravans down the trade routes.

"Leader Wei, it's not a trick, is it?" one of them said, turning to their superior with uncertainty and hope in their eyes.

A man with a scarred upper lip and short brown hair looked intensely at the Heavenly Interface. His face broke out into a smile, like a child who had found a new toy to play with. Wei's heart wanted to leap out of his chest.

He spoke to the group, commanding their attention. "This is no trick." His qi leaked out slightly, making the battle-hardened bandits shiver in fear. "This is an *opportunity*."

"But if everybody has it . . ." one of them spoke hesitantly. He seemed reproachful of the Heavenly Interface, as if thinking about its implications for the world.

"So what if everyone does? We can use it better. This tool, it'll be what takes us from mountain bandits to something bigger." Leader Wei's enthusiasm was palpable. Even the men who enjoyed the system's clear and crisp view of their cultivation progress didn't understand why he was so overjoyed.

"If we use this right, that Jade Mist Serpent will no longer be a threat to us!" Wei continued. "Think! Can a beast hold a candle to us with this? Our name will spread, and I will cement myself as the Crimson Gale when we separate its head from its body!"

They mulled it over for a second and realized it was true. With the ability to cultivate at a faster pace with the Heavenly Interface's support, defeating the legendary Spirit Beast of Jade Mist Valley wouldn't be a pipe dream.

"Let's not waste any more time! We'll arm ourselves, and once I've reached the peak of the Spirit Ascension stage, that wretched serpent won't stand a chance," Wei said. His laugh echoed over the hills. Leader Wei knew that the Heavenly Interface would be the key to unlocking his full potential.

Together, the Ravaging Tempests hastened their efforts under their leader's guidance. They knew that so long as they followed Leader Wei, they would succeed.

The Emerald Spirit Forest was a vast expanse of lush greenery and mystical energy that drew many cultivators from all over the continent. With an affinity for nature and life energies, the province was home to many Spirit Beasts, perhaps the most famous of them all being the World Tree.

It had stood tall for centuries and witnessed the rise and fall of kingdoms, sects, and empires throughout history. Sometimes it was even the catalyst for such events.

The World Tree was five hundred li in diameter, and it pierced the clouds with ease, seemingly to no end, a colossal monument to the ancient world. Its branches stretched out like the arms of a benevolent deity providing shelter and nourishment to all who sought them out. Its leaves shimmered with a vibrant, otherworldly green. Its roots seemed to hold the very fabric of the province together.

For years it had lain dormant. And in a way, it was for the best. Whispers from the locals claimed that every time it was roused, a major event occurred. Whether it was a boon or disaster, the World Tree's awakening was synonymous with the turning wheels of fate.

So it was no surprise that the Heavenly Interface's descent made the entity stir from its slumber. It was subtle, but the presence could be felt throughout the province. The deep, resonant hum of energy made the Emerald Spirit Forest abuzz with activity.

A connection to the world itself . . . The very essence of cultivation that permeates all living beings . . .

It took some time to absorb the information it saw and felt. The World Tree could feel the emotions, the flourishing sects, and the cities in turmoil. Even the Spirit Beasts that called the Emerald Spirit Forest their home were intrigued by the magic persistently appearing in their vision.

This Heavenly Interface . . . the World Tree intoned. Some beings could hear the ancient one's voice, like a whisper in the back of their head. Cultivators who frequented the area would go on to claim the World Tree was responsible for the Celestial Convergence, hearing its introspection from wherever they were.

It will bridge the gap between mortal and celestial.

It observed the civilians on their land experimenting with the system. Their bewilderment transformed into something more as they realized that the faraway stories of cultivators and defying the heavens weren't as distant anymore.

But it shall also bring chaos and destruction. Those who seek to exploit this power . . .

It knew the power would be used for many good deeds, as well as many evil ones. From mortal to cultivator, those who brimmed with greed and ambition outnumbered those who sought to use the Heavenly Interface for pure reasons.

The energy in the air seemed to thicken as the World Tree processed and interpreted the Heavenly Interface's purpose, as well as its role in the grand scheme of events. A few cultivators who used the branches of the World Tree to meditate suffered as the ancient being gathered its power to swear an ancient oath. Like an avalanche, it was inevitable. The World Tree was far from a being that could be challenged; it was a force of nature given sentience.

I will strike them down myself if it comes to it.

The powerful voice faded not too long afterward. The World Tree knew its time had yet to come. It prepared itself for slumber once again, but it couldn't help but ask one more thing before it fell asleep.

What great force could have brought the Heavenly Interface into existence?

Kai was not pondering the mysteries of the universe, nor was he engaged in an epic battle or deep meditation.

Instead, he was knee-deep in the dirt, tending to his small garden with great care. With a watering can in one hand and a hoe in the other, he whistled a cheerful tune as he watered the plants and removed weeds. His face, tanned slightly by the constant work under the sun, playfully mimicked the exaggerated demeanor and speech of the cultivators in the stories he read daily, and he talked to himself with an air of arrogance and condescension.

"Ha, you dare to encroach upon my territory, little weed? You're courting death!" Kai declared dramatically, plucking a weed from the soil and tossing it aside.

He continued his performance, pretending to be an all-powerful cultivator addressing a lowly junior. "Kneel before me, lowly plant, and kowtow to acknowledge my superiority! Only then shall I bestow upon you the blessings of water and sunlight!"

With a smirk, Kai gently poured water onto the plants, nurturing them with the life-giving liquid. "Heavenly Elixir of Life, descend upon these humble beings and grant them the strength to grow and flourish!"

Little did he know that his life was about to change forever and that he would soon be thrust into a world of celestial beings, monstrous cultivators, and the enigmatic Heavenly Interface.

And so, in the most unassuming and unexpected of circumstances, our story began with Kai, the herbalist who would one day walk the path to greatness in a world forever changed by the rise of the Heavenly Interface.

CHAPTER TWO

Dreaming Gardener Kai

A re you talking to the plants again?" a feminine voice said from behind me. I turned to see who it was.

She stood a short distance away, just past the fence, and was clearly holding in a laugh. She had her hair styled in a loose braid that dropped past her shoulders and soft, rounded facial features. I flushed lightly upon being caught mimicking the young master act I had been working so hard to perfect.

Lan-Yin's warm brown eyes looked at me with mild amusement. I got up slowly, searching for the right thing to say.

"No, just . . . I'm just preparing for the day when the Whispering Wind Sect finally sees my innate talent and recruits me as their disciple!"

Doubling down. That should save me some face. Great thinking, Kai.

Lan-Yin giggled madly, raising her sleeved arm to cover her smile. My heart skipped a beat. Although I never bothered to tell her, I had a massive crush on her when we were younger. But I'm past that now. She was already betrothed to Wang Jun.

No room for some gardening brat like me to interfere.

"There you go again. This is why we've been poking fun at you since we were kids. Remember Yang Tao's nickname for you? Kowtow Kai?"

I rolled my eyes, resisting the urge to crawl away and hide in embarrassment. It certainly didn't help my efforts when she brought up old memories from our childhood.

Times of our youth replayed in my head, the days when everyone played together, but I was content acting out my fantasy of being a master cultivator, armed with a sword. Or rather a nice-looking stick and pretending to continue my gallant adventures across the continent to slay Spirit Beasts and wayward bandits. But due to transportation issues, I had to limit the scope of my imagination to the confines of the village.

"Ugh. What do you want, Lan-Yin? I don't assume you came here just to humiliate this young master?" I turned my nose up, putting away the watering can and hoe. Nailing the haughty voice and demeanor had taken quite some time, but I was sure I had it down pat, even if I hadn't seen a young master before.

Lan-Yin opened the fenced gate and let herself in, carefully avoiding the plants I had carefully laid out. She appraised my garden with an impressed stare. It was neat, organized, and flourishing. Nobody in the village knew about plants more than I did. Except maybe the Village Head, Elder Ming. He's been around and even helped kickstart this place back when my parents were in charge.

"I wanted to buy some ginseng. Grandmother's come down with something."

I frowned, remembering Lan-Yin's grandmother. She was the nicest of all the village elders and played cultivator with me when nobody else wanted to. Her candied apples were the best! Hearing about the frail woman's situation made me sad, as I knew she was getting older.

"Coming right up." I whistled, turning serious for a moment as I took Lan-Yin to my home, which doubled as my shop. It was a small, modest space with a rustic charm. Wooden shelves lined with various plants and medicinal products covered the sides, and along the countertop were woven baskets and clayware jars holding fruits and vegetables.

The interior was well lit by paper lanterns that I'd decorated with simple patterns.

It smelled earthy and herbal inside, providing the shop with a relaxing atmosphere. It was easy to get people to buy more when they had their guard down, after all. An extra sale or two didn't hurt anybody, right?

"Tell me about what she's got. I can give you something more than just ginseng, if you need it."

Lan-Yin tilted her head cutely. A few strands of hair fell down, making her look even more beautiful than before.

Kai, that is a betrothed woman. Have some decorum!

I put my thoughts away and listened to Lan-Yin. Hearing about her grandmother's symptoms and physical appearance, I guessed she had a flu or something of a similar nature. I glanced around, searching for something that could help alleviate her grandmother's illness.

"Ginger, ginseng, green onion, and goji berries," I informed Yang-Lin, meticulously placing the items into her basket. "Brew a tea from these ingredients, and it should help her condition. If it's insufficient, add some honey to the mix."

Lan-Yin appeared mildly impressed by my swiftness. *Naturally! I am an erudite scholar! I've read hundreds of books by this point in my life.*

Sure, most of the books I read were tales of legendary cultivators and their butt-kicking adventures, but that's beside the point. I hadn't been able to maintain a store like this without acquiring extensive herbal and medicinal knowledge.

"Thank you, Kai. How much do I owe you for these?"

"For the disgrace you've inflicted upon me, addressing me with such contemptible monikers like 'Kowtow Kai,' it shall cost you a silver coin! Hopefully this will teach you a lesson in respecting your betters."

Lan-Yin rolled her eyes, fully aware that the price I quoted was lower than it should have been. But I had a soft spot for Lan-Yin and, in particular, her grandmother. They were good people.

"Honorable Dreaming Gardener, I am forever indebted to you." She bowed deeply, playing along with my performance. I couldn't help but grin. "I shall etch this lesson into my heart. For now, I have truly tasted the bitterness of fear."

I bade her farewell, and she left me in the shop with my thoughts.

There was plenty of gardening to do, but I felt a bit explorative. Picking up my gear, which consisted of a woven basket, a leather pouch, a small knife, and some rolled-up cloth, I was ready to find some herbs in the forest.

I opened the gate and closed it behind me, leaving my humble abode to make my way down to the village. It was a short walk, and I took a moment to enjoy the warmth of the sun bearing down on my back. It was a bit humid, but I didn't mind. So long as it wasn't cold. I hated the cold. I'd been trying to figure out a way to build a greenhouse to grow some plants during the winter, but glass was still way too expensive. Fifty silver for a single pane? I'd have to sell everything in my shop to have even a tiny greenhouse!

All too soon, I reached the cobbled main streets of Gentle Wind Village. I was met with the same old sights I'd seen my whole life: wooden houses with thatched roofs and plenty of shops and markets out in the open selling their wares. It was fishing season, so I could see many boats off in the distance collecting a variety of sea creatures. *I should buy some on my way back.*

I greeted my fellow villagers with a smile, and they returned it with the same vigor.

"Morning, Kai!" old Mrs. Wang called out as she hung her laundry. "Going herb-hunting?"

I chuckled and nodded. "Yes, Mrs. Wang. Looking for the Celestial Star Lotus of Immortality. I've got a good feeling about today."

She laughed, shaking her head as she got up on her tippy-toes to hang another article of clothing. "Ah, little Kai. You've grown so big and so have your dreams. Best of luck as always, dear."

As I continued down the cobbled streets, I saw a group of children playing near the village square. Upon spotting me, they ran toward me, their eyes gleaming with curiosity and excitement.

"Hey, Kowtow Kai! Are you going to find that super-rare plant today?" asked little Xiao Bao, the youngest of the bunch.

I chuckled, playing along with their teasing. "Ah, my young friends, today might be the day I finally uncover the Celestial Star Lotus! And when I do, I shall share its miraculous properties with the village so you can truly become an immortal cultivator like yours truly!"

With a flourish, I struck a pose, covering the bottom half of my face with my sleeve. The children exchanged excited glances and began chattering among themselves, their imaginations running wild.

"Wow, Kai, you're so cool! I want to be like you when I grow up!" said a girl named Mei-Li, her eyes sparkling with admiration.

I laughed, ruffling her hair. "Well, young one, to be like me, you must study hard, respect your elders, and always dream big!"

With a final wave, I left the children behind, their enthusiastic voices fading into the distance. Just a few steps later, I approached the blacksmith's shop, where Master Qiang was hard at work.

He was tall and muscular, wearing a simple leather apron as he worked on the anvil. He was tall with graying hair, and a bushy beard framed his sweaty face. As he wiped the sweat from his brow, he caught sight of me and grinned, shouting in a boisterous voice, "Kai! Getting more plants for your quest to defy the heavens?"

He was a little too loud. I turned my nose up and did my best to look down on him, even though he towered over me. Somehow, I managed to make it work. "You may mock me now, but the day shall come when you will lament your folly. In that moment, you will rue not having crafted a divine weapon for Kai, who shall have ascended to the Essence Awakening stage!"

Master Qiang chuckled and I waved goodbye.

Other people nodded in acknowledging me, and I returned the gesture. I could see Lan-Yin's home a few paces away. It brought back good memories of when we were children and used her home as the gathering spot for games and such. I shook my head and passed through without a word, bringing my leisure walk to a brisk jog. I didn't want to be out for too long.

As I left the confines of the village, I could hear the sounds of children from afar, role-playing and acting, much like I used to. Not to brag, but I was sure that I played a factor in popularizing the young-master act. They teased me like always, but the villagers meant well. All in good fun. They were there when things got rough and had come together to help me get the garden shop running when my parents passed. I remembered Master Qiang handcrafting the hoe I used to this day! I would never forget their favor, even if they poked fun at my dream of being a cultivator.

I entered the Whispering Leaves Forest. It was rich with plants, herbs, and wildlife, but I never had to worry about anything overly dangerous lurking within. We were on the Tranquil Breeze Coast, after all. Anything akin to a Spirit Beast would have starved to death from how lacking the place was in innate qi. So the animals were just regular animals, and I was sure I could fend off the likes of a wolf with my knife. I was quite adept with it, if I did say so myself.

The trees were tall and ancient, providing ample shade and relief from the summer heat. As I walked deeper into the forest, I couldn't help but remember my childhood dream of becoming a cultivator. I thought about the stories I had read about legendary cultivators who traveled the world, slaying Spirit Beasts and protecting the weak. While I knew that becoming a cultivator was far out of reach for someone like me, a small part of me still clung to that dream. I wanted to find a way to prove my worth and maybe even catch the attention of the Whispering Wind Sect or some other sect, even if I'd only ever seen one disciple pass by this part of the province.

I let out a quiet chuckle, thinking about the absurdity of the idea. "Imagine if I found the Celestial Star Lotus here," I mused to myself. "That would get their attention. But who am I kidding? I don't think that's even a real herb." Shaking my head, I let out a soft sigh as I began my task of foraging for some good herbs.

The area was filled with the scent of damp earth and the sweet aroma of blooming flowers. Out of all the places nearby, the Whispering Leaves Forest was my favorite. It was my sanctuary, a place where I could escape from all the noise and just be myself.

I still remembered the time I tried to meditate here. I didn't have half a clue of what I was doing. Staying still was a challenge! And cultivators could do that for months on end? Without food or water? Crazy. I even got crapped on by a bird while I was attempting it.

Glancing at the towering branches, I made sure there were no birds looking to repeat the event. Thankfully, they seemed to have moved themselves elsewhere for the time being.

Focusing on my task, I began searching. It didn't take long for me to find my first batch of plants. I spotted a group of luminescent flowers a short distance away. Moonbeam Petals! I was running pretty low on my supply, as kids had been bugging me for the paste that soothed mosquito stings and whatnot. Taking my knife out, I cut the stem just below the flower head, leaving the roots and the rest of the stem intact. Had to make sure they survived and grew back in the future, after all. That was a gardener's duty! Preserve the environment and make sure we had a way of collecting some more for the next time we needed it.

It was a simple life, which I didn't mind all too much. Becoming a cultivator was far out of reach, and although I'd never turn down the opportunity, spending my days in this village wasn't so bad. I'd need to find a woman to settle down with, however. Running the shop by myself did get dull at times.

As I hummed quietly, foraging and placing the Moonbeam Petals in my basket, something moved in the corner of my eye. It was so quick, I thought it was a trick of the light.

But just a few paces away, I saw a butterfly with iridescent wings, shimmering in the dappled sunlight. It was unlike anything I'd seen in my entire life. But I had read of its likeness described in a book. It was a rare creature, exclusive to the Tranquil Breeze Coast. It was one of the few that could take advantage of the qi in the surroundings because of its diminutive size. The butterfly could evolve and grow into something more. A Spirit Beast. A weak one, but a beast nonetheless.

The Azure Moonlight Flutter.

CHAPTER THREE

Chasing Butterflies

My heart skipped a beat upon seeing the creature. They had said it was a creature of great fortune, with only one other person in our village having seen it for themselves. It stood out like a sore thumb from the lush greenery, its wings shimmering like the purest sapphire.

It was a sight to behold. I knew that it wasn't much compared to the fantastical Spirit Beasts like the Jade Mist Serpent. But it was the first time I'd seen anything remotely close to the books I had read. The Azure Moonlight Flutter seemed to leave a trail of glitter as it flitted among the trees. Another awe-inspiring sight of what nature had to offer.

"Wow," I whispered to myself. *I need to get that damn butterfly!*

The coins I could get from selling it would be enough to make some headway on that greenhouse for the winter! Determination and desire surged within my body as I stared at the Azure Moonlight Flutter.

Little butterfly, you will be a stepping stone for this young master's goals!

I ruffled through my leather pouch, which contained a few tools and knick-knacks. Every other second, I glanced back at the butterfly, hoping it hadn't moved from its position.

I carefully bruised the Moonbeam Petals, rolling them delicately between my fingers to release the essential oils within them and intensify their fragrance. I placed them inside a cloth, securing them with a bit of vine from a nearby tree. It was tight enough to keep the rolled petals from falling but had enough room to let the scent waft over me.

I shook the petals over my head, and the aroma of jasmine and a hint of vanilla spread through the air. My bruising technique really helped make the scent even stronger, enough to cover the distance between me and the Azure Moonlight Flutter.

After a few seconds, the blue butterfly began making its way toward me, following a nonlinear flight pattern. I hadn't thought I'd be trying to capture an insect today, otherwise I would've gone ahead and brought a net designed for the task. But a cloth should be more than enough to keep the butterfly steady before I could deposit it into a glass jar. I'd worked with plenty of delicate plants before, so handling the Azure Moonlight Flutter shouldn't be too much of a problem.

Right?

With every beat of its wings, it drew closer and closer. My arms were twitching in anticipation, waiting for the moment it landed on my Moonbeam Petal bait to try to grab ahold of it.

There was a fleeting thought that crossed my mind, wondering if the Azure Moonlight Flutter could somehow aid me in my pursuit of cultivation. I quickly dismissed the notion, as I knew that they were unlike other Spirit Beasts whose bodies held immense value due to their Beast Cores. This ethereal creature was a mere butterfly that had managed to absorb a trace of qi, a far cry from the mythical beasts spoken of in ancient tales.

But it would go for a nice sum if I could capture it. Alive, preferably. Maybe I could even figure out a way to breed them in my garden! I had plenty of plants to keep it nice and happy in my home.

Almost as if it sensed my overwhelming desire, the Azure Moonlight Flutter recoiled from the Moonbeam Petal essence I had laid out for it and darted away, deeper into the forest. I gaped at the sheer speed the butterfly retreated with and the faint glimmering trail in its wake.

It left me alone in the clearing for a few seconds, and I could hear my dream of having a nice, fancy greenhouse collapsing into pieces.

"My money! Come back here!"

I followed the trail it left, letting my feet carry me through the Whispering Leaves Forest. That damn butterfly was fast when it wanted to be. I wouldn't exactly call myself a slouch, but it took all I had to keep up with its swift retreat.

Dreaming Gardener was one of the many monikers bestowed upon me. Indeed, I was a gardener who dared to dream. In my fantasies, I envisioned grand escapades where I would chase after ancient Spirit Beasts, journeying across perilous hills and valleys before cornering the ferocious creature that had tormented the common folk for ages. Such grand visions filled my mind time and again.

Kai, a prodigy who appeared only once in a century, in his majestic dark red robes and wielding a divine weapon, would vanquish the Jade Mist Serpent.

Yet here I was, utterly exhausted from chasing a mere butterfly. My robes had become soiled with grime and dirt. Fortuitously, I had chosen my attire wisely— dark maroon with black undertones, which made the stains less conspicuous. Such was the sagacity of I, Kowtow Kai!

But really, this was getting annoying.

I didn't know how long it had been since I continued the chase. Sometimes I lost sight of it but followed its glimmering trail to get an idea of where it went.

But I kept catching glimpses of it again, enough to keep me committed. I quickly realized I ventured from the route I always took, but it was too late to stop. I would capture the Azure Moonlight Flutter or die trying!

Well, "dying" was a bit extreme. Maybe if I completely lost sight of it, then I'd consider going back home.

The chase continued, and I was starting to feel the strain. My breathing became heavier, and my running form became disjointed as I reached the point of total exhaustion. Eventually, I fell to my knees.

I had no clue where I was. Judging from how long I'd been running, I could be several li away from the village. Getting back would be a mighty pain.

I'd forgotten to bring a water canteen with me as well. Of all the days—!

No. That damn Azure Moonlight Flutter had to stop eventually. It was too late to turn back.

I pushed off from my kneeling position and ran through the forest. The butterfly's trail had seemingly gone cold. The glimmering had dwindled as I recovered from exhaustion, but it was faint enough for me to see and move forward. The sound of rushing water attracted my ears. I didn't recall a body of water being nearby, but it should've been enough to satiate my thirst.

As I continued, I couldn't help but notice the distinct aura that enveloped the area. The forest seemed to radiate a serene tranquility that was unlike anything I had ever experienced elsewhere in the forest. The trees stood tall and proud, their bark free from any signs of scarring or damage. The canopy above was dense, with sunlight filtering through the leaves, casting a myriad of dappled patterns onto the forest floor. The air was crisp and pure, devoid of any trace of human disturbance.

The vegetation was lush and vibrant, with a diverse array of plants I had thought were scarce. Wildflowers in a dazzling array of colors adorned the ground, while the melodious songs of birds filled the air. Even the undergrowth seemed to be arranged in a harmonious symphony, orchestrated by an unseen force.

It was as if I had stumbled upon a long-lost sanctuary, a hidden gem tucked away from the prying eyes of humanity.

But this wasn't what I came for! Where was that damn butterfly?

As I continued, I stumbled upon a breathtaking sight—a clearing with a mesmerizing waterfall, its crystal-clear waters cascading gracefully down the rocky cliffside. The Azure Moonlight Flutter danced in the air.

"Damn you!" I pointed at the insect flying around in circles. "You've led me on a goose chase for too long! You're mine!"

The Azure Moonlight Flutter continued to ignore me. I glanced at the water. It would be a pain to capture it while it was floating there, close to the waterfall. My clothes would get wet! Then I'd have to trudge back home drenched and miserable.

I took off my robes, making sure to do so as quickly as possible while keeping an eye on the Azure Moonlight Flutter. With nothing covering my privates, I grimaced, knowing that it would look absurd from an outsider's perspective.

I prayed that my theory of this place being barren of humans was correct. I didn't want anybody seeing me naked chasing after a butterfly like some sort of madman.

But just as I finished neatly folding my clothes off to the side, I watched as the Azure Moonlight Flutter flew into the cascading waterfall and disappeared.

"MY GREENHOUSE!"

My heart sank. That Spirit Beast would sooner commit suicide via a waterfall's downpour than let me profit off its existence. How terrible! I wasn't even going to kill the thing, just keep it in a jar and sell it to the highest bidder!

I stood there for a moment, lamenting the loss of such a beautiful being and the fortune it might have brought me. I hoped that playing a part in its demise wouldn't result in having some horrible curse put on me.

But as I was about to turn back, something caught my eye. The glimmering trail the butterfly had left behind seemed to extend past the waterfall and farther into the distance, inside where I had thought the butterfly had been crushed. It was only because of the clarity of the water that I was able to spot the telltale glimmer of the Azure Moonlight Flutter. Curiosity piqued, I approached the waterfall, squinting as I tried to make sense of what I was seeing.

As I got closer, I realized that something was off. The waterfall still appeared as a normal cascade of water, but the fact that the glimmering trail extended beyond it made me question my initial assumption. From what I could tell, only stone and dirt lay behind the wall of water. Could the Azure Moonlight Flutter have survived the force of the waterfall? Or was there something more to this scene than what met the eye?

I approached the downpour and reluctantly pushed my hand into it, expecting to find a flat surface. But instead, something shimmered, and I fell flat on my face. *Ow.* That would leave a mark.

Drenched in water, I spotted the glimmering trail leading deeper into a cave. No, this wasn't natural. There were stairs! This was manmade! And from the look of it, it had been untouched for years—decades, even. I shook my head and squeezed the water out of my hair. I turned to look back at the waterfall. Waving my hand through it caused a small shimmer, and I drew back, seeing that there was some sort of illusion in place.

"Something more than an Azure Moonlight Flutter . . . Could it have led me to the secret base of a martial master? Maybe the Wind Sage used to live here . . ."

Ah, who am I kidding? I shouldn't get ahead of myself. Let me just see if I can find that butterfly once and for all. There would have been some traces around here if the Wind Sage had actually come around. He wasn't that ancient. Probably a century old at most.

But still, the idea of finding something in this cave formation intrigued me. Maybe not a cave master looking for a disciple, but who knows?

"Azure Moonlight Flutter, you will not escape me that easily!"

Determined to capture the elusive butterfly, I followed the glimmering trail deeper into the cave. The farther I ventured, the more uneasy I felt. The air was damp, and the darkness seemed to close in around me, making the cave feel even more claustrophobic than it already was. Yet the trail continued, and I couldn't help but be drawn farther in, my curiosity piqued by the mysterious environment.

As I delved deeper, I began to notice something strange. The walls of the cave were etched with markings and symbols unlike any language I had ever seen. It was clear that this place was no ordinary cave. It had once been the site of a lost civilization, their secrets and stories hidden away beneath layers of dust and time.

Or some sort of crazed scholar went ahead and hid his archive here.

I couldn't help but let my imagination run wild as I whispered to myself, "Could this be a secret hideout of a legendary cultivator? Or maybe the tomb of an ancient king?"

Ancient artifacts lay scattered about, covered in cobwebs and grime. Some were broken, others still intact, but all of them seemed to hold a deep connection to the past. I couldn't help but wonder what had happened to the people who once lived here, what drove them to create such a hidden sanctuary. They didn't emit any sort of qi or energy. But even then, my skin prickled upon being so close. I could tell they were unlike anything I'd seen.

As I ventured farther, the cave opened up into a larger chamber. The air grew colder, and an eerie silence settled over me. There, floating atop a pedestal in the center of the chamber, was the Azure Moonlight Flutter. It seemed to be drawn to an artifact that rested beneath it—a large, intricately carved stone tablet. The tablet was adorned with the same mysterious symbols I had seen etched into the cave walls, yet they seemed to hold a greater significance here.

I stared at the artifact, my imagination running wild once more. "This . . . this must be some sort of . . . legendary treasure? An ancient cultivator's legacy? Maybe . . ."

The Azure Moonlight Flutter continued to float above the artifact, seemingly unaffected by my presence. I cautiously approached it, my heart pounding in my chest. As I reached out to capture the creature, I couldn't help but wonder if it had brought me here for a reason.

The Azure Moonlight Flutter finally in my grasp, I gazed at the mysterious artifact before me. For some reason, the butterfly on my palm didn't seem as eye-catching. I knew that I had stumbled upon something extraordinary, though the true nature of it was beyond my comprehension. My life as a humble gardener had been simple, but now, with this discovery, maybe I . . .

I chuckled nervously. "This is how it usually goes, right? I touch the pedestal and a flashing light overcomes me?" I asked the butterfly in my palm, but it seemed content to just stare at me with an eerie intelligence. Seeing no response, I gulped down my anxieties and got closer to the pedestal marked with engravings of a lost language.

"Well, here goes nothing."

I placed my palm on the tablet and closed my eyes, waiting for something to happen.

CHAPTER FOUR

Path to Ascension

My heart thudded wildly, bracing for some sort of impact or great flash of light. But nothing happened. I warily opened my eyes, seeing that the ancient pedestal was inert. I felt disappointed. Damn my overactive imagination! I had such high hopes.

I glanced at it again, hoping to find some sort of clue to the artifact's purpose. The Azure Moonlight Flutter stood still on my hand, a great contrast to when it recoiled and ran away from me. It seemed content to stay where it was, but I wouldn't be able to figure out the artifact with only one hand. I ushered it toward my shoulder, letting it crawl onto my right side while I inspected the pedestal.

I had no clue what the hell I was doing. I perused my memories for any instance in cultivator stories where they came across an ancient relic. What had they done?

I gave the artifact a hug. Nothing. My naked body touched the entire pedestal, and I shivered, cheek pressed onto the cold, dusty surface. I sighed. If there was an ancient spirit contained in this, it was likely cursing me and my bloodline for letting my privates touch the hallowed artifact. But seeing as how lightning didn't smite me on the spot, I supposed it was okay.

"A sacrifice of blood, perhaps?"

I withdrew my plant-cutting knife and winced, letting a few drops of blood spill from the tip of my finger. With bated breath, I watched as the life-giving liquid fell onto the engravings. Once again, the artifact was dormant.

"What do you think, little butterfly?"

The Azure Moonlight Flutter had nothing to contribute apart from silence, so I decided to close my eyes and think. Bare-assed with my legs crossed, I brainstormed ways the artifact could be activated. An idea popped into my head, one so clear that I didn't know why I hadn't thought of it sooner.

"Qi! I should put my qi into the artifact! It's probably been starved of energy being stuck on the Tranquil Breeze Coast!"

There was only one problem with that method.

How did one use qi?

Inner energy? It was easy to talk about it. But trying to use it as a mortal was a whole other matter. There was a reason why solo cultivators like the Wind Sage were so rare. Unlocking one's qi reserves required guidance, talent, luck, and skill. I'd heard that even the weakest mortal had a speck of qi, but they would never learn to access or use it without supreme effort and being properly guided by a manual or some sort of instructor.

Okay, let me see . . . I just feel it, right? Visualize it as a ball of dormant energy within myself. That was how my favorite author, Liang Feng, described it. I took a deep breath and calmed my mind. My eyes snapped open, and I extended my hand forward, shouting at the top of my lungs, "HA!"

Nothing. Not even a twitch. I tensed up and tried to force it out of my palm. Gritting my teeth and squeezing as hard as I could, I thought for a moment that I was going to lose control of my bowels.

"Grrgh! Ha . . . ! Just a little bit . . . !"

These weren't noises a good boy would make.

With every attempt being a miserable failure, I gave up and set my hand down on the pedestal. I panted lightly and decided to rest my weight on the support for a brief moment. The Azure Moonlight Flutter floated onto my hand, and I watched as it rested perfectly atop my knuckle. The intricate pattern on its wings glowed a deep blue.

Before I could react, a rush of energy flowed from my hand and into the rest of my body. Just as soon as it came, a feeling of being drained occurred, and the artifact hummed in response.

The little butterfly had given me its energy! This truly was a fated encounter. My dreams of being a cultivator weren't so ridiculous after all. I would ascend past my mortal vessel, and then—

DING!

A loud noise similar to a bell rang across the cavern formation, and I looked around in bewilderment, expecting something to happen. The sound echoed for several seconds until it became just a faint whisper.

But nothing came to pass. The pedestal went back to being dormant, and the dust around the artifact hadn't even been disturbed. What exactly was that noise?

WE ILLUMINATE THE PATH TO ASCENSION.

A NEW ERA.

HIDDEN PATHS AWAIT.

I flinched violently upon seeing the blue box of text appear before my eyes. Path to Ascension? I'd never heard of anything like this happening before. Was this the guidance of an ancestor? Ancient knowledge from millennia past that would unlock my full potential?

The Azure Moonlight Flutter seemed tired, resting on my hand upside down and lying still.

Was it some manner of a reincarnated cultivator trapped in the form of a butterfly? As I observed it for a few moments, a screen popped up once again.

Name: Azure Moonlight Flutter
Race: Mystical Butterfly
Affinity: Wood
Cultivation Rank: Qi Initiation Stage—Rank 1
Special Abilities:
Moonlight Empowerment—Gains increased power and vitality
under the moonlight.
Qi Siphon—Can absorb small amounts of qi from its
surroundings to sustain itself.
Qi Transfer—Can imbue living beings with energy by transferring its qi,
providing a small boost to those who receive it.

Bond Level: 1 (Acquaintance)—The Azure Moonlight Flutter is
familiar with you but does not yet possess a deep connection.

"What type of sorcery is this?"

It was not a heaven-defying ability that enabled me to advance my cultivation at unparalleled speeds, nor was it a divine blessing that bestowed upon me the physique of a martial expert.

Another screen popped up before me.

Heavenly Interface: Kai Liu

Perk(s):

Interface Manipulator—Allows manipulation of the
Heavenly Interface and access to special features.

Race: Human

Vitality: Sufficient

Primary

Affinity: Wood

Cultivation Rank: Mortal Realm—Rank 1

Qi: Mortal Realm

Mind: Mortal Realm

Body: Mortal Realm

Skills

Herbalism: Level 8 (. . .)

Gardening: Level 9 (. . .)

Cultivation Techniques: N/A

"Little butterfly, I've received the greatest boon from you! I'll be able to accomplish my dream of being a cultivator!"

It wasn't what I expected, but perhaps that was a blessing in disguise. Heavenly Interface . . . It tracked my general information and presented it in a comprehensive manner. The heavens were smiling down upon me. There was no question of what I was: a mortal. But with this, I could achieve so many things. I just knew it. I eagerly glanced over my information and noted down everything I had.

"Herbalism and Gardening. Fair. I am not sure what the eight represents. But that Interface Manipulator skill . . . Does it mean I am able to interact with this?"

I tried to touch the screen, but my hand passed through it like a mirage. Perhaps it was mentally controlled? Those special features it told of weren't specified. *Let me try. Herbalism.*

Herbalism (Level 8): A skill that grants knowledge and understanding of various plants, their properties, and their uses in medicine and alchemy. Herbalism enables the user to identify, harvest, and process plants effectively.
Next Stage: Spiritual Herbalism
Requirements:
Qi Initiation Stage—Rank 1
Herbalism Proficiency—Level 10
Infuse qi into a plant successfully.
Find a plant that inherently possesses qi.

Interesting! I can enhance my current skills with existing ones. I see the potential here. Let me see the other skill. Gardening.

Gardening (Level 9): A skill that imparts knowledge and expertise in cultivating, nurturing, and managing various plants and gardens. Gardening allows the user to optimize the growth of plants, increasing their quality and yield.

Next Stage: Nature's Attunement
Requirements:
Qi Initiation Stage—Rank 1
Gardening Proficiency—Level 10
Acquire the Wood Affinity.
Successfully grow a plant with qi.

Most curious! Excitement bubbled in my chest. It wasn't the rise to power I imagined my debut as a cultivator would be, but it gave me the path to strengthen myself. If I did things correctly, I could take both skills to the next stage in one fell swoop. I already completed a few requirements. My interface said I had a Wood Affinity. I'm assuming it's because of my background in gardening, but alas, the Heavenly Interface didn't seem keen on answering that question.

I glanced around the cavern I was in for anything of interest, but everything remained the same. Compared to the artifact in the center, everything else didn't hold that aura of mystique. They were just remnants of a long-lost civilization.

But they were the ones that had given me this power. The least I could do was pay my respects. I would return again.

I bowed my head to the pedestal in silence, mentally apologizing for putting my privates on the surface in the midst of figuring out how to activate the artifact.

"Come on, little butterfly. Let's go back up and polish these skills of mine!"

I sneezed and shivered, feeling the cold creep into my bones after being naked for so long.

". . . And grab my clothes, as well."

I spent a few hours roaming around. Retracing my steps was easy, evidenced by the trail I had left chasing the Azure Moonlight Flutter. But I wasn't going to just go home so easily.

First, I had to do what the Heavenly Interface said! Off in the less-explored parts of the Tranquil Breeze Coast, I had a much higher chance of finding some sort of qi plant lying around somewhere. They were incredibly rare, especially considering the nature of the province. There was a reason why I coveted the Azure Moonlight Flutter.

Speaking of the Spirit Beast, I had laid it comfortably on a nearby leaf. It willingly left my arm and crawled underneath a plant, seemingly tired from the transfer of energy it had given me. I had developed some sort of obligation toward it. Let it be known that this young master repaid all his debts twofold and grievances by a hundredfold!

But returning to the qi plants, I knew there were only two native to the province. The Breezesong Fruit and the Moonlit Grace Lily. The problem with the first was that it had no recorded instances of existing in the Whispering Leaves

Forest. Last I recall, it was found by a villager and harvested about three decades ago, closer to Crescent Bay City. They used it to get their son initiated into the sect or some other thing like that, but the point of the matter was that I had no business finding the fruit in the vicinity.

The Moonlit Grace Lily, however, I knew very well. Not only was it found here, but I had a special attachment to that particular species. Memorized the entry in my botanical encyclopedia, I did!

"A perennial plant with long, slender, and slightly curved leaves that grow in a radial pattern from its base. The leaves have a dark green hue with a faint silvery sheen, making them appear as if they are glowing under the moonlight," I recited dutifully, harvesting any plants of interest in the area by the waterfall. Even if they weren't a qi plant, most of them were hard to find in my usual foraging spots.

In addition to being one of the most potent medicinal plants in the province, the Moonlit Grace Lily held the power to calm emotional turmoil. Memories of my childhood illness came flooding back to me. A fever so severe, it made me believe that I was going to die. My body was cold and clammy, despite being wrapped in layers, and the pain shooting up my legs kept me awake at night. Our usual medicines offered no relief.

Under the full moon's gentle glow, my mother prepared a concoction using the last Moonlit Grace Lily in our possession, harnessing the flower's peak potency. I can still recall the taste of the elixir: a delicate, floral sweetness, accompanied by a cooling sensation that spread through my entire body, bringing relief in mere moments. Though I felt rejuvenated, my mother insisted I rest and let my body heal. She sat by my side, her voice like a gentle breeze, as she sang an ancient lullaby to calm me into a peaceful slumber.

"Sleep, my dear, and worry not, for Moonlit Grace will soothe your thoughts. Wrapped in lily's tender hold, you'll awaken strong and bold."

That sparked my appreciation for gardening. Who knew that measly plants could bring upon such a powerful effect?

The memory of my mother and her gentle lullaby made me smile fondly. It would be simpler to arrange a carriage to the Whispering Winds Sect and pay a high sum to fulfill the Herbalism requirement. However, I wanted to honor the cherished memory of my mother's care by taking my first step toward becoming a cultivator with the Moonlit Grace Lily.

I would ascend on my own terms, forging a story that would be uniquely mine, one that future generations would remember with awe!

Today is the day I, Kai Liu, begin my quest to defy the heavens!

CHAPTER FIVE

Return to the Village

"Tianyi, I've done it!"

> *Herbalism has reached level 9.*

I spent far too long in the forest. The sky had already gone dark, and my only sources of light were the moon and the Azure Moonlight Flutter's glittering wings. I had given it a name: Tianyi. A regal title!

After all, I couldn't call it "little butterfly" every single time. My decision to call it that had stuck and even its name changed when I observed the Spirit Beast's status once more.

The butterfly in question was now active, fluttering around as I worked in the clearing with a pile of various herbs and plants I collected during my outing. I lined them all up in neat portions, where I had been studying them for the past two hours.

From right to left, I had Misty Dew Grass, Skyreach Flower, Moonbeam Petals, and Nightshade Flowers. All fairly uncommon herbs, but I found a significant amount from foraging in the area. I knew what each one of them did, and I was aware of the few combinations I could make with them. I was limited by the tools I had at my disposal, but with the Nightshade and the Misty Dew, I was able to create a fairly potent sleeping aid.

Then I added the Moonbeam Petals to it and ingested it.

Now, I knew it sounded stupid. But I had seen what the Heavenly Interface said. I needed my Herbalism skills to reach a certain level. How would one improve their level in a given skill? By pushing it to its limits! So I did it the way I knew how: by experimenting and documenting the results. I discovered that adding Moonbeam Petals made the concoction work much quicker, and I fell flat on my face within fifteen minutes of drinking it. Not the smartest idea, but I woke up an hour later to continue. Tianyi had stood guard, protecting me from any evil-doers while I was unconscious. A steadfast and reliable companion, she was!

I repeated the process a few more times. But I made sure to pay attention to my every move. The way I cut using my knife, how I ground herbs, and even how I stored them! They were all actions I did without much thought, but I was determined to see if my thought process would make a difference. And it did, in the form of my Herbalism skill reaching the next level. My genius knew no bounds!

In all honesty, I was close to giving up. I breathed a sigh of relief as soon it came, and I packed up my items and got ready to go home. I glanced at Tianyi and wondered if she would follow me. The Azure Moonlight Flutter was content to stay nearby, occasionally darting out of sight but always coming back.

I wouldn't take her with me by force. The Spirit Beast was responsible for this course of events, and I had much to thank her for. Tianyi could be independent or accompany me, whatever she wished!

But I hoped she would—she would be a fine addition to my garden, and the companionship was nice. Someone I could talk to in my haughty young-master tone without fear of judgment or embarrassment. Tianyi was the only one I could count on. Except for my plants. But they didn't really count, I thought.

Not to mention the looks on the villagers' faces! Kai the Spirit Beast Hunter, that's what they'd call me from now on!

"Tianyi, will you be coming with me?" I called out. "I can accommodate you. My plants have superior nectar to the ones grown here."

The butterfly seemed enthused, glowing slightly in response to my words. I was certain that Tianyi was not an ordinary Spirit Beast. She must have been some sort of reincarnated cultivator! A divine ancestor was willing to help her descendant! I would treat her most lavishly with nectar from the finest of flowers.

With the Azure Moonlight Flutter at my side, I carefully retraced my steps back to the village.

The lights were still on in the village. I could see them from a distance, still active despite being past midnight. It had taken me nearly an hour to find my way back, getting lost and having to return to my original position a few times. My clothes were a ragged mess, and my hair was tangled up. A warm bath was needed!

As I drew closer to the village, I saw people huddled in a group near the entrance, discussing something animatedly. Master Qiang was among them. I knew for a fact he was the sort to turn early! It was unusual for the villagers to be gathered like this so late at night, especially when they had fields to tend to early in the morning.

Curiosity piqued, I approached the crowd and tried to listen in on their conversation. Their voices were a mix of excitement, confusion, and disbelief.

"I can't believe it! I received the Heavenly Interface too!" Master Qiang said in his gruff tone.

"Mine says I have a Fishing skill at level three," another chimed in, looking both proud and bewildered. He was one of the younger fishermen, and I couldn't recall his name at the moment. I was merely stunned at what I was hearing.

"Is this some kind of divine blessing? Why would it happen to all of us?" an elder questioned, stroking his beard thoughtfully.

As I listened to the villagers' excited chatter about their Heavenly Interfaces, my heart continued to sink. It seemed as though everyone else had received skills that were much more interesting and useful than mine, especially among those my age.

"I got a level four Carpentry skill!" one of the teenagers announced, grinning from ear to ear. He was much younger than me, but to think he was skilled enough to possess levels in the trade! Li Wei, if I remember. It had only been a year or so since he began taking up his family's business.

"And I have level five in Blacksmithing!" another chimed in, flexing his arms to show off. It was Wang Jun. I hadn't gotten the chance to see him in some time, and he looked as mighty as an ox. Out of all the people in the village, he was the only one that rivaled Master Qiang in size. The two of them, standing side by side, resembled towering mountains guarding our village.

Master Qiang, the village blacksmith, whose broad shoulders and powerful arms were the result of years of hard labor, was now inspecting his Heavenly Interface. He let out a hearty laugh, revealing that he had received a level ten Smithing skill. His eyes sparkled with excitement, a flame that wasn't there before.

"I feel like an apprentice again! Come, Wang Jun, let's go see if we can further them!"

The more they spoke, the more disappointed I felt. My Herbalism and Gardening skills paled in comparison to the amazing abilities my peers had received. I had thought that the Heavenly Interface would make me unique and special, but now it seemed that I was just one among many. One of them turned and asked me if I had received the enigmatic message the others did.

As I shared my experiences with the villagers, they did express some interest in Tianyi, the Azure Moonlight Flutter that followed me. I didn't mention the ruins, deciding to keep it a secret for myself. However, their attention was quickly drawn back to the Heavenly Interface, as they were too preoccupied with their own newfound abilities to focus on anything else. Tianyi, sensing my disappointment, fluttered closer to me.

Around us, the village was abuzz with activity. A group of elderly women sat outside, discussing their new skills in hushed voices. Mrs. Wang was among them, mentioning her Cooking skill with a proud smile. She had always been a talented cook, and now, with the Heavenly Interface, her dishes would likely become even more exquisite.

With a heavy heart, I excused myself from the crowd and trudged back to my home, longing for a warm bath to wash away the day's events. My shop was exactly the same as I left it, and I carefully opened the fence gate to let myself in. The Azure Moonlight Flutter wandered aimlessly for some time before entering my home. She provided a nice touch of glamor to my home, making it a bit more mystical than before.

As I prepared the bath, I couldn't help but talk to Tianyi while I waited for the water to warm up. I placed some chamomile to steep in the water.

"You know, Tianyi, I thought the Heavenly Interface would make me special. But it seems everyone has it now," I muttered, sinking into the warm water. "Still, it's good for the village, right? And it's not like I'm completely ordinary . . . I'll just have to work harder and prove that I can be the best with the Heavenly Interface."

Tianyi seemed to nod in agreement, its wings shimmering softly as it settled on the edge of the bathtub.

"Yes, you're right," I continued, feeling a little more determined. "I may not have flashy combat skills or incredible crafting abilities, but Herbalism has its strengths! I'll make the most of my skills, and show everyone that even someone like me can become great!"

With a newfound sense of purpose, I pondered the impact of the Heavenly Interface on Spirit Beasts like Tianyi. Were they also granted skills and abilities through the Heavenly Interface, or were they exempt from its influence? How far did its effects go? Was it just here in the village, the province, or even the entire world?

"Tell me, Tianyi, has it affected you too?" I asked, knowing full well that the butterfly couldn't respond. "If it has, then that means the entire cultivation world, both human and beast, will be changed forever."

Tianyi's wings twitched as if considering my words.

It made me think; was I the one who caused it? Or was it some sort of cruel coincidence that occurred the moment I touched that artifact and infused it with qi?

I couldn't help but feel a sense of wonder and anticipation about the idea of being part of such a monumental change in the cultivation world. Despite the challenges ahead, I was determined to carve my own path and rise above the ordinary.

As I soaked in the bath, I couldn't help but think about how the appearance of the Heavenly Interface would impact the cultivators and sects of the world. I specifically thought about the Whispering Winds Sect and even those of other provinces. How would they react to such a sudden and unexpected change? Would they embrace the Heavenly Interface or treat it with suspicion and caution? Inspiring cultivators like me would not sit idly.

I imagined the various sects scrambling to understand the new power and how to use it to their advantage. The balance of power within the Jianghu would be thrown into disarray as everyone attempted to adapt and thrive in this new era. Even the powerhouses would have to move. Some sects might find their previous advantages diminished, while others could rise in prominence thanks to the mysterious power of the Heavenly Interface. I was almost certain of it.

Well, as far as I know from the books I read. Any news or gossip would take some time to reach the village, considering how remote it was.

This shift in power dynamics and the possible impact on Spirit Beasts only served to fuel my curiosity and excitement about the Heavenly Interface.

I knew that the road ahead would be filled with countless challenges and surprises. But who was I? Kai Liu, a budding young prodigy who would take the world by storm!

"I will not be daunted so easily," I declared, rising from the bath with renewed vigor. "With my newfound determination, the support of my mysterious companion, and the power of the Heavenly Interface, I am more than ready to face whatever the future has in store!"

As I stepped out of the wooden tub, my enthusiasm was short-lived as my foot slipped on the wet floor. I tumbled forward, landing with a painful crash on the hard ground. Tianyi fluttered in the air after I disturbed her peace.

"Perhaps I should focus on mastering the art of exiting the bathtub before I conquer the Jianghu," I muttered, rubbing my bruised ego and sore body.

CHAPTER SIX

Quests

Several days had gone by since the Day of Awakening, the term coined by people around the world for the extraordinary event.

Since then, I've made some progress in my skills and noted some startling differences in my interface compared to other people's.

I talked with the other villagers, and none of them had a clue on how to further progress their skills to the next stage. They didn't even know what the next stage of their skills would be called! It seemed mine was more helpful than I initially thought it was. But that was just the beginning.

Wondering what other things I could do with my Heavenly Interface, I poked and prodded it mentally as much as I could. And in turn, I was greeted with more boxes of information and quests.

Quest: Body Refinement
—Run the perimeter of Gentle Wind Village without stopping to rest. (1/5)
—Commit to the horse stance for ten minutes without stopping to rest. (0/5)
—Squat 250 times without stopping to rest. (1/5)

Quest: Mind Refinement
—Perform Visualization Training for one hour. (2/5)
—Meditate for one hour without losing focus. (2/5)
—Solve a mathematical equation without any external aid. (5/5)

To my delight, I received quests after inquiring about ways to enhance my mind and body, which were still at the mortal realm, which I assumed was the lowest realm. The interface provided me with various tasks and challenges, pushing me to strengthen my mental and physical fortitude.

I had begun almost immediately. I almost blacked out attempting to run the entirety of the village's perimeter, but I had done the challenge. But it humbled me to know that such a simple task left me in such a dire state. I was a physically active, able-bodied young man! To think Kai Liu would be felled by mere running. The interface showed me just how much it would truly take to become a cultivator. I had been shallow and neglected to understand the actual work it took to get there.

After squatting for hundreds of times, I didn't even have the capacity to do the second task. My legs shook madly, and I was forced to give up and try again the next day. But even now, I could hardly hold that stance! I'd have to work toward it and complete the other two in the meantime.

Over the past few days, I'd been trying to do the horse stance for ten minutes, but even with all my strength I couldn't make it. My legs were so unaccustomed to that sort of training. This was something that would require constant effort.

Same for the Mind Refinement quest! They were odd, telling me to do a thing called Visualization Training. It had given me a short prompt, explaining that it was a matter of imagining objects, scenes, and scenarios in vivid detail. Not a challenge for the Dreaming Gardener! That was my specialty, and I could even do it while I was running the shop. Mathematical equations were easy for a genius like me, I did them on a daily basis for the shop's finances!

So with these quests, I continued my daily life. The shop never had many customers, but my garden always needed maintenance!

The villagers noticed me running around, but they knew that something as magnificent as the Heavenly Interface would probably inspire me. They just chalked it up to "Kai being Kai."

Some of the younger children followed along, trying to see what else the Heavenly Interface had to offer. But most of the villagers had gone back to their usual lives. From what they said, the Heavenly Interface didn't play much of a part in their day-to-day, and unlike mine, the interface only showed and tracked their progress.

However, a handful of people, driven by ambition and determination, were emboldened by the Heavenly Interface's presence—people like me.

"Kai! Sorry to interrupt your meditatin', but here's the staff you ordered."

I opened my eyes. It was Wang Jun. His smile was wide and boisterous. He wore a white bandana, covered in soot and dirt from toiling away in the forges with Master Qiang. Wang Jun was always a boisterous man with an upbeat personality.

I got up from my position on the dirt floor, stretching my back after being in the same position for quite some time. Meditating was one of the tasks given to me, and I decided to do it in the garden where I felt most at peace. Being in nature would surely help me gather energy, or something like that.

Opening the fence gate to allow Wang Jun in, he handed me the clothed item and I nearly tipped over due to the unexpected weight.

Unwrapping the cloth, it revealed a simple iron staff of good quality. The weapon was about my height, and heavy enough that holding it by its end was impossible for my current physical strength. But that's where my training comes in! It wouldn't do to train like it was a hobby, but I should invest in the necessary equipment to further my skills! One day, I'll be able to wield this like it is lighter than air.

Swords were no good; they were too sharp, and I'd likely cut myself trying to handle them for training. But a staff? It was perfect for my needs and would be versatile enough to serve multiple purposes!

"Thank you, mighty blacksmith! You've performed a critical mission, and now I'll be able to train as a proper cultivator should. Come! Let me give you some tea and some more for Master Qiang."

"I'd appreciate that!"

I led him into the shop, where Tianyi rested peacefully on a perch I had mounted up by the windowsill. She glimmered beautifully, as always. Wang Jun whistled, admiring the Spirit Beast while I prepared some tea.

"So you're really taking that cultivator stuff seriously, eh? That Heavenly Interface must've lit a fire under your ass!"

"Indeed, indeed! Would you say the same for yourself, Wang Jun?" I responded, handing him a warm cup. He muttered out a word of thanks and drank with me. I pushed out a chair and sat back, enjoying the peaceful afternoon. It had been a while since I caught up with him, especially since he was betrothed to Lan-Yin and went under Master Qiang as an apprentice. We were quite close, so it was good to see him well and healthy.

"I'd say so. Y'know, Master Qiang has been going nonstop since it came out." He leaned in closer with a small grin. "And I received a quest from it."

My eyes widened as I sipped my tea. The quest system was something that everyone had, it seemed. "And what did it entail? I've got some of my own as well."

"It tells me to craft twenty different kinds of tools and armor. The staff was actually one of them, so I hope you enjoy it."

"I can tell even from a glance it is of good quality! Let me know when you complete your quest; I want to know what you get from it!"

Our conversation continued into more miscellaneous subjects. It has given me much to think about.

"We got an uptick of orders from as far as Crescent Bay City! The merchants have been going on about the Silent Moon Sect starting problems." He said, rolling his shoulder back and wincing. It looks like he had been hard at work prior to coming here.

I perked up at that information. Crescent Bay City was the district capital of the Tranquil Breeze Coast. I had wanted to save up and visit the city myself at least once, but life had gotten in the way of things. Hearing problems about the Silent Moon Sect made me frown. They were quite a prestigious sect.

"What did they say about the Silent Moon Sect?"

"Just the usual, recruiting talented individuals to become cultivators. There's been more of them coming out of the woodwork with the Interface 'n all that. Whispering Winds Sect and the Silent Moon's disciples have been getting into a lot of fights, apparently."

That was a concern. The Heavenly Interface had done a lot of good, but with it being given to everyone, problems were bound to arise. Those with ambition, whether it was for good or evil, would find success being guided by the Heavenly Interface. I sighed, thinking about the power struggles that would come as a result of the powerful magic. I felt partially responsible, but what could I do? As far as I knew, there was no way to take it back.

Shaking my head at such thoughts, I turned the conversation to lighter topics. Thinking about those conflicts from far away would do us no benefit after all.

Giving him a few herbs that helped eliminate fatigue, I sent him off while I resumed my training. With the staff in my hand, I tried to practice some swings and strikes. They were clumsy, and my balance was off. Contrary to other times, the Heavenly Interface didn't seem keen on helping me out here. But I would prevail! Perhaps the Village Head would have some books for me to learn more about wielding a staff. I glanced at the biggest quest yet, which I had no clue how to start.

> *Quest: Cultivation Technique (Wood)*
> *—Find five different areas that have sufficient wood qi in the surroundings and meditate in them for one hour. (0/5)*
> *-Areas with sufficient wood qi will be marked with a glowing yellow orb only visible to you.*

Where would I find one? Maybe it was easy for someone outside of the Tranquil Breeze Coast, but it was impossible for me! There was a reason why Tianyi was the only Spirit Beast I'd ever encountered. It's also why finding the Moonlit Grace Lily was so difficult. The innate qi in the environment was far too low to accommodate any cultivators. Only those in the heart of the province could cultivate properly.

After several more minutes of swinging the staff around clumsily, I sighed and put it down. My body was covered in sweat. My progress was lacking, and I had far more questions than answers.

I needed to find a way to unlock my qi reserves! I hadn't been able to since Tianyi gave me some, and she hadn't repeated it since. It would be the key to getting on track with all the other quests I had, especially my Gardening skill. There were so many things I needed to learn, and even the Heavenly Interface wouldn't be able to give me all the answers.

I tidied myself, rinsing my body with water before embarking on a journey to the village square. I would need to consult the Village Head.

"Elder Ming! I require your expertise!"

I waited patiently at his door until it slid open to reveal a tall, slim man with a stooped posture. His silvery hair was tied in a neat bun, and his beard was well-groomed. The Village Head seemed curious at my entrance.

"If it isn't little Kai. What can I do for you today?"

"I would like your help in regard to my quest of being a cultivator!"

He whacked me on the head lightly, and I cursed. His face was impassive as usual. Village Head had barely aged since I was a young child.

"Still on about that, aren't you?" He sighed, retracting his hand and allowing me in.

"The Heavenly Interface was a sign from above, Village Head! I've been training properly now under its guidance!"

"Hardheaded brat!" He ruffled my hair, leaving it an undignified mess.

Village Head, or rather, Elder Ming, was always against my dream of being a cultivator. He was once part of a sect, although he never mentioned which it was, before leaving the path of cultivation and settling down here in the Gentle Wind Village. He had been here for decades, so he couldn't have been too far into his journey before he stopped.

He always told me, even from a young age, that it wasn't a path one should seek so easily. Elder Ming warned me of the danger, the rigors of training, and the pressure set upon you by being a disciple. He even warned me about the way those of lower status were treated within sects; it was one of the major reasons why I didn't run to one and beg to be let into the Whispering Winds Sect or the Silent Moon Sect. When I begged him to train me in the ways of cultivation, he flat-out refused, saying he couldn't give a child something so dangerous, citing a problem called Qi Deviation as being too risky.

I know his resistance came from a place of concern, but I knew what I wanted. Being a gardener was okay, but I wanted to live a life of freedom and travel. Being a cultivator would grant me that luxury, and I was more than determined to get it. He probably thought I wasn't taking it seriously or didn't understand the consequences, but I did! I acted as an overconfident fool at times, but I knew where I stood and just how much work it'd take to get to where I wanted to be.

"Please, Elder Ming." I bowed my head. "I wish to learn. I want to understand just what it takes to be a cultivator."

"Raise your head, Kai."

I complied, and he hit me with another chop to the head. I could tell he was a retired cultivator, those strikes packed a serious punch despite his frame!

"Don't think that being a cultivator is so easy! You don't get that way overnight, even with that Interface's help. You need consistency and practice, built upon years and years, along with the right guidance!"

"That's why I'm here, Elder Ming! Come on, you've refused to teach me since I was a kid! What do I have to do to prove to you that I'm serious about this?"

He scratched his chin, looking at me with an appraising eye. I stood there with a determined expression on my face. Elder Ming closed his eyes and sighed, seemingly giving up on trying to convince me. It wasn't the first time I tried to convince him to teach me or give me guidance, but I suppose this was the only time where I bothered him so much about it.

"Well, I know I can't stop you. If anything, you'd get yourself killed doing something reckless, so I'll give you a test."

The old man who spent his life walking around the village had a certain pressure around him that made me nervous, but I smiled in the face of it all.

I looked at him with a determined expression on my face. Whatever challenge he gave, I, Kai Liu, would be up for the task! Whatever it may be!

CHAPTER SEVEN

Challenge and Purpose

The sun was already setting as Elder Ming led me to a clearing on the outskirts of Gentle Wind Village. The grass swayed gently, and the air carried the fresh scent of earth and dew. I was excited to finally start my training under the guidance of Elder Ming, but I could tell he was still a bit hesitant.

"All right, let me see these quests the Heavenly Interface gave you," Elder Ming said, his voice firm but curious. I didn't hesitate to tell him the list of challenges for both body and mind refinement. He examined the lists for a moment, his eyebrows knitting together in what seemed like disapproval.

"These challenges . . . they're hardly a proper test for a cultivator," he scoffed. "You want to be a cultivator, don't you, Kai? The real path requires much more than what this interface is asking of you."

I stared at him, feeling slightly discouraged but determined to prove myself. "I'll do whatever it takes, Elder Ming. Just tell me what to do."

He nodded, a glimmer of respect in his eyes. "Very well. We'll start with the body refinement tasks, but we'll make them more challenging."

Elder Ming picked up a couple of large rocks from the ground and handed them to me. "Instead of just holding the horse stance for ten minutes, I want you to do it with these rocks on your shoulders."

I hesitated for a moment, then nodded, gripping the rocks in my hands. I got into the horse stance, lowering my hips while keeping my back straight. Elder Ming placed the rocks on my shoulders, and I felt my muscles strain under the additional weight. I focused my mind on the task, using my determination to push through the discomfort.

As the seconds ticked by, the weight of the rocks seemed to multiply, and my legs quivered in protest. Sweat poured down my forehead, and I could feel my body wanting to give up. But every time I felt like collapsing, I reminded myself of my dream to become a cultivator, and it gave me the strength to keep going.

Elder Ming warned me when my form strayed from perfection, forcing me to straighten my back and raise my legs.

Finally, after what felt like an eternity, Elder Ming told me to stop. It wasn't even a fraction of the time necessary to complete the challenge. My legs gave out from under me, and I fell to the ground, gasping for breath.

"Good work, Kai," Elder Ming said, his voice holding a hint of surprise. "Now let's move on to the mind-refinement tasks. The first one was Visualization Training, wasn't it?"

For the next several hours, Elder Ming pushed me harder than I had ever been pushed before. He had me perform the Visualization Training while holding a handstand, forcing me to maintain both physical and mental focus. I couldn't even do a handstand, so he allowed me to use the wall as a support. He quizzed me on increasingly complex mathematical equations while I jogged laps around the clearing.

As I struggled through each task, Elder Ming explained the importance of having a strong body to cultivate qi. "You see, Kai, a weak body cannot hold and maintain the qi necessary for cultivation. It's like trying to fill a cracked vase with water—it will simply leak out and be wasted. By strengthening your body, you create a proper vessel for qi, allowing it to flow and be cultivated within you."

His words resonated with me, and I understood the significance of these challenges. It wasn't just about completing tasks like a checklist for the Interface; it was about creating a strong foundation for my cultivation journey. Perhaps I was taking it too lightly. These challenges were difficult; I don't think even someone like Wang Jun could do it to completion despite his blessed physicality. Much less a gardener like me. I didn't even manage to do half of what he set out, but Elder Ming hadn't even discussed the word "failure" since I began. Just quiet encouragement and the occasional criticism. Aside from smacking me in the head when I first came, he was a gentle instructor.

By the time we finished our training, the moon was high in the sky, casting a soft glow over the clearing. My body ached, and my mind felt stretched to its limits, but I had never felt more alive. The training I had put myself through over the past few days was nothing in comparison to the Village Head's regimen. Having a proper mentor was truly a blessing.

"Thank you, Elder Ming," I said, my voice hoarse from exhaustion. "I feel like I've learned so much already. Is this what they had you do in your sect? You never did tell me which one you belonged to."

Elder Ming nodded, a hint of a smile on his lips. His eyes were wistful, as though he was remembering a particularly fond memory from long ago.

"There's no use talking about the past. It holds no use in the present. Stand up!"

I gathered myself and stood at attention, ramrod straight. He examined my body, and I discarded my top halfway into training as it was drenched in sweat.

"You've done well, but there's still one more thing we need to cover today. Sit down and cross your legs. We're going to meditate. This will be the first step in unlocking your qi."

Truly?! He was actually going to teach me?

Seeing no hint of a joke, I followed his instructions, my body protesting as I settled into a seated position. Elder Ming sat across from me, his eyes closed and his breathing steady.

"Now I'll teach you how to circulate qi," he said, opening his eyes. "As a mortal, you don't have access to your own qi yet, so I'll push some of mine into your body to help you understand the process. Imagine your body as a series of rivers and streams, and qi as the water that flows through them. The goal is to guide the water through the rivers and streams without it overflowing or becoming stagnant."

I nodded, my brow furrowed in concentration as I tried to visualize what he was describing.

Elder Ming placed his hands on my shoulders and began to slowly push his qi into my body. At first, I didn't feel anything, but then I felt a gentle warmth spreading through my veins. It was like sunlight on a cold winter morning, comforting and invigorating at the same time. It was more pronounced than when Tianyi exchanged her energy with me to activate the artifact.

As the qi flowed through me, I could feel it following the pathways Elder Ming described, like water through a network of rivers. I focused my mind on guiding the qi, making sure it flowed smoothly and without obstruction. It was a delicate balance, and I found myself completely absorbed in the task. Unlike my past experience with meditation, where I had difficulties clearing my mind, I was focused utterly on guiding the energy Elder Ming put into my body.

At one point, I felt the qi building up near my stomach, and a sudden pressure caused me to let out a loud, unexpected burp. Both Elder Ming and I opened our eyes, startled by the interruption. For a moment, we stared at each other, then burst into laughter, our earlier seriousness forgotten.

Once we had composed ourselves, Elder Ming continued with the lesson. "That's a good example of what can happen if you don't properly circulate the qi. Sometimes the consequences aren't as light. The key is to maintain a balance, allowing the energy to flow smoothly regardless of how much time or attention it takes. Understand, little Kai?"

We continued to meditate, Elder Ming guiding me in the process of circulating the qi. By the end of our session, I felt a sense of harmony within my body that I had never experienced before. My mind was clear, and my muscles, though still aching, felt more relaxed.

As we rose from our meditation, I thanked Elder Ming once more, a newfound appreciation for the world of cultivation filling me. I was eager to continue my training and unlock the potential within me, step by step. I thanked him profusely and promised him some tea leaves for our training session tomorrow. He laughed and shooed me away.

"Rest is important as well. Visit me the day after and we can continue your test."

As I walked through the village, I couldn't help but notice the warm interactions between the villagers. Families shared hearty meals together, children chased each other through the narrow streets, and friends exchanged laughter and stories. These scenes of camaraderie and love filled me with bittersweet longing. Memories of my mother and father resurfaced, sobering me up after the training with Elder Ming.

I hope they looked kindly upon me, wherever they were. Your son was going strong, living his life to the fullest. I won't let myself be bound to being a simple gardener.

I'll become an immortal!

Lost in my thoughts, I ran into Lan-Yin once again. She had a basket of freshly picked fruits balanced on her hip, her hair was tied up in a neat bun. Her eyes sparkled with amusement as she looked at my worn-out and bruised form.

"Kai, what happened to you?" she asked with a mixture of amusement and concern.

I puffed out my chest and replied with mock arrogance, "I am training with Elder Ming, learning the way of cultivation. Soon I will be the most powerful young master in the land!"

Lan-Yin rolled her eyes, chuckling. "Oh, really? Kowtow Kai, the mighty cultivator? I suppose I should bow down to you right now!"

We laughed together, and for a moment, the pain in my body seemed to fade away. I asked how her grandmother was, and she told me that the ingredients I gave her improved the woman's health. I was glad to hear that. But then Lan-Yin's gaze turned more serious. "In all honesty, Kai, why are you trying so hard to be a cultivator?"

I thought about it for a moment before answering. "Freedom, I suppose."

That's all it was, really. There was something so poignant about being a free man with no obligations and no worry except his next destination. I lived in the village my entire life, eked out a respectable living for myself, but then what?

I had no family. No significant other holding me down to this village. Living here would give me a life of comfort, peace, and tranquility. But would I be truly satisfied with that? I didn't know. My heart yearned for something outside of here. I wanted to see the world for all it had to offer. The volcanoes at the Crimson Flame Peaks. The legendary World Tree in the Emerald Spirit Forest. Glimmering shores of the Sapphire Sea Isles. I've heard so much, read so much, but I have yet to take a step out of the place I called home. Being a cultivator would give me the freedom and security needed to explore the world and places outside of this province.

She looked at me thoughtfully, her eyes filled with warmth. My answer was of few words, but she seemed to understand the depth behind them. "Well, if that's what you truly want, then I'll support you, Kai. Just promise me one thing."

"What is it?"

"Promise me you'll come back to visit us, no matter how far your journey takes you."

I nodded, my heart swelling with gratitude. I may not have a family, but I had a community here in the Gentle Wind Village. One that I wouldn't forget even if I wanted to. "That's a foregone conclusion. I will return bearing gifts from my travels! Legendary elixirs, mythical artifacts!"

With a smile and a wave, we parted ways, and I continued on my way home.

The scent of various flowers and herbs filled the air as I entered the shop, a comforting reminder of home. I made my way to my room, exhaustion weighing heavily on my shoulders.

As I pushed open the door, I was greeted by the sight of Tianyi, the Azure Moonlight Flutter. She was perched gracefully atop a potted plant, her delicate wings shimmering with the ethereal beauty of moonlight. I still remembered she possessed a certain skill that strengthened her under the guise of the celestial body, and I could see that Tianyi's colors were much more vivid than before. She flitted over to me, her gentle presence a soothing balm to my aching body.

"Hello, Tianyi," I whispered, smiling warmly. She responded with a soft flutter of her wings as if acknowledging my greeting. My body begged for rest, and I couldn't resist its call any longer. "I will leave the door open for you should you require some nectar in the garden outside. This young master needs his rest."

Carefully nudging the butterfly to her spot on the windowsill, I refilled her bowl which contained some sugar water. Tianyi would not go hungry so long as I could help it!

I collapsed onto my bed, my mind drifting to the challenges that awaited me the next day, and soon, I was engulfed by the comforting embrace of sleep. Something passed my vision, another blue box, but my eyelids seemed to weigh as much as the sky, and darkness took over.

I awoke the next morning, astonished to find my body feeling revitalized, with only the faintest hint of soreness lingering from the previous day's training. I blinked away the remnants of sleep, glancing around my room to discern the reason for my unexpected recovery.

You have deepened your bond with the Spirit Beast, Tianyi.

You have discovered a hidden ability possessed by the Azure
Moonlight Flutter—Qi Haven.

Qi Haven: Transforms frequented areas into concentrated qi zones,
boosting recovery and cultivation efficiency for those
within its boundaries.

Level: 2 (Friend)—Tianyi has developed a closer relationship with you,
displaying increased trust and willingness to assist in your
cultivation journey.

My eyes settled on Tianyi, who was resting on my windowsill, her wings pulsing gently as they emanated a faint but steady stream of qi. I realized that it was her healing energy that had contributed to my recovery. A broad grin spread across my face as I leaped out of bed.

"Ah, the heavens themselves are guiding me on the path to ascension!" I proclaimed dramatically, gesturing grandly toward the sky. It was a beautiful day today. "Surely, I am destined for greatness, for it is I, Kai, the illustrious cultivator-to-be, who shall conquer the world of cultivation and leave my mark on the annals of history!"

Filled with enthusiasm, I strode over to my beloved plants, greeting them with the same grandiosity I had displayed earlier. "Greetings, my loyal subjects! Today, your esteemed master shall embark on a noble journey toward the pinnacle of cultivation! Fear not, for I shall return victorious, and together, we shall bask in the glorious light of my triumph!"

My plants, of course, did not respond, but I couldn't help but feel a surge of motivation coursing through me, fueled by my recovery.

After I completed my daily tasks around the shop, I would travel back into the forest. It was time to focus on my Herbalism and Gardening skills.

CHAPTER EIGHT

Tianyi, the Azure Moonlight Flutter

There was another advantage of Tianyi's Qi Haven skill that I realized as soon as I exited my house.

Her presence had made my home qualified for the Cultivation Technique quest, which required me to find an area with sufficient wood qi and meditate in it for one hour. That was made clear by the glowing yellow orb floating just above my garden.

I was roused by that information, and I did my best to complete my daily tasks around the shop before I began meditating. Tending to the plants was a peaceful, though slightly tedious, activity. I had some difficulty doing it as a child, but I framed it in a way that made me feel obligated to attend to them with the same attention I did every day.

The plants were alive, and I was the one responsible for them. Neglecting even a plant, for something as simple as not being able to move or talk, was the height of foolishness!

Talking to them, and giving them individual names, all played to giving me a small, but treasured attachment that kept me consistent with caring for my garden. Even those retired elders in the village couldn't make a garden as nice as mine! And they have all the time in the world to care for them. Had it not been for my aspiring dream to be a cultivator, I would've been the greatest gardener under the heavens!

Ahem, it seemed I was getting ahead of myself.

Then came harvesting, stocking, and organizing the shop and cleaning my tools. I'd have to take a look and see if I could gather up some new seeds, the merchants from out of town would likely have some for me to purchase.

All in all, my mundane tasks took me about an hour to do. Maybe it was me being overeager, but I finished up quite quickly in comparison to other days. No customers out in the distance, so I took it as my chance to meditate and complete the first part of my cultivation quest.

As I crossed my legs, I envisioned the circulation of qi that Elder Ming showed me. But it was supremely difficult without his guidance. I could remember the pathways, likening them to a network of rivers. But actually manifesting any sort of energy was a moot point. I didn't feel anything like I did when Elder Ming was doing it. There was still something I lacked.

Despite it all, I continued to sit cross-legged, uninterrupted. I tried to keep my mind clear and serene. Breathing in the smell of the plants and herbs all around me, with the wind flowing through my hair, it made the job incredibly easy. Keeping track of whether I'd been doing it for an hour was the rough part, but I guessed it as best I could and added some time on top of what I already did.

By the time I opened my eyes, I had made my first step toward gathering my first cultivation technique.

> —*Find five different areas that have sufficient wood qi in the surrounding and meditate in them for one hour. (1/5)*

A few customers strolled in, keeping me busy. I changed the hours of my shop so I had enough time to go about doing my tasks, but if I was really shorthanded, I could always ask Lan-Yin to run it for me. She helped at times, and I paid her handsomely for her efforts. Thanks to my careful budgeting, I was able to use her services when needed.

I glanced around, making sure that Tianyi was all good while I prepared for my expedition. She never drifted too far from the house, occasionally exploring the garden and feeding on the nectar, but the butterfly seemed content here.

"Will you be coming with me to the forest, Tianyi?" I asked. I would continue my search for a plant with qi. Going closer to the waterfall where I found the artifact that triggered the Heavenly Interface seemed like a good place to start. I wanted to visit there again anyway.

The Azure Moonlight Flutter moved from its spot on the windowsill and landed lightly on my shoulder. I grinned and pointed out of the house. Carrying a water canteen and some extra tools to properly harvest whatever herbs I found, I was ready to go.

"ONWARD!"

With Tianyi perched on my shoulder, we ventured into the village square. The sun was warm on my skin, and the sounds of conversation and laughter filled the air. As we walked through the bustling market, I overheard a group of villagers discussing something unusual.

"Did you hear about Li's chickens?" one woman asked, her brows furrowed with concern. "They've been acting really strange lately. I wonder what's causing it."

"Yeah, and it's not just his chickens. A lot of the farm animals have been restless and agitated these past few days. Some are even refusing to eat," a man chimed in.

I couldn't help but be curious about this unusual behavior. Pausing for a moment, I pondered whether it could have something to do with the Heavenly Interface or the creatures lurking in the forest. After a brief moment of contemplation, I decided to keep this information in mind as I continued on my journey.

Again, for as long as I remembered, there was nothing in the forest outside of mundane animals. Tianyi was likely the only Spirit Beast within a hundred li of the village.

Soon enough, Tianyi and I reached the edge of the forest. As we walked deeper into the woods, the atmosphere began to change. The air grew colder, and the sounds of the forest seemed strangely muted. Even the vibrant colors of the plants and flowers appeared somewhat subdued. Tianyi, who had been happily fluttering around me, suddenly grew still and unwilling to leave my shoulder.

As we ventured further, Tianyi's behavior became odd. I tried to soothe her, gently stroking her delicate wings.

Tianyi and I ventured deeper into the forest, the sunlight filtering through the dense canopy above us. As we walked, I noticed how eerily quiet it was. The usual cacophony of birdsong and rustling leaves was strangely absent, replaced by an unnerving silence that made my skin prickle with unease. It felt as if the forest was holding its breath, waiting for something to happen.

Despite the unsettling atmosphere, the forest was exactly as I remembered it—the moss-covered stones, the twisted roots snaking across the forest floor, and the smell of damp earth and decay. I tried to offset my nervousness by acting boldly, striding confidently through the undergrowth with Tianyi still perched on my shoulder.

"No creature to fear here, Tianyi. In fact, I am the most dangerous one here. My entire body is a lethal weapon, I say. So if a hungry beast were to try its luck . . . it would find its head separated from its shoulders!"

In an effort to reassure myself, I gripped the knife I used to harvest plants tightly in my hand. The familiar weight of the tool in my grasp provided some small comfort, but I couldn't shake the feeling that something was amiss.

As we continued on our path, the silence of the forest was only broken by the occasional snap of a twig or the rustling of leaves as we disturbed them. The farther we traveled, the more pronounced the sense of unease became. Tianyi's trembling had not subsided, and I found myself casting wary glances around as if expecting danger to materialize from the shadows at any moment.

Finally, after what felt like an eternity, the sound of rushing water reached my ears. We were getting closer to the waterfall where I had discovered the artifact that triggered the Heavenly Interface. As we approached, the atmosphere seemed to shift slightly. While the silence remained, the tension in the air seemed to lessen, as if the forest was finally exhaling a long-held breath.

The waterfall came into view, cascading down the rocks in a shimmering curtain of mist and spray. I couldn't help but be struck by the beauty of the scene, even as my mind remained preoccupied with the strangeness of the forest.

"All right, Tianyi, be careful, now. Don't get wet."

I lifted my robe to avoid getting it wet while the butterfly fluttered around in a hurried manner. She seemed partial to sticking closer to me, but I didn't want to get any water on her. I didn't know how durable a Spirit Beast was, but I didn't exactly think the Azure Moonlight Flutters were known for their toughness.

Approaching the spot where the mirage was, I leaned forward expecting no resistance to enter the secret tunnel.

Instead, my forehead met with solid stone, and I almost stumbled backward into the water, cradling my head in agony.

"Ahh . . . ! Dear heavens, Tianyi, I see two of you!" I groaned, rubbing my aching forehead.

The injury wasn't the most pressing matter; the tunnel leading into where I had seen the artifact was gone. It was as if the very entrance to the mysterious ruins had vanished without a trace. I couldn't make sense of it; the hidden chamber had been so real, so vivid in my memory. That was no illusion. It was where I had my fateful meeting with Tianyi.

I touched the spot where the entrance should have been, only to be met with water and rock. I felt around, trying to see if it was blocked, but to no avail. The smooth stone surface offered no indication that a passageway had ever existed there.

"Was it all just an illusion, Tianyi?" I asked the butterfly. "Did I imagine the entire thing?"

Tianyi fluttered her wings as if to offer some comfort, but she remained silent. I couldn't help but feel a pang of disappointment. The discovery of the mysterious ruins had ignited a spark of hope and excitement within me, and now it seemed to be snuffed out just as quickly. I had hoped it would allow me to gain some further insight into this Heavenly Interface and what it had to offer. Much of it was still shrouded in mystery, after all.

I took a moment to gather my thoughts, trying to recall every detail of the hidden chamber as I attempted to make sense of its sudden disappearance. The intricate carvings, the musty scent, and the sense of profoundness when I glanced at the stone pedestal in the very center of the ruins, all of it felt so real, yet here I was, standing before a blank wall of unyielding rock.

"Could it be a hidden mechanism?" I mused, not wanting to give up on the possibility that the secret chamber still existed. "Maybe there's a specific way to access it."

I started to examine the area more closely, searching for any clues or hidden switches that might reveal the entrance once more. I pressed and prodded the stone surface, tapped on the rocks surrounding the waterfall, and even tried speaking to the waterfall as I ran out of ideas.

But no matter what I tried, the entrance remained stubbornly hidden, leaving me feeling more perplexed and disheartened than ever.

"Why would it vanish like this, Tianyi?" I asked, my voice barely above a whisper. "What am I missing?"

A rustling in the bushes alerted me to the presence of something nearby. Instinctively, I gripped my knife tighter and scanned the undergrowth for any sign of movement. Tianyi, who had been fluttering anxiously, suddenly froze in place, her wings quivering.

From the shadows, an unusually large crow stepped out into the open, its black feathers glistening in the dappled sunlight. Its beady eyes bore an unnerving intelligence, and it seemed to be studying us with great interest. The crow seemed to be drawn to Tianyi, and I could tell that it coveted the Azure Moonlight Flutter for more than just nutritional value.

For a moment, I thought it was a Spirit Beast. One thing they all seemingly possessed was greater intelligence. But it didn't hold the same, mystical feel that Tianyi had. Perhaps it was on the cusp of becoming one?

Before I could react, the crow lunged at us, beak open and talons extended. I swiped at it with my knife, but the bird easily dodged my attack and took to the air, circling us and cawing mockingly. Any concern I had about the missing entryway was gone.

"Get back, you vile creature!" I shouted, swinging my knife in a futile attempt to fend off the crow. "You won't lay a single talon on Tianyi!"

The chase was on. The intelligent crow led us on a wild pursuit deeper into the forest, constantly out of reach but never far from sight. I was impressed by its cunning, as it seemed to have a plan to separate Tianyi from me. The crow would occasionally swoop in for a strike, forcing me to swing wildly with my knife, only to retreat once more and lead us farther into the woods. I kept the butterfly close, cupping her in my hands and preventing the agile avian from picking her off.

As we raced through the forest, the crow's attacks grew more daring and persistent, aiming to wear us down and catch us off guard.

"Argh!" A wound opened up across my shoulder, as the crow's talons ripped open my robe.

Tianyi clung to my shoulder, her tiny body trembling with fear, and I could feel her desire to escape with each passing moment.

I cursed my weakness. Being unable to fend off a crow, even with uncanny intelligence, was shameful. The only caveat so far was the constant physical training I've endured keeping me sharp against the bird's constant attacks. The crow's talons were sharp, cutting open another wound on my cheek. It would've been difficult to fend it off by myself, but protecting my butterfly companion at the same time added another layer of challenge.

Despite my best efforts to shake off our pursuer, the crow continued to hound us, its intelligence and persistence pushing me to my limits. With every near miss and desperate lunge, I could feel my resolve and energy waning. I stumbled on a root, and I only had just enough time to extend my arms and prevent Tianyi from being crushed by my weight. But it meant she was vulnerable to attack, and the dastardly bird knew it.

Finally, the crow made its move. It swooped in, talons extended, and managed to get ahold of Tianyi's wings. I could see the damage the crow's sharp talons had inflicted on her, and I snapped.

"UNHAND HER!"

In a burst of adrenaline-fueled fury, I charged at the crow and managed to land a decisive blow with my knife just as it caught her, slicing through its wing and sending it crashing to the forest floor. The bird let out a final, pitiful caw before succumbing to its injuries and lying dead.

I rushed to Tianyi's side, cradling her in my hands as I examined the damage. Her wings were badly torn and bent, and she was barely moving. I cursed and looked around for a spot where I could set her down and treat her. Damn it all! I had no clue how to treat a butterfly's grievous wounds! And I sincerely doubted anyone else in the village did either. It would take me hours to get back, especially considering that I ran even farther off the familiar path. I was well and truly lost in the forest this time around.

I would have to heal Tianyi myself.

The fact that she was still alive after being caught in that crow's talons was a miracle, a testament to her title as a Spirit Beast. But it was just enough to keep her from the jaws of death.

I cupped her into my hands as gently as I could, but then I noticed a yellow glowing orb from a small distance away. I recognized it immediately; it was identical to the one outside my porch! An area with wood qi!

> *Qi Siphon: Can absorb small amounts of qi*
> *from its surroundings to sustain itself.*

Her skill Qi Siphon should work here! I laid her down as close as I could to the glowing orb, where I surmised the innate qi was at its strongest, and searched for a flower of some sort that could be used as her bed. Just underneath the yellow orb, I spotted another item of interest.

A Moonlit Grace Lily.

Under the gentle warmth of the early-afternoon sun, I carefully cradled Tianyi in my palm, her delicate azure wings quivering ever so slightly. As I approached the Moonlit Grace Lily, its vibrant petals swayed gently in the breeze atop the grassy hill. With the utmost care, I lowered her onto the soft, velvety petals, which seemed to embrace her tiny form. The plant's subtle mystical aura enveloped her, and I could see her tense body gradually relax, her wings settling down to rest. With shaking fingers, I carefully smoothed out her wings, wincing at the spots where the crow had left its mark.

At that moment, as the Moonlit Grace Lily's soothing energy began to work its magic on Tianyi, a pang of guilt and shame washed over me. The cultivation quests and the pressures of my journey seemed to fade into insignificance. Despite all that she had done for me, I had been unable to protect her when she needed me most.

No—I wouldn't sit here mourning my weakness. It was time for me to do something for her. To save Tianyi.

CHAPTER NINE

First Steps

My heart raced as I stood there, watching Tianyi's fragile form resting on the Moonlit Grace Lily. I couldn't just stand idly by, waiting for the flower to do all the work. In my desperation to save her, I racked my brain for a solution, feeling the weight of helplessness bearing down on me. I recalled the time when Tianyi had selflessly transferred her own energy to me when we were trying to activate the stone pedestal in the ancient ruins. If only I could do the same for her now.

With nothing left to lose, I closed my eyes and took a deep breath, trying to focus on my inner energy. I remembered Elder Ming's teachings about visualizing the pathways within my body as a series of rivers and streams, flowing through me and connecting each part of me to the others. My brows furrowed as I concentrated, trying to grasp the elusive concept that had evaded me for so long.

At first, all I could sense was darkness and the distant sound of my own heartbeat. But as I focused more intently, the darkness began to fade, replaced by a faint shimmering light. I could feel the energy pathways in my body, like tiny threads of light weaving through me. They were weak, barely perceptible, but they were there.

Desperate to unlock my qi reserves, I concentrated harder, recalling the sensation I felt when Tianyi shared her energy with me. My mind's eye traced the path of my internal rivers and streams, willing the energy to flow through them, to break free of their confines and surge forth.

Slowly, as if responding to my desperate pleas, the energy within me began to awaken. I felt it gradually building, like the first drops of water forming a gentle stream. The sensation grew stronger, my inner rivers swelling with newfound power, until finally, I felt a breakthrough. My inner qi, previously dormant and untapped, now coursed through me, a torrent of energy waiting to be directed.

You can now access your qi.
Your qi has transcended into the next stage, Qi Initiation Stage—Rank 1.

With my heart pounding in my chest, I dismissed the slew of boxes and placed my hand near Tianyi, focusing on channeling my newfound qi toward her. A warm, soothing flow of energy emanated from me, enveloping her in a comforting embrace. As my own strength mingled with the healing power of the Moonlit Grace Lily, I could see her condition improving, her wings straightening out and her aura regaining its luster.

My manipulation wasn't as precise, and some of it spilled onto the Moonlit Grace Lily, but it seemed to strengthen the subtle aura around it, releasing a fragrant smell that soothed my nerves.

My body was covered in sweat and I gasped out in exhaustion. That move had taken a significant amount of my energy, and I was beginning to feel lightheaded.

But . . . I did it! I unlocked my qi reserves! Not even a day after Elder Ming guided me, I was able to do it on my own! I was a genius!

Ha ha . . . Ha . . .

I fell onto the grass and collapsed, my surroundings becoming fainter and fainter. Trying to open my eyes was an impossible task, and I let sleep claim me.

I shot awake, my stupor vanishing as I searched for Tianyi. The overhead moon had shown me just how much time had gone by since I passed out. Using my qi was no joke!

She was no longer lying atop the Moonlit Grace Lily, and I feared that another crow may have taken its chance to capture her once more. But the glimmering motes of light from my peripheral vision showed that wasn't the case.

Name: Tianyi
Race: Mystical Butterfly
Affinity: Wood
Cultivation Rank: Qi Initiation Stage—Rank 2

Bond Level: 3 (Close Companion)—Tianyi has formed a deep bond with you,
displaying loyalty and commitment to your shared journey.
Her abilities may strengthen in response to your connection, and
she will be more attuned to your emotions and needs. Additional abilities or
enhancements may become available as your bond continues to grow.

I could see she grew stronger. Her cultivation rank had increased, and so had the bond level, which showed just how much closer we got. It seemed quite silly, having such a deep connection with a butterfly, but what was wrong with that?

Kai Liu always repaid his debts! Regardless of who it was for.

A foreign feeling echoed in my head, which felt like . . . agreement? I turned to Tianyi, who was fluttering away with her wings more vibrant than ever.

"Are you able to talk to me, Tianyi?"

The foreign feeling appeared once again, but I could sense it was closer to affirmation. I've never heard of such a thing!

This new connection between us was truly odd, and I'd have to take some time getting used to it. After confirming her well-being and the Moonlit Grace Lily, I sat down and observed my quests. The area had many resources I could use to fulfill several requirements in regard to my path as a cultivator.

> *Herbalism (Level 9): A skill that grants knowledge and understanding*
> *of various plants, their properties, and uses in medicine and alchemy.*
> *Herbalism enables the user to identify, harvest, and process plants effectively.*
> *Next Stage: Spiritual Herbalism*
> *Requirements:*
> *Qi Initiation Stage—Rank 1*
> *Herbalism Proficiency—Level 10*
> *Infuse qi into a plant successfully.*
> *Find a plant that inherently possesses qi.*

> *Quest: Cultivation Technique (Wood)*
> *—Find five different areas that have sufficient wood qi in the*
> *surroundings and meditate in them for one hour. (1/5)*
> *—Areas with sufficient wood qi will be marked with a*
> *glowing yellow orb only visible to you.*

The Moonlit Grace Lily was a plant with qi. I also had plans of taking it with me back home. Having it in the same spot where there was sufficient wood qi for my cultivation technique quest seemed too good to be true, but I realized that areas where the Moonlit Grace Lily can grow overlapped with areas that had sufficient wood qi. It made sense, I supposed.

"Tianyi, I'll be meditating. Make sure to alert me of any presences nearby!"

I was giddy; I had unlocked my qi reserves, and now all I had to do was circulate them and take advantage of the qi in the surrounding area.

I crossed my legs and resumed the same position I did when Elder Ming taught me, and I could feel the strands of energy this time. They weren't as dense or firm as the one Village Head showed me, but it was my own, and I felt particularly proud of that.

With the goal of meditating and cultivating at the same time, I let things flow. The sound of my heartbeat began to increase, getting louder and louder, but I stayed my pace and tried to keep going.

Time passed, although I didn't for how long. Meditating was more fun this way, circulating the small tendrils of energy throughout my body and just getting used to it. It gave me something to focus on. Although I couldn't really—

"Grhhk!"

I felt a shooting pain right where my heart should've been, which snapped me out of my meditation. My chest tightened, and I could hardly breathe. Fear gripped me as the pain intensified, and I instinctively knew something had gone wrong. I remembered Elder Ming warning me about the improper circulation of qi—could this be the dreaded Qi Deviation?

Panic welled up inside me, and I gasped for breath. Desperation gnawed at me as I recalled Elder Ming's teachings, trying to figure out what I had done wrong and how to fix it. The pain was unbearable, but I knew I had to act fast or the consequences could be fatal.

My struggle alerted Tianyi and she darted over to my side, fluttering frantically. I tried to speak, but no words came out.

She seemed to sense my predicament and quickly began to circle me, her wings glowing with a soft, healing light. As she did, I could feel the soothing energy she emitted seeping into me, helping to alleviate some of the pain and stabilize my erratic qi. It was much more prominent than before. It was as though she doused the flame in my heart with cool water, allowing me to regain some control of my qi.

With Tianyi's support, I took slow, deep breaths. My focus shifted to the pathways within my body, and I cautiously guided the energy back to where it belonged, ensuring that I didn't aggravate my condition further. That was far too close. I wouldn't even know where I'd be without the butterfly's timely intervention.

After what felt like an eternity, the pain finally subsided, and my breathing returned to normal. I slumped back onto the ground, utterly exhausted, and looked up at Tianyi, gratitude shining in my eyes.

"Thank you, Tianyi. You saved me," I whispered, my voice barely audible. "I suppose I shouldn't be so distracted when cultivating . . ."

Tianyi fluttered closer, her wings brushing against my cheek in a gentle, comforting gesture. I could sense her concern and relief through our bond, and it warmed my heart to know that she cared so deeply for me.

Determined not to repeat the same mistake, I resumed my meditation, but this time, I decided not to circulate my qi. Instead, I simply focused on keeping my focus on a single point.

Before I knew it, enough time had passed for me to get some progression on the cultivation technique quest. I got up and stretched my arms, feeling Tianyi resting on my shoulder. I harvested the Moonlit Grace Lily as carefully as I could, keeping it as whole as possible. I wanted to grow more of the qi plant, and with Tianyi's Qi Haven skill, I had a feeling it would have ample energy in its surroundings to grow.

I did the best I could to navigate the forest, but with the darkness and unfamiliarity of my surroundings, it made it difficult to rely on my knowledge. Tianyi seemed comfortable moving forward, a far cry from when we initially entered the forest. I supposed that was a good sign. Through our connection, I could feel her beckoning me, almost as if she knew the way back home. Her glimmering trail made it easy to follow her every step of the way.

What a day. I had imagined it to be a simple one, but it was far more chaotic and hectic than I ever thought it'd be. But I received great boons and deepened my bond with Tianyi, so I didn't mind.

My thoughts were drawn to the bird. It was the first of its kind I had seen. Crows were not unusual, but one so aggressive and intelligent was far from the norm. Could it be related to the Heavenly Interface? If everyone, including animals and humans, got it, then that would mean . . .

I glanced at Tianyi. Her cultivation rank had increased by one stage. Perhaps she could evolve into a higher form as well?

Within an hour of walking, I finally came across the end of the forest, with the village in sight. I thanked the Azure Moonlight Flutter for her services and made my way back home, careful not to disturb the others when it was so late at night. I scratched the wound on my cheek, feeling a slight twinge of pain as I did so. I wondered how I'd explain such a thing to Elder Ming. An aspiring cultivator, injured by a bird. Bah!

I had been getting myself into too much trouble during my excursions into the forest. Perhaps it was time for me to learn how to use that iron staff I had Wang Jun make? It wasn't too bad of an idea.

My garden knife was far too unwieldy, and I needed a reliable weapon if I were to keep going back into the forest. There was no guarantee that the animals would stay as peaceful as they were now. The crow was just one example. I couldn't imagine if a boar or some other manner of beast had decided to attack me. I shivered, knowing it wouldn't have ended well.

Upon reaching my garden, I selected a spot that I felt would be ideal for the Moonlit Grace Lily. I chose an area with rich soil, surrounded by other plants, which would help nurture and support the flower's growth. Additionally, I ensured that the location was bathed in ample moonlight, as I knew the Moonlit Grace Lily thrived under such conditions.

Before planting the Moonlit Grace Lily, I carefully prepared the soil, removing any debris and weeds that could potentially harm the delicate plant. I then dug a small hole, gently placing the flower's roots into the earth and covering them with soil. I don't have too much information in regard to the sort of nutrients it needed, but I could guess it needed more than a regular plant.

I glanced at my hands. Perhaps I could imbue it with some energy? I was a bit apprehensive, considering the fact that even circulating my qi nearly led me to having a heart attack. But I glanced over at Tianyi and knew she'd likely be able to help me if the same thing happened again.

Cautiously, I manipulated the tendrils of energy from the core of my body and guided them past my arm and into my palm. I closed my eyes in deep focus, trying to make sure that I didn't undergo any sort of Qi Deviation. As qi flowed out of my palm, I could see the Moonlit Grace Lily being imbued with it and standing up somewhat straighter.

I let out another breath and stopped the transfer of energy. That was easier than I thought. It felt natural to do it . . . Perhaps it had something to do with my affinity toward wood qi. I would have to ask Elder Ming.

Flopping onto my bed, I went to sleep bearing more questions than ever. From the disappearance of the ruins to the path of my cultivation, there was so much to learn. But all would be answered in time.

Just as soon as I rested.

CHAPTER TEN

Mind Refinement

I returned to Elder Ming in the afternoon, shortly after completing all my daily tasks. Watering my garden and paying special attention to the lily I had brought back home took precedence over all. I brought Tianyi with me to training as well. The Village Head seemed interested in my new companion, and she greeted him by fluttering around his face. I could see she liked Elder Ming.

After giving him some tea leaves, the first thing I told about him was the new skill I learned: Qi Manipulation. He almost dropped the teacup in his hands.

"You unlocked your qi reserves?!" Elder Ming said, his eyebrows rising in astonishment. "Show me. I don't believe you."

I sat down and cycled my qi throughout my body. I had no hesitation as I did it, knowing he and Tianyi would be able to help me if I were to undergo Qi Deviation. He watched in amazement, and he slapped me on the head once again.

"Ow! What's that for?!"

"Foolish boy! You could've sent yourself into Qi Deviation! This is dangerous without my super—"

"I did, actually." He gaped in horror upon hearing that. "But Tianyi helped me. She stabilized my condition before it got too serious. See? I'm fine! I'm a genius, right, Elder Ming?"

Elder Ming was far from amused. He began lecturing me about the importance of cultivating qi under proper supervision, including several painful taps to the head with a cane. Funny. I had never seen him use it to help walk, only to hit me and other children when we were being unruly. His lips were set in a firm line as he spoke in a low voice.

"Kai, I must warn you. Your body is not suited to being a cultivator. It is barely qualified to be a martial artist." He shook his head and closed his eyes. "Your qi circulatory system is thinner than the average person. Do you know what this means?"

"Uh, I'll have to work much harder to become a cultivator?"

"Well, yes, but it also means your qi won't flow as efficiently in your body. Every time you cultivate, you have a much higher chance of suffering from Qi Deviation. Far more than the average person would. Your journey will put you at great peril for even the simplest of moves like circulating your qi."

What the hell? My talent was third-rate? I was likely to die from meditating? No way! But I saw the look in Elder Ming's eyes. He was completely serious, and I had seen the effects of it myself.

"B-but there's ways to go about it, yes? I can still become a cultivator?"

Elder Ming's eyes sharpened. "You can, but it won't be easy. I will teach you the basics, but I can tell you right now that anything more advanced won't work for you the same it worked for me."

"I won't back down, Elder Ming. You already know I'm willing to do whatever it takes."

"Then let's get to it! The first step to making you fit to be a cultivator is refining your body! Grab those rocks! We're going back to the hills!"

"Yes, Master!"

And so my training continued.

We finished much quicker this time, although it took well into the evening to complete my training. My body and mind were stretched to their limits, but I was happy. Elder Ming had told me of my constraints, but wasn't the point of cultivation overcoming one's limitations?

He shooed me away, deep in thought. It seemed as though he was slightly distracted during our training session. I had much to think about as well.

Quest: Body Refinement
—Run the perimeter of Gentle Wind Village without stopping to rest. (2/5)
—Commit to the horse stance for ten minutes without stopping to rest. (1/5)
—Squat 250 times without stopping to rest. (2/5)

Quest: Mind Refinement
—Perform Visualization Training for one hour. (3/5)
—Meditate for one hour without losing focus. (4/5)
—Solve a mathematical equation without any external aid. (5/5)

Quest: Cultivation Technique (Wood)
—Find five different areas that have sufficient wood qi in the surroundings and meditate in them for one hour. (2/5)
—Areas with sufficient wood qi will be marked with a glowing yellow orb only visible to you.

I was almost done these quests. I wanted to see what I'd get for their completion. I was excited, but I knew the rest of my evening should be devoted to expanding upon my other skills: Gardening, Herbalism, and the new Qi Manipulation.

Yes, Elder Ming warned me against doing anything too foolhardy, but there were other ways to manipulate my qi aside from circulation. Like qi infusion! I noticed just how easy it was for me to do in comparison. Maybe I had a knack for that sort of thing.

My thoughts were interrupted by the heat of the forge. It seemed Master Qiang and Wang Jun were hard at work.

"Wang Jun! Master Qiang! How goes it?" I asked, letting my presence be known. It had been some time since I last saw either of them.

Wang Jun looked tired, but he bore a hearty smile. Master Qiang, on the other hand, had his usual stern expression, although he seemed to be in a good mood as he supervised his apprentice at work.

"Kai, it's been a while! We're just finishing up some orders from the nearby city," Wang Jun replied, wiping the sweat off his brow.

"I see you've made some progress with that cultivator training," Master Qiang observed, his eyes briefly flicking over my body. Was it that visible? I flexed my biceps, they were more defined than before, but it was hard to tell for me.

"Yeah, I've been learning a lot from Elder Ming. But how about you, Wang Jun? How's that quest of yours?" I asked, genuinely curious about his achievement.

Wang Jun's face lit up, and he nodded enthusiastically. "I finished it! It was a difficult challenge, but the results were well worth it. Let me tell you . . ."

He spoke to me about the tribulations he faced. Making twenty different kinds of weapons and armor truly challenged Wang Jun. But upon completion, he received a free level to his Blacksmithing skill! He showed off his weapons and compared the difference to the ones he made when he first began the quest, and although it was minor, I could see they were of greater quality.

I supposed that was how my quests would go. It made me more motivated to complete them. In fact, I could complete the Mind Refinement task as soon as I got home! If it were to grant me a reward like that, I suppose it would make me smarter and perhaps even help with my other quests!

"Ha ha! Wang Jun, I applaud your effort. You are a fine blacksmith. I will come by to have my tools maintained by you in the future."

He grinned sheepishly and seemed caught off guard by my compliment. Ah, I could never bring myself to dislike Wang Jun. He was as kind as he was big.

"Of course, but it may take some time. Those orders from Crescent Bay City keep coming. We've got a back order of close to fifty weapons due by the week's end!"

I raised my brow. It seemed as though the cities were gearing up for war. "Is there something going on?"

Master Qiang butted in, holding one of the swords he forged. The tall man held it up to the light with a critiquing eye. "There's been a rise of Spirit Beasts, bandit sightings, and just about every sort of trouble you could think of. I didn't think such a thing would be a problem round here. Nobody bothered when we had nothing to offer. But now, with the Heavenly Interface?"

The question went unanswered, as he swung the blade with practiced ease. I flinched backward, fearing that the blade would cut me. Master Qiang had a profound understanding of the weapons he created, and I didn't need to know how high his Blacksmithing skill was to see that. He had been the village blacksmith longer than I'd been alive. He mumbled something about it being off-balance before focusing his attention back on me.

"I guess you were right about being a cultivator, Kai," Master Qiang mumbled. "The world's getting a little more dangerous. We should be gearing up as well. This place won't be as quiet as it used to be, if my hunch is right."

I heard about life in other provinces. Power and conflict went hand in hand. Spirit Beast attacks, wayward bandits, wars between sects, and even whispers of demonic cultivators were common. But they were mitigated by the presence of so many powerful sects and cultivators that people of other provinces still managed to live a somewhat peaceful life. But we had nothing close to that. Our village was out of the way, with minimal defenses and no ties to any of the major or minor sects in the Tranquil Breeze Coast. If the Gentle Wind Village didn't prepare accordingly . . .

I swallowed nervously. Even Wang Jun seemed unnerved by what his master was implying.

"But! That's all an old man's worries!" His serious expression morphed into a stupid grin, and Master Qiang slapped me on the shoulder. "Come see me next time for your tools. It's been a couple years since you got them fixed up, right, Kowtow Kai?"

I left them with a smile and wave. But my thoughts were filled with other worries. Although the Day of Awakening was considered a blessing for all, maybe I shouldn't have been so lax in regard to my cultivation. That had been a trigger, not just for me, but for many throughout the world. People would move, and my cozy little life here in the village would be affected.

What if a Spirit Beast were to attack my village? Not just an intelligent crow? Or a group of bandits empowered by the Heavenly Interface? I looked to Tianyi. The memory of nearly losing her to that damn bird came to the forefront of my mind.

I tried to calm myself down. I was being too pessimistic. We were on the outskirts of the Tranquil Breeze Coast. No bandit or beast would try anything here. It was too far out, and we had nothing to offer. But if a third party ever turned their eyes to my village . . .

"It's simple, isn't it, Tianyi?" I asked her. "I simply become strong enough to ward off any threat that comes our way."

Our village had no real defense against outside threats. Perhaps the Village Head, who was once a cultivator, could fend off an invasion. But the thought of leaving it all to him felt like ash on my tongue.

Kai, protector of the Gentle Wind Village. That had a nice ring to it as well.

It would be a nice title to begin my journey. A goal to work toward before I explored the rest of the world.

Before this village could fend for itself in this new world, I would be their shield.

Three hours passed. I devoted my evening to mediation and Visualization Training. I felt more at peace meditating here at home, surrounded by the subtle wood qi provided by Tianyi's Qi Haven skill. I opened my eyes to a message from my interface.

> *Quest: Mind Refinement has been completed.*
> *Due to your status as Interface Manipulator, your rewards*
> *will be adjusted accordingly.*

Before I could question what was going on, a gentle warmth spread from the back of my head and eventually encompassed it. As though a veil had been lifted, I felt an immeasurable amount of mental clarity I hadn't had before.

> *Your mind is growing more powerful.*
> *You now have access to your own Memory Palace.*

I instinctively knew what the message entailed, even if I had never seen or heard of a Memory Palace. But it was pretty self-explanatory. I went back into the recesses of my mind, creating an endless expanse that came easily, thanks to my Visualization Training.

This was a Memory Palace. My Memory Palace. A place where I could recall and access any piece of information I'd ever learned. I grinned internally; this would be an incredible boon toward progressing my skills!

All right, let's see here. Let's go over the current potions and elixirs I know how to make. I can start experimenting from there.

My Memory Palace shaped itself according to my needs, creating a massive pile of books. I frowned. I needed to organize this place into something less mundane. Perhaps a library? No, that wouldn't do. Maybe something in line with who I am. Although I was a scholar, I wasn't particularly fond of rows upon rows of books. Perhaps . . .

I focused my mental energy on my surroundings, giving birth to a luxurious garden. A massive tree sat in the middle, growing large enough to blanket my entire vision. Branches upon branches sprouted from the trunk, some longer than others.

A tree of knowledge. Specifically, the one containing all my knowledge about herbs and plants. I'd need to make a separate tree for other disciplines, but this was good to start with. I looked over specific branches, instinctually knowing what each one represented. The ones that stemmed from the trunk were the foundation of my knowledge: soil knowledge, plant anatomy, identification, and so much more.

When I visualized it, it was truly awe-inspiring to see how much knowledge I'd accumulated. I had been around plants all my life, and the buildup of this information had been spread over years and years. I wondered what Elder Ming's looked like. Or even Wang Jun. Did his expertise in smithing go as deep as mine did for herbs?

I imagined mine in the future as something akin to the World Tree in size. It would pierce the skies and into the heavens! Once I became a cultivator, all the knowledge I had would be stored here, steadily growing and unfurling its roots.

I finally found the branch I was looking for, the one on medicinal properties and the usage of plants. It spread farther than most of the branches, and every single one I touched gave me an inkling of the knowledge behind it. The way my Memory Palace manifested itself to my desires was both an unconscious and a conscious action. This ability was incredibly profound.

Reviewing all my knowledge in regard to herbs took some time, but when I opened my eyes, only half an hour had passed. It felt like I had been there for hours, just going over potential ideas and ruminating about combinations I hadn't thought of.

With my entire store and garden in my grasp, I could experiment how I pleased. Perhaps I'd make a revolutionary elixir with what I had. Then I'd make a fortune off that product. And then I could use it to buy pills and elixirs to get stronger. Ha! If I accumulated more plants, I could probably make those pills and elixirs myself.

It all clicked into place. My plan for defying the heavens has solidified into something of worth! Nothing could stop me!

"He he he he . . . HA HA HA HA!"

My house was filled with evil cackles as I, Kai Liu, resolved to become the greatest herbalist and cultivator the Gentle Wind Village had ever seen!

CHAPTER ELEVEN

Experiments

I ended up spending most of my night in my Memory Palace. It was somewhat a poor idea in retrospect, as I wasn't truly resting while in this state. Physically, I was fine, but I felt mentally drained. I created several trees relating to each major discipline in my life, the most recent of which was in regard to my cultivating journey.

It was small, but I knew with time they would grow to surpass even the World Tree in size!

My time experimenting with new potions and herbal combinations was well spent. By combining milk thistle and Cleansing Lotus, I made a concoction that could detoxify a person's body! Although it was weak, it would be a great hangover cure for the folks down in the village. This was just one of the four successful recipes I'd created, but they'd need some further testing and refining to get a working product. Perhaps Elder Ming would enjoy this energy-boosting tonic of mine. Those old bones weren't getting any younger.

My little projects had been rewarded with a satisfying message from the Heavenly Interface.

Herbalism has reached level 10.
Your skill has reached the qualifications to evolve to the
next stage, Spiritual Herbalism.
Spiritual Herbalism grants you two new abilities.
Essence Extraction—You can extract the spiritual essence of plants for the
creation of pills and elixirs.
Spiritual Plant Cultivation—You can infuse plants with your qi,
increasing their potency or imbuing them with new properties.

The sun dawned on me, tired and victorious. The knowledge I currently had within me seemed to extend and lengthen into ways I didn't think of prior. It bridged the gap between my understanding of qi as well as herbalism, and I glanced over at my hands with a gut feeling about how to accomplish the extraction and infusion of plants.

This . . . This was incredible!

The Heavenly Interface was building upon the foundation of knowledge I already had. Whoever created this must've been quite the powerful cultivator; if this was what it was like for other disciplines like blacksmithing, carpentry, or fishing, they would've had to condense the knowledge of entire civilizations into this little box.

It made me wonder who or what could've made the Heavenly Interface. Was it some sort of immortal at the Spirit Ascension Stage? A martial god who descended from the heavens and shared this power to mortals? The interface was powerful beyond belief. It made me think back to the ruins that disappeared and why it was left there untouched until I came along.

I shook my head at such thoughts. Those answers would come with time. *For now, let me try these new skills out.*

It was my day off, so the shop would be open for the whole day. I opened the door and inhaled the smell of earth and fresh herbs, shouting at the top of my lungs, "Good morning!"

The first skill I was going to try out was Spiritual Plant Cultivation. It seemed to be an offshoot of my Qi Manipulation skill, or more specifically, the act of infusion, which I did with the Moonlit Grace Lily some time ago. I didn't know what the difference would be, but I was hoping for something good.

I knelt beside my ginseng. They were one of the slowest among my crops to grow, which was why I'd dedicated an entire section of my garden to it. This particular batch was supposed to be fully matured by next year, but they'd been growing a bit faster than I'd expected. Perhaps it was the effect of Tianyi's Qi Haven skill. There were very few places where ginseng could grow naturally while being saturated with qi. I placed my palm toward it and did the same thing I did with the Moonlit Grace Lily.

For some reason, my energy was far more responsive than I last remembered. The flow felt less forced as it transferred from my arm to the ginseng plant. I let it go for a few seconds before I paused and observed it again. The once-green leaves took on a brighter, almost-luminescent shade, reflecting the energy that now coursed through every part of the plant. Although the real prize was the root itself, I couldn't take it out prematurely. It would take some time for the plant to be ready for harvesting. Maybe within a few months, if this accelerated growth kept up.

Monitoring my reserves, I could gauge it took about a tenth of my energy in those few seconds of infusion. I frowned and looked at my entire patch of ginseng plants, knowing I wouldn't have nearly enough to infuse them all today. I decided to start with the first row, recover, and assess which other plants I would try afterward.

The act of infusing the plants with my qi wasn't as draining as I'd thought. In fact, it felt invigorating. Like it was a natural motion. I ended up having some leftover energy and decided to save it, lest I pass out. I watered the rest of my flourishing garden before sitting down to rest and meditate. Early in the morning surrounded by a garden teeming with life, this was probably a better spot to cultivate than whatever those disciples had in other sects!

I could feel Tianyi's presence even without opening my eyes. Maybe it was due to my deep bond with her, but I could clearly visualize her fluttering around, taking note of the freshly watered flowers, and absorbing some nectar. She continued to get closer until finally landing on my shoulder.

Her delicate touch was barely noticeable, but the moment she settled there, I felt a warm, tingling sensation begin to spread through my body.

From my shoulder, the warmth radiated outward, filling my limbs and coursing through my veins. It was as if a gentle, soothing energy was washing over me, seeping into my very core. I closed my eyes, focusing on the sensation and allowing it to envelop me completely.

The process was subtle and almost imperceptible, but as Tianyi drew on the qi in our surroundings, she transferred some of that energy into me. It was a slow, gradual process, but I could feel my exhaustion lifting, replaced by a renewed sense of vitality and strength.

As the minutes passed, the warmth within me continued to grow, and I felt my qi reserves slowly recovering. It wasn't a complete restoration, but it was enough to give me a newfound sense of clarity and focus. My mind felt sharper, my body lighter, and my spirit rejuvenated.

I felt a profound connection to my surroundings, as if I was one with the elements around me.

Tianyi fluttered off my shoulder, her work complete. I gave her a thumbs-up, knowing that her presence was the biggest boon to my cultivation journey. She seemed to understand my silent thanks as she bobbed gently in the air before resuming her dance among the flowers.

"Well, it seems more of you will be getting this blessing of qi," I declared to all my crops. The effect of qi on plants wasn't something I really knew, but from the looks of it, they'd be growing bigger, faster, and better than they would without.

I would need to study the effects more. My gardening skill wouldn't improve without further knowledge. How much of the effects contributed to being in an area with wood qi? Which of them was a result of my Spiritual Plant Cultivation?

Once I finished infusing my selected plants with qi, I'd go ahead and try the Essence Extraction skill. I had an inkling of what it did, but I needed to see it for myself.

"Thank you. Come again!" I waved farewell to my customer. They were the first to come around today, so I had the benefit of showing them some of the new concoctions I'd created. I sold the energy-boosting tonic and told them it was at a discount so long as they came back and told me of its effects. That was business, baby! If it were better than I'd thought, I could use it to sell some of my products to the merchants and make a profit by having them sold to other cities.

My dream of a greenhouse before winter may not be out of reach.

Returning inside, I placed my freshly harvested mint plant on the table. Now was the time to test my extraction skill. I placed my hands by the herb and tried to recall what knowledge the Heavenly Interface had given me. It was similar to qi infusion but in reverse.

I just needed to find the point from which I could take the plant's essence . . . Come on . . .

There!

A dull blue tendril of energy escaped the plant. It was far more corporeal than I thought it'd be. It coalesced into a small orb the size of a marble in my palm, and I quickly realized I had no place to store it. I wasn't keen on absorbing a mint plant's essence into my body. With my left hand preoccupied, I scrambled for a vial of some sort in my shop to contain it with.

Carefully, I let the blue essence of the mint plant flow into the vial. I sealed it and watched in awe as the essence swished around like a liquid. My eyes caught the herb that I extracted from; it seemed listless compared to before, as if it had gone stale. I held it to my nose and smelled it, still catching traces of that minty scent, but it was much fainter than before. They were still usable, but it wasn't of good quality anymore. I couldn't sell it to customers unless they were looking for plants to use in compost or mulch.

I took a plant's essence. *This is so cool!*

Unlike infusion, this one used very little of my energy to accomplish. I went about and grabbed a handful of herbs throughout my shop and began extraction.

Chamomile for calming teas. The essence it made was a soft, white, and soothing liquid that seemed more potent than when it was in plant form. In all honesty, it seemed to rival the Moonlit Grace Lily in that aspect, although the healing properties were minimal in comparison.

Ginger was a staple ingredient for its invigorating and warming properties. When I extracted its essence, it had a light brown hue and an intense fragrance.

Lavender, eucalyptus, and elderberry were just a few more of the plants I chose to extract from. I made sure to take the ones I had an excess of. Although I was highly tempted to try extracting the Moonlit Grace Lily, I needed to wait until it was mature enough for me to collect seeds as well as stems for even more of the rare qi plant.

But that was one of the greatest skills gardening bestowed upon me: patience. Whether it took weeks, days, or months, with consistent effort, these plants of mine would grow into what I envisioned them to be.

Perhaps I should've taken a page from my gardening and incorporated it into my path as a cultivator. Slow and steady won the race, after all.

If I wanted to cultivate these thin qi circulatory systems of mine, I'd need to have a good foundation to start off with. No shortcuts. Strengthening my body, mind, and qi would require consistency. I'd learn how to make pills and elixirs and grow a beautiful garden. Kai's Garden Shop would become a garden emporium.

So what if it took months or years? Cultivators had plenty of time to work with. I just needed to stay the course and remain faithful to what I knew. I didn't have access to pills and mentors like those sects, but what I did have was freedom.

"All right, Tianyi. We're going to save up and get a greenhouse. Let's make some more potions today."

I spent about an hour fiddling with the essences, mixing some together along with a few ingredients. My entire shop was filled with intense fragrances as the extracted ingredients reacted with one another. I took a sip of the potion I was making and hummed with pleasure. Even as a drink, it was delicious. But the effects of the purple concoction I made didn't end there. Elderberries were known for their immune-boosting properties, and the combination of willow bark and chamomile turned it into a pain-relief potion. Any aches and pains I had from the previous day, as minor as they were, disappeared like a bad dream.

I had to make more. I had to sell these.

While I wrote down the effects and ingredients I used in my own notebook, the familiar jingle of a customer entering my shop alerted me. I turned to see Lan-Yin with a smile on her face.

"How go things, Dreaming Gardener?"

"Lan-Yin! Just the person I wanted to see!" I greeted her enthusiastically, unable to keep the grin off my face. "Anybody in the village feeling ill? Tired? Down with the flu?"

She seemed surprised by my exuberance, which was even greater than it usually was. But Lan-Yin couldn't know about everything I'd been doing the past few days. The brown-haired girl put a finger to her chin, trying to think of an answer.

"Well . . . Xiao Bao's been coughing an awful lot. Elder Wen's been complaining about his back, like always. But that's about it. Why?"

"Perfect . . . Let me write that down. What were you here for?"

"Not much. Just wanted some ingredients for tonight's dinner. Could I have some chili and bamboo shoots?"

I acquiesced and handed her the ingredients she needed, and I put away the coins she gave me. Looking at my variety of new concoctions, I selected the ones I was most confident in alongside the products that would help with little Xiao Bao's and Elder Wen's problems. An idea was brewing in my head, and I wanted to go out there and test it as soon as possible.

Tianyi seemed content to stay home, so I bade her farewell and tagged along with Lan-Yin, carrying several of my new potions and the essences with me. I would give some to Xiao Bao and Elder Wen, but I'd be seeing if I can sell my products to the traveling merchant Huan. To do that, I'd need proof that my concoctions worked. And I was certain they did, but one could not convince a merchant with just their word alone.

It would have to be through action.

"You seem . . . enthusiastic. I suppose your cultivation journey's going well?" she teased, giving me a slight bump with her hip. But my core and lower body were immensely stable now in comparison to even a week before. The horse stance and squats I'd been doing were having an incredible effect. That small hit would've made me stumble before, but I barely even reacted, except for a small grin.

"Couldn't be better. Elder Ming's training is keeping me sharp. Soon I'll be the size of Wang Jun!" I declared.

Lan-Yin giggled and we delved into more pleasant topics. Although we were all teenagers, hers and Wang Jun's betrothal still forced responsibilities upon them. Nevertheless, Lan-Yin seemed happy for the stability it would provide, and Wang Jun was growing into a fine man.

"So, do you think he's gonna take Master Qiang's title as village blacksmith anytime soon?" I asked, genuinely curious about how their relationship was progressing.

Lan-Yin shrugged, a hint of uncertainty in her eyes. "I think so. He's been working really hard lately. Even with all the orders they've been receiving, he's still managed to be attentive to me. It's . . . nice, actually."

I smiled, happy for her. But the corners of my mouth turned more upward, into a cheeky grin. "That's good to hear. I will provide you both with energy-boosting tonics for the night your marriage is official."

She stuttered madly and blushed, slapping me on the shoulder several times and shouting out "Stupid Kai!" and other rude monikers. I howled like a hyena, trying to fend her off while carrying my stash of potions and essences.

"Honestly, you're so perverted." She paused for a moment, her expression turning mischievous. "And what about you? Are you too busy being a cultivator to have a girl of your own? Or rather, you couldn't find one and gave up!"

Oof. That was a low blow.

I laughed, putting on a comically serious face. "Ah, the life of a young master is fraught with peril and responsibility! I must tend to my ever-growing garden, cultivate my inner self, and create wondrous elixirs and potions! How could I possibly find time for love in such a hectic life?"

Lan-Yin laughed, shaking her head. "You're ridiculous, you know that?"

"I do my best," I replied, grinning.

As our conversation carried on, I waved off any names she pointed out when thinking of girls compatible with me in the village. They were all perfectly good women, but I aspired for a jade beauty, a female cultivator who could match or surpass me in wit and strength. Lan-Yin rolled her eyes, seemingly giving up and shaking her head at my absurd desire. The pleasantries continued until we arrived at the village square.

CHAPTER TWELVE

Validation

As I entered the village square, I bade farewell to Lan-Yin, agreeing to meet her again in a short while. My heart raced with anticipation as I approached the traveling merchant's makeshift shop. Huan's trading post was a colorful assortment of tents and makeshift stalls, adorned with banners and signs displaying various wares. The vibrant colors and bustling atmosphere were a stark contrast to the tranquil surroundings of Gentle Wind Village.

A large, central tent housed Huan's most valuable items, while smaller stalls were scattered around it, showcasing more common products. The scent of exotic herbs and spices filled the air, a testament to the variety of goods Huan had brought with him. As I walked closer, I could see Huan, a middle-aged man with a neatly trimmed beard, engaged in lively conversation with a group of villagers.

I took a deep breath and approached Huan, who greeted me with a warm smile. "Ah, young Kai! What can I do for you today? Are you here to buy some herbs or perhaps a new tool for your gardening?"

I shook my head. "Actually, Huan, I'm here to sell you some of my own products." I revealed the potions I had crafted, neatly arranged in small glass bottles.

Huan raised an eyebrow, his interest piqued but skeptical. "You've made these yourself, Kai? What do they do?"

As I began to explain the properties of each potion, Lan-Yin arrived with Xiao Bao, a young child coughing gently, and Elder Wen, whose back ached from years of labor. They were the perfect test subjects for my potions. I had asked her to come bring them for me just before we separated, and she seemed content to watch my antics as well. Curiosity gleamed in her eyes, and the rest of the villagers seemed interested in what I had to say.

"This one is a cough suppressant and should alleviate Xiao Bao's cough," I said nervously, handing the small blue vial to the boy. "And this one is a pain-relieving balm for Elder Wen's back." I passed a small jar filled with creamy ointment to the elder.

Lan-Yin helped me apply the potions as I carefully explained their proper usage. I felt a mixture of excitement and anxiety as we waited for the results, silently hoping that my knowledge and skills were sufficient. This was my first test with other people, and I only made certain that the effects wouldn't be adverse. I waited anxiously, expecting them to work immediately.

After a few moments, the effects became apparent. Xiao Bao's cough subsided, and he smiled brightly, relief shining in his eyes. Elder Wen straightened up, a look of surprise and gratitude on his face as his pain seemed to have vanished. The other villagers present murmured in awe, and I felt so happy, I was about to explode.

Huan observed the transformation with growing interest, his skepticism replaced by amazement. "Kai, these potions are incredible. I never knew you possessed such talent," he exclaimed, a hint of newfound respect in his voice. "How'd you do it?"

"The Interface gave me access to some amazing knowledge. These were made from the very plants I found here in the forest or grown in my garden. But only I can create them."

I grabbed an herb from my basket, it was the elderberry. As I closed my eyes and focused, a stream of essence escaped it and coalesced into my palm, stunning the audience and making them gasp.

"Behold, this is my new skill. I can extract a plant's very essence and utilize it in my recipes, creating even more potent concoctions that work better than the original, despite using the same ingredients I always had."

People clamored over my basket of goods, examining the essences with wonderment. I proudly showed the elderberry essence in my palm to all those who wished to see, and Xiao Bao poked it, almost as if in a trance, and watched it fluctuate slightly. I promptly placed it in the vial containing the rest of my elderberry essence for later use.

"What do you think? Will these products be suitable for sale, esteemed merchant?" I grinned, my confidence at an all-time high. After such a display, there was no way he could refuse.

"I'll have to see it for myself . . . But, Kai, I see the potential of this. I see the potential of *you*." Huan said with a particular glint in his eye. He seemed to be doing calculations in his head on the potential profits he'd reap from this. "Can you come tomorrow and present this again? There's someone very important coming tomorrow."

My curiosity was piqued. "Who's coming, Huan?"

Huan's eyes lit up with excitement. "Xiao Yun, the daughter of the head of the Azure Silk Trading Company, is arriving tomorrow to assess the potential for opening a permanent outpost here in Gentle Wind Village. As you know, I work for them, and if she's impressed with your products, it could mean a great opportunity for you."

I couldn't believe my luck—the chance to showcase my skills and potions to someone so influential could change everything for me. My back straightened and my eyes didn't waver as I made contact with his.

"Fear not, Huan! This young master will prepare a performance the likes of which has never been seen before!" I declared, my voice rich with enthusiasm and certainty. "I shall weave a performance so mesmerizing that all who bear witness will be left utterly spellbound, their minds captivated by the sheer brilliance on display!"

He laughed. So did the other villagers. But it wasn't like how it used to be. They were no longer laughing at me. They were laughing with me. I looked to Lan-Yin and I could see the shock and awe in her eyes, to which I responded with a foxy smirk and a thumbs-up.

"Excellent!" Huan clapped his hands together. "She'll be here in the morning, so make sure you're ready. Bring your best potions and be prepared to demonstrate your abilities. And don't forget that amazing skill of yours!"

I nodded, my mind racing with thoughts of the opportunities that lay ahead. "Thank you for the opportunity, Huan. I won't let you down."

As I parted ways with Huan, I couldn't help but feel a surge of excitement and anticipation. Tomorrow could be the start of a new chapter in my life as an alchemist and cultivator.

I managed to sell a bunch of my potions and extracts on the spot, and my coin purse was much heftier than before. Lan-Yin closed in on me and grabbed a hold of my shoulders, shaking me violently.

"Kai, that was amazing! That skill of yours is magical! It's like you're a cultivator!"

"No, it's not like I'm a cultivator." I settled her down with a serious expression before transforming it back into a shit-eating grin. "I *am* a cultivator!"

We circled each other like a bunch of hooligans, the excitement is contagious. The crowd had dispersed, so it was just us two outside of Huan's outpost making a fool of ourselves.

As the sun began to set, I realized that I needed advice on how to present my potions and elixirs to Xiao Yun. There was only one person in the village who had the wisdom and experience to guide me in this endeavor—Elder Ming. The Village Head would know how to approach this conundrum of mine.

I bade farewell to Lan-Yin, promising to catch up with her later, and made my way to Elder Ming's home. The cobblestone path leading to his house was familiar to me; I had walked it countless times seeking his guidance and company. The village was bathed in the warm, golden glow of the setting sun, casting long shadows on the ground.

As I walked, I couldn't help but feel a mixture of excitement and anxiety. Tomorrow would be a turning point in my life, and I wanted to make the best impression possible. Elder Ming had always been there for me, offering his wisdom and support, and I knew I could rely on him now.

I reached Elder Ming's home close to the center of the village and knocked on the door, my heart racing with anticipation.

"Come in, young Kai," Elder Ming called out before I even had a chance to announce my presence. His intuition was uncanny. Perhaps it was his cultivator senses at work?

I stepped inside the dimly lit room, the scent of incense and old scrolls filling the air. Elder Ming sat in a corner, his wise, aged eyes studying me intently.

"You seem to be carrying a heavy burden today, my boy," he said warmly. "What has brought you to my doorstep?"

I explained the situation with the Azure Silk Trading Company and my desire to make a good impression on Xiao Yun.

Elder Ming listened intently, nodding from time to time, and when I finished, he stroked his beard thoughtfully. Then his eyes twinkled as he looked at me.

"Ha! The best thing you can do to sell to them is to simply be you, Kai," Elder Ming said with a chuckle. His eyes sparkled with wisdom as he continued, "You possess a unique talent and a sincere heart. Trust in yourself and your abilities, and others will be naturally drawn to your cause. It's as simple as that."

His words resonated deeply within me, filling me with newfound confidence. "Thank you, Elder Ming."

Just be me, huh?

He patted my shoulder, his eyes full of warmth and understanding. "Go on, young Kai. Show them what you are capable of. I have faith in you."

I bowed my head in gratitude. "Thank you, Elder Ming. I will do my best."

I hesitated for a moment, unsure of how to bring up the topic of our usual training sessions. "Elder Ming, I was wondering if we could move our training sessions to the afternoon for tomorrow, just for this one time. I need the morning to prepare for my presentation to Xiao Yun and the Azure Silk Trading Company."

Elder Ming's eyes twinkled, and he nodded. "Of course, my boy. Your presentation is important, and I understand that you must focus on it. We shall resume our training in the afternoon. I wish you the best of luck."

"Thank you, Elder Ming. Your understanding means a lot to me." With a final bow, I left his home, my heart full of gratitude and determination.

As I returned to my garden shop, the evening sky painted in hues of pink and orange, I felt a sense of peace and contentment wash over me. The gentle breeze carried the sweet scent of flowers, and I could feel the magic of the world around me.

I paused for a moment, gazing out at the horizon and reflecting on the twists and turns my life had taken. I thought back to my early days. Mourning the loss of my parents, picking up the pieces, the long hours spent poring over scrolls, and the countless times I had failed and picked myself back up. Even before the Day of Awakening, I had worked harder than the rest of my peers. Nobody expected me to keep the shop running, much less have it flourishing the way it was now. My journey had been fraught with obstacles and setbacks, yet somehow I managed to persevere.

As I stood there, contemplating the future that lay before me, a mixture of fear and excitement swirled within my chest. What if my presentation failed to impress Xiao Yun? What if I stumbled over my words or made a fool of myself in front of everyone? The thought of failure weighed heavily on my mind, causing my heart to race and my palms to sweat.

With a deep breath, I steeled myself for the challenges that lay ahead, resolving to face them head-on and give it my all. I knew that no matter the outcome, I could hold my head high and be proud of the person I had become. And with Elder Ming's guidance and Lan-Yin, Wang-Jun, and the rest of the other villagers supporting me, I felt more confident than ever that I could seize this opportunity and make the most of it.

I opened the door to my shop, greeted by the familiar sight of Tianyi fluttering about the room. Her vibrant wings shimmered in the fading light, and I could feel her contentment through our bond.

"Tianyi, you wouldn't believe what happened today!" I exclaimed, my voice filled with excitement. I shared the events of the day with her, and she fluttered around, listening to the sound of my voice.

As I settled down at my workbench, surrounded by herbs and plants, I felt a sense of purpose and determination. With Tianyi by my side, I began to scrawl notes in my notebook, listing the potions and elixirs I would present to Xiao Yun, along with detailed explanations of their properties and effects.

I carefully collected the necessary herbs and plants from my shelves, placing them on my workbench, ready for tomorrow's preparations. This young master was going up in the world.

My name shall ring throughout the heavens. Kai Liu, cultivator and master herbalist, coveted by the finest beauties on the continent. I'd prove Lan-Yin wrong someday.

That comment she made about my inability to find a woman still hurt.

There was much to prepare, but I already had an idea of how it was going to go. The framework of my plan was already being built.

Prepare yourself, Xiao Yun, for you will be witness to the greatest presentation you'll ever see!

CHAPTER THIRTEEN

Showtime

As the first rays of sunlight filtered through the trees, I stood in the village square, my heart pounding with a mixture of excitement and nerves. My meticulously prepared potions and elixirs were neatly arranged on a large table before me, their vibrant colors shimmering in the morning light. I had spent the entire night refining my presentation, ensuring that every detail was perfect. I even delved into my Memory Palace when I was brainstorming, going through my memory trees to make sure I left no stone unturned. But despite my thorough preparation, I couldn't shake the nagging feeling of anxiety that gripped my chest.

Tianyi sensed my unease and fluttered onto my shoulder, her soft wings brushing against my cheek in a comforting gesture. As her delicate form settled, I felt a gentle surge of qi flow into my body, soothing my nerves and filling me with a sense of calm. I looked at her in surprise, marveling at the potency of her newfound abilities.

"Your abilities seem different, Tianyi," I whispered in awe. "Is this the influence of the Moonlit Grace Lily? It's incredible!"

Something akin to positivity reverberated through our connection. I couldn't help but smile, my worries momentarily forgotten as I basked in her comforting presence. I had brought her along with me, she would give me the aura of mystique I needed to make my presentation that much better. I wondered if Lan-Yin and Wang Jun would come. I was half expecting them, but in my rush to create the presentation, I forgot to tell them to come. Some support would be nice.

My anxiety eased slightly, accepting things as they were. Whatever happened, I would take it in stride.

If Xiao Yun didn't see the worth in my products, it didn't mean the presentation was for naught. It simply meant that the Azure Silk Trading Company failed to see my value. Me—Kai Liu, the finest cultivator in the Tranquil Breeze Coast. I am giving them the opportunity to ride my coattails before I ascend.

The village square was bustling with activity, people haggling over prices and admiring the exotic wares on display at Huan's trading outpost. I was seated in the center of it all at the merchant's behest, and I sat there with all my products on the table covered by a fine silk cloth. He said that they'd be here any moment and was waiting by the road. The scent of freshly baked bread and grilled meat wafted through the air, mingling with the earthy fragrance of herbs and the sweet aroma of flowers. The cacophony of voices, laughter, and the clatter of hooves on cobblestones filled the air, creating a lively and vibrant atmosphere.

Most of the villagers heard of my products and clamored for them, although I told them I couldn't sell any until my presentation was done. I had to negotiate the prices, and I had a full understanding of how much it cost to produce my elixirs. Five silver per potion was the goal. I'd get the value I deserved.

My hard work and knowledge would finally pay off here. I turned to my interface, glancing over my stats as of now.

Heavenly Interface: Kai Liu
Perk(s):
Interface Manipulator—Allows manipulation of the
Heavenly Interface and access to special features.
Race: Human
Vitality: Sufficient
Primary
Affinity—Wood
Cultivation Rank: Mortal Realm—Rank 2
Qi: Qi Initiation Stage—Rank 1
Mind: Mortal Realm—Rank 1
Body: Mortal Realm
Skills
Spiritual Herbalism—Level 1 (. . .)
Gardening—Level 10 (. . .)
Cultivation Techniques: N/A

I reached the tenth level in Gardening, but it hadn't evolved yet.

The only requirement I was not confident I'd reached was the last one. Growing a plant with qi? I'd been infusing my qi into my plants since I'd learned the skill. I did it at the same frequency with which I watered my garden, but it seemed I hadn't fulfilled it. Perhaps it meant I needed to wait until the plant infused with qi was fully mature? I thought back to my garden and remembered there were a few that would be ready for harvest by next week. I'll infuse those and wait until then.

If this deal went through, I'd be able to build the greenhouse of my dreams. I'd be able to expand my garden and house more plants. Maybe I could even use it to secure some more qi plants for myself.

Calm down, Kai. The merchants hadn't even arrived yet! I couldn't get ahead of myself. *Focus on the prize.*

"She's here!" I heard Huan cry out, alerting me out of my stupor.

I felt a surge of anticipation ripple through the air. Everyone's voices became muted as the rhythmic sound of hoofbeats approached, and I turned to see a magnificent horse-drawn carriage with blue undertones making its way toward us. The craftsmanship was exquisite, with intricate designs etched into the gleaming wood, and the azure silk curtains billowed gently in the breeze.

The carriage came to a halt, and the door opened to reveal four individuals. I could see Xiao Yun, the daughter of the head of the Azure Silk Trading Company, sitting elegantly within the carriage. Her long, flowing hair cascaded down her back like a silken waterfall, and her eyes sparkled with intelligence and curiosity. She was beautiful. If Lan-Yin was pretty, she was drop-dead gorgeous. My cheeks would've flushed upon seeing her, but I was too focused on my presentation to care.

Before she could step out, Huan, seemingly harried, approached the carriage with enthusiasm. He bowed before addressing her. "Lady Xiao Yun, welcome to the Gentle Wind Village. I am Huan, the merchant in charge of this trading outpost. It is an honor to have you grace us with your presence."

Xiao Yun stepped out of the carriage, her movements as graceful as a swan. Behind her, two attendants followed, each carrying various scrolls and implements. They were clearly well trained and skilled, their movements fluid and coordinated as they assisted Xiao Yun.

The fourth individual, a mysterious escort wearing a bamboo hat that obscured his face, stepped out of the carriage last. His posture was relaxed, yet there was an unmistakable air of power and authority that emanated from him, sending a shiver down my spine. I couldn't help but wonder about his identity and the purpose of his presence here. A guard of some sort?

As the group approached, I felt a sense of calm wash over me. Huan was talking animatedly and gestured toward me, drawing the woman's attention to me. The hours of preparation and hard work had led to this moment, and I was determined to make the most of this opportunity. I greeted Xiao Yun with a confident smile, my eyes meeting hers without hesitation.

It was time.

"Lady Xiao Yun, it is a pleasure to meet you. I am Kai, a humble herbalist. I have prepared a selection of my finest potions and elixirs, and I humbly request an audience to showcase my work to you."

Xiao Yun studied me for a moment before nodding, a hint of a smile playing on her lips. "Very well, Kai. I am intrigued by your request and curious to see what you have to offer."

With her permission, I began my presentation. I picked up the first potion, a modest but effective energy-boosting tonic. "This, Lady Xiao Yun, is the Invigorating Dawn Tonic. It is formulated from the essence of the Morning Dew grass and ginger, which I have personally collected from the surrounding forest. A single sip can reinvigorate the body and mind, providing a much-needed burst of energy for those who toil long hours. It relieves fatigue immediately, and . . ."

As I continued, I showcased various other creations, such as the Tranquil Night Elixir, a sleep aid derived from the essence of the Dreamweaver Vine, and the Vigor's Reprieve, a hangover potion crafted from the Rejuvenating Marrow Root. Every single one I had given a grandiose name, befitting of their effects. I was certain anything short of cultivator medicine fell short of what I made.

Throughout my presentation, I emphasized my knowledge of the local herbs and plants, explaining how I had unlocked their true potential by extracting their essences to create more potent effects. The gathered crowd listened with rapt attention, their eyes widening in surprise and admiration as I revealed the secrets of my craft.

While I presented my potions, Tianyi, my butterfly companion, fluttered gracefully around the table, her vibrant wings shimmering in the sunlight. Xiao Yun's eyes followed her movements, and she remarked, "What a beautiful creature. I've never seen an Azure Moonlight Flutter before. It's truly mesmerizing."

I smiled, feeling a surge of pride for my companion. "Thank you, Lady Xiao Yun. Tianyi is a treasured companion."

As my presentation drew to a close, I could see the curiosity and admiration in Xiao Yun's eyes. "Your creations, while seemingly mundane, are truly remarkable, Kai. May I see that one? The Invigorating Dawn Tonic?"

I handed it to her with both hands, and she examined it with a critiquing eye.

As I watched her carefully handle the Invigorating Dawn Tonic, the captivating hues of golden yellow and soft orange swirling within the elegant glass vial. She gently swirled the semitransparent liquid, allowing the fine particles of Morning Dew Herb and ginger to dance in the light. The container seemed to capture the essence of a sunrise. She deftly uncorked the vial, and as the aroma of the potent ingredients filled the air, I could almost feel the rejuvenating energy that awaited her with just a single sip.

It was the most potent version of my energy-boosting tonics while also being the most impressive-looking one. I was glad she picked it out of all the ones I brought.

Xiao Yun turned to the man wearing a bamboo hat behind her and offered the concoction. Without a word, he drank the thing in one gulp, and I anxiously awaited his reaction.

". . . It's given me a boost of energy. Any fatigue I had just left my body, as minor as it was." He said in an impressed tone. I still couldn't see his features, except his mouth. Who was he? Perhaps he was a famous cultivator?

Xiao Yun seemed to take his words into account, crossing her arms and looking at the rest of my wares while humming quietly.

Huan, who had been standing nearby, chimed in. "I can personally attest to the efficacy of Kai's potions. I used them yesterday and found them to be quite potent. Kai holds great potential in alchemy, and I believe his work will only continue to improve."

My heart swelled with gratitude for Huan's endorsement. I had not expected him to speak on my behalf, but his words carried weight in this negotiation.

Xiao Yun finally turned to me, her eyes sparkling with interest. "Your work is indeed impressive, Kai. I must admit, I didn't expect to find such talent in a small village like this. Your dedication to your craft is evident, and your creations have potential. The Azure Silk Trading Company would be interested in discussing a possible partnership with you."

A wave of relief washed over me, and I could hardly contain my excitement. This was the moment I had been waiting for, the opportunity to make a name for myself and secure a better future. I bowed deeply, my voice filled with gratitude. "Thank you, Lady Xiao Yun. I am honored by your words and would be delighted to work with the Azure Silk Trading Company."

She nodded and gestured to one of her attendants, who handed her a scroll. "Very well, Kai. We will negotiate a contract detailing the terms of our partnership. Once the terms are agreed upon, we can proceed with establishing a working relationship. I believe your potions and elixirs could prove popular in the markets we serve. Let's work on this tomorrow. I'll need to discuss this further with my advisers, as well as Huan, for referring you to us."

I couldn't believe it. My hard work and persistence had finally paid off. As I watched Xiao Yun and her entourage depart, I couldn't help but feel a sense of pride and accomplishment swelling within me. The support of my friends, my cultivation journey, and my bond with Tianyi all led me to this pivotal moment. The villagers showered me with praise, and I felt like I was on top of the world. I bowed to Xiao Yun and the group before they headed off, and noticed the man in the bamboo hat facing me, his gaze fixated on me for a brief moment. But before I could question it, he turned away.

Huh.

As I turned to begin packing up my wares, I noticed Lan-Yin and Wang Jun among the crowd, their faces beaming with pride and happiness. The blacksmith looked like he was just pulled away from the forge, still covered in soot and ash. I smiled at them, knowing that their support had helped me reach this point. My cheeks were beginning to hurt from how much I was smiling. I had done it! I wanted to shout and make a fool of myself, but the merchants hadn't left the vicinity yet.

There was much work to be done. With the Azure Silk Trading Company's backing, I would be able to create my dream greenhouse, expand my garden, and explore new cultivation techniques. The path to greatness awaited, and I was ready to embrace it with open arms.

But first, I was going to celebrate!

CHAPTER FOURTEEN

Body Refinement

I celebrated at Lan-Yin's family-owned teahouse, the Soaring Swallow. It was one of the oldest establishments here, run by her family for generations.

The interior of the Soaring Swallow Teahouse was a perfect blend of traditional charm and homely warmth. As soon as I stepped inside, I was greeted by the rich aroma of freshly brewed tea, accompanied by the soft chatter of villagers and the occasional tinkling laughter. Whenever I felt like treating myself, this was the place to go.

The teahouse was furnished with low, sturdy wooden tables and comfortable cushions, allowing patrons to sit cross-legged on the floor in a traditional manner. The tables were spaced out evenly, providing ample room for quiet conversations and lively debates alike. At the center of the teahouse, there was a small stage where talented musicians and storytellers occasionally performed.

Behind a beautifully carved wooden counter, Lan-Yin's family members could be seen skillfully preparing a wide variety of teas, from fragrant jasmine and calming chamomile to robust oolong and earthy pu-erh. They occasionally purchased my herbs, but due to the amount they required, they usually sourced them from Huan in bulk.

"Look at Kai. Now he's moving up in life! Any plans on going to the big city?"

Wang Jun clashed his cup with mine, and we drank the rice wine. Lan-Yin was out in the back, helping prepare the food and beverages, while I chatted amicably with her betrothed. I held myself back, knowing I'd have to go and train later with the Village Head. It wouldn't do to show up inebriated!

"Perhaps, but maybe farther along in the future. I'd like to take it one step at a time, y'know? Patience is key," I said, grabbing a steamed dumpling and stuffing it into my mouth. Delicious!

"Indeed, indeed. When you go out there and make a name for yourself, don't forget us! We'll be cheering you on, Kowtow Kai!"

I gave him a playful shove, looking over to the corner of the table where Tianyi was sitting. I requested a small cup of sugar water for her, and the butterfly sat there celebrating with us in her own way.

Our little feast came to a quick end, with both of us extremely satisfied. As I hungrily reached for the last plate of steamed dumplings, I couldn't help but notice how my appetite had grown recently. Keeping up with the much larger Wang Jun, I found myself devouring almost the same amount of food as he did. It was a stark contrast to my usual modest diet. I covered my mouth and burped quietly, slapping my stomach in satisfaction. Lan-Yin strolled toward us, carrying a small tray, collecting the empty dishes with a small smile on her face.

"Looks like you boys enjoyed the food."

"Incredibly so! Thank you again for the meal. How much will it be, Lan-Yin?" I replied, whipping out my coin purse and collecting the silver coins.

"It's on the house, Kai. Don't worry about it."

"Ah, come on! You don't think this young master can pay for his meal? At least take this much."

I tried to offer her a handful of coins, but she sternly refused. Lan-Yin was always stubborn when it came to this. I rolled my eyes and pocketed the money, but I left several of the coins behind on the table as I got up.

"Well, thanks again, guys. I'll have to go train with the Village Head now. I did tell him I was going to come in the afternoon."

Wang Jun's eyebrows furrowed in surprise. "You're going to train? Right after eating? You're going to puke your guts out!"

"Yeah, shouldn't you sit down and wait for a bit?" Lan-Yin asked.

I smirked at them, letting Tianyi perch on my shoulder. "Greatness waits for no one! I will seize it with my own two hands."

I bade them farewell and whistled as I made my way to Elder Ming's home. He'll probably celebrate with me as well! I quickened the pace and got to his front door within minutes. Today, I was going to complete my body refinement quest.

I found myself overflowing with energy, feeling better than I ever had before. As I assessed the tasks ahead, I grew confident that I could complete them before the sun set. Had my Invigorating Dawn Tonic been more effective than I anticipated? I had taken one of my concoctions as a result of working late into the night and sacrificing sleep, but it seemed to have imbued my body with an extraordinary vitality.

I knocked on Elder Ming's door, eager to begin my training. After a few moments, the door creaked open, and Elder Ming appeared, his warm smile greeting me. He inclined his head to Tianyi, and she returned the greeting with a wave of her wings.

"Ah, Kai! How was your presentation?" he said, clapping me on the shoulder.

"They're interested. I'm going to negotiate the contract with them tomorrow. Thank you for helping me, Elder Ming."

Elder Ming chuckled and waved off my modesty. "You have the talent and determination, Kai. I just gave you a nudge in the right direction."

I grinned and took a deep breath, feeling the energy coursing through my body. As we walked into his house, I began my request. "Elder Ming, I was wondering if I could try to complete the body refinement quests today. I feel stronger than ever, and I believe completing them is more important than ever."

Elder Ming raised an eyebrow, asking me what I had left to complete. "Those aren't easy to do with your level of training, Kai. How do you know it's going to help you?"

I nodded firmly. "Yes, Elder Ming. I can do this. I completed the mind refinement quests just yesterday, and now I unlocked the ability to create a Memory Palace."

His eyebrows shot up once he heard that. Elder Ming looked at me in disbelief.

"A Memory Palace? Are you sure?"

"Certain, Elder Ming. The Interface told me it was the reward for completing my quest. I spent the past few nights constructing them into the shape of trees!"

The more I explained, the higher up his eyebrows went. I feared they would disappear into his hairline and never come back. I chuckled nervously. I didn't think I'd seen the Village Head this floored in quite a long time, so I asked him what was wrong.

"Er, is that something I shouldn't have done?"

"No, no." He waved off my worries. "It's just . . . rare for an ability like that to manifest. Especially when you're at the fledgling stages of cultivation."

"Ah! So I'm a genius is that what you're saying? I'm exceptional among the disciples in the Qi Initiation stage! HA HA HA—"

Elder Ming chopped me on the head, and I rubbed the spot and quieted down immediately. He scratched his beard and was thinking deeply.

"A Memory Palace isn't a requirement for all cultivators to have. But the higher you go, and the more knowledge you accumulate, it becomes something less unusual. But at the Qi Initiation stage? Unless it was an ability from birth, this is unheard of."

"When does it become an ability that is commonplace?"

". . . Around the Essence Awakening stage? At that point, it basically becomes a requirement."

Essence Awakening stage? That's an entire realm ahead of where I was. I thought only sect elders were at that stage.

As far as I knew, there were only a handful of people who reached that cultivation rank, including the Wind Sage, still in the Tranquil Breeze Coast. And only those of that rank could use the Memory Palace?

I didn't know it was such a powerful thing. Although my body may not have had the greatest talent in martial arts history, my mind would. I was never one for brawls in the first place. I would conquer the world using my cleverness and then become God Emperor of—

Before my daydreams could continue, Elder Ming chopped me on the head once again in the same spot he had just a few moments ago.

"Elder Ming, please. This is the most important part of my body as a cultivator. What was that for?"

"I could see you conjuring up some nonsense in your head," he said gruffly. "Well, I'll put that aside for now. You want to finish your body refinement quests? I'll be there to guide you through it. Let's go!"

We moved to the outskirts of the village, and I began my first task: running the perimeter of Gentle Wind Village without stopping to rest. My legs felt strong, and my breath was steady as I completed the laps, feeling a sense of accomplishment with each one. Tianyi floated ahead of me, keeping pace as I ran along the boundaries of the village. I barely broke a sweat.

"Come on, pick up the rocks! You're not struggling with these tasks. Push yourself and overcome your limits."

Next, I committed to the horse stance, my legs trembling slightly as I pushed past the ten-minute mark. Elder Ming watched me closely, offering words of encouragement and advice as I struggled to maintain my form. I got a ten-minute break in between each set, and I was forced to disrobe due to how much I was sweating. Tianyi perched herself on my shoulder once more, and I felt my body recovering a bit faster than usual. A thin stream of energy was entering my circulatory system. An idea sparked in my head.

Crossing my legs, I began meditating and circulated my qi alongside Tianyi. What I could retain from my surroundings, although small, was enough to freshen myself before Elder Ming shouted for me to continue. I grabbed the rocks and assumed the stance, gritting my teeth.

I am rooted in the earth, unyielding as the trees.
With each breath, I draw strength from the natural world around me.
The pain I feel now is a testament to the power I will gain.

I repeated a variety of phrases in my head, keeping myself focused on the task without wavering. *Journey through the Elements* by Zi Chen was full of fantastical lines like that. I thought I should reread it. Perhaps later tonight? As a treat to cele—

"Focus! Strength is not just in the body, but also in the mind and spirit."

Elder Ming tapped my backside and forced it upright, snapping me out of my idling thoughts.

It took me almost an hour and a half to finish. I failed to accomplish the horse stance set once and required an even longer break before attempting it. That extra time to meditate gave me just what I needed to push through. Now it was time for the last set of tasks: squats.

I approached it with determination, my legs already feeling heavy from the previous challenges. But I knew I couldn't give up now. Elder Ming stood by my side, offering words of encouragement and guidance as I began my squats. Tianyi remained perched on my shoulder, her presence providing me with additional strength and motivation.

As I lowered myself down and then pushed back up, I counted each squat in my head. I could feel the strain in my leg muscles, but I refused to give in. My breathing grew heavier, and sweat poured down my face, but I continued to push through the pain and fatigue. The Invigorating Dawn's effects had disappeared a long time ago. I've been operating on persistence and sheer will.

"One hundred . . . two hundred . . . Just fifty more to go," I muttered under my breath, my voice barely audible. Elder Ming nodded in approval, seeing the determination in my eyes.

As I approached the final ten squats, my body screamed for me to stop. But I gritted my teeth and pushed through the pain, reminding myself of my goal to complete my body refinement quest. With a final burst of energy, I completed the last squat and collapsed onto the ground, completely exhausted.

Elder Ming smiled at me, a look of pride in his eyes. "Well done, Kai. I knew you could do it."

I lay on the ground, panting heavily, my body aching all over. But despite the pain, I felt an overwhelming sense of accomplishment. I had completed my body refinement quest, and I knew that this would only make me stronger in the long run.

> *Quest: Body Refinement has been completed.*
> *Due to your status as Interface Manipulator, your rewards*
> *will be adjusted accordingly.*
> *You completed the quest with additional challenges.*
> *Your efforts do not go unnoticed.*

> *Your body is growing more powerful.*
> *Your qi circulatory systems are more robust, able to*
> *handle the rigors of cultivation.*
> *You can now utilize the skill Rooted Banyan Stance.*

And just like that, everything in my mind clicked.

CHAPTER FIFTEEN

Rooted Banyan Stance

It felt as if my mind was struck by a bolt of lightning, and I could suddenly see the world with newfound clarity. It was as though an invisible thread had woven together the fragments of my knowledge, forming a cohesive tapestry of understanding. My heart raced, excitement surging through me as I realized how the different aspects of my learning—cultivation, martial arts, and the natural world—were intertwined and complementary.

Was this what enlightenment felt like?

My mind raced, adjusting to the connection made between my knowledge in various topics. Laying out the basis of my cultivation, the muscles worked when in the horse stance, and even my information pertaining to trees, all culminating into the Rooted Banyan Stance.

What was a banyan?

The banyan tree wasn't native to this part of the Tranquil Breeze Coast, although we had one several li from the village. It was the only one of its kind in the area. I had always been intrigued by banyan trees, with their sprawling roots and massive trunks that seemed to convey a sense of ancient wisdom and unwavering strength. Their aerial roots growing downward from the branches, eventually reaching the ground and forming additional trunks. They were never known for their ability to withstand cold temperatures, but this one lived for decades and was still going strong. My mother said it housed some sort of forest spirit, which is why it lived for so long.

The first time visiting it as a child, I could remember feeling so infinitesimally small. No other structure in the village or forest matched it in size. Whenever I visualized the World Tree of the Emerald Spirit Forest, it always drew back to the first time I saw a banyan tree. That dense network of roots and trunks that provided the tree with remarkable stability, making it appear as if it could withstand the most violent of storms and the test of time, made me realize that it will remain long after I'm gone. Firm and unyielding.

Elder Ming spoke of practice. The horse stance was integral for a martial artist; strength, stability, and endurance being put to the test by holding yourself in the right position. Through his guidance, I perfected my form and learned how to utilize my core to better endure the training.

When I circulated my qi through my body, it was merely for cultivating and recovering my energy. It never enhanced my body the way I envisioned cultivators could, being able to withstand mighty blows that could rend a mortal to pieces. But with this—

I scrambled to my feet, straightening myself before spreading my lower body till it was wider than my shoulders. My toes pointed straight ahead. I lowered my abdomen until my thighs were parallel to the ground. My body was fatigued and I shook slightly getting into position, despite not having rocks weighing me down.

"Kai, are you all right?" Elder Ming asked, slightly concerned. I suppose I was quiet for too long, trying to digest everything that I received.

As I looked down, the image of the banyan's massive roots digging into the very earth overlaid itself onto my lower body, digging deep and keeping me anchored in place. My arms and torso, like the sprawling branches and trunk, capable of withstanding any blow.

Drawing qi came as naturally as breathing as I did this. I moved into position and the energy enveloped my body, a thin layer that was invisible to the naked eye.

A sharp outtake of breath, squeezing my core, and the tightening of every muscle in my body as qi fully manifested across every inch of my body.

Instantly, I knew that this was the Rooted Banyan Stance.

My first technique. A *cultivator* technique. I turned to the Village Head with an ecstatic smile on my face. He seemed dumbfounded at what he just saw, and his jaw hung slightly open seeing the move I just performed.

"Elder Ming, look! I've discovered a new technique!"

"Kai, you fool! How many times have I warned you about recklessly using your qi? Qi Deviation is a serious matter, not something to be taken lightly."

He reared his cane back to smack me on the top of my head, but I was prepared. Getting into position, I unleashed my technique within a second's notice.

"ROOTED BANYAN STANCE!"

I shouted it aloud, although I didn't need to. It seemed right.

The feeling of stability and strength filled me once more, and I tightened my muscles in preparation for the blow. The cane slapped across my head with enough force to make a thwacking noise, but the sensation of pain that followed it was absent. Being hit but not feeling pain was truly odd. The impact was there, but it was muted.

INVINCIBLE! I WAS INVINCIBLE UNDER THE HEAVENS!

I looked at my teacher with a smirk as I let go of my stance. His face turned red, and before I could get a word out, something blurred just below the corner of my vision.

CRACK!

I already let go of my stance and relaxed, expecting that initial strike to be the end of it. But as I stared at the foot placed firmly where my groin was, I sorely regretted that course of action.

The Village Head kicked me in the balls!

My mouth was open in a silent scream, and I collapsed to the floor completely and utterly defeated, where Elder Ming proceeded to continue beating me with his cane.

"Eld—Master! Master Ming! This disciple ha—urk!" I hastily covered myself, trying to make Elder Ming see reason. "The disciple has learned his lesson! MERCY! MERCY! TIANYIIIII—!"

Following the beating, Elder Ming provided me with a stern lecture in regard to Qi Deviation. We returned to his home, where the townspeople murmured about my questionable state. It was a humbling experience. This day was truly one of the highest highs and the lowest lows.

As we continued our journey, the cool breeze caressed my face, providing a momentary respite from the sting of Elder Ming's words and my own embarrassment. The sun had begun its descent toward the horizon, casting a warm golden hue over the village. He led me into the house and I trudged in like a cow going to a slaughter.

"Listen! Forcing your qi to circulate in such a manner for advanced techniques, without the necessary preparations and guidance, can cause irreversible harm. To begin with, your body was not suited for cultivation," Elder Ming said, tapping his cane gently on the drawing of the qi circulatory system. He traced around the lower abdomen, where the dantian was located. "Should your qi reach this point, you shall find yourself no more than a crimson smear upon the wall."

"But if I subject myself to it multiple times, won't my circulatory systems get stronger as a result?"

Elder Ming's previous impression as an all-knowing sage was gone. His neatly tied hair was sticking out, and his clothes were ruffled. The old geezer looked ready to keel over as soon as I spoke. I moved to pour some of the calming herbal tea into his cup and pushed him to drink, seriously worrying he'd get some sort of heart attack.

Honestly, what the hell was wrong with him? Beating me up over a little qi manipulation. Feh! I wouldn't be felled by something as simple as that. That wasn't what fate had in store for me.

The drink seemed to soothe his irritation. Tianyi, as spirited as ever, floated around me and provided a nice touch to the interior of his home. She eventually landed on Elder Ming's shoulder and glowed, and the tension on his shoulders went away ever so slightly.

"Ha—What would your parents say . . . Your mother would've tried to poison me if she knew I was teaching you cultivation techniques."

I frowned. Although I knew my parents and the Village Head were close, it wasn't often he spoke of them. "I don't think so. I think they'd be quite proud. I'm following my dreams. Being true to myself. Is that so wrong?"

His lips tightened ever so slightly.

"Kai, you must understand. The world of cultivation is not the glittering dream you believe it to be. There is far more beneath the surface than meets the eye."

He gazed out his open window with a small sigh, as if to reminisce. I remained silent, and he continued his thoughts.

"Politics, greed, and revenge. People assert themselves over others and commit unspeakable acts, simply because they are perceived as weak. The Jianghu is not a place to be trifled with."

I gritted my teeth. I wasn't a fool. Does he think I don't know that? The way sects look down on the common people? The atrocities committed by demonic cultivators in other provinces? Although my dream was built on stories and fairy tales, they were not built on ones that kept away from the dark side of pursuing cultivation. If anything, they emphasized it.

"But how do you know, Elder Ming? How terrible can the Jianghu be? Is there no joy to be found in overcoming your limits? Growing stronger day by day?"

"That which you speak of, no. But it is not the personal growth that is perilous. It is the people with whom you become entwined." Elder Ming intoned gravely. "May I share a story with you, young Kai?"

I nodded and let him continue.

"When I was but a mere child, I became a third-class disciple. The name of the sect is irrelevant here," he said gruffly, seeing the look in my eye once he mentioned being a disciple. "It is not an interesting story. Abandoned at their doorstep, they raised me and taught me their ways. It was simple."

Elder Ming was an orphan? He was abandoned at birth? That's . . . sobering to think about. At least I had the chance to be with my parents. He never even knew who they were.

"I had friends. Talented ones. They pushed me and helped me strive for greatness on our journey. They were my sworn brothers. But alas, life is never that simple. One of the second-class disciples, our senior, consumed by jealousy of my sworn brother potentially taking his position as the next sect leader, sought a method to suppress him."

The Village Head looked calm, although his eyes were downcast for most of his retelling. His gaze seemed far off. He raised his robe and showed me his abdomen. In the area around where his dantian was, the skin had a network of faint, spiderweb-like cracks. Discolored, appearing as a mix of red, purple, and even blackish hues. It looked familiar. I glanced over to the diagram he had on the table and saw that the shape of the injury matched that of the pathways in the area.

"They attacked us while we were meditating. There are ways of doing it while being vigilant, but who would be in their own home? I was struck first, and the pain . . ." he murmured softly. His eyes didn't hold any resentment, but bitterness of an untold degree. "I would not wish that on my worst enemy."

I widened my eyes. That was preposterous. I disliked their attitude toward those of outsiders, but . . . something like a senior disciple colluding to bring down someone younger than them never even crossed my mind. That was like me breaking Wang Jun's arm because he was getting too good at blacksmithing.

I felt a deep sense of disillusionment. The sects were supposed to be bastions of knowledge and mutual support, places where cultivators could grow and learn together. But the dark side of human nature seemed to taint even these sanctuaries. I clenched my fists, wondering if this was more of a common problem than I thought.

Even in the deepest, darkest pit of my heart, I could say I never wished ill upon anybody in my village, much less acted upon it. Were there times when I was jealous or angry? Of course. But to do something despite knowing the consequences . . . it was despicable. An ugly feeling welled up within me. Terrible anger but also pity at what Elder Ming had gone through.

"My sworn brother managed to fend off the initial attacks. I wasn't there to see it. But when I came to, it was him, carrying me in his arms while covered in blood. But it wasn't his. He had murdered the second-class disciples and ran from the sect with me in tow."

There was much to digest from what Elder Ming said. A third-class disciple? At my age, I'd be the oldest among them in a normal sect. They were usually young children. Second-class disciples were at least a decade older than them, with years of martial arts training and experience under their belt. The gap between a third and second-class disciple, even if the former was a talent beyond compare, was the equivalent of comparing a puddle to a lake.

But a single one managed to kill a coordinated group?

It was so ludicrous. I almost questioned the validity of his story, but I knew he would never lie about something so serious. His injuries, as well as the solemn way he talked, showed me just how genuine it was. I could only remain silent and gulp down my questions as he continued the retelling of his past.

"We were hunted down and I was only a burden to him. Had he been by himself, escaping the province, away from prying eyes would've been a simple task. But we ran into the first-class disciples and we were separated from each other."

As Elder Ming revealed his story, I felt my heart twist with sympathy and sorrow for the man who had become like a mentor to me. My eyes widened, and I felt a shiver run down my spine as I listened to his words. It was as if the shadows of his past had taken form around us, making the room feel colder and darker. Even Tianyi's aura felt muted, and she quietly remained by the Village Head's shoulder.

"That is not to say your pity is what I desire. I share this tale to show you how easily destruction can be wrought and how difficult it can be to rebuild. My body, once capable of withstanding the rigors of cultivator training, was nearly destroyed," Elder Ming said, his eyes steely. "Your situation is far more precarious. Even the slightest misstep could lead to your demise."

"But I'm careful, Elder Ming," I said softly. "Tianyi stays by my side as I cultivate. Nobody in this village would disturb me so recklessly as they did to you."

"Do you truly believe, Kai, that not a single soul would harbor ill intent? Jealousy? Annoyance? To be human is to err." He shook his head. I refused to believe it. The idea of someone from the village committing such a heinous act. But Elder Ming believed his sect was a safe space as well. I could see what he was trying to say. "Many believe that cultivators transcend their humanity when they gain these powers. But in truth, it only serves to magnify their humanity. Whether they are virtuous or wicked, their true nature is amplified when given great power. And unfortunately, the Jianghu tends to be more ruthless. It is nothing like you have ever experienced before."

Elder Ming was speaking the truth. I had never experienced such conflict in my life. I grew up in a sheltered environment here in the Gentle Wind Village. Even if I was aware of the horrors in the Jianghu, there was no way for me to fully understand the extent.

". . . Then isn't it a good thing you're here to teach me?" I said. "Had I tried to learn all this on my own, I would've died from Qi Deviation or gotten deceived by those who wish to hurt me. You know how I am, Elder Ming. I would've embarked on a journey out of the village eventually. Better to know the pitfalls now rather than later, correct?"

He smiled, although it seemed quite different from the other ones he wore. Elder Ming grabbed me by the hair and yanked me across the table. Tianyi flew into the air as we caused a ruckus in the Village Head's home.

"Only if you heed my words, you foolish boy! Listen to your teacher! Don't! Use! Your! Qi!"

He emphasized each word by shaking my head. This eccentric old man! How could he be so strong? His meridians were damaged! He even showed me! It didn't make sense for him to be overpowering me like this!

"All right, Elder Ming. I'll listen to you," I said reluctantly, still rubbing the sore spot on my head once he let go. "I won't use my qi without your guidance. I'll only meditate and use the Rooted Banyan Stance here."

Although, infusing my garden with qi or extracting plant essence was an entirely different matter. Those didn't count, right?

The conversation turned back to him lecturing me on what I was forbidden to do without supervision, but the tension from before was broken. I listened to Elder Ming and took his words more seriously. There was a story behind every lesson he taught me, and I'd hold off on completing my quests for now.

CHAPTER SIXTEEN

The Escort

I didn't return home until late at night. I spent a long time discussing my future with Elder Ming. How I was going to train and manage my garden shop at the same time. It was tumultuous, but I hashed out an outline that had me doing longer, more rigorous training sessions every other day, followed by a day of rest with cultivation and meditation at the Village Head's home, where he could monitor my progress and I minimized the risk to myself. It also allowed me to train every day, which was important.

Either way, my mornings would be where the bulk of my training happened. Anything involving the usage of techniques and qi circulation was to be done with the Village Head present, although it was for his sake more than it was for mine. Aside from that one instance when I cultivated in the forest, I hadn't suffered from any reflux or deviation. He told me if I was consistent, it wouldn't take long for me to be able to cultivate without the risk of Qi Deviation at minute disturbances.

It was a busy schedule. Elder Ming was incredibly accommodating, and he knew just how much it took to keep the shop running as it was. I should look into hiring someone to run the shop while I was away. Perhaps Lan-Yin would be up for it? Although she worked part-time at the Soaring Swallow, I didn't think she'd refuse.

We celebrated the deal I made with Xiao Yun, the daughter of the Azure Silk Trading Company, eating red bean buns that he saved for special occasions. I bade him farewell. Tianyi seemed to linger but eventually came with me to go back home. I suppose she liked Elder Ming's home. It had a cozy feel to it, and the smell of old scrolls permeated the area. It was very nostalgic.

The stars glittered in the night sky, casting an ethereal glow over the land below. The cool, gentle breeze carried the faint scent of blooming flowers and damp earth, a constant reminder that spring was in full swing. I couldn't help but smile as I walked down the worn dirt path, my thoughts swirling with a mixture of excitement and anxiety. Tomorrow was going to be a big day, and there was so much to do.

"Ha, so much to do. So little time."

I looked up to the moonlit sky with my hands placed behind my head. It was going to be a bit hectic tomorrow, negotiating the terms of my contract. I was tempted to sleep after such a long and tiring day, but I needed to create more stock in advance for the deal with the merchants. I had about twenty-five bottles fit for sale, with five varying effects and purposes. They were the ones I considered a success. After all, making a new recipe didn't always mean it was good. Even if I was using extracted essences.

I would need to mention my qi-infused plants. Although I should probably wait until some of them are ready to harvest. I need to mark down the differences between regular ones and those I infused with energy.

"Tianyi, could you turn into a human and become my assistant?" I asked her. She fluttered questioningly. "Although I appreciate how you are now, it'd be nice to have some help around the shop."

> *Your companion, Tianyi, cannot transform until she reaches*
> *Essence Awakening Stage—Rank 1.*

That was new. I read the notification with a mix of intrigue and bemusement.

My eyes turned toward the butterfly floating around me, glowing softly under the illumination of moonlight. Essence Awakening Stage? A butterfly?

Imagining Tianyi with a cultivation rank equivalent of a sect elder was horrifying to think about. Would she be able to conjure up powerful wind blasts with a flap of her wings? Or maybe her healing powers would become potent enough to rejuvenate those on the verge of death. Although I didn't know how to strengthen her, it was definitely possible. She moved up a rank when she took in the Moonlit Grace Lily's energy. It seemed to have a permanent effect on her. I didn't want to replicate it, since that required her being injured, but . . .

The night was eerily quiet, as if the world itself was holding its breath. The only sound that accompanied my footsteps was the soft fluttering of Tianyi's wings as she floated beside me, her luminescent form casting a comforting glow over the darkened path. I knew I was going to have a long night ahead of me, but I couldn't shake the feeling that something important was going to happen.

As I continued to ramble on to Tianyi, I noticed her fluttering had become a bit more erratic. Did she seem . . . nervous? It was strange because Tianyi was usually quite placid. The only other time I had seen her act this way was when we were in the forest, right before we were ambushed by that crow.

A strong sense of foreboding washed over me, and I knew something was amiss.

I instantly felt a shiver run down my spine, and my heart began to race. Was it possible that we were being watched or followed? I tried to keep my composure, but it was difficult. With all that talk with Elder Ming about people with ill intent, I became paranoid.

I slowed my pace, my eyes darting around the area, searching for any signs of danger. My hands trembled slightly, and I clenched my fists to steady them. I was afraid, and I couldn't help but think about how all the training I had gone through felt like it was for nothing. I was still just as vulnerable and inexperienced as I was before.

No, I had a trick up my sleeve. The Rooted Banyan Stance. I was fully capable of defending myself.

Tianyi's behavior continued to worry me. The closer we got to home, the more her tiny body trembled and remained close to my shoulder, barely even twitching the rest of the way home. I knew I had to do something, but what? My mind raced with possibilities, but nothing seemed like the right move.

As we reached the entrance to my home, I hesitated, my hand hovering over the door. Was it safe to go inside? Or would I be walking into a trap? I felt like I was teetering on the edge of a cliff, unsure whether to jump or step back.

"Tianyi, are you sensing something I'm not?" I whispered, my voice shaking. She didn't respond, but the feeling of nervousness fed into my telepathic bond with her. There was definitely something wrong.

I took a deep breath, trying to steady my racing heart. Okay, I thought, I can do this. I've trained for moments like this, right? I just need to be cautious and smart about my actions. I know where I put my staff. It was behind the door of my bedroom. If anything, I could get it within moments.

Despite my inner pep talk, my hand still trembled as I slowly pushed the door open, my senses on high alert. I tried to channel the same confidence that I had when I pretended to be an arrogant young master, but the feeling of fear and dread continued to cling to me.

As I stepped inside, I carefully surveyed the room, looking for any signs of intruders or traps. Everything seemed normal, but the unsettling feeling in my gut persisted. I knew I couldn't ignore my instincts or Tianyi's behavior.

"Okay, Tianyi, let's do a thorough sweep of the shop," I whispered, my voice barely audible. We moved cautiously from room to room, our nerves taut like a bowstring.

The tension in the air continued to build, and every little sound made me jump. My heart pounded in my ears, and I couldn't help but think that all my training had been for naught. I still felt like an amateur, stumbling in the dark, unsure of what to do next.

As we approached the last room, my bedroom, the atmosphere felt even heavier, and the fear that had been gnawing at me threatened to consume me entirely. I had to force myself to breathe and take one step at a time, my entire body tensed, ready to face whatever was waiting for me behind that door.

I reached out a shaky hand and slowly pushed the door open, bracing myself for whatever horror might lie within. But as the door creaked open, revealing the dimly lit room, there was nothing out of the ordinary. No intruders, no traps, just my simple bedroom, exactly as I had left it.

My legs gave out, and I collapsed onto the mattress with a small sigh.

Damn it all to hell. There was no way I was sleeping tonight. I'd just spend my time making the potions.

"Excuse me—"

I screamed like a girl upon hearing the unfamiliar voice, shooting up into the air and grabbing my iron staff. The stranger, standing at the entrance of my shop, flinched violently upon my reaction.

"I come in peace!"

He took off his bamboo hat and revealed a handsome face with white skin and a sharp jawline. His eyes were a deep shade of green and were opened wide, with his hands up in the air in a placating gesture. Once I got ahold of myself, I recognized him by his outfit. The only one among the Azure Silk Trading Company who wore a bamboo hat with green-and-white robes.

"You—you're that guy! The escort who drank my potion!"

The escort nodded and relaxed, bowing lightly. "Yes, this one's name is Feng Wu, second-class disciple of the Verdant Lotus Sect. I apologize for my intrusion."

I was surprised to hear that. A second-class disciple? Of the Verdant Lotus Sect? I heard the name in passing, although they were never as popular as the Whispering Winds Sect or the Silent Moon Sect. He gave off an aura of quiet strength. He was calm and composed, and was a far cry from what I expected when dealing with members of a sect.

I half expected him to beat me up. Although, I don't think someone affiliated with the merchants would do so. He seemed reasonable.

"Yeah . . . It's all right. But what business do you have with me? Our agreement was to meet in the morning, no?"

My guard was raised. Dealing with cultivators, in real life, was not as simple a matter as it seemed. Feng Wu glanced at my shoulder, where Tianyi was sitting. I shielded her from view, and he seemed to snap out of focus and answered my question, as calm as ever.

"I am not here on Lady Xiao Yun's behalf. I was passing by and noticed this area was laden with qi. It is a rarity to see one, especially here in the outskirts of the region. I wanted to ask for permission to cultivate, outside in the garden.

I will be quiet when doing so." He asked courteously, dipping his head and clasping his hands in front of him. A polite request.

I lowered my staff. It seemed he didn't wish me harm. Nor did he covet Tianyi. I glanced at her and she seemed fine, although still a bit shaky after the events that transpired. I suppose she was triggered by the fact that someone was watching us. Once he revealed himself, it seemed as though the butterfly calmed down significantly.

Despite the initial scare, the tension in the room began to dissipate as I allowed myself to relax. I had always been the cautious type, perhaps overly so, but my paranoia had saved me from trouble on more than one occasion. It was hard to say whether my instincts were well founded or if I was just overly nervous, but I couldn't shake the feeling that there was more to this situation than met the eye. I resolved to stay on guard, just in case.

". . . Sure. You have my permission. Would you like some tea?"

I decided to trust him. For now. It wasn't often that I got a chance to interact with a cultivator, after all. The last one I saw was a third-class disciple from the Whispering Winds Sect several years ago. He was a bit of an asshole, which colored my thoughts on sects in general, but I suppose they weren't all bad. Perhaps I'd get to pick his brain.

Feng Wu raised his head and nodded. I got to prepare two cups. Since we were both going to be active for the night, I decided on making green tea with some goji berries and ginger. Nothing too crazy.

We sat in my small shop, the warm glow of the lanterns casting flickering shadows on the walls. The scent of the tea, both earthy and sweet, filled the room as the steam rose from the cups. It was a simple moment, two strangers sharing tea under the same roof.

I carefully poured the steaming tea into two cups, inhaling the fragrant aroma before setting the cups on the table.

"Please, have a seat," I said, gesturing toward a chair.

"Thank you," Feng Wu replied, settling down with the same grace and poise he seemed to exhibit in everything he did. I couldn't help but admire his elegant movements, so different from my own clumsy, dirt-streaked life.

As we sipped our tea, I couldn't help but let my curiosity get the better of me. "So, Feng Wu, I've heard of the Whispering Winds Sect and the Silent Moon Sect, but not much about your sect, the Verdant Lotus Sect. What's it like?"

Feng Wu took a sip of his tea before answering, "The Verdant Lotus Sect is a smaller sect situated west of Crescent Bay City. Our cultivation techniques are primarily based on the principles of nature and growth, and we strive to maintain a harmonious relationship with the natural world. While our elders and disciples may not be as prominent as the other sects in the province, we are still among the best."

He seemed to puff up upon talking about the sect.

I found myself more and more intrigued. "That's awesome. And what about you? What brought you to the Verdant Lotus Sect?"

Feng Wu's eyes seemed to soften as he began, "I was born into a humble family of herbalists. My parents instilled in me a deep appreciation for nature and its wonders."

He paused, taking another sip of tea, and I couldn't help but feel a kinship with Feng Wu. His story felt familiar, yet I was eager to know more.

"When I was twelve," he continued, "our village was attacked by bandits, and we lost everything. The Verdant Lotus Sect intervened, saving the village and offering aid to the survivors. Recognizing my innate talent and potential, they invited me to join them as a disciple. I accepted, driven by a desire to protect my family and seek a better life."

I couldn't contain my excitement. I leaned in closer. "Your martial arts skills must be incredible, then. You know, I've always been interested in the world of cultivators, but I never had the chance to see one in action. Would you mind showing me some of your moves?"

Feng Wu raised an eyebrow, but a smile tugged at the corner of his lips. "Very well, I can show you some basic forms. Consider it thanks for allowing me to cultivate here. But I must remind you that cultivation is a lifelong journey, and what I will show you is only a glimpse of what our sect elders can perform."

We went out into the clearing, a little further away past the fenced area where my plants grew. I watched from a small distance, making sure not to blink for fear of missing the cultivator's moves. I would see for myself just how far I was from my goal. My goal of becoming a cultivator.

Feng Wu fell into his combat stance, with his palms open, and one arm tucked close to his body and another placed in front of him. He let out a small breath, and his face became impassive. He made wide, sweeping motions, and I could feel the pulse of qi as he entered into a state of flow. Every movement was graceful, practiced, and sharp.

A series of rapid strikes unfolded from where he stood, stepping into the blows and giving them enough power to break a man's ribs. I could see it. Had there been a person standing before him, Feng Wu's palm strikes would've done incredible damage. Coming from all angles at speeds I could barely perceive, I saw just how poorly I understood the strength of a second-class disciple.

Elder Ming's sworn brother killed a group of people like this? As a child?

The intricate dance was punctuated by a sweeping low kick, and a downward palm strike to the floor, leaving a small indentation where Feng Wu hit. I gaped in astonishment, as the man returned to his original stance and let out a small breath. His ponytail was barely disturbed, and a single strand of hair fell down his forehead as he turned to me.

"That was the first stance of the Lotus Palm. A staple technique of ours. What do you think?"

I stood there, slack-jawed. My new technique, the Rooted Banyan Stance, seemed to pale in comparison. I don't think I would be able to withstand a quarter of those hits even if I was using it!

". . . That was incredible! I didn't know palm techniques could be so powerful. You know, I read something like that in *Chronicles of Zhen Lu*, where they came across an old master that used something called the Heavenly Palm. With the way they described it, I'm thinking they used your sect's technique as inspiration. But I've heard the Whispering Wind Sect also—"

The man seemed taken aback by my enthusiasm, momentarily lost for words as his eyes widened in surprise. I couldn't help it, though. My excitement bubbled up like a gushing spring, fueled by my desire to become a cultivator. We talked under the silvery glow of the moon, our voices weaving together in the still night air. We delved into the intricacies of cultivation techniques, the subtle differences between sects, and the legends that had been passed down for generations.

And so, I met my first friend outside of the village. A well-mannered cultivator by the name of Feng Wu.

CHAPTER SEVENTEEN

New Features

I gulped, swallowing down my nervousness as I faced off against the largest challenge in the nineteen years I've lived. Tianyi was absent, and I missed her calming presence greatly.

Feng Wu smirked from the corner of the room, and I glared at him before refocusing on the two people before me.

Mei Liling and Liang Chen, the two people who accompanied Lady Xiao Yun as her advisers stood before me. The cultivator provided me with some background information about them during our conversation, highlighting their expertise and roles in the Azure Silk Trading Company. It was an enlightening discussion that covered a wide span of topics, which left us with little time to actually do what we wanted to. I only got a few hours to prepare for the presentation, and Feng Wu barely got the opportunity to cultivate.

I felt like I was on the verge of collapsing. Having already consumed another Invigorating Dawn Tonic to keep me awake, I found it increasingly difficult to ignore the warning signals my body was sending me. My eyelids felt heavy, and my muscles ached, desperate for rest and recovery.

Mei Liling was an older woman who took a more advisory and consultative role after working for the Azure Silk Trading Company for more than thirteen years. Feng Wu mentioned her expertise in alchemy. Liang Chen, the vice leader of finance within the same merchant company, was known for being a shrewd but fair man. Their reputations as reliable businessmen and businesswomen preceded them, which made me thankful. I did not have the mental capacity to engage in verbal sparring.

If they offered me a deal above five silver a potion, it would be a glorious victory. Then I'd sleep until tomorrow.

The burden of steering the conversation fell squarely on my shoulders. In hindsight, perhaps I should have sought more guidance about how to proceed after delivering my presentation instead of focusing solely on preparing for it.

Despite my inner turmoil, the older woman greeted me with a small smile. She looked over at the products I brought, each of which I provided a timely explanation for. It was a rehash of the presentation I made yesterday. My voice seemed a bit monotone, so I took a deep breath and did my best to put some energy into my explanations. Mei Liling was quite knowledgeable and asked me pointed questions about the specifics of the potion. I enjoyed the conversation and watched as Liang Chen observed beside her, exchanging occasional glances and writing down something on his notepad.

First, the Invigorating Dawn Tonic, a potent brew that infused the body with a burst of energy, making the consumer feel as if they were reborn with the rising sun. Next, a soothing ointment that alleviated pain, fortified by the refreshing essence of mint and wormwood, renowned for its restorative properties. Then there was the calming elixir, a concoction using the tranquilizing properties of lavender and chamomile, known to enhance sleep quality and reduce night tremors. The elderberry potion, a proven remedy for the common cold, had been tested on Xiao Bao during my presentation, showcasing its efficacy. Last but certainly not least, a vial of goji berry essence that honed one's focus to razor-sharp levels. Five vials of each, elegantly packaged and meticulously labeled, nestled within a box carved from the finest oak.

I was planning on experimenting with certain combinations, like the goji berry and the Invigorating Dawn Tonic to create an even more powerful elixir that could awaken the dead, but it would have to wait for later.

I glanced at Mei Liling and Liang Chen, gauging their reactions to my explanations. Mei Liling's eyes seemed to shimmer with interest and curiosity, while Liang Chen maintained a more stoic demeanor. I couldn't help but feel a sense of pride as I spoke about my creations, showcasing the fruits of my labor and dedication. They were my pride and joy. Although I'd consider them prototypes as of now, they were perfectly serviceable products as they were. I'd refine the recipe for them as I produced more.

Mei Liling seemed satisfied by my answers and deferred to Liang Chen, and he turned to face me.

"We've looked over the products you have and would like to offer you a price of five silver per potion."

That was exactly what I wanted. But I didn't show it in my face. I kept my face impassive. The desire to fall asleep likely helped produce an even better blank face than I would've been able to do if I was well rested.

It was common knowledge that whenever merchants provided a price, it was a gauge to determine whether the person was a sucker or not. Although the degree to which they ripped someone off depended on the merchant's code of morality (which was usually ambiguous).

When I first began running my shop independently and bought from the traveling merchants, they thought I was an easy mark. I mean, I was a child. It was easy to underestimate me.

But not anymore. Kai Liu was a savvy negotiator, talented herbalist, and future cultivator.

"The price seems a bit lacking compared to the quality of the products I'm offering. I believe that the essences used differentiate it from most of the products in the market, no?"

I watched their faces closely, searching for any flicker of reaction. I knew I had a strong point, but it was all about how well I could sell it. My products weren't simply concoctions of herbs and elements; they were the culmination of painstaking research, expertise, and an innovative approach to alchemy. The essences I used set my potions apart from the rest, elevating them to a higher level of quality and potency. As I spoke, I tried to convey my passion for my craft, hoping that the sincerity in my words would resonate with them and demonstrate the true value of what I had to offer.

It was a string of back-and-forth negotiations. I held my ground, but in my head, I knew I already won. I was simply seeing if I could aim for any higher. It came down to the rarity of my skill, which was the ability to extract plant essences that made my products much more special. They were moderately better than anything you could get in the area, but it was about the potential I held. What if I extracted qi-based plants like the Moonlit Grace Lily? Or the ones in my garden growing in a Qi Haven?

They were what-ifs, but it was pretty clear to me that Mei Liling was here to determine my qualifications, and for her knowledge of alchemy to identify any weaknesses or areas for improvement in my products, and use these as bargaining chips to negotiate a lower price. But something like extracted essence was unheard of. I didn't know much about other regions, but something like this ability should be valued highly.

In the end, we came to a satisfactory conclusion.

"Six silver for the four potions, and seven silver per Invigorating Dawn Potion." Liang Chen muttered, putting the final touches to the contract he drafted up. He handed it to me for a final revision and I gave it a thorough look.

A message from the Interface appeared before my eyes.

A contract has been created.
IN WITNESS WHEREOF, the parties hereto have executed this Agreement.
Kai, Alchemist

> *Liang Chen, Executive, Azure Silk Trading Company*
> *Mei Liling, Executive, Azure Silk Trading Company*
> *Witnessed by:*
> *Feng Wu, Second-Class Disciple, Verdant Lotus Sect*
> ***Y/N?***

I stood there, frozen. The two older advisors looked at me with concern and Mei Liling spoke.

"Is there something wrong?"

"Ah, um, I . . ." I floundered, trying to think of a way to explain what I was seeing. "I received a message from the Interface. It just lists out what you've written on the contract, and it looks like it is prompting me for an answer. Do you know of this?"

They looked at each other and then back at me, shaking their heads. "We're afraid we don't. No prompt has risen from our ends, and the Heavenly Interface has not been seen to trigger when forming a contract."

I looked around hesitantly. The contract seemed straightforward; there wasn't even anything discussing penalties or punishment. But the appearance of the contract in the interface unsettled me. Without much thought, I decided to accept the terms.

> *You have made your first contract.*
> *Quest: Contract Fulfillment (Production)*
> *—Complete the terms of your contract.*

Everybody in the room seemed to get a similar notification, their eyes flitting down to read a text invisible to my eyes.

"This is . . . unexpected." Liang Chen said, coughing slightly. "There doesn't seem to be any drawbacks to the contract we have created, but I suppose this makes it more concrete."

I wasn't planning on reneging on the contract, but the Heavenly Interface's interference provided me with even more incentive not to. What would happen if I failed the quest? Would it strike me with lightning? Kill me on the spot? Take my funds?

"If there's anything, please don't hesitate to contact me. This is new for me as well," I confessed. Bowing my head and clasping my hands, I gave them my farewell. "Now I will go and rest. Please excuse me."

It was still early in the morning when I left the merchants with a copy of my contract. I stumbled out of the tent they set up, putting my hand up to block my eyes from the sunlight.

I needed to sleep, *now*! Just a small nap would do.

The trek back home felt like a dream, my exhausted mind barely registering the scenery that passed by. The cobblestone streets and familiar faces of the villagers seemed to blend together in a hazy kaleidoscope as I stumbled my way toward the sanctuary of my home.

Seeing Tianyi brought a sense of peace and calm, knowing that I was truly home. The innate qi in the air lifted me slightly, releasing the tension from my shoulders that I held after negotiations. I looked around my room, taking in the familiar surroundings that I had grown to cherish. The neatly arranged shelves of herbs, the soft glow of the lanterns, and the comforting scent of lavender all served as a soothing balm to my frayed nerves. As I lay in bed, I couldn't help but feel a sense of accomplishment, having faced one of the most challenging situations in my life and emerging victorious.

I fell into my bed in a boneless heap. My mind was far too out of sorts to think of anything else other than sleep.

With that, I succumbed to the darkness.

A dim glow visible through my eyelids stirred me from my deep sleep, and as I opened my eyes, a delicate, glimmering butterfly hovered just above my nose. The overwhelming fatigue I had experienced earlier seemed to have vanished without a trace. My body, which had been sore from pushing its limits during my training with Elder Ming, now felt as light as a feather.

Bewildered, I wondered how long I had been asleep. What time could it possibly be?

Curious, I opened my door to find the birds outside chirping merrily, while the sun shone brightly in an unblemished sky. This struck me as odd, and a nagging feeling of unease began to well up in my gut as I glanced around the village.

Could it be possible that I had slept all the way through to the next day?

"Dammit! I missed morning training!" I exclaimed in frustration.

Hastily, I changed into a fresh robe and rinsed my face before sprinting back toward Gentle Wind Village. Judging by the sun's position, it must have been around noon by now, which meant I was several hours late for my morning training with the Village Head. The disorientation I felt was staggering; I had barely awoken, yet here I was, dashing through the village like a madman.

As I sped along the cobbled pathway, I deftly sidestepped Mrs. Wang as she turned a corner, shouting my apologies before quickly continuing on my way. I waved at the children playing in the street, giving them all an enthusiastic thumbs-up as I dashed past them.

Realizing that this was the first day of my new training schedule made the situation all the more embarrassing. This was hardly the behavior befitting of a cultivator.

This was the price I had to pay for pushing myself so relentlessly. I needed to find a more sustainable balance between my various commitments. The idea of hiring Lan-Yin to run the store in my absence became increasingly attractive, as managing everything on my own was proving to be quite the challenge.

I knocked on Elder Ming's door, and he opened it up after a minute or so. I immediately bowed my head to apologize.

"My apologies, Elder Ming! I overslept because of yesterday and missed today's training! Do with me as you see fit!"

"What are you talking about? Weren't we supposed to begin your new schedule tomorrow?"

I glanced upward in total confusion. It finally sunk in that I wasn't actually late for my training, nor had I slept for a full day. My nap was only a few hours at most, but I supposed it was enough to completely eliminate any and all fatigue from my body. I looked down in disbelief. That was how refreshed I was; the thought that my slumber was anything less than the entire day didn't register in my head.

Elder Ming sighed, seeing the look on my face.

"You brat. I suppose that's another thing I might as well teach you. Resting is just as important in your training than the actual training itself. Come in!"

He ushered me inside, and I asked him an innocuous question.

"Don't you have anything better to do as the Village Head?"

Elder Ming snorted. "The Gentle Wind Village runs itself fine, Kai. Don't worry about me. I have plenty of time to knock some sense into that thick skull of yours."

Despite Elder Ming's advanced age and frail-looking body, he moved around the furniture in his home with surprising grace and agility. He created a cozy, serene space for me to relax and unwind. Once he had finished, he beckoned me to join him.

"Now, Kai, the first thing you need to understand is that life is a delicate balance of effort and rest. You have been pushing yourself too hard, and that is not the way. I no longer doubt your ability to work hard, but now you must value harmony in all aspects of life. As much as you train and learn, you must also find time to rest and rejuvenate your body and mind."

I sat down on one of the comfortable cushions Elder Ming had arranged on the floor. He poured me a cup of tea from a beautifully crafted teapot. "Drink it slowly, and let your body and mind find peace."

As I sipped the tea, I could feel the tension in my muscles begin to dissipate, and my mind grew more tranquil. Elder Ming, with a gentle voice and a hint of a smile, guided me through some simple breathing exercises. "Breathe in deeply, filling your lungs with the life-giving air around you. Now release the breath slowly, letting go of any tension or stress you may be holding on to. No need to circulate your qi. This is purely for relaxation, understand?"

I followed Elder Ming's instructions, focusing on my breath and feeling my body grow lighter with each exhalation. He continued, "Now close your eyes and imagine yourself in a place of serenity—a place where you feel completely at peace. It could be a forest, a beach, or even a quiet room. Let your mind wander and explore this place, allowing yourself to release any worries or concerns."

I closed my eyes, and my mind immediately brought me to my home garden. Surrounded by my plants, I felt the warmth of the sun on my skin, and the soft scent of flowers filled the air. With the help of my Memory Palace, visualizing my garden was as easy as breathing.

After some time, Elder Ming gently tapped my shoulder, bringing me back to the present. "Ah, there you are," he said with a warm smile. "Remember, Kai, balance is the key to a fulfilling life. When you find yourself overwhelmed or exhausted, take the time to rest and recuperate. This will not only make you a better cultivator but also help you maintain harmony in your life."

Elder Ming paused for a moment, allowing his words to sink in. Then, with a twinkle in his eyes, he continued, "You see, Kai, the journey of life is like the path of a river. It may twist and turn, sometimes flowing smoothly, other times rushing with great force. But the river always finds its way, just as we must find our way through life's challenges. Balance is the key to navigating these currents."

The Village Head could get oddly philosophical and profound at times like these. And then there were other times when he beat me with a cane or kicked me in the groin. I wondered if he had a split-personality disorder.

But I nodded regardless, feeling a newfound appreciation for the importance of rest and relaxation. It hadn't even been a full month since the Day of Awakening. But the me from before seemed unrecognizable. There had been too many changes in such a short span of time. No wonder I was so disoriented. Progress was good, but burning myself out like a candle in the process wasn't worth it.

Perhaps I should take this time to read. Elder Ming always had entertaining novels on his shelf. Perhaps this was my chance.

As we continued our conversation, Elder Ming shared more wisdom with me. "In life, there are times when we must be like the bamboo—strong and resilient, bending with the wind but never breaking. And there are times when we must be like the willow—soft and yielding, allowing life to flow around us. Knowing when to be strong and when to be soft is the essence of balance."

Elder Ming graciously allowed me to stay in his home while he went about his day. I made sure to keep his house nice and tidy, going up to his bookshelf and picking the most interesting title to read. *Ha, I can't believe it. I haven't read a proper book in ages. Not since I first saw Tianyi.*

Ascending the Jade Dragon Mountain: A Tale of Immortal Pursuits. A grand title. You shall be worthy of my attention today, little novel.

I picked it from the shelf, dusting away the forest-green cover, and enjoyed the present.

A new skill has been created.
Reading (Level 1): A skill that grants the ability to read books slightly faster and more efficiently than an average person. Reading enables the user to understand and retain information from books within their current knowledge scope and known languages.
Next Stage: Accelerated Reading
Requirements:
Reading Proficiency—Level 10
Accumulate fifty hours of reading.
Read a total of thirty books.
Develop a basic understanding of at least three different subjects you didn't know before.

I sighed aloud. Work never failed to find me, did it?

CHAPTER EIGHTEEN

Calm Before the Storm

A week had passed, and I'd made significant alterations to my daily routine. I was still in an adjustment period, but the strain I imposed on my body and mind through constant training and experimentation was decreasing day by day.

During the day, I honed my skills with Elder Ming, while my evenings were spent concocting potions and elixirs, expanding my understanding of herbs, and nurturing my garden. To relax, I indulged in reading and enjoyed Wang Jun's company. Our bond strengthened as we frequented the Soaring Swallow to share drinks and discuss our aspirations and responsibilities.

I decided to hire Lan-Yin to hold down the store while I gallivanted. I paid her a fair wage and broke down how I operated the store. She was quick on the uptake and by the middle of the week, she was already independently running the shop. The girl was reliable, and she greatly enjoyed the peace and quiet of my shop in comparison to the hectic nature of running the only teahouse in the village.

This gave me the opportunity to focus on the things I truly enjoyed doing: training and gardening!

My plants flourished remarkably over the week, thanks to Tianyi's Qi Haven skill, my energy infusion, and the meticulous care I provided. Contrary to my initial prediction that the ginseng would be harvest-ready in a few months, it would actually mature by the month's end. I planned to keep some on hand to observe its potential. Cultivating potent ginseng held immense value, rivaling or even surpassing qi-based plants in terms of creating pills and elixirs to enhance one's strength or qi. Tales of millennia-old ginseng transforming mortals into all-powerful cultivators left a strong imprint on my mind.

Speaking of qi, I had figured out a way to complete the quest without having to venture into the forest. It was purely an accident. Tianyi came with me almost every time I went to Elder Ming's house, and it became a second home of sorts.

Even in the times I wasn't training, I would come to return or borrow some more books to read. The Village Head didn't have any family, and I realized just how lonely it was for him. He was a quiet man and rarely asked for help. I made sure to accompany him whenever I could. It was the least I could do for my master.

And with that, I came to realize Tianyi's Qi Haven skill now affected Elder Ming's home, making it qualified as an area with sufficient wood qi for me to meditate in. I was in the midst of helping him clean the floors and reorganize the shelves when a bright yellow orb appeared out of nowhere, scaring the daylights out of me and making me scream like an infant.

It was the perfect sequence of events, and I took advantage of it, circulating my inner qi under my master's supervision. I could feel my pathways becoming more resilient. The amount of qi I could unleash when infusing was larger than before. Although it wasn't by a wide margin, it was enough for me to notice.

> *Quest: Cultivation Technique (Wood)*
> *—Find five different areas that have sufficient wood qi in the*
> *surroundings and meditate in them for one hour. (3/5)*
> *—Areas with sufficient wood qi will be marked with a glowing*
> *yellow orb only visible to you.*

Day by day, I was becoming stronger. I had a glimpse of what a cultivator should be capable of, thanks to Feng Wu's demonstration. He left shortly afterward, but he said that he would likely come back and visit someday. I hoped so. It would be nice to see him once I become a full-fledged martial artist and surprise him with techniques of my own. I began training with my staff, incorporating some basic training that focused on the fundamentals. Elder Ming mentioned that he wasn't a staff user by any means, but he had seen wielders in action during his time as a cultivator and had a clear vision of what they used to do when they trained.

I focused on mastering the proper grip techniques for the staff, both forward and reverse, while learning to transition smoothly between them. I also became familiar with the staff's length and the mechanics of wielding it effectively.

Alongside weapons training, Elder Ming began imparting the basics of hand-to-hand combat to me as well. Punching, kicking, and everything in between. I was sure that I was ready to tackle it now, with my mind and body now at the first rank of the mortal realm according to the Heavenly Interface.

Tianyi, Elder Ming, and I all ventured far from the village to visit the banyan, several li away from the village. It had been years since I last saw it, but it remained unchanged by the rigors of time.

I requested for our morning training to take place here because I felt like being near the mighty tree would give me some sort of inspiration. I avoided it for so long, a somber reminder of what was before my parents died. But I wanted to grow and emulate the banyan: strong, unwavering, and able to stand the test of time.

It also acted as another place for Tianyi to activate her Qi Haven skill. If she frequented the area with me for long periods of time, it would create another zone and bring me closer to getting my second cultivation technique. I was excited to know what it was.

But I had to focus on the task at hand. With the transition from endurance and strength training to actual combat, I had to learn how to actually fight. It was my first time learning how to fight against a human. I didn't recall ever engaging in fisticuffs with anybody as a child.

As the sun gently peeked over the horizon, bathing the serene forest in a warm orange light, we stood under the ancient banyan tree. Elder Ming gazed at me with a tender smile, his eyes resembling autumn leaves as they crinkled.

"Now, Kai, we shall begin with a simple exercise," he said, his voice calm and energized. "I want you to try to strike me. Do not worry about hurting me; I am more resilient than I appear."

I hesitated for a moment, uncertainty creeping into my heart. The idea of attacking such an elderly person felt wrong, but I remembered the nimbleness I had seen him display before. So, I took a deep breath and steadied myself, remembering how he beat me with a cane and struck me in the groin.

Dropping low to the ground, I lunged at Elder Ming and drew my fist back. To my surprise, he deftly sidestepped the attack, chuckling softly. "Your speed is impressive, but your predictability leaves much to be desired. Again!"

I gritted my teeth and tried once more, this time attempting to tackle his midsection. Elder Ming effortlessly leaned back, avoiding the attempt by a hair's breadth. "Too slow, Kai," he said, his voice leisurely and patient. "You must learn to flow like the wind, swift and unpredictable. Do you see? I am not moving any faster than you are."

It was true. Elder Ming still had his hands clasped together behind him, making simple moves to avoid me.

Frustration bubbled within me as I launched a flurry of punches and kicks at Elder Ming, each one dodged or parried with ease. It was as if he could read my every move before I even made it.

As I attacked, Elder Ming continued to speak, his voice never losing its calm demeanor. "Your stance is too rigid, Kai. You must learn to be like the banyan tree, rooted yet flexible, bending but never breaking."

My breaths grew heavier, my muscles screaming in protest as I desperately tried to land a single hit on my elderly master. I was getting dragged into it, but I couldn't help it. Every blow was just missed by a millimeter. I fell into the trap that if I were to go just a bit faster, I'd catch him. But each attempt was met with the same outcome: failure. Finally, I felt my legs give out beneath me, and I collapsed onto the ground, gasping for air.

Elder Ming looked down at me, his expression kind and understanding. "Do not be disheartened, young Kai. This is only the beginning of your journey. I'll be teaching you how to incorporate what you just saw into your own fighting style. This is why I emphasize footwork."

As I lay there, panting and exhausted, I couldn't help but feel a newfound respect for Elder Ming and the path of cultivation I had chosen to follow. I knew that I had much to learn, but I also knew that I was determined to grow.

After a bit of rest, he educated me on the proper way to throw a punch. The way to involve my lower body during the movement. Adding rotational force to increase power. Making the punch more efficient to avoid telegraphing and wasting stamina.

It was such a simple move. I didn't know just how much thought went into a straight punch.

The more I learned, the more I realized how out of my depth I was without Elder Ming's guidance. I wouldn't have made even half the progress without him. But because of his support, I'm growing and developing at a rate far beyond what I could've imagined.

"Now, your Rooted Banyan Stance . . . We'll need to gather some more information."

I stood, ready to unleash my technique at a moment's notice, and at Elder Ming's behest, I let the qi pour out from my body as I clenched my core muscles as tightly as possible. With my iron staff in hand, he swung the end at my thigh. It made a terrible noise, but the impact was muted. The feeling of being struck but feeling minimal pain took some time getting used to.

Elder Ming stood there silently, observing me as I released the stance.

The technique was costly in terms of qi. Making it protect my entire body took entirely more than I was capable of handling. Even those three seconds it took to hold the Rooted Banyan Stance wiped out half of my reserves.

Then there was the issue of being unable to move. I was forced to tense every portion of my body, drop down into the horse stance, and leave my hands tucked away at my sides. We experimented with the technique being maintained in other positions, such as the form of a punch, but my body couldn't grasp it. The qi barely circulated through my body, and the defensive benefits were cut down to a fraction of its initial effectiveness.

It felt humbling. The technique was perfect for withstanding blows. Honestly, I was pretty sure I could take a palm strike or two from Feng Wu with it. But it was very situational. How often would I stand there and allow my opponent to strike me? What's to say they would stop at one blow? I voiced all these worries to my master and he placed a supporting hand on my shoulder.

"Ah, Kai. You gaze at the world through a narrow lens. The fact that you can utilize the move, even if just a bit, when you're in a different position, is like planting the seed of potential, waiting to sprout into a towering tree. Striking somebody at the point of impact, powered by the Rooted Banyan Stance, would be like a wave crashing against the shore, its force multiplied."

My eyes widened. I didn't view it like that. "So you're saying that the Rooted Banyan Stance isn't limited to defense? I can use it to create offense?"

"Correct. As the ancient sages once said, defense is the foundation of offense. From it springs opportunity. With the versatility of your skill, it can be wielded to seize those chances. All it requires is your creativity and diligence," Elder Ming said with a small smile on his face. "Come, let us forge ahead in refining your technique. Your qi reserves shall deepen and expand the more you deplete and replenish them."

Our early-morning training continued, and even with so much left to learn, I couldn't help but feel excited for my own potential. Something about Elder Ming's words struck a chord with me.

His wisdom, steeped in ancient teachings, had a way of illuminating the path before me, casting away the shadows of doubt and uncertainty. As I trained under his guidance, I began to understand that the journey of cultivation was not merely about honing my skills or amassing power, but also about discovering my own inner strength and the boundless possibilities that lay within.

The towering banyan tree provided us respite from the sun, casting its cooling shade over our training ground.

CHAPTER NINETEEN

Dao

The days flew by like the summer breeze. Being so engrossed in multiple projects did that, I suppose.

My first shipment for the Azure Silk Trading Company was set for today, so I took a break from training today in order to accomplish this with Elder Ming's blessing. All he told me to do for today's training was to begin comprehending the dao. I'd heard the term in many of the books I'd read, but it was always vague, and they varied greatly from book to book. I knew that the Whispering Wind Sect had its own interpretation of the dao, but I didn't remember what it was fully.

As usual, the old man gave me another cryptic riddle to decipher. And it was harder to understand than usual as well.

The dao is not something you can grasp with your mind alone. It is something you experience and feel, like the wind on your face or the earth beneath your feet. It's in every breath you take, in every step you make, and in every moment of your life. It's what guides your every action and shapes your understanding of the world.

It seemed quite critical to my training as a cultivator, so I asked him what his interpretation of the dao was. It'd be easier to make an answer if I had something to base it on.

He gave me that little chuckle and simply pointed to a lit candle, telling me that was what he learned in his sect. When I pestered him for more answers, he threatened to beat me with his cane. Whatever. I'd figure it out on my own. It would give me an excuse to read, and I'd be able to evolve it to the next stage within time.

Reading (Level 4): A skill that grants the ability to read books slightly faster and more efficiently than an average person. Reading enables the user to understand and retain information from books within their current knowledge scope and known languages.
Next Stage: Accelerated Reading

Requirements:
Reading Proficiency—Level 10
Accumulate fifty hours of reading.
Read a total of thirty books.
Develop a basic understanding of at least three different subjects
you didn't know before.

It would be a long time before I ran out of books to read. Elder Ming's home was filled to the brim, although I mainly kept to the books chronicling the tales of cultivators, real or fictional.

Huan's voice disrupted my next line of thinking as I neared his outpost. The area where the traveling merchant had set up was now more permanent, but it was still a work in progress. Planks of wood and blocks of stone were still strewn around, and I had to be careful navigating through them as I carried an entire crate of product with my hands.

"Oh my goodness! Set it down! Set it down!"

I did what I was told, hearing the frantic tone in his voice. Being careful not to strain myself, I bent my knees and tilted forward in a controlled manner so the inside of the crate didn't shake too violently. Phew! That was a good workout!

Huan looked at me as though I were a madman.

"You don't have a cart?" he exclaimed, bending down to try and pick up the crate himself. The older man, although he was far from thin or weak, struggled mightily and gave up. "Why would you carry all the products by yourself?"

I scratched the back of my neck, glancing upward. "Well, the one I had at the shop is far too small. It would've broken. Besides, this was a good way to get the blood flowing."

The merchant shook his head, wiping sweat from his brow as the summer heat bared down on us. Luckily, I was used to this. My skin was always tanned from doing work outside my garden, and I held up well against the sun. In fact, I always felt more energized being outside.

"There's still a second crate back at home so I'll come back and—"

"A second crate?" Huan asked, his eyes bulging out. He lifted the lid and counted out how much there was under his breath before looking up at me in astonishment. "There's about a hundred and fifty potions in here . . . Is the second one—?"

"Yeah, it's about the same size. I got a bit over excited during production. If I remember correctly, I made three hundred and forty-six in total. Make sure to count carefully while I'm getting the other one."

Before I could turn around, Huan grabbed me by the shoulder and shook his head, pointing at a cart left untouched by his shop.

"Go, use it. For my sake, at least," he muttered.

I shrugged and thanked him for the wooden cart. It was large and spacious, enough to fit the crate from my shop with ease. I hummed to myself, calculating the profit from this deal. About six silver per potion multiplied by three hundred equaled to 1,800 hundred silver. Or, converted to gold, almost twenty gold coins.

The tantalizing clink of coins echoed in my mind. That was insane. I don't think I ever had that much in a lump sum. In particularly profitable seasons, I amassed about two to three gold, but maintaining the shop and buying ingredients were large expenses.

My dream of having a greenhouse was close. I'd be able to grow anything I'd want, even during the winter. I only had one window in the house, so imagining an entire section expanded upon my garden covered by a ceiling composed entirely of glass was interesting. Excitement bubbled in my stomach, and I hastened my pace.

It was remarkably easy to bring the cart back up to my shop. Too easy, in fact. I looked around for a moment, and I spotted what I was looking for.

Three heavy rocks. Each one about the size of my head. They added enough heft to the cart that would allow me to work up a sweat. If I wasn't going to train with Elder Ming, I'd make up for it. I realized early on there were ways of training that didn't require qi.

If my past self could see me right now, he'd think I was insane. But he would also see how muscular and handsome I was and wouldn't complain at all. The overall muscle development compared to before was astounding. I was not Wang Jun, but from an aesthetic perspective, I could say I was his match. *Jade beauties, here I come!*

I pushed through and made it back home within a few minutes. Tianyi was out and about in the garden, circling through placidly. I was always worried about the idea of her being picked off by a pesky bird, but they seemed to pose no threat to her. That crow in the forest was exceptionally smart and fast, but it barely managed to catch her. Tianyi had gone up a cultivation rank, and although she rarely utilized it, she was incredibly fast.

"Tianyi, is your patrol going well? No dastardly invaders?"

She responded in the affirmative through our mental link, and I nodded and went inside to collect my crate. Lan-Yin wasn't supposed to come until this afternoon, so it was just me maintaining the shop until then. I'd need to drop this off and come back here quickly, in case any customers were waiting. The rumors about my tonics, balms, and potions spread through the village like wildfire, and they were my most popular product. Even the essences were being bought out. The Soaring Swallow purchased some so as to infuse their products with a light flavor. I gave them a discount, of course. It didn't take much for me to extract the essences, and it was good practice.

I loaded up the last box onto my cart, making sure to be careful as I set it down. Once it was secured, I went back toward the village.

During my walk, I thought about what exactly Elder Ming meant by contemplating the dao.

Dao. The path. *My* path.

My path to cultivation? That was fairly simple, in my opinion. Attain great power, ascend to greater heights, and become free to travel the world as I pleased. Enjoy the sights, cities, and delicacies without holding back.

I'd have fantastical resources only cultivators from farther provinces could access. I'd share them with the village and those in need. I never quite understood hoarding that sort of wealth, especially when a mere droplet would revitalize an entire province like our own.

But for some reason, I didn't think that's what Elder Ming meant when he asked me to comprehend the dao.

I had the entire day ahead to ponder over a fitting response.. Maybe I'd ask Wang Jun and Lan-Yin when I came across them.

It didn't take long for me to reach the merchant outpost, especially with a cart speeding up the process. Huan told me the payment would be ready by tomorrow and to come and collect it then. Once that came in, I'd have to ask the carpenters about how much it'd cost to have one built. By the looks of it, I could afford to build the greenhouse with another month's worth of shipments being sold. It would be a sizable one.

One of the main challenges in running the herbal shop was how limited I was during winter; it wasn't a profitable season, and my ability to grow plants year-round was restricted. Foraging in the cold was essential when inventory ran low, but with a greenhouse, I might never need to forage again. Gone would be the days when I froze my fingers off in search of anything edible or usable.

I strolled through the village with my hands on the back of my head. Out of habit, I went to the forge. It was as active as ever; I don't know how their neighbors slept with the constant sound of clanging metal. I greatly appreciated the peace and quiet I had at my shop.

"Kai! How are things?" Wang Jun asked, turning to look at me with his face covered in soot. Maybe it was a hallucination, but I swear he'd gotten taller. His bulky frame had filled out even more, and he was already larger than his master. Calling him an ox was not so far removed from the truth.

"Eh, busy as usual. Running the shop and keeping up with training never gets easier." I sighed. "But I wanted to ask you a question."

"I'm here to talk, so long as you don't mind me working while I'm at it. Master Qiang's gonna kill me if I'm behind on the orders," he muttered quietly.

"What's your dao?"

He turned to me with a brief look of confusion. "What?"

I pursed my lips for a moment, trying to think of the best way to put it in a way he'd understand. "Like your way of life. What do you believe in? The foundation upon which you operate on."

"Kai, that's a bit of a heavy question to ask while I'm hammering away here." Wang Jun replied, remaining silent for a few seconds as he thought of an answer. "Maybe for me, I'd say it's being able to control your destiny."

I leaned in, interested in what he had to say. Despite others often mistaking Wang Jun for a simpleton, I knew he was far from it. From a young age, he'd been quite sophisticated. His skill in calligraphy was unmatched, and he had a graceful touch for someone that was so large and heavy-handed. In fact, he helped me write up some signs for the shop when we were younger.

"See this sword?" He held it out for me. It was clearly a work in progress, but the quality was undeniable. "It used to be just a hunk of iron. But with enough heat and a steady hand, it becomes something more. Master Qiang told me a lot about how blacksmithing isn't just a job. It's a lifestyle. It's something I apply to in my day-to-day life. If I keep putting effort, with time I'll bring my vision to life."

"Huh." That was a pretty thoughtful answer. "You're much more introspective than you look, Wang Jun."

"What's that supposed to mean?"

I laughed at him, giving the taller man a pat on the back. "I'm joking, I'm joking! I've known you since we were kids. I know you hated how people thought you'd be some sort of warrior. Feels like you and I should've switched bodies."

He rolled his eyes. "I wouldn't be able to get any smithing done with your scrawny arms, Dreaming Gardener!"

I turned my nose up at him. "You'll come to regret that once I'm a cultivator, Wang Jun. I'll face-slap you in front of the village and bring shame upon your family for a thousand generations!"

After a small round of bickering, I thanked him for his time and went off back to the garden. I got an example of what a dao is from Wang Jun, and I feel like it gave me a bit more understanding in terms of what it meant. It helped to verbalize what I meant when asking what his dao was.

A way of life. How I interpreted it in my own, individual way.

If Wang Jun compared his dao to smithing, I supposed mine would be based on something related to gardening.

Wang Jun's assertion that our destiny could be shaped by relentless effort and a clear vision resonated with me. Yet his metaphor of the sword didn't quite align with my own perspective. Instead, my thoughts wandered to a seedling breaking through the earth, reaching for the sky. Growth and transformation, to me, were intertwined as deeply as roots in the ground.

There were times, however, when, despite our best efforts, external circumstances seemed to conspire against us. Plagues, droughts, various unpredictable calamities could all too easily devastate our carefully nurtured growth. Yet I had come to see a profound truth in these cycles of life and death.

Nothing lasted forever. Not even the mighty banyan tree, deeply rooted and formidable, was immune to the passage of time. Sooner or later, it, too, would fall. But even in its demise, there was a promise of rebirth. A single seed, born from the fallen giant, would sprout, unfurl its leaves, and strive for the heavens.

What was my path?

It was one of continuous growth. But it was not a linear path. I'd spent the first nineteen years of my life imagining rather than doing. It wasn't until I'd met Tianyi that I started pursuing cultivation. Ups and downs, a constant cycle of failure and success.

But day by day, I grew closer to my goals. Maybe I wouldn't make much progress within a week. Or a month. But within a year? A decade?

Eventually, I'd bloom into something that could reach the heavens themselves. I'd bear fruit and give back to all those who have yet to reach the level I had. *Give back to the earth, and it will give back to you.*

That was my path. A blossoming path.

CHAPTER TWENTY

Cultivation Method

Lan-Yin, what's your dao?"

"Huh?"

She paused her work, staring at me in the same way Wang Jun had. Married couples really did act alike.

I dramatically raised my hands. "Your way of living, the belief that guides your every action. Every thought. It's the very air we breathe, the ground that settles on our feet. That is the dao."

"Is this another one of those nonsensical quotes from your cultivator books?"

"They are not nonsensical!" I gasped, as though she'd committed blasphemy of the highest order. "Humor me, Lan-Yin! What's your philosophy?"

She gave me a half-hearted shrug. "I don't know, my family? Being in the present?"

"Gah, maybe something a little more profound? Even Wang Jun had something nice to answer the question with."

The girl rolled her eyes at me. "You don't pay me to answer that. Now, can you help me put this up? It's heavy."

I sighed. Another one that was unable to comprehend the dao. I guessed some weren't blessed with the insight to do so. No matter.

Her shrug may have been half-hearted, but the message was clear—she didn't care much for philosophical inquiries. Her focus was on the present, the tasks at hand, her family, her duties. To her, life was simple and straightforward. The tangible world around her was the priority, not the complex intricacies of one's belief systems.

The small display of potions and elixirs was perched just above my head. Accommodating the essences and potions on my shelves took a bit of planning. Lan-Yin was quite skilled at designing, especially when considering how customers would enter the store. They would see my new products the moment they entered my shop. Although she wasn't helpful when it came to contemplating philosophy, she was quite good at interior design.

As we worked on the display of potions, the scent of different herbs filled the air. It was a mix of bitter and sweet, spicy and cool, each scent distinctive yet mingling seamlessly with the others. The smell of the herbs was heady and intoxicating.

After hashing out any last-minute tasks for her to do, I went out into the garden where Tianyi rested. She seemed to notice my intent and fluttered toward me, happily perched on her spot by my right shoulder. With my iron staff on my other hand, it was time to complete one of the tasks I'd been looking forward to all day.

Completing the cultivation quest.

> *Quest: Cultivation Technique (Wood)*
> *—Find five different areas that have sufficient wood qi in the surroundings and meditate in them for one hour. (4/5)*
> *—Areas with sufficient wood qi will be marked with a glowing yellow orb only visible to you.*

After Elder Ming's home became saturated in qi thanks to Tianyi's skill, I decided to measure just how long it took for the skill to take effect. I counted it at the banyan tree where I'd hosted my hand-to-hand combat sessions with the Village Head, and I realized exactly how long it took.

It was nearly three days of Tianyi's presence. But obviously, I didn't stick around at the tree for consecutive days, and neither did she. It was over the course of half a month. Tianyi's skill was powerful. From what I could see, the Qi Haven didn't fade so long as she revisited the area at least once a week. My shop and the surrounding area was always teeming with energy, and since I lounged frequently at Elder Ming's home, it became another place where I could cultivate my qi without holding back.

The Village Head appreciated Tianyi's presence. His posture and energy improved since Tianyi regularly attended our meetings, and he gave her a small plate of sugar water by his dining table as thanks. How beautiful.

With that knowledge, I searched for the appropriate place where I could complete the quest. It could've been anywhere, from Master Qiang's forge or just a small distance away from my shop for convenience. But I had a better idea.

My feet carried me through the village and farther into the coast, where the fishing boats were. The smell of seafood and saltwater greeted my nose. It was far more intense here, and I waved to the locals. They cooed at Tianyi, admiring her glimmering wings. She had become a celebrity of sorts among the inhabitants of Gentle Wind Village. The delicate Spirit Beast preened under the attention, and I could feel her smugness through our link.

I didn't know how smart Tianyi was, but clearly she could comprehend other people's words. I wondered if she'd be able to formulate words if our bond grew deeper, or if she went up another cultivation rank.

We went past the fish market. With the upcoming deposit I'd receive from the Azure Silk Trading Company and the completion of my quest, I'd celebrate with a hearty meal after I was done. The fishermen would be carrying loads of salmon, and I'd need plenty if I were to eat it. I'd invite Wang Jun and Lan-Yin for dinner, since salmon was one of the few dishes I knew how to cook.

I ended up at the beach. It was far from hustle and bustle, and for good reason. This area was barren during this time of the year. The beach was a place of tranquility, a place where the sea met the land, where the sky met the earth. The sun shone brightly, casting a warm glow on the white sandy beach. The waves lapped gently at the shore, rhythmically washing over the fine grains of sand, each wave leaving behind a frothy trail as it receded. The serenity of the beach, coupled with its significance in my life, made it the perfect place to meditate.

It was also the place where we held our funeral rites for those who passed on. The body is placed on a boat with mementos from their life as well as gifts that their family believed they should take with them to the afterlife. Once it was all laid out, the boat would be set adrift at a high tide, with everyone watching as they're carried off further than the eye can see.

This was where I had said my last goodbyes to my parents.

It was a place of significance to me, as well as most of the village. At the end of the summer, we'll be hosting the annual Feast of Tides event, where we celebrate life, death, and rebirth. I know that Elder Ming has already begun coordinating with most of the village folk with summer coming to a close.

I'd been spending more time here with Tianyi by my side. It was a quiet area, and not extremely far like the banyan tree. It was ideal and had an especially beautiful view under the moonlit sky.

A place of life and death. To honor my parents.

There was no better place to complete this quest. Today was the day, according to my calculations, that Tianyi's Qi Haven skill would be triggered.

And so I went about my own training, a quick warm-up to get the blood flowing throughout my body, followed by staff practice.

My first exercise was two hundred downward swings. It was the most basic move, and therefore the most important. I didn't think it'd be so difficult. But when done with an iron staff, doing a hundred was a difficult task. My forearms felt like they were on fire, and my shoulders felt like lead after the first training session. Getting it up to two hundred swings was no easy feat, and it showed in the transformation of my upper body.

I had gotten used to training without a robe. My body, which was fairly average prior to training, now had definition and untold strength. I exhaled with every swing, sweat pouring down my face as I neared the end of the set. Each strike of the staff echoed through the quiet morning, each thud a testament to my dedication. I could feel the resistance of the air, the strain in my muscles, and the sharp intake of breath as I drove the staff down. It was a symphony of exertion and willpower, each move building upon the last.

Hands grasping the staff firmly but not tightly. Making sure to stay loose until the point of impact to reduce the amount of energy used per swing. Imagining the staff as an extension of my arm.

These were just the few things that I had to remember during my training. Some I learned through constant repetition and adjustment, but the most important thing was my attention to detail. From the first rep to the last, I made constant adjustments. A slight twist to my foot. The timing of my swing. The distance between my hands as I held the staff. They all made minute differences to my form that added up over time.

With a small exhale, I concluded my two hundred swings and sat down to rest. Being so close to the ocean helped cool me off, and I splashed myself with some water and ran it through my hair. It was getting terribly long now. Tying it up into a ponytail would be a good idea.

"Well, on to the next set."

I repeated the two hundred swings for different moves. One-handed downward swings. Overhead strike. The straight thrust.

By the time I finished, I could barely hold my hands over my head even without the staff.

I flopped to the sandy beach floor and glanced at Tianyi. She was content to flutter around, close to where the sand transitioned into the earth. Keeping focus throughout my training was important, but I couldn't help but glance over at the butterfly just in case the yellow orb appeared. I sat down and meditated, trying my best to keep my mind off things. I delved into my Memory Palace and reviewed the numerous training exercises I did with Elder Ming. He rotated through plenty, from ones that tested my core, conditioned my fists and feet, or even my ability to block and defend.

I was limited in what I could do by myself and without the usage of qi, but I settled on a few for today that I could do. Holding the advanced form of the horse stance, which was just making myself drop into an even deeper squat. I hung my arms limply over my staff and kept it on my neck as an additional weight.

Twenty minutes passed until I could no longer hold it. Training without Elder Ming wasn't as intense, but I had a good understanding of how much I needed to get better. There wasn't anybody to tell me what I should do and why. Feng Wu's display of martial prowess stuck in my mind as a baseline of what I should be capable of, but it was still a far goal to reach. My physical capabilities were slowly bridging the gap, but the difference in technique was like a massive chasm. The idea of entering a sect entered my mind once more, but I brushed it off as soon as it appeared.

A glow of light just from the corner of my vision caught my attention, and I turned around to see that after almost two hours on the coast, the yellow orb I had been waiting for finally appeared. My fatigue temporarily forgotten, I jogged over and giddily began meditating. It took me a few minutes to settle the excitement bubbling up within my gut as I tried to focus.

Breathe in, breathe out. Focus on the present, and cleanse my mind of thoughts about the past or future. Only the present was what mattered most.

The soft, nigh-imperceptible touch of Tianyi on my shoulder was followed by qi circulating through my body, chipping away at the fatigue and soreness built up from today's training session.

As I settled into my meditative state, the rhythmic lullaby of the sea immediately captured my attention. The gentle ebb and flow of the waves against the shore created a soothing, repetitive melody. Every so often, a wave crashed against a nearby rock formation, the sharper sound punctuating the steady rhythm, a stark reminder of the sea's untamed power.

I took a deep breath, the salty tang of the sea air filling my nostrils. It was a scent so familiar and yet so complex, carrying hints of seaweed and fish. As I exhaled, I imagined my stress and worries being carried away on the sea breeze.

Beneath me, the sand was cool and slightly damp. It conformed to my body, grounding me and connecting me to the earth. I could feel the faint vibrations of the earth beneath me, the subtle movements that were usually overlooked in the bustle of daily life.

The cries of seagulls echoed in the distance, their calls blending with the softer sounds of other seabirds. Every so often, the splash and chitter of a sea otter or the blow of a distant whale added another layer to the symphony of natural sounds.

As I delved deeper into my meditation, I became aware of the ebb and flow of the sea's own immense energy, a powerful yet calming presence that mirrored my own breath. All these sensations blended together into a tapestry of awareness that kept me firmly anchored in the present moment. As I meditated, I felt a deep sense of peace and connection with the world around me, a reminder of my place in the grand scheme of things.

And when I opened my eyes, it was to a message. My quest was complete.

Quest: Cultivation Technique (Wood)
Due to your status as Interface Manipulator,
your rewards will be adjusted accordingly.
The mentorship you received from an elder with a fire alignment
has influenced your reward.

> *Your qi is transforming.*
> *Your pathways are now stronger and more resistant to*
> *status ailments such as Qi Reflux and Qi Deviation.*
> *You can now utilize the skill Crimson Lotus*
> *Purification Technique.*

A sensation akin to a sudden lightning strike flooded my consciousness, as if a vast tome of ancient knowledge had been abruptly dropped into my mind. The Crimson Lotus Purification technique, it permeated my thoughts, effortlessly weaving itself into my understanding of the world. Just like that instance with the Rooted Banyan Stance.

No, it was far more profound.

I felt it, the life force around me, the pulsating rhythms of nature, the inherent vitality of the wood-aligned qi that I'd been nurturing since I'd started on this path. The budding contemplations I had about my dao were brought to the forefront of my mind. Suddenly, the cryptic response of Elder Ming when I asked him what his dao was started to make sense, their true meanings surfacing from the depths of my comprehension. A candle. But he didn't point at that; he pointed at what made it so significant.

The flame.

I could see it now, the essence of wood, the ceaseless growth, the tenacious persistence, the budding potential. And there, intertwining with it, the fire. It was not mere destruction; it was a purification process, a renewing flame that burned away the old and unnecessary to make room for the new. This was the balance, the harmonious dance between creation and destruction, growth and rebirth.

Suddenly, everything clicked into place, like the pieces of a puzzle that I'd been trying to solve for ages. Elder Ming's teachings up until now taught me about the transformative nature of flame, its ability to cleanse and purify, to induce change.

This cultivation technique, this Crimson Lotus Purification, it was not just about harnessing the vitality of wood or the destructive power of fire. It was about combining them, learning to cultivate life energy like a thriving, ever-growing tree, and then purifying it, burning away the impurities, in the way of a cleansing, revitalizing fire.

It was about the cycle of life, about understanding that in nature, even destruction was a form of creation, that rebirth followed death, and that growth and decay were two sides of the same coin. This was what my master was trying to teach me, and this was what the Crimson Lotus Purification embodied.

This wasn't just a technique. It was a new perspective, a new way of understanding the universe and my place within it. I felt like I'd taken a significant step on my journey of cultivation.

I let out a breathless sigh as my mind tried to process all the information. And once it was all digested, I picked up Tianyi and ran off to the fish market. It was time to celebrate, and I needed to pull Wang Jun and Lan-Yin together for a grand feast.

CHAPTER TWENTY-ONE

Drunken Celebration

Cheers!"

All three of us raised a toast and clinked our cups together. We all dug into the meal before us with gusto. I had bought an excess of salmon and decided to cook them in various ways. I went with the way I knew best: seasoning it with soy sauce, ginger, and my favorite spices and steaming them until thoroughly cooked.

Lan-Yin took part in the cooking, fileting the fish and turning them into finely cut strips. She went back to her teahouse to make the sauce she needed to create kuai.

Wang Jun brought out alcohol. Rice wine, made by Master Qiang himself. Turned out the mighty blacksmith had the tendency to make his own alcohol. It was delicious to boot. I'd have to ask the older man later if I could buy some of his stock for future use.

"Ah, this hits the spot. We should do this more often," Wang Jun said, a satisfied grin lighting up his face as he gulped down his cup in one go. I chuckled in response, matching his enthusiasm.

The aroma of ginger and soy sauce wafted through the air as we tucked into the tender salmon. The flavor was a delightful mixture of sweet and salty, each bite melting on our tongues. Lan-Yin's kuai was equally scrumptious, the finely cut strips of fish bathed in her special sauce, offering a unique tanginess that complemented the salmon beautifully. The rich flavor of the rice wine was the perfect finish, its robust body filling our mouths with a warm, smooth sensation.

"If we continue at this rate, we'll have reason to celebrate every day!"

At my declaration, Lan-Yin turned to look at me, her hand idly hovering over a strip of raw salmon. A curious gleam sparkled in her eyes as she spoke. "So, does this mean you're at the first stage of cultivation? The initiation stage, or whatever you call it?"

Her question hung in the air, drawing an amused smile from me. "Not exactly. But the method I learned will surely get me there soon enough!"

My mind, body, and qi have been stagnant according to the Heavenly Interface, but that was far from what it felt like to me. Perhaps there was a major difference between this rank and the next. I knew it, though. With a cultivation method, I wouldn't be so idle. The one I was taught by Elder Ming was as basic as it got, and I knew it was because of my poor qi circulatory system; anything more advanced would've sent me into Qi Deviation or something worse.

But when I understood it so intimately, I felt that the chances of me going through Qi Deviation were low. I never encountered issues with the Rooted Banyan Stance, unless I experimented with it. I wouldn't test the Crimson Lotus Purification technique until I met with Elder Ming tomorrow morning, no matter how tempted I was. A promise I made was worth its weight in gold. Wait—I didn't think promises held any weight, physically speaking. No matter. The point was that I would keep my promise to him.

"I'm proud of you, Kai. You've come a really long way in such a short span of time. Aren't you a genius, all things considered?"

"Don't push it, Wang Jun." Lan-Yin scoffed but smiled at me in a teasing manner. "He'll get a bigger head than he does now, and we won't hear the end of it."

I smiled bashfully. Being called a genius was . . . It felt odd. From my perspective, I was slow. I overlaid the vision of Feng Wu's movements over mine whenever I trained; it was incomparable. But from those who didn't train in martial arts, my progress must've seemed explosive.

"I have Elder Ming to thank for that. He's the one who helped me understand where to focus my efforts. All I had to do was follow his lead," I said, grabbing a slice of raw salmon and chewing quietly. Delicious!

There was a pause in the conversation, and I raised my head to both of them staring at me with a dumbfounded look in their eyes. I became a bit defensive.

"What?"

Lan-Yin turned to her betrothed and whispered, but I could hear it clearly. "Has our young master swallowed a humble pill? He's unusually modest tonight."

"I know, right? Maybe he's going to die soon."

"You jerks!" I blushed. Was it really that bad? I thought everyone knew that young-master act was a joke. "You've doomed your family to a thousand face-slaps!"

The rest of the night continued pleasantly. We talked about the daily happenings around the village. Lan-Yin was always up to date on the gossip, but I heard more about what was going on from Wang Jun outside the village. The orders from outside of the village never ceased. Master Qiang's shop was extremely well known throughout the province, it seemed.

With multiple bottles of alcohol emptied, I brought up another topic I'd been considering since I came back home.

"Have you guys ever considered learning how to use your qi?"

"Us? We're not martial artists, Kai! And I have no plans of defying the heavens either." Lan-Yin chuckled. Wang Jun nodded, his face flushed. What a lightweight.

"You don't have to be a cultivator to use your qi. Think about it." I stopped slouching in my seat and sobered up slightly. "Even without the training, I use my qi to help me with gardening! I don't feel sore or tired after working all day. I think you guys should. What have you used the Heavenly Interface for since it arrived?"

"Nothing, really," she said. "What's there to use? We're not cultivators."

"I've gotten a couple of quests for my blacksmithing. It helped me get a little better than I would've otherwise," Wang Jun said, chipping into the conversation with a quip of his own.

"That's what I'm saying! Isn't this the whole point of the Heavenly Interface coming down? We can use these skills and techniques that only cultivators had. But it gives us the ability to tap into our qi! Wang Jun! Imagine!" I took my chopstick and pretended it was a hammer. "You're in the forge, but you don't get tired. Your strikes remain as steadfast as they did when you first stepped in. How much more work could you get done?"

". . . Maybe at least twice as fast. The last few weapons take a lot of my energy to make. And I can't send out half-assed items, so it takes me more time."

I turned to Lan-Yin. "Isn't it difficult being the only waitress at the Soaring Swallow? What if you had the body of a cultivator? Wouldn't it be so much easier?"

My speech seemed to give them some thought, and in my drunken stupor, I raised my fist and boldly proclaimed, "Cultivator training isn't just for fighting! Gardening, blacksmithing, hospitality! We could make our lives easier, and now we have the ability to do it with the Heavenly Interface!"

"Yeah, but how? Unlike you, we can't exactly spend half our day meditating and contemplating the dao," Wang Jun said. It was true. He spent half the day, minimum, at the forge. They didn't have the leisure like I did to commit my time to cultivation. "How would we fit this into our daily life?"

"You could join me at Elder Ming's morning training. I don't think he'd mind. Something as simple as meditating would do wonders for your mental strength! Under his guidance, he could teach you how to circulate your qi."

Ever since I received the Heavenly Interface, I asked why it gave it to everybody. Cultivator or mortal, they gave them the ability to track their cultivation progress. But it didn't limit itself to just cultivation! The evidence was right in the skills section. Even something as simple as reading was classified as one. I didn't think the ancestors who made such a mighty spell would do it for no reason. From the very first message it gave, it hinted at its purpose.

> ### *WE ILLUMINATE THE PATH TO ASCENSION.*

Equality. Power to those who seek it. Illuminating the path to all, regardless of their stature, talent, or alignment.

Wouldn't life be better if everybody was given the resources to succeed? Limiting the usage of qi to martial techniques was a stupid idea. Growing, creating, building—there was so much it could be used for.

I didn't know what my role was. Bearing the title of Interface Manipulator was a mysterious yet heavy responsibility. I couldn't credit my progress to just my efforts. It felt like the Interface was pushing me toward something. It gave me quests, rewards, and functions that nobody else had. But why?

It didn't feel right to hoard this knowledge for myself. Teaching my fellow villagers how to use it, guiding them on its utilization to make their lives easier . . . Perhaps I would be the one to show them. The knowledge that all these sects desperately hoarded, I would give freely.

They left my house well past midnight, and although they didn't make any commitment, I could see on their face that the idea of learning how to cultivate intrigued them. I mean, how couldn't it? If I told myself a month ago that my garden would be growing like this just because of meditating here and there, I would've done it within a heartbeat.

"Ha! What a great day, Tianyi." As I cleaned up the dishes, my gaze kept wandering over to Tianyi, sitting quietly in her corner. We'd fallen into a routine of sorts. I'd wake up, bring her to Elder Ming's, train, go home, do my daily garden maintenance, leave her here with Lan-Yin while I went about doing errands and additional training. Rinse and repeat. Sometimes she tagged along for the entirety of my day; others, she didn't.

Even though our interaction was mostly limited to telepathic communication, I felt a kinship with her. Perhaps it was her constant presence or the soft hum of her aura that filled the room, but being around her felt comforting, homey. The moonlight seemed to highlight her intricate wing patterns, adding an ethereal glow to her, making her seem almost . . . magical. "You know, I think I could do with some company in the garden tomorrow," I mused aloud, not really expecting a response from the butterfly.

Maybe I was seeing things, but I swear the glowing aura around her had gotten stronger.

Nothing seemed to change in the description the interface gave me, so I shrugged it off. Our bond hadn't changed since that fateful day in the forest. Perhaps that was the key to helping her grow and cultivate.

But how did one get closer to a butterfly?

"So . . ." I kicked up a chair and sat by Tianyi's corner facing the windowsill. "Is there anything you'd like in your sugar water, aside from . . . well, sugar?"

She turned to face me, her wings unmoving. Nothing came through our telepathic link, but I could almost hear her asking if I was really giving an open-ended question to a butterfly.

"Ah, here. Let me make it easier for you." I went over to the bookshelf in my bedroom, fishing out an encyclopedia that contained several diagrams of fruits, plants, and herbs. Flipping it to the pages where I thought Tianyi would like the most, I pointed and asked her, "Peach?"

A strong sense of agreement washed over me, and I nodded. The charade continued for a long while. Tianyi didn't seem very picky. Or maybe she didn't understand what I was saying at all and just responded at random. I didn't know how a Spirit Beast understood human language—or the diagrams in my book.

Butterflies couldn't eat, only drink. Perhaps some sort of mash for Tianyi would suffice. I could ask the elders in the village for any overripe fruits and make it into a paste that she could lick.

As I thought deeply about what I could give her, the butterfly fluttered over to the empty cups I had left out from Master Qiang's rice wine. She unfurled her proboscis and began dipping it into the small amount left. I watched in astonishment as Tianyi consumed the rice wine.

Was she going to be okay?

Contrary to expectations, I was not an all-knowing genius. I had no idea if alcohol was something butterflies could ingest. But Tianyi seemed to be fine. It'd be quite a terrible event for her to just drop dead from alcohol consumption.

The feeling that came through our telepathic link was similar to happiness. But a bit more . . . buzzed? It was colored with that warm feeling I often received in my stomach after drinking alcohol.

Tianyi was drunk.

After observing her for a few more minutes and making sure that her condition was stable, I cleaned up the cups and kept a tight seal on the last bottle of rice wine that Wang Jun had left for me.

I learned something new about Tianyi today: She was a heavyweight. She could drink her body weight in rice wine and stay standing. Maybe? She was oddly still, and I had to coax her back into the nest she made for herself on one of my shelves.

"I've heard of Spirit Beasts that like alcohol, but a butterfly? This is too much," I told myself, getting comfy on my bed as I went to sleep. I stared at the ceiling, pondering my next steps for the future.

Was I ready to shoulder the responsibilities that came with these newfound abilities? I felt a sense of duty to share my knowledge with my fellow villagers, to empower them to enhance their own lives. But with that came a weight of responsibility that I hadn't expected. The role of a teacher, of a leader, was not one I had ever envisioned for myself.

But it shouldn't be a challenge. I am Kai Liu, and my name will ring throughout the heavens. Helping the Gentle Wind Village during these times of uncertainty was a simple matter.

With that determination in mind, I closed my eyes and dreamed.

CHAPTER TWENTY-TWO

Crimson Lotus Purification

You," Elder Ming began, seeming on the brink of voicing some thought, yet he restrained himself, shutting his eyes in an expression of patient resignation. "It is no longer within me to be astounded. I direct you toward meditation, toward finding your path, and you come back with a new technique. You know, Kai, if I were to ask you to forage in the forest, I wouldn't be surprised if you came back cradling a phoenix egg."

I didn't think he'd appreciate it if I revealed that time I went to the forest and triggered the Heavenly Interface, so I kept my mouth shut and continued cultivating. His mutterings faded as I returned to the circulation of energy.

> *Crimson Lotus Purification Technique (Level 1): A sophisticated cultivation method that harmoniously blends the essence of the wood element's growth and the purifying power of the flame element. This technique allows the cultivator to draw in and accumulate energy from their surroundings at a slow pace, resembling the gradual unfolding of a crimson lotus. The gathered energy is then purified, removing any impurities or harmful constituents in the user's body, before integrating it into their reserves. The cultivator can regulate the extent of purification, providing a finely tuned balance between cultivation speed and quality.*

The cultivation method was incredible. It was faster than the basic one I was taught, but whenever I accumulated a sufficient amount, it was whittled down to a fraction of pure energy. I added it to my reserves and opened my eyes. Everything felt clearer, and I had produced an incredible amount of heat as I cultivated. It was like a fever, and sweat covered my body.

"How's that, Elder Ming?"

He was monitoring my condition, partially to prevent Qi Deviation and to see how it worked. I recited the information from the interface, but he needed to check its capabilities for himself.

"The speed at which you cultivate is . . . slow. Incredibly so. It refines it down further, shedding away any impurities until it's a fraction of what you collected."

"So, is that a good thing . . . ?"

"Imagine your body as a vast vessel," he began. "Many cultivators see their bodies as immense oceans, capable of holding an enormous amount of qi. They don't worry about the quality of the qi they gather; they just keep pouring in more and more, like a torrential rain. They believe the sheer volume would eventually lead them to transcendence."

He then glanced at me, his gaze piercing. "But you, Kai, you're not like them. Your vessel is not an ocean but a small cup."

His words were like a pebble dropped in a quiet pond, creating ripples in my understanding. He was right. My body's capacity for qi was far smaller than others due to my weak qi circulatory system. Even though I told him my condition improved as a result of our training, it was still well below average. He mentioned that there were elders in the village who had more physical aptitude than I did.

"With a small cup," he continued, "you can't simply fill it with rainwater. You must be selective, fill it with the finest nectar. It is not about quantity, Kai, but quality. The slower accumulation of qi, the process of its purification, might be seen as a curse by many, but for you, it is a blessing in disguise."

He turned his back, facing the sun as he did so. "Your body is your vessel, Kai. Treat it with care. Fill it with the purest qi, nurture it, and in time, it will surely transcend to the next rank. Don't see your limitations as shackles. They are the keys to a path less tread. The path that is yours."

I was encouraged by his words, although his mention of how exceptionally slow my cultivation method was concerned me. I didn't have a baseline, except for the simplest one that wasn't classified as a technique. I asked him another question.

"Elder Ming," I hesitated, "you used to be a disciple, right? I'm curious about your cultivation method. How did it work?"

His eyes held a glimmer of mirth. "You probably wouldn't recognize the name even if I told you, but it is known as the Phoenix Blaze Resurgence."

"The Phoenix Blaze Resurgence," I echoed, letting the unfamiliar words roll off my tongue. "Sounds powerful."

"It has its merits," he said, the corners of his eyes crinkling with a smile. "It's based on the principles of my sect, which fundamentally revolves around the flame."

"But . . . how does it compare to mine in terms of gathering qi?" I couldn't help but ask. It wasn't a matter of competition, but rather understanding our relative positions in the vast world of cultivation.

Elder Ming considered the question for a moment before replying, "If we were to compare, it gathers qi at roughly tenfold the rate of your Crimson Lotus Purification Technique."

"Tenfold . . ." The amount echoed in my mind, daunting but also strangely motivating. So the amount Elder Ming could collect in a day was worth over a week's worth of mine?

"However, do not despair, Kai," he quickly added. "Remember, our paths are different, and so is our approach. Just like your technique, the Phoenix Blaze Resurgence also draws from the flame element. But while yours focuses on the purification aspect, harnessing the flame to refine the energy, mine emphasizes the rebirth aspect, harnessing the flame to continuously replenish and renew the qi. Both methods carry their own beauty and uniqueness, just like two flames from the same fire."

Two flames from the same fire, I mused. Despite our different paths, there was an uncanny sense of connectedness. It was a comforting thought, knowing that my technique was not an isolated instance, but part of a greater, more intricate tapestry of cultivation methods.

Again, I was reminded of patience. If I acted hastily, the foundation of my cultivation would be ruined. The idea of spending years building something that would take another months irked me, but those were the cards I was dealt.

There would be no half measures here. If I was going to fill this vessel of mine with energy, it would be with the purest. I could make a garden wherever I pleased, but I'd only be satisfied if it were made on the finest soil rich in nutrients.

Elder Ming left me to my cultivation, and I spent hours accumulating the energy from my surroundings. It wasn't innate, but a part of Tianyi's Qi Haven skill. She exuded an aura that provided the environment with energy, and my technique was slowly but surely collecting it within my body.

I kept going until I could go no farther; the ball I had accumulated was of significant size, and the qi in Elder Ming's home had all but dried up. If I had to compare it to something, it was the size of Wang Jun's head.

But unlike his cranium, it was full of impurities. Throughout the process, it purified the mass bit by bit. But now I focused fully on filtering out the impure qi.

Each moment spent in cultivating was akin to an expert bonsai gardener delicately pruning their treasured tree. The impure qi was like excessive branches and leaves that needed to be trimmed away for the true beauty of the tree to shine. I needed to ensure every leaf—every sliver of qi—was as close to perfection as it could be.

The ball of energy within me began to shrink. As though an invisible hand was pruning it, the impurities were slowly whittled away. The process was slow and arduous, but I didn't waver. Like a meticulous gardener inspecting each leaf, I examined each bit of qi, casting off what was impure, retaining only the purest essence.

Gradually, the ball reduced to a fraction of its original size. It was painstaking work, and at times, I could feel frustration gnawing at the edges of my patience.

I could almost feel the purity of the qi left within me. It felt as if I was holding a small diamond, sparkling with brilliance and purity in the vast emptiness of my internal world. It was smaller than what I had started with, but it was more pure, more potent. It was a drop of nectar gleaned from a vast ocean, and it was mine.

This was the path Elder Ming had guided me toward. It was a path of patience and meticulousness. It was the path of the gardener, creating something beautiful and pure from what seemed ordinary and excessive.

There was a certain madness to it, a fervor that was as intoxicating as it was frightening. Yet I embraced it, for half measures were never an option. Not for me. Not now.

I couldn't afford to be content with the impure and the ordinary. I needed the purest and the best. I needed perfection, and I would attain it, even if I had to tear it bit by bit from the vast expanse of the universe. Because this was my choice. My path. And on this path, there was no room for mediocrity.

After all, the ones who revolutionized the world weren't those who walked the beaten path. They were the ones who ventured into the wilderness, fought the monsters, and emerged victorious. They were the ones who dared to question, dared to strive, and dared to become more than what the world expected them to be.

That ball had become the size of a millet seed, and I placed it into my dantian, the core where my qi resided.

The moment it made contact with my core, I felt a rush like never before—a sensation akin to a searing iron meeting ice. I could feel the energy immediately starting to work, its purifying nature tearing at everything I had built so far, like a tempest raging against an unsteady fortress.

Every imperfection, every fault line within my core began to dissolve under the relentless onslaught of the pure qi. It was like introducing a river into a stagnant pond, the fresh, vibrant water pushing away the murky liquid, bringing with it a wave of new life.

The impurities were stripped away, eroded to their very core. I could feel it happening on a cellular level, a thorough cleanse unlike any I had experienced before. It was pain and euphoria, torment and liberation, all wrapped into one dizzying package. It felt as if I was being torn apart and put back together, piece by piece, molecule by molecule.

And then came the manifestation. I could feel my skin start to perspire. But it wasn't sweat that seeped out of my pores. It was a viscous black liquid. It clung to my skin, as if reluctant to leave the confines of my body. It was almost sentient, a sticky, smelly substance that was a testament to the impurities that had been living within me. The sight was revolting, the smell even more so. But beneath the initial disgust, I could feel a sense of profound satisfaction.

This was the physical representation of my body's impurities. It was proof of my progress, evidence that my relentless pursuit of purity was not in vain. This was the price I paid for perfection, and as I stood there, the black ooze dripping from my body, I knew without a doubt that I would gladly pay it again.

My body, my vessel, was cleansed, renewed, and ready to be filled with even purer qi.

As I took a deep breath, feeling the clean, vibrant qi circulating in my core, I knew I had taken a step farther on the path I had chosen.

"Kai, what ha—Urgh! Blech!"

My eyes snapped over to Elder Ming. The day passed by without me knowing and it was already evening. He had quietly left me to my own devices, monitoring me and making sure nothing disturbed my cultivation. His face was one of immense disgust and confusion.

"Sorry, do you mind getting me a towel?"

"Out! We're going to the river! Oh my heavens, did you defecate yourself?"

While pinching his nose, Elder Ming ushered me out of his home. It was bad. I fully understood his reaction. Even Tianyi seemed hesitant to fly near me, eliciting a feeling of revulsion through our link.

I passed through the village, dutifully avoiding the common areas due to my . . . condition. But even then, there were complaints.

"Did you forget to clean the pigpen?" an accusing voice said from farther into the village.

Xiao Bao's house was close by, and I could hear whines from outside. "Mom, it smells like when Grandpa removes his boots after farming!"

"Ah, the unmistakable fragrance of youthful indiscretion. Reminds me of my first attempt at brewing rice wine. Didn't end well, I tell ya!"

Every comment served to color my cheeks and hasten my pace before the villagers realized the smell was coming from me.

It wouldn't do to get another nickname. Kowtow Kai was bad enough. I could already imagine what Lan-Yin and Wang Jun would call me.

CHAPTER TWENTY-THREE

Guardian of the Garden

I watched him, my wings shimmering in the sunlight, perched on a leaf. His name was Kai, and he was . . . my friend.

His movements flowed like water, his emotions a kaleidoscope of radiant hues that I could sense, vibrant and ever-changing. It was him, always him, who filled my day with these colors.

I took to the skies, going higher until I could see home from a different angle—a burst of color and life, constantly in motion. His garden, our garden, was a haven of nectar-rich flowers and sunlit leaves, filled with the aroma of growth.

> *Qi Haven has reached level 11.*

Something glowed and appeared before me, as mysterious as the night sky, its foreign rhythms weaving into my existence. The patterns on the blue shape before my body imparted an understanding to me that I had grown stronger. The aura I exuded into my surroundings became slightly denser, further enriching the environment. It was the least I could do for the home I was provided with.

I fluttered to another plant, my wings dusting the petals with an invisible, calming essence. I didn't quite understand the pulsing, blue shape or its cryptic echoes, but I knew it had something to do with the strange new vigor in me. Before I met Kai, I was less. But ever since I met him, flickers of understanding came and went, becoming more and more pronounced until it became a default state of existence.

It was thanks to Kai, and this . . . Interface. It was thanks to them I could live comfortably, growing and becoming something more than what I once was.

A moment of tranquility passed. I found peace in the gentle rustling of the leaves, the familiar hum of the insects, the harmonious symphony of the garden.

Then, in the midst of the serenity, a dissonant note struck, a ripple disturbing the calm waters of my existence.

As a silhouette cast a shadow over our garden, an ominous feeling built up in my thorax like a desperate drum. Its massive form was adorned with a tapestry of feathers, each meticulously designed for its dance with the wind. Like blades of grass fluttering in a breeze, these appendages rippled and flowed, painting a hypnotic portrait against the sapphire backdrop of the sky. Its beady eyes scanned the foliage, its presence a storm on the horizon of my emotions. Panic welled within me, a crippling force, a vivid flashback to talons, pain, and a brush with death. Yet beneath the surging fear, a spark of defiance flared up. This was our garden, our sanctuary, and I wouldn't let it be defiled.

Bracing myself, I took flight, the wind whistling past my wings as I confronted the interloper and readied myself. My proboscis was no match for the pointed beak and sharp talons. The bird dwarfed me in size, its wingspan a canopy of feathers against the sun. The realization chilled me to the bone. I was a butterfly, a creature of nectar and light, unversed in the harsh dance of predator and prey.

I had come here unprepared.

Dread seeped into my heart as the reality of my predicament hit me. I was weaponless, hopelessly outmatched. The scales that armored my body were nothing more than fragile, gossamer shields against the feathered menace. I felt a pang of helplessness, of frustration. How could I protect our home, our sanctuary, if I couldn't even protect myself?

No. I wouldn't let myself give up so easily. I would not allow Kai's garden to be defiled by intruders!

Desperation fueled my mind. And then a faint memory, a thread of hope wove its way through the despair. I remembered Kai. How diligently he trained every day, how he harnessed his qi, focusing it throughout his body and protecting him from harm's way.

An idea sparked, like a stray sunbeam piercing through a canopy. Could I do the same? Could I channel my qi and become a weapon to strike down my opponent?

There was no time to ponder. The beast swooped, its beak a gleaming spear aimed at my frail form. It was a scene from my nightmares, yet with the promise of pain all too real. I summoned every ounce of qi, focusing it into my wings, pouring every drop of energy I could muster. The residual qi from my surroundings grew thinner and thinner, coalescing into my body. It was unfamiliar; it felt clumsy. I was not used to storing it within my body like this.

My wings hummed, pulsing with a newfound vitality. I was fast. Faster than I had ever been. Faster than the wind, faster than the bird's strike. I dodged, my wings a blur of blue and white. The bird cawed in surprise, its lethal strike evaded so easily.

I didn't have the luxury of relief. I needed to strike. A voice in me screamed to flee, to run and gain Kai's support, but I steeled myself. I could not rely on him for everything. Channeling the qi, I soared straight at the bird. It cawed, flapping its wings to escape, but I was too fast, too desperate.

In a rush of adrenaline and mana, I sliced through the air. The edges of my wings, imbued with the power of qi, met the bird's surprised form. There was resistance, a fleeting moment of shock. Then, with a heartbreaking screech, the bird split into two, a shower of feathers cascading down to the earth.

> *You have learned a new skill:*
> *Qi Infusion: Infuse your body with qi,*
> *strengthening and making it faster.*

In the aftermath of the brutal clash, I hovered, the world around me eerily silent. The echo of the battle reverberated in the air.

The Interface pulsed within me, acknowledging my victory, acknowledging my courage.

The surge of triumph was short-lived, overshadowed by a wealth of emotions—confusion, pride, and fear. In the cruel world of the natural order, the butterfly should be the prey. We should flutter by flowers and avoid the talons and beaks of our predators.

But I was different. I was more. I had done the unthinkable, defied the norms of the natural world. The corpse of my defeated enemy fell to the ground, beside Kai as he tended to the garden and elicited a shriek of terror.

Thoughts whirled through me, a whirlwind of introspection. I had defied my nature, broken the shackles of my existence as a mere butterfly, and emerged victorious. I contemplated the price of this power, the weight of this responsibility.

> *Quest: Butterfly Guardian*
> *—Successfully defend Kai's home from intruders five times.*

An ethereal echo resounded within me, the Interface stirring. I was given a quest, a command, and a purpose: Protect home. The intention was as clear as the sunlit sky. The notion filled me with newfound confidence, intertwining with my instinctual love for this sanctuary.

Kai's terror and confusion echoed through our bond. His familiar presence soothed me, washing away the remnants of the fierce battle. I approached from above, his gaze going between me and the slain beast.

He would no longer have to carry the burden of being this land's sole guardian. I would become his aide, even if it meant shattering the natural order and defying what the heavens willed.

With that declaration, something stirred within me.

The feeling of urgency, helplessness, and anxiety washed over me for nearly half a minute, and I didn't know if it was instinct warning me of danger like when Feng Wu came to my house or something else. My nerves were frayed, and I immediately stopped watering my plants and searched around the area, to see nothing amiss.

I almost pissed my pants when the bisected corpse of a bird dropped beside me. I was already jumpy as it was.

Tianyi came down from the sky, pushing away the feelings of urgency and replacing it with pride and determination. Our emotional bond was the source of those negative feelings just a minute ago.

But that didn't explain how she managed to kill a damn bird. She cut it clean in half.

The aura around her had gotten stronger, and I could see drops of blood forming at the tip of her wing. There was no doubt she was the one responsible for it.

"Tianyi, are you okay?" I asked, trying to keep the worry out of my voice. She didn't seem hurt, but the lingering traces of desperation and fear still echoed in our bond.

Tianyi fluttered a moment longer before landing softly on my shoulder. Her wings were less vibrant, almost translucent from exertion. I breathed a sigh of relief. She was okay.

"Let's go," I said, gently picking her up and placing her on my palm.

Her minuscule weight was nothing to me. Never would I have expected her to take on a bird and win. She had always been frail, especially after that crow attack in the forest. But today, she had proven me wrong. Tianyi was a powerful Spirit Beast and deserved recognition.

I brought her to a secluded part of my garden, where a single Moonlit Grace Lily plant flourished. Its petals glowed with an ethereal light, their calming aura spreading tranquility in the vicinity. It was almost fully mature, and soon I'd be able to harvest it and plant more of them. But it would be Tianyi's bed for now.

"This will help," I said, placing her on one of the blossoming lilies. "Rest, Tianyi."

She gave a slight nod before her wings started to shimmer, exuding an almost imperceptible glow. I watched as the healing essence of the Moonlit Grace Lily flowed into her, reinvigorating her worn-out form.

"You did well today, Tianyi," I spoke, my voice low but full of admiration. Her wings shone a bit brighter at my words. I didn't understand it all, but her feelings were clear as day to me. She was exhausted but proud—proud of protecting our home.

"Never thought I'd see the day when my little butterfly would turn into a fierce warrior," I chuckled, trying to lighten the mood. I was still in shock.

She fluttered her wings, a butterfly's equivalent of a shrug, but there was a sense of humor in her response.

"And don't think I didn't notice your new trick. Qi Infusion, huh? Where did you learn that?" I questioned, a playful smirk on my face. Was it from me? Although I wasn't half-bad at Qi Infusion, there was no way I could use it in a combat setting yet. But Tianyi used it to defeat a bird twice her size?

Maybe I'm not the genius in this village . . .

Tianyi didn't respond, only tilted her head at me. Of course, she couldn't verbally reply, but the sensation of curiosity and amusement flowed through our bond. It seemed she was quite pleased with her new trick.

"We'll make a true warrior out of you yet," I mused, reaching out to lightly stroke her wings. She didn't shy away, instead leaning into the touch. It was comforting, familiar.

"Rest up, Tianyi. We've had quite the day".

She gave another slight flutter of her wings, this time a confirmation.

"Yes, more to come indeed," I murmured, glancing at the fallen bird again. I would bury it in the garden. Its body would be nutrients for my plants and continue the cycle of nature.

As I walked away, leaving Tianyi to rest and recover, I couldn't help but wonder at the unexpected turn of events.

A warrior butterfly. Who would've thought?

As if in response, a soft breeze rustled the leaves around us, carrying with it a gentle yet determined flutter. My guardian butterfly, standing her ground.

I thought it'd be a good time to take the day off, but now I had to worry about Tianyi becoming stronger than me. I should've reviewed my knowledge in my Memory Palace. See if there's anything I could glean about the Azure Moonlight Flutter. There were so many things we didn't know about them because unlike other Spirit Beasts, they didn't have anything noteworthy to harvest, aside from the aesthetic beauty of their wings.

But Tianyi was living proof they were gems hidden in broad daylight. With Qi Haven and Qi Infusion, she was shaping up to be an incredible creature in her own right.

I had a legendary Spirit Beast as my companion. The Chronicles of Kai and Tianyi. The heroes of the Tranquil Breeze Coast.

Our journey had just begun.

CHAPTER TWENTY-FOUR

Alchemy

It was only a week after I had sent out my shipment of goods to the Azure Silk Trading Company. I hadn't received any news from Huan in regard to how they were doing, but I was confident it was going great. I've been producing and refining the formula for my existing tonics. It turns out I was limited in what I could produce using the ingredients on hand. There were only so many I could create using common herbs. I'd require more exotic items for new discoveries.

I eyed the ginseng growing outside, as well as the Moonlit Grace Lily. I had high expectations for what I could create with them. I'd already gone over the theoretical combinations in my head, the preparation required, and what the effects would be.

Right now, my products were only of use to regular people. They were more potent than regular medicine. But plants imbued with qi would allow me to penetrate the market for cultivator items. Pills, elixirs, and more!

The difference in price would be night and day. If my theories were proven right, a ginseng root's essence, combined with other ingredients and refined into a pill would be enough to pay off the garden house. I'd be a tycoon. This was my first batch of home-grown ginseng, and I'd meticulously cared for them for the past three and a half years. Before all these events, I'd thought it'd be another half a year before they were ready for harvest, but they thrived under the existing conditions and were incredibly potent, even from a glance.

But more significantly, a pill created from the ginseng root would likely serve to augment my qi reserves. This root was primarily associated with yang energy, a harmonious match for my own alignment of wood and flame. Elder Ming's been especially helpful, and even gave me a book on the history of pill-refining and elixirs. If I consumed one, it would accelerate my growth.

My plans for the Moonlit Grace Lily were quite different, however.

They'd be used to create medicine. I've been doing research and making up theoretical combinations that could cure any illness that could sprout up from this corner of the province. Once it matured fully, I'd propagate it and make sure everything was in place for me to continue creating medicine using the Moonlit Grace Lily. And with my essence extraction skill, I could extend the shelf life of my potions and make sure it remained effective for as long as possible. Elder Ming gave me the books I needed to get started on alchemy, but I'd have to experiment and discover it on my own.

He was my martial arts teacher, and someone I could come to for guidance in all aspects of life, but it seemed as though the path to herbalism, alchemy, and science was mine alone. If anything, I'd need to utilize the Heavenly Interface more to further my skills in the field. Quests would be responsible for filling the gap left by sufficient guidance.

It would solve the main problem we had here in Gentle Wind Village of not having access to doctors and healers once I learned how to refine and create potions, pills, and elixirs. Nobody would have to go through the things I had.

The memories of my childhood still felt fresh and vivid as I stared at the Moonlit Grace Lily. It wasn't the lack of food or the hard work that made those years difficult, but the loss of my parents. Memories of those times washed over me.

They both had fallen victim to the Moonshadow Lung Rot, a disease that resulted from contact with the saliva of the elusive Moonshadow Bat, a creature that had a habit of leaving its infectious saliva on the night-blooming flowers, just like the one my mother had picked.

My parents had used the last elixir we had to cure my fever when I was just a child. They had no idea that they would contract the lung rot and be left without a cure. In the end, they chose to isolate themselves from the village to protect everyone else, including me. I stayed with Lan-Yin's family at the Soaring Swallow, waiting for the day I could return home.

Even with the support of the entire village, it was near impossible to find a cure. The doctors from Crescent Bay City would take a month to reach our village, and even then, acquiring the Moonlit Grace Lily or a medicinal equivalent was unaffordable. Elder Ming, blessed with a strong constitution due to his background as a cultivator, was able to visit them periodically and deliver food. Everybody in the village provided all they could for my mother and father. They were beloved figures in the village and were the ones who held extensive medicinal knowledge from running the shop.

I remembered the desperation of those days—my innocent eyes unable to comprehend why my parents were slowly wilting away, my small hands rummaging through the forest to find a cure, a Moonlit Grace Lily, anything that could save them. But no matter how much I searched, it was always in vain.

The guilt still gnawed at me. The fact that I had taken such a precious resource from them was a burden that I would carry for the rest of my life. But now I saw an opportunity, a chance to make amends.

To me, harnessing the Moonlit Grace Lily to develop accessible medicine for the villagers was far more than a mere business venture. It was a promise to my parents, a vow to ensure that no one else in Gentle Wind Village would ever have to suffer from a disease that they couldn't cure.

"I swear to you, Mother, Father," I whispered, my hand hovering above the Moonlit Grace Lily, "no one in Gentle Wind Village will suffer as you did. The only thing they're allowed to die from is old age."

A heavy silence hung in the air. It was a vow made in solitude, yet it carried the weight of a promise, echoing across the land that bore witness to my oath. I knew then, looking at the ginseng and the Moonlit Grace Lily, that I wasn't just a cultivator or an alchemist, but also a healer. I held in my hands the power to change lives, to protect my village, and to honor the memory of my parents.

Tianyi fluttered toward me. The Azure Moonlight Flutter and my dearest companion. It was hard to think a butterfly was the key to all these fortunes coming my way. Without her, I would've never found the ancient ruins hidden behind the waterfall. There would've been no Qi Haven and, subsequently, no opportunity for me to advance and hone my skills as a cultivator and herbalist.

I stroked her wings and smiled softly.

"Thank you, Tianyi. It wouldn't have been possible without you."

And it wouldn't have been possible without my effort and brilliance. It takes a genius to recognize all these opportunities coming my way and make something out of it.

A wave of happiness flowed through our emotional connection, and I decided to give her a special treat: Master Qiang's rice wine. I'd learned over time that she greatly enjoys alcohol. Perhaps it was the nature of Spirit Beasts. Either way, I popped open the bottle and poured a small amount into her cup, which included mashed overripe fruit. They would combine into a mixture perfect for Tianyi's taste.

Although leaving out the bowl constantly in the sun was beginning to attract pests. There were more insects crawling in and out of my home, which wasn't rare, but I did notice the uptick since I began leaving out the mashed fruit for Tianyi. Perhaps I should move it outside.

Just then, I saw a tiny spider coming through a crack on the floor. A subtle glow from Tianyi alerted me, and I flinched. Before I could even realize what was going on, she blurred from the edge of the cup.

The eight-legged insect on the floor was sliced in half, its abdomen separated in an instant. It struggled weakly for a few moments before going still, and I watched the Spirit Beast flutter back to her place on the cup and extend her proboscis to feed.

I suppose leaving the bowl inside would be best. Especially if I wanted to avoid bird carcasses outside where my garden was.

Before I could ruminate over the implications of Tianyi's promotion on the food chain, a voice from behind alerted me.

"Looks like you've been up to a lot, haven't you, Kai?"

I turned around and saw an unfamiliar figure before me. But the striking, green and white robes made me recognize him immediately, even with a bamboo hat covering his face.

"Feng Wu!"

He took off his hat and held it by his side, revealing his striking green eyes.

"Hello, Kai," he greeted me, his voice steady and calm. His gaze swept across my flourishing garden. It wasn't just the ginseng and the Moonlit Grace Lily that captured his attention, but the whole of the qi-infused greenery I'd so painstakingly nurtured. "Impressive," he murmured. "Your garden has truly blossomed."

His gaze turned to me, subtly appraising. His eyebrows rose just slightly. "And it appears you have as well," he added.

I grinned, scratching the back of my neck. "Well, a few things have changed, I suppose." I didn't need to ask what he meant. The changes within me, both in my body and in my qi, were tangible and evident. It was hardly surprising he'd noticed.

His gaze landed on Tianyi, and this time his eyes widened visibly. "Well, I'll be," he muttered, reaching out to gently stroke the vibrant creature. Unlike with most people, Tianyi didn't shy away, instead fluttering closer to Feng Wu to allow him to touch her wings. She was comfortable around him and thankfully didn't see him as an intruder. I wouldn't know what to do if she unleashed that trick of hers on a person.

"You've been nurturing her well, Kai," he said, a note of admiration in his voice.

I couldn't help but feel a spark of pride. "I try my best," I replied.

He nodded, stepping back to give us some space. His tone shifted, a clear sign that pleasantries were over. "I heard the potions you sent to Crescent Bay City were massively popular. Sold out within the first three days of them being distributed. You've done well, Kai. Very well."

Three days. The information was more than I could have hoped for. A pleased grin split my face. "I had a feeling they would do well," I answered, trying to keep my voice steady and composed.

He chuckled at my response, a light sound that echoed pleasantly in the still afternoon air. "Modesty suits you, Kai," he replied, eyes twinkling in good humor.

But as quickly as the jovial atmosphere descended, it dissipated. I knew that cultivators didn't visit tranquil villages like Gentle Wind out of sheer leisure, not even those who'd previously shared a close camaraderie with the villagers. There was a certain, tangible gravity in the air that hinted at more serious matters.

"Why are you here, Feng Wu?" I asked him, my voice taking on a serious undertone.

"Well, my sect has taken an interest in you after hearing of your potions. Would you happen to know about the Grand Alchemy Gauntlet?"

The name took me some time to recognize. Yes, I knew the Grand Alchemy Gauntlet. But only in passing. It was a contest that accepted contestants from all over the province to showcase their talents in alchemy. It was held every five years. It slipped my mind that it was happening this year.

I nodded, my heart pounding in my chest. My mind started to whir, piecing together what his purpose could be here.

"I see," he acknowledged, taking a deep breath as though preparing himself. "On behalf of the Verdant Lotus Sect, I am here to formally extend an invitation to you. We wish for you to participate in the upcoming Grand Alchemy Gauntlet."

His words echoed in my head, each syllable sounding incredibly surreal.

Feng Wu continued, "Moreover, the Verdant Lotus Sect is willing to sponsor your entry, along with providing the necessary training and preparation required for the contest."

His words hung in the air, heavy with promise and expectations. An invitation to the Grand Alchemy Gauntlet, backed by the Verdant Lotus Sect. The opportunity was immense, and the possibilities endless.

"B-but you do realize I'm a herbalist, right? Although I'm flattered by your evaluation of me, I don't know how I'd fare against other alchemists in a provincial contest. Is there a reason why you're having me take the spot rather than one of the members of your sect?"

I confessed my thoughts despite my initial elation. It was insane to me that they'd be willing to sponsor my entry and even train me for such a thing. I mean, the Verdant Lotus Sect was known primarily for its alchemy. I doubted they had a shortage of talent there.

"You're correct on that point, but the gauntlet has some restrictions: those in the second rank of the Qi Initiation Stage and above are barred from entering, effectively barring our second-class disciples from participating. And unfortunately, our sect has nobody else suitable to take the spot. Among our third-class disciples, none of them are particularly interested in alchemy or showed an inclination toward it."

The offer was tantalizing beyond compare. Hadn't I just mentioned how difficult it was for me to expand upon my expertise in alchemy with the resources I had on hand? It was as if the world just bent over to cater to my whims. Getting access to their facilities and guidance from one of the greatest sects in the land would be a massive boon.

"But." I wasn't fooled so easily. They'd demand something of me in return. I couldn't just receive this amount of goodwill without giving anything in exchange. "What's the incentive of the sect to let an outsider like me in so easily?"

Feng Wu met my eyes with a steady gaze, his answer prepared. "This is an investment. The Verdant Lotus Sect recognizes potential when we see it. Right now, you are a budding alchemist with an already proven track record. Your concoctions sold out within three days in Crescent Bay City—that's not a small feat."

He paused, letting his words sink in. Then: "It's true, we have alchemists within our sect, but your background in herbalism and potential to combine both worlds to create unique products are invaluable. Especially considering the rising tensions within the province, people with your skills are highly sought after."

"Furthermore," he added, "the Jianghu is a dynamic and shifting world. We often foster relationships and alliances with those showing great promise. We see you as a worthy investment, a chance to have an ally who can rise to prominence in the future. Our sect can help provide the resources and guidance you require to flourish even further in your field. In return, you'll represent our sect in the Grand Alchemy Gauntlet, and if you win, our sect gains prestige and recognition."

His reasoning made sense. I wasn't just a lone alchemist making potions and elixirs. I was someone who was demonstrating rapid growth and had the potential to make significant strides in the field of alchemy. That was an asset, especially in these turbulent times.

There was no question that this was a significant opportunity. However, I had to consider the consequences and the expectations that would come with it. The pressure, the responsibility, and the potential changes it could bring to my life. But looking at the bigger picture, the advantages outweigh my concerns.

"If I agree to this," I started, feeling a nervous excitement coursing through my veins, "what would be the next steps?" My mind raced with the possibilities this could open up for me.

"Well, we'd take you to our sect and have you learn as much as possible in order to prepare for the tournament, and then once it concludes, we'd like to establish some sort of deal with you. The details would be further expanded upon when you meet our elders."

I swallowed. This was it. My debut into the world of cultivation. But I remembered what I had here. My friends. My shop. Elder Ming. This was a decision I couldn't make lightly. The rest of my projects would likely need to go on hold while I prepared for the tournament.

". . . Give me some time to think. I need to consult others about this before I make a decision."

"I understand. But I hope that you'll have your answer ready by tomorrow."

With that, Feng Wu left me and Tianyi to sit in contemplative silence.

CHAPTER TWENTY-FIVE

Advice

With the echoes of Feng Wu's words still ringing in my ears, I found myself meandering toward Elder Ming's quaint abode in the center of the village.

The midafternoon sun washed the pathway in a soft, warm light, casting long shadows that danced in the gentle breeze. It was a familiar and comforting sight. A reminder that, despite the monumental proposition placed in front of me, life still persisted in its ordinary rhythm.

As I stepped onto the cobbled path leading to Ming's house, the smell of potent herbs wafted into my nostrils, a comforting blend of ginseng, mugwort, and a hint of something subtly sweet—angelica root, perhaps.

Elder Ming sat outside his house, a gentle look on his face as he patiently ground herbs. He looked up after I gently opened the door. "Kai," he said warmly, the lines on his face deepening with his smile. "What brings you here?"

I took a deep breath, my mind swirling with thoughts and doubts. "I need some advice, Elder Ming. Feng Wu visited me today."

His eyebrows raised a fraction, the surprise reflected in his dark eyes. "Feng Wu? From the Verdant Lotus Sect?"

I nodded, taking a seat opposite him. "Yes. He brought a proposition. They want me to represent them in the Grand Alchemy Gauntlet. They're even willing to sponsor my entry and provide me with training."

His surprise gave way to contemplation, a deep furrow forming between his brows. "That's a considerable offer, Kai. The Grand Alchemy Gauntlet . . . It's a prestigious contest. A big step from being a village herbalist."

"Yes, and that's what worries me. Elder, I've never even stepped out of the village. I know nothing about what life is like out there."

A small, understanding smile tugged at his lips. "Yes, it will be your first time venturing out of Gentle Wind Village. It's only natural to feel apprehensive."

"I'm not just worried for myself," I confessed. "I've responsibilities here . . . I worry about what leaving would mean for all of it."

After so many years in the village, I grew accustomed to being the one people approached for medicine and salves. It was a natural process; after my parents passed, there was nobody who knew more about herbs and their effects aside from Elder Ming. Being absent for two months may not seem like much, but that's more than enough time for illness and disease to spread. Nothing on the level of Moonshadow Lung Rot had occurred since, but who knew when it would strike again?

Elder Ming paused his grinding, looking at me with a knowing gaze. "Change is a part of life, Kai," he began, his voice soft yet firm. "It's scary, often overwhelming. But it is also the path to growth. This opportunity . . . It's a chance for you to test your abilities, to push your boundaries."

He resumed his grinding, the rhythmic scraping sound echoing in the stillness. "The village will manage. It always has. Your shop will survive, and I can help maintain it, if need be."

His words gave me comfort, but they also brought forth a surge of uncertainty. I had grown so comfortable with my life in the village, with the routine and familiarity. But I also yearned for more, for a chance to grow, to expand my knowledge and skills in herbalism and cultivation.

I didn't think I'd hesitate like this when an opportunity to experience the world was just a step away.

Elder Ming's voice broke my chain of thought. "Remember, Kai, this journey won't just be about alchemy or the contest. It will be a test of your convictions, your values. Outside the comfort of our village, you will face challenges that will question your principles. It's your actions in those moments that will define you, not the accolades or the accomplishments."

His gaze was stern, yet there was a softness to his words. It was a reminder of what lay ahead, of the daunting and exciting world beyond the confines of Gentle Wind Village. A world I was being offered a chance to explore.

"But in the end, it's your decision, Kai," he concluded, his eyes softening. "You need to decide what's right for you, what aligns with your heart's desires. No matter your choice, know that we will support you."

I nodded, a knot of emotions tightening in my chest. His words echoed my fears, my hopes, and my doubts. They were a mirror to my own thoughts, a reflection of the crossroads I stood before.

For a long moment, we sat in silence, the only sound was the gentle rustle of leaves and the rhythmic grinding of Elder Ming's pestle.

"Thank you, Elder Ming," I murmured, standing up from my seat. "I've got a lot to think about."

His smile returned, a touch of reassurance in his dark eyes. "Take your time, Kai. And remember, the path to wisdom often begins with a single question."

With a nod, I turned away from his house, stepping back onto the path that would lead me back home. As I walked away, Elder Ming's words rang in my ears, a testament to the difficult choice that lay ahead of me. An opportunity to compete in the Grand Alchemy Gauntlet and train with the Verdant Lotus Sect was alluring, but the road that led there was rife with uncertainties. And as much as I yearned to rise to the challenge, I was equally wary of what it would mean for my life in the village, for Tianyi and for me.

It was a long walk home, but it gave me the space to reflect. Reflect on my life in the village, my desires, and the daunting opportunity that lay before me. I felt a pull toward the unknown, a pull that was equal parts exhilarating and terrifying. The time had come for me to make a decision, and I knew I had to do it with my eyes open and my heart prepared to face the consequences, whatever they may be.

The clinking of metal on metal guided my steps toward a familiar part of the village: the forge. Like Elder Ming's abode, this place was a sanctuary of another sort, filled with the sharp, intoxicating scent of iron and the rhythmic harmony of hammer meeting anvil.

My eyes landed on Wang Jun, his tall and burly figure hunched over a glowing piece of metal. Sweat poured down his face, dripping onto the sweltering coals, but his focus remained unbroken. This was the dedication of an apprentice blacksmith, and a friend who shared my journey from boyhood to the cusp of manhood.

"Wang Jun!" I called over the din of the forge, stepping toward him. "Master Qiang!"

The gruff, tall blacksmith turned away from his anvil and waved at me. "Y'here to bother my apprentice again, Kowtow Kai?"

Wang Jun looked up, the heat from the forge making his face glow. A broad grin spread across his face as he recognized me. "Kai! What brings you here in the middle of the day?"

I stepped closer, the heat of the forge washing over me. "I need your advice, Wang Jun. It's about an offer I received."

His eyebrows rose in surprise, curiosity burning bright in his eyes. He set down his hammer, gesturing for me to continue. Master Qiang shook his head, bemoaning the amount of orders but ultimately didn't stop his apprentice from listening to my woes.

I took a deep breath, explaining the proposition from Feng Wu and the Verdant Lotus Sect, the opportunity to compete in the Grand Alchemy Gauntlet, and my doubts about leaving the village.

Wang Jun listened attentively, his eyes reflecting a range of emotions—surprise, awe, and finally, excitement. "Kai, this is incredible! You've got the opportunity of a lifetime here," he said, a determined look on his face.

"I know, but I'm also afraid. They'll teach me as much as they can, but . . ." I started, my voice trailing off. "I'd be competing with people from all over the province. What if I disappoint them?"

He waved away my concerns with a broad sweep of his hand. "Kai, we've spent our entire lives in this village. There's nobody more qualified than you are to be an alchemist. It's only been a few months and I've watched you become someone incredible. Don't let fear hold you back."

He glanced back at the forge, his eyes reflecting the fiery glow. "When I was given the chance to apprentice under Master Qiang, I had my doubts too. But look at me now, learning and growing every day. It's an experience, Kai. When you're afraid to jump, that's exactly when you do it. Or so he says."

"Exactly!" Master Qiang exclaimed, raising his muscled arm and pumping his fist in agreement.

"What I'm trying to say is, don't be so hard on yourself. You're the Gentle Wind Village's herbal prodigy. Even if it's not a victory, I think you'll have a strong showing that can impress anybody down there in Crescent Bay!"

His words were like a balm, easing some of the unease in my heart. I smiled at him, feeling a spark of confidence rekindle within me. "Thank you, Wang Jun. You've given me a lot to think about."

He nodded, clapping me on the shoulder with a grin. "Just promise me one thing, Kai. When you go out there and win that Gauntlet, bring me back a souvenir, all right?"

I laughed, nodding in agreement. "That's a promise, Wang Jun. I'll be back with some cultivator artifacts for you!"

"I'm not a cultivator! Get me a new hammer or something!"

As I stepped away from the forge, the echo of Wang Jun's words stayed with me, igniting a sense of adventure within me. Maybe I could face the unknown, maybe I could embrace this challenge and emerge victorious. And so, with newfound confidence, I made my way back to the shop, ready to face what lay ahead.

I returned home and worked diligently. My mind was almost made up. But if I were to leave for two months, I wouldn't do it so callously. Preparations were necessary.

"Come, Tianyi! We're going to make some potions!"

With renewed enthusiasm, I delved back into my garden and moved before the sun went down.

I looked at my hands—hands that, after training so diligently, moved with a grace and precision that I once could only dream of. They were steady and precise. My newfound strength and speed were awe-inspiring, and I marveled at how cultivation had honed my skills, not just in alchemy, but in all aspects of life.

My fingers danced over the leaves of a Moonbeam Petal plant. A gentle tug was enough to free the flower from its stem, and it lay nestled in my hand, its ethereal glow pulsating softly. A quick glance was all it took to find the next one, and the next. In the past, it would have taken me an hour to harvest these delicate flowers, but now it was a matter of minutes.

Next, I moved to the Misty Dew Grass, its slender stalks glistening with droplets that sparkled in the sunlight. The process of collecting the dew was intricate and slow, a test of patience and skill. But the water was vital to my potions—a natural essence imbued with the plant's unique healing properties.

I picked the Nightshade Flowers last, their dark beauty both captivating and intimidating. They were one of my subtle favorites, giving my garden a nice and vibrant touch of purple.

Between these uncommon herbs were the traditional ones—mint, goji berries, wormwood, and more. Each had its place in the vast tapestry of herbalism. As my hands deftly moved through the garden, I appreciated how they intertwined to create the world I was a part of.

With my harvest complete, I headed back to my shop. It was time to extract the essence I needed.

Even from a glance, it was easy to tell my plants were much higher quality than anywhere else. Huan's herbs couldn't compare with how fresh mine were. The lavender's color had become so intense, it looked as though it were glowing. The smell was extremely fragrant. My constant infusion of qi into my plants had borne fruit; even the most common ones growing in my garden looked magical.

With the harvested plants spread across my table, I took a moment to appreciate the sight before me. It was a beautiful array of nature's gifts, each with its unique properties. My gaze first landed on the lavender, its delicate, fragrant blossoms seeming to vibrate with energy. And so, I decided to start with it.

I reached out my hand, hovering it above the lavender. I concentrated on the feeling I'd had, that sense of drawing forth its essence, like pulling on a thread that was deeply woven within. I could feel the qi within me shifting, aligning with my intent.

A moment passed, and then I felt it—a steady pulse beneath my fingertips. I latched onto it, drawing it out. I saw a swirl of violet energy begin to rise from the lavender. It was a strange, beautiful sight, even more pronounced than my first time doing it. The essence swirled and twirled, finally coalescing into an orb in my palm.

With my other hand, I quickly found an empty vial, and gently guided the lavender's essence into it. It flowed like a stream of light, pooling at the bottom of the vial. The lavender plant on the table seemed to have lost some of its luster, its vibrant color faded, and its aroma diminished.

Next came the Misty Dew Grass. I focused again, drawing out the essence as I did before. This time, the energy emerged as a dewy, green orb, shimmering like morning dew under the sunlight. The process repeated for the willow bark, with a woody, earthy essence, and finally, the chamomile, its essence a soothing, golden glow.

Each extracted essence filled a vial, standing on my table like a testament to my newfound ability. The feeling of accomplishment washed over me, yet with it came a pang of sadness. The vibrant plants were now a shadow of their former selves. I knew I had to find a way to use them wisely, to honor the life that had been gifted to them.

My shop was filled with an array of scents—the calming lavender, the soothing chamomile, the fresh Misty Dew Grass, and the grounding willow bark. It was a symphony of fragrances, each note bringing comfort and healing. With my table filled with these precious essences, I felt a sense of awe. I had always been able to work with herbs, but never like this.

With these vials of pure, unadulterated plant essence, I could concoct potions and elixirs of unprecedented potency. The possibilities were endless, and for the first time in a long time, I felt excited for the future. If I were to leave the village, I wanted to leave something beneficial behind. The essence was my first step in doing so.

"Kai, sorry I'm late. What're you up to?" The door opened to reveal Lan-Yin. She seemed harried, although ultimately relieved to be here. I glanced outside. The hours had passed so quickly when I was engrossed in making potions, and the sun was already setting past the horizon. "Oh, essences! Need help sorting them out and labeling?"

"I'd greatly appreciate that. I also need your support, Lan-Yin," I said, puffing up my chest. "This young master will be participating in the Grand Alchemy Gauntlet!"

"Oh, I heard that from Wang Jun just before I came. Think you're up for the challenge, arrogant young master?" she teased.

"Indubitably! But alas, that will leave this village without my expertise. So I'd like to have you maintain my shop and garden during the time I'm away. You'll be compensated handsomely, of course."

Lan-Yin rolled up her sleeves and began collecting the essences piling up on my table. Over the past week, she'd been getting more and more familiar with the ingredients I used and what they were for. Although it was pretty simple, I wanted to educate her so if any illnesses arose while I was gone, she'd know what would be best suited for the task.

She accepted the fact I'd be going to the contest without much thought. For some reason, I expected more pushback from her when I mentioned the contest. But she seemed quite casual about the entire thing. Almost like it was a foregone conclusion that I'd go. She was always a bit of a mother-hen type out of our friend group. When I asked her why, all Lan-Yin responded with was:

"Well, you'll just win and come back after, right? Just make sure not to piss off any cultivators and I think you'll be all right."

I don't think she fully understood the extent of the contest. But that casual belief that I'd win the contest made me hold back from correcting her. I just swallowed my anxieties and grinned.

"Yes! Victory isn't something to be earned; it's a right! A right only given to me, Kai Liu!"

She rolled her eyes, putting away the neatly organized box of essences away into a shelf.

With further discussion being pushed back to a later date, I helped organize the shop and departed for the evening. I needed to do my afternoon training. For routine and peace of mind.

I went down to the sandy shores, going through the motions and let my mind focus on the task at hand. The constant effort and pushing of limits is exactly what I needed to keep me in my right mind. And after an hour of diligent training, I sat with Tianyi and began to cultivate.

The Crimson Lotus Purification technique. With Elder Ming's permission to practice responsibly, I could do it in my own time. It'd be an opportunity for me, especially if I were to go to the Verdant Lotus Sect and their training grounds. I'd be able to accumulate more and more qi.

The cyclical process of collecting and purifying the qi in the environment with Tianyi's natural ability made the process much easier. The energy in my body was infinitesimally small, but incredibly pure. Like a perfectly forged gem sitting within my dantian. After two hours, I opened my eyes to the moon shining overhead. Under its light, Tianyi's presence seemed to intensify.

Once morning arrived, I'd have my answer for Feng Wu.

CHAPTER TWENTY-SIX

Meet My Friend

It took me some time to find Feng Wu. He was resting by the shore, cultivating quietly to the sound of waves. As if detecting my presence, he opened his eyes and from a glance he already knew my answer to the Verdant Lotus Sect's offer.

Our dialogue was quick and short, although I did want to introduce him to Elder Ming and the others. He was a cultivator! And a second-class disciple at that. For most of the younger generation in the village, it was the first time they'd seen someone of his caliber!

First, I visited Wang Jun and Master Qiang at the forge with the disciple in tow. But on my way there, a gaggle of children stopped us right in front of Mrs. Wang's home. I immediately had an idea.

"Peasants, remove yourselves from the path of this young master and his entourage!" I declared, shooing them out of the way. Contrary to my words, the children didn't shy away and instead drew closer with rising interest on their faces.

Xiao Bao, the youngest and rowdiest of the bunch, wiped the snot from his face and pointed at Feng Wu. "Who's this guy?!"

"He is the honored guest of our village, the second-class disciple of the Verdant Lotus Sect, Feng Wu," I replied, trying to keep a straight face.

Feng Wu, catching onto the act, played along. With an imperious air, he swept a bow in their direction. His sharp and impeccable appearance gave him an air of mystique and grandeur. "At your service, young masters and ladies," he said, his voice filled with feigned pomp and circumstance.

Xiao Bao's eyes widened in admiration, while Mei-Li, a shy girl usually found hiding behind the others, blushed fiercely. "He's . . . handsome," she whispered to her sister, but loud enough for all to hear.

Feng Wu, in response, looked slightly taken aback but recovered quickly with a gentle smile. "Thank you, young lady. That's quite a compliment."

The children erupted into giggles, pushing Mei-Li forward. She stumbled, her face now a bright red. "I . . . I want to be a cultivator too," she stammered, looking up at Feng Wu with sparkling eyes.

Feng Wu bent down to her level, a soft smile playing on his lips. "Then work hard, young lady. Cultivation is a path of dedication and discipline, but it can also be very rewarding. Perhaps, one day, I will see you at the Verdant Lotus Sect."

The promise elicited excited squeals from the children, their eyes all filled with dreams of grandeur. Even Xiao Bao seemed taken by the idea, his usual rowdy nature replaced by a determined glint in his eyes.

"Well, then, children," I said, trying to regain control of the situation. "The esteemed disciple Feng Wu and I have important business to attend to. But before we go, do you all promise to work hard and follow your dreams, just like Mei-Li?"

The children nodded enthusiastically, the joy and excitement in their faces reflecting the impact of this unusual encounter. As we continued on our way, I turned to Feng Wu, laughing. "Thank you, you've just become the hero of our village's younger generation."

Feng Wu chuckled, his eyes shining with uncharacteristic warmth. "As long as it inspires them to reach for their dreams," he responded, looking back at the children who were still buzzing with excitement.

Wang Jun and Master Qiang were hard at work in the forge, as always. They were likely growing tired of my constant visits, but they seemed quite surprised by the company I had brought with me. The large, older blacksmith still had the height advantage, but Feng Wu's posture didn't make him seem small at all in comparison to the largest men in the village.

"Master Qiang! This is Feng Wu, an esteemed disciple of the Verdant Lotus Sect! He'll be the one escorting me for the Grand Alchemy Gauntlet!"

He looked at him with an inspecting eye, before finally speaking. "You need some armor?"

Feng Wu glanced at Master Qiang, his eyes assessing the strong and rough hands of the blacksmith. "I might, indeed," he said, a hint of a smile tugging at the corner of his mouth. "Though I am more interested in acquiring good quality weapons and utility wares. The Verdant Lotus Sect always has a need for fine craftsmanship."

Master Qiang's eyes gleamed with interest. "Aye, I reckon we can strike a deal. Quality wares for a fair price."

While the two continued their conversation, I pulled Wang Jun aside. He was watching Feng Wu with eyes full of admiration. "He looks every bit the part of an esteemed cultivator, doesn't he?" I asked.

"He's impressive, that's for sure," Wang Jun replied, still unable to take his eyes off Feng Wu. "You're going to be learning from him?"

"Maybe," I replied with a laugh. "Who knows? Maybe during our journey we'll trade pointers!"

The two of us shared a moment of silence before Wang Jun suddenly threw his arms around me. "You're gonna do great, Kai!" he said, his voice muffled against my shoulder. His hug was warm, and I was certain some of the soot had rubbed off on my dark-red robes. Thank goodness they didn't show stains so easily. "Just promise me one thing, okay? When you're a famous cultivator, don't forget about your old friend Wang Jun."

"I'd never," I responded, returning his hug. "And we're celebrating tonight, right? Drinks at the usual spot?"

Wang Jun's laughter echoed in the blacksmith shop. "You know it! First round's on me."

As we separated, I noticed Feng Wu watching us, a thoughtful expression on his face.

As we left the forge, Feng Wu turned to me, his gaze steady. "How much time do you require to arrange your affairs?"

His question was reasonable, but it hung heavily in the air between us. I hadn't truly considered what leaving would mean, what I would need to do before I could go. There was much to think about.

First, there was Lan-Yin and Elder Ming. They'd need to know about the garden shop, how to care for the various plants, and how to utilize the right ingredients for the right sicknesses. The garden was not just a hobby of mine; it was a lifeline for many villagers who depended on the remedies it produced.

Next, I'd have to ensure my obligations to the Azure Silk Trading Company were fulfilled. My ongoing potion contract with them was a significant commitment that I couldn't simply abandon. I'd have to accelerate my production, working long hours to ensure I left them in a good position.

And beyond all that, there were personal matters. Saying goodbye to friends, preparing myself mentally for the journey, and ensuring I left nothing unresolved.

I looked at Feng Wu, who had remained silent as I pondered his question. I met his gaze with a resolute nod. "I believe I can have everything in order within a week," I replied.

Feng Wu nodded in understanding, a look of approval in his eyes. "A week it is," he confirmed. "I will wait for you, Kai. Make sure to leave nothing behind that could hold you back."

Walking toward the heart of the village, Feng Wu and I moved in comfortable silence. Ahead, perched on a small hill, was the modest abode of Elder Ming, the Village Head and my mentor.

"Feng Wu, I'd like you to meet Elder Ming," I introduced as we approached the house. "He's my master, and cared for me since I was a child."

As we entered, Elder Ming was seated at his usual spot by the window, gazing out at the distant fields with a meditative look. His old yet sharp eyes turned to us, scanning Feng Wu with almost palpable intensity.

"Ah, so this is the disciple of the Verdant Lotus Sect. Welcome, young man." His voice was calm, betraying none of the curiosity I knew was simmering beneath his exterior.

"Thank you, Elder Ming," Feng Wu bowed slightly, showing the due respect. He was always composed, but I noticed a hint of wariness in his stance. Elder Ming was not someone to be taken lightly. Even though from a logical standpoint, I knew that Elder Ming was old and injured while Feng Wu was a cultivator in the prime of his life, but for some reason it felt like he was . . . cautious?

"Kai tells me you'll be taking him to the Grand Alchemy Gauntlet," Elder Ming started, his eyes never leaving Feng Wu.

"Yes, Elder Ming. He has much potential. He would benefit greatly from the competition and training with our sect." Feng Wu responded, the respect in his voice unwavering.

Elder Ming's gaze hardened subtly, "And what do you stand to gain from this? It's rare to see a disciple of the Verdant Lotus Sect in this part of the world, much less one so invested in our Kai."

I watched Feng Wu carefully as he responded, "Kai's talent is rare and unique. It's in the best interest of the alchemical world that he receives the right training and exposure."

Elder Ming nodded slowly, his penetrating gaze never leaving Feng Wu. "Indeed, Kai is a precious gem. But as a Village Head and his mentor, it's my duty to ensure that he is not exploited."

Feng Wu didn't flinch at the thinly veiled warning. "I understand, Elder Ming. My intentions are honorable. We at the Verdant Lotus Sect believe in nurturing talent, not exploiting it. I assure you, Kai will be treated with the respect and care he deserves."

As they conversed, I found myself lost in their exchange. I wasn't oblivious to the gravity of their conversation, but the layers of meaning that seemed so obvious to them felt out of my grasp.

Elder Ming finally broke his gaze, turning to me with a soft smile. "I trust your judgment, Kai. Always have. Remember, this is your journey. Be sure to make the most out of it."

His words, simple yet profound, served as a reminder of why I was embarking on this journey. It was more than a competition or an opportunity to learn from the best. It was my chance to explore the vast world of alchemy beyond the confines of our village, to see how far I could go with my talent. Hearing him give me his blessings made me relax, and ease the tension from my shoulders.

With renewed determination, I responded and bowed, my hands clasped together in front of me. "I understand, Elder Ming. I promise to make you proud."

As we left Elder Ming's house, a strange silence settled between Feng Wu and me.

I took him to the Soaring Swallow Teahouse, where Lan-Yin worked to serve the few seated. She noticed me immediately, raising a brow at Feng Wu beside me. But she seemed to have an inkling of who he was. I had spent last evening talking to her about my meeting and subsequent offer.

"Lan-Yin, meet Feng Wu, the disciple of the Verdant Lotus Sect I was telling you about," I introduced him, keeping my voice low to not draw too much attention from the other customers.

A blush spread across Lan-Yin's face as she glanced up at Feng Wu, the handsome stranger who stood a head taller than most of the men in our village. "Nice to meet you," she said shyly, "What can I get you?"

Feng Wu gave a polite smile and ordered a cup of jasmine tea. We found an empty corner in the teahouse and sat down on the low cushions, the soft chatter of villagers providing a comfortable background noise.

"Kai," Feng Wu broke the silence, his gaze serious, "I need to know how committed you are to this. Training and cultivation will not be easy, and it'll take time."

"I'm ready," I responded, meeting his gaze squarely. "But I have a concern. What if my cultivation rank becomes too high? Would that make me ineligible for the Grand Alchemy Gauntlet?"

A faint, amused smile appeared on Feng Wu's face. "At your current level, it would take about three or four years of rigorous cultivation to reach the second rank of the Qi Initiation Stage. For the competition, you have nothing to worry about. Scaling the cultivation ranks isn't as easy as you think."

His words brought relief, but I couldn't resist the curiosity. "What about you, Feng Wu? What's your cultivation level?"

"I'm at the fourth stage of the Qi Initiation Stage," he replied without hesitation.

My eyes widened. It was already at the realm of superhuman. I've heard of fourth-stage cultivators that could split boulders in half. The protagonist of *The Storm Sage Chronicles* was a similar rank, and he could conjure up such powerful gusts of wind using a fan that it could cause gouges in the ground. Was Feng Wu at that level already?

"But the Sect Leader . . . he's at a different realm," Feng Wu continued, "He's at the third stage of the Essence Awakening Stage. It took him forty-five years of consistent cultivation to reach that stage."

The Essence Awakening Stage. I've heard the rumors. Elders who could form pure qi to make barriers and manipulate objects. Elder Ming once told me that the Whispering Wind Sect elders use it in the festival in Crescent Bay City to fly in the air and perform acrobatics in the sky!

It made me wonder just how powerful those of higher cultivation ranks were. The Wind Sage was hailed as a legend who equaled the power of a sect just by himself. Surely he was at the Spirit Ascension Stage? Or even higher? At this point in time, even reaching the Essence Awakening Stage would require significant effort.

I asked Feng Wu, but he shrugged. Nobody he knew had seen the Wind Sage before.

"I doubt those of the Whispering Wind Sect have seen him either. And they share the same elemental alignment! He's a recluse, probably in closed cultivation for the past few decades." He muttered.

I frowned. Closed cultivation seemed really, really lame. I mean, who'd want to shut themselves off in a secluded area for an undisclosed amount of time, only to get the slightest bit stronger? Wouldn't it make sense to just go out, train, and polish your skills against the world? Meditation was a foundational part of cultivation, but I couldn't see myself doing that sort of thing to get stronger.

But before I could ask him more about the intricacies of cultivation, a notification from the Heavenly Interface arrived.

> *Your skill has reached the qualifications to evolve to the next stage,*
> *Nature's Attunement.*

CHAPTER TWENTY-SEVEN

Nature's Attunement

> *Nature's Attunement grants you two new abilities.*
> *Plant Whisperer—You develop a deeper connection with plants,*
> *enabling them to communicate with you on a spiritual level and*
> *understand their needs and properties.*
> *Earthly Root Connection—When surrounded by nature,*
> *you can draw forth additional strength and utilize it as your own.*
> *Increases cultivation and recovery speed in areas of nature.*

I hurriedly excused myself from the meeting with Feng Wu, dropping several coins that would be more than enough to pay for the meal. The burning desire to test out my new abilities from my skill evolution hastened my steps back to the shop.

Nature's Attunement! What a powerful sounding skill!

Once I had crossed the threshold into my garden, I stood still for a moment, letting the familiar scents of the herbs and plants wash over me. The fragrant notes of the Moonlit Grace Lily, the fresh scent of ginseng, the calming aroma of lavender, the sharp tang of rosemary; they all swirled around me, creating a symphony of scents that was both grounding and exhilarating. I stared at the only qi-based plant in my garden, which seemed to reach maturity before my very eyes. The soft, white undertone of the lily was great enough to be visible in the daylight.

Clad in my dark-red robes, which fluttered softly in the breeze, I took a deep breath and reached out with my senses. Plant Whisperer, the first skill the Interface gave me. That instinctive knowledge on how to use it came to the forefront of my mind. It felt as though my mind had touched something vast and ancient, a consciousness that sprawled outward in every direction.

Closing my eyes, I allowed my senses to roam freely among my green companions, feeling their subtle vibrations, the flow of their sap, and the beat of their silent hearts. It was a sensation of unity, of being one with the natural world around me. I resisted the urge to cry, and whispered quietly into the air.

"It's so beautiful . . ."

As if responding to an invisible signal, the vitality around me seemed to grow stronger, more palpable. The energy of life that had been flowing quietly beneath the surface of the soil, within the roots of plants, and the leaves rustling above me suddenly became accessible, like a vast well of vitality that I could draw from.

My robes, taking on a deeper shade of red in the sunlight, billowed around me as an invisible force seemed to ripple through the garden. I felt my energy reserves swelling, my qi surging within my meridians. The plants seemed to respond to this, their energies dancing along with mine in an intricate harmony.

Even my recovery speed seemed to increase. The weariness from the long day, the small pangs of soreness from training, all seemed to wash away, replaced by a rejuvenating energy that made me feel alive, stronger, more connected. It was as though the essence of the earth and the plants had intertwined with my own, empowering me, enhancing my cultivation.

I opened my eyes, the world around me seeming brighter, richer. I looked at my hands, feeling a new sense of strength coursing within me. I couldn't help but smile, the connection with nature I had always felt now intensified and given a tangible form. My garden, my plants, the earth beneath my feet—they were no longer just a part of my environment, but extensions of myself, allies in my journey of cultivation.

With great reluctance, I withdrew from my garden and stepped backward until Earthly Root Connection no longer worked.

As I moved away from the garden, I could feel the tether of connection thinning, like a rubber band being stretched, but not snapping. My senses, which were just a moment ago, supercharged by my proximity to the garden, started to dim, but I was not left bereft. I still carried the afterglow of that connection, a part of me deeply ingrained and attuned with the rhythm of nature. It felt as though I had left a piece of my soul back in the garden, forever connected with the plants and earth.

I carried the scent of the garden with me, a sweet and green aroma that felt like a comforting embrace. The vibrant memories of the thriving plant life, the gentle rustle of leaves, the quiet whisper of the wind, they all accompanied me as I moved further away, serving as a grounding reminder of the connection I now held with the natural world.

Drawing away from my garden, I realized that it didn't feel as though I was missing or lacking something. Quite the opposite, in fact. It felt like I was something more, as if my boundaries had expanded beyond my physical self.

Tianyi's form flew up to greet me as soon as I opened the door.

"Guess who just got stronger!"

She didn't respond, as always. But instead waited for me to continue talking.

"That's right! It's me! Let's strike while the iron is hot and cultivate!"

I eased myself into the lotus position, feeling my mind focus wholly on the task at hand. The energy in my surroundings seemed to accumulate at significantly higher speeds. With Tianyi's presence enhancing me, the amount which I drew in from my environment seemingly doubled.

But even then . . . growth was slow. I observed the bundle of qi within me, and knew that only a fraction would remain once I began purifying it. But nevertheless, progress was progress. Even if it's a single step, that was one more step than I did yesterday.

Inhaling deeply, I began the process and delved deeper into the confines of my mind. There was no time to waste.

The week I had to get my affairs in order went by like a breeze.

My garden was now in the care of Lan-Yin, Elder Ming, and Wang Jun.

Three pairs of hands I trusted more than anyone. I had written, rewritten, and then written again the Encyclopedia of Kai's Garden, a comprehensive guide detailing how to care for each and every plant, and how to identify any potential issues they might have. I made sure it was simple enough for anyone to understand, while detailed enough to leave no room for error. Had it not been for my Invigorating Dawn Tonic, I wouldn't have had the time to do this while balancing out the rest of my duties.

With the departure looming closer, I spent one last afternoon in my garden, harvesting a few herbs and roots I planned on taking with me. I gently placed multiple boxes and bags filled with various items on my sturdy wooden cart I had prepared for the journey.

I knelt down to touch the soil, feeling the essence of each plant with the skill Nature's Attunement had granted me. I couldn't resist smiling as I spoke to the plants, telling them about my journey, my worries, my hopes.

"I'll be away for a while, my friends," I murmured, gently patting the vibrant leaves of a ginseng plant. "But don't worry, you're in good hands. Lan-Yin, Elder Ming, and Wang Jun will take care of you all."

The plants, of course, did not verbally respond. Yet, I could sense their understanding, a wave of serene acceptance radiating back. It was as if they were telling me, *"Go, Kai. We will be here when you return."*

It was strange, in a way, to find comfort in the silent communion with plants. Yet, it felt more natural and soothing than any words could have been.

Among the boxes and bags of various herbs and essences, there was a special one, carefully wrapped and placed at a safe spot on the cart placed securely beside the iron staff Wang Jun made for me. A bottle of essence like silvery moonlight. The extracted essence of the Moonlit Grace Lily. I glanced over at the spot where the mature plant once bloomed, now replaced with bulbs that have yet to erupt from the ground.

I covered them with rich, fertile soil, their tops just peeking out from beneath the earth. I could feel their vitality, their eagerness to grow and flourish under my care. They were small and delicate, their potential hidden within the protective layers of their shells.

"You are my star pupils! Make sure to grow and train diligently! Come, Tianyi."

After saying my goodbyes, I placed my hands on the handle of the cart, feeling the coarse grain of the wood against my palm. Tianyi's mesmerizing wings passed by me, fluttering around in circles. With a soft sigh, I began to push the cart laden with potions toward the village.

The journey to the village was quiet, filled only with the gentle rustling of leaves in the wind and the steady creaking of the wooden cart's wheels. The further I moved away from my garden, the more the connection thinned, but it never fully disappeared. I could still feel the echo of the garden's vitality in the back of my mind, a gentle hum that soothed my worries.

Once I reached the village, I made my way toward Huan the merchant. His eyes lit up when he saw me approach, his gaze quickly taking in the cart full of herbs and roots.

"Ah, Kai!" he exclaimed, a wide grin stretching across his face. "What do we have here? More potions, perhaps?"

"Indeed, Huan," I responded, a smile mirroring his own on my face. "This is the half we agreed upon for this month. The second half will be delivered from the Verdant Lotus Sect's address."

As the sun began to set, casting a golden hue over the village, I found myself chatting with Huan, discussing trade, herbs, and the impending journey. With every passing moment, the reality of my impending journey was sinking in, bringing with it a mix of anticipation and trepidation. But I knew that I was ready to face whatever lay ahead, fortified by the power of my garden and the connections I had nurtured.

"Ready to go, Kai?"

I turned my head to see Wang Jun smiling brightly at me at the entrance of the shop. I pulled him into a hug and saw more familiar faces bearing down on me.

Elder Ming and Lan-Yin. Master Qiang. Xiao Bao and his ragtag group of friends. Mrs. Wang. It seemed as though a quarter of the village had personally come down to greet me. Tianyi stayed on my shoulder, her antennae twitching at the amount of people around.

Two sturdy horses were led forward by Elder Wen. The animals were strong and healthy, their coats gleaming in the last light of the setting sun. Their eyes were bright and intelligent, their flanks powerful and their hooves sturdy.

"We know your cart is filled with all kinds of delicate stuff, Kai. Can't have you pulling that all the way to the city. These fellas here will help you," he said, patting one of the horses affectionately. "They're strong and reliable. They'll get you there safely."

I stepped forward and ran my hand over their silky manes, my smile growing wider. "Thank you. I promise I will take good care of them."

The people started to approach me, each of them carrying small bundles and packages. They placed them one by one into the cart, their eyes shining with good-will and anticipation. A small bag filled with spiced biscuits from Mrs. Wang, a spinning top from Xiao Bao, a sturdy flask of Master Qiang's potent rice wine. There were scarves, cloaks, medicinal herbs, jars of pickled vegetables, and even a small jade amulet that Elder Ming placed in my hand with a stern expression.

"Protection," he said, his voice gruff. But his eyes were kind, filled with a warmth that nearly brought tears to my eyes.

As I accepted their gifts, each one a token of love and support, I swallowed the lump that had formed in my throat. These were not just my friends, they were my family, and they had been there for me when I had lost everything.

But I wasn't about to let them see me weep. I straightened up, wearing a flamboyant grin on my face, my eyes twinkling with mirth and determination.

"Worry not, my dear people!" I declared, sweeping my hand in a grand gesture. "When I return, I'll be carrying with me the victory of the tournament and elixirs of untold power! Not a soul in the village will ever complain of aches or illness!"

The square filled with hearty laughter, echoing off the buildings and into the darkening sky. Some of the younger children began cheering and clapping, their small voices full of excitement. The atmosphere was warm and joyous, a true reflection of the camaraderie and love that bound us all together.

"I'll remember all your faces," I said, my voice carrying over the clamor. "Mark this day as the rise of Kai Liu!"

The villagers hollered and cheered, their voices ringing in the twilight, echoing my promise back to me. Gone were the rolled eyes or quiet scoffs of times past. I watched as their faces filled with expectation and belief. I would not leave them disappointed.

Feng Wu, staying away from the crowd, made eye-contact with me and smiled. Beckoning his head, the crowd spread apart to let me pass through. The cart I had brought hooked up to the steeds Elder Wen provided.

As I settled the last of the gifts into the cart and thanked everyone profusely for their generous presents, Feng Wu appeared at my side. The regal-looking cultivator seemed to be infected with the general merriment of the atmosphere, his lips curved into a small smile.

"Are you ready, Kai?" he asked, more of a formality than anything.

I turned to him, my grin still wide on my face, and replied, "More ready than I'll ever be."

Taking the reins of the horses in one hand, I waved my free hand toward the villagers. "Let's get moving! We've got a tournament to win!"

With Feng Wu at my side, we began our journey through the village, the sturdy horses obediently pulling the loaded cart. We passed familiar buildings, waved at familiar faces. The baker kneaded his dough, the tailor meticulously threading his needle—all paused to wave at us or call out their well-wishes. The children who were running around playing tag halted their game to cheer for us. A sense of joy and excitement filled the air.

Everywhere we went, people sent us off with cheers and waves. Some of the villagers had even climbed onto their rooftops to bid us farewell, their voices echoing through Gentle Wind Village. It was overwhelming, the attention, the goodwill. But I held my head high, a wave of pride washing over me.

Embarrassment niggled at me. I was just a herbalist, after all, not a hero heading into battle. I shook my head, the feeling being overshadowed by a sense of gratitude and affection for these wonderful people.

I'd show them their belief wasn't in vain! Kai Liu, victor of the Grand Alchemy Gauntlet!

We walked on, slowly leaving the village behind. With each step, I felt the familiar surroundings becoming a little less familiar, the cheers growing a little fainter. Yet, the crowd followed us to the village borders, their cheers and good wishes filling the crisp afternoon air. Lan-Yin, Wang Jun, and Elder Ming at the forefront of the crowd.

As we crossed the village borders, I turned back one last time. There they were, still cheering, still waving, their smiles wide and bright. My heart clenched at the sight, a lump forming in my throat.

A wave of homesickness washed over me as the village became a mere speck on the horizon, disappearing from sight.

Ahead of me lay the unknown, a path I had never walked before. The journey, the tournament, the challenges—they all awaited me. A strange mix of trepidation and enthusiasm settled within me. My hand tightened around the reins, my steps becoming more determined.

With a resolute nod, I turned back to face the road ahead, my heart pounding with anticipation and resolve.

I was ready. Ready for the journey, ready for the challenges, ready for whatever was to come.

CHAPTER TWENTY-EIGHT

The First Day

The journey began just as the sun started to paint the horizon with hues of orange and red. Feng Wu and I led our horses at a leisurely pace, the load they carried light enough not to strain them but heavy enough to remind us of the purpose of our journey. The path to Crescent Bay City was well-trodden, a testament to the constant travel and trade that flowed between the village and the city. As we put the familiar sights and sounds of Gentle Wind Village behind us, the world began to unfurl with new landscapes that took my breath away.

Despite my mind spinning with fantasies of the grand adventures we might encounter, the first day of our journey was astonishingly mundane. I had envisaged bandit attacks, villages under siege, mythical Spirit Beasts emerging from the wilderness. Instead, all we came across were fellow travelers, rolling hills blanketed with verdant green, and quiet brooks babbling in the midday sun. The Tranquil Breeze Province, it seemed, lived up to its name.

By the time the sun began to dip, we'd made good progress. We set up camp by a gently murmuring stream, its water clear and cold, reflecting the first twinkling stars of the evening. The horses grazed nearby while Feng Wu and I unpacked our belongings. As we lit a small fire and the inviting aroma of our cooking dinner filled the air, I turned to Feng Wu.

"Who will take the first watch tonight?" I asked, my mind still filled with the thrilling prospect of a nighttime attack. A seasoned traveler and cultivator like Feng Wu must have come across some dangers during his journeys.

Feng Wu laughed, a sound as light and carefree as the wind rustling through the trees. "Kai, in all my years of traveling these roads, there has never been a need for a night watch. But nevertheless, I'll be alert in case there is one."

His words took me aback. I blinked, incredulous, as he continued.

"The Tranquil Breeze Coast is named so for a reason. It's one of the most peaceful provinces in the whole empire. The most excitement we might come across could be a raccoon rummaging through our food supply."

His light-hearted tone, the twinkle in his eyes, and his nonchalant demeanor did much to reassure me. It was strange, but his words stirred a mixed sense of disappointment and relief within me. Tianyi's emotions rolled through our connection, and I could sense the curiosity from her as she explored the greenery around, her tiny wings contrasting with the various plants and herbs around.

Still, I chose to enjoy the serenity of the moment. The fire crackled and sparked, casting dancing shadows against the darkening landscape. The scent of roasting meat and herbs was mouthwatering, a pleasant reminder of the comforts I'd brought from home. As a taoist, Feng Wu turned down my meat skewers in exchange for a humble meal of rice and vegetables.

"Do not worry, Kai. Cultivators don't need as much food as a regular person."

That didn't seem very fun. Even if I was a cultivator, how could I abstain from delicious food? Just the thought made me wince. I would live life to its fullest! Experience the finest cuisine, charm the most beautiful women! Jade beauties!

We spent the rest of the evening in comfortable silence. We talked about mundane topics. He mentioned visiting his village just prior to this and getting the chance to spend time with his parents. It seemed surreal, the fact that we came from such similar backgrounds. There was a small pang of bitterness when I remembered that despite our similarities, his parents were still alive.

I wondered how mine would've reacted to all these wonderful things I've accomplished since their passing.

As the night drew in, the darkness blanketing the sky, Feng Wu retreated to a quiet spot near the edge of our camp. He began to stretch, his movements slow and precise. I watched as he took up a martial stance, his palms extended in front of him as though holding an invisible sphere.

The Lotus Palm. The Verdant Lotus Sect's hand-to-hand martial art.

His palms moved in a fluid, circular motion, a representation of the ever-changing and cyclical nature of life. His form was exquisite; every movement was smooth, like water flowing over smooth pebbles, strong and relentless yet incredibly gentle. Despite the darkness, a faint green aura seemed to emanate from him, giving him a mystical, otherworldly air. It was as sharp as I last remembered.

I watched in awe, the firelight reflecting in his eyes, his body moving like a dance to a silent tune. It was fascinating and inspirational to see the raw power and control he demonstrated, a clear depiction of his high level of cultivation.

Emboldened by Feng Wu's movements, I decided to take initiative. Even without Elder Ming's guidance, I had a strong foundation. I had trained under his watchful eyes for over a month, practicing my stances and improving my physique.

I moved to a clear area away from Feng Wu, taking a deep breath as I focused on the exercises Elder Ming had ingrained in me. There were no advanced techniques or secret arts, just a series of grueling conditioning exercises to strengthen my body and discipline my mind.

My training consisted of relentless repetitions of various exercises, and the dreaded horse stance. I remembered Elder Ming's stern face and harsh voice echoing in my mind: *A strong mind needs a strong body, Kai. A weak body will only hinder your progress.*

Sweat started to bead on my forehead, my muscles protesting. Yet I refused to slow down. Every drop of sweat, every twinge of pain, brought me closer to my goal. As I glanced off to the side, I could see Feng Wu going even faster without a single pause.

I pressed on, my body falling into a rhythm. Each movement, each breath, was a step toward the strength I craved. The night air around me was cooling, soothing against my heated skin.

By the time I finished my routine, I was drenched in sweat, my muscles aching yet oddly invigorated. Panting slightly, I dropped onto the grass, allowing my body to rest. I looked up at the stars.

Looking up at the star-studded sky, I felt my breath hitch at the ethereal sight. Each twinkling light was a world unto itself, distant yet familiar, echoing the very essence of my journey. I felt a strange connection with the earth. Faint but there. It revitalized my body, the grass curling inward as if embracing me. The effect of Nature's Attunement wasn't as prominent, but it seemed as though I got stronger being in nature's presence.

The sounds of shuffling grass made me turn my head, with my gaze landing on Feng Wu. He was standing nearby, a serene look on his face as he studied me. The glow of the firelight danced in his eyes, accentuating the depth of his gaze.

"That was quite impressive, Kai," he remarked, his voice calm, not even a hint of exertion apparent. The fact that he was not even winded, while I was gasping for breath, spoke volumes about the gap between us.

My lips curved into a grateful smile, my chest puffing up at his words. However, I knew I still had a long way to go. A sudden idea dawned on me, a spark lighting up in my mind.

"Feng Wu," I began, my voice firm, "Would you . . . would you trade pointers with me?"

His eyebrows arched slightly in surprise. Then a slow smile spread across his face, changing his aura from a calm brook to a playful breeze.

"You are relentless, Kai," he responded, his tone teasing. He reached into his satchel and pulled out a small flask. With a flourish, he handed it to me. "Here, take this. It's a revitalizing elixir. Rest for a while before we spar."

I gratefully took the flask, the cold touch of its surface soothing against my sweaty palm. As the liquid went down my throat, I paused and stared at the cultivator, who was smirking playfully.

"This is water," I deadpanned.

"It is quite revitalizing after your training, is it not?"

I barked out a laugh and returned it to Feng Wu. I leaned back against a tree, allowing the "elixir" to do its work. As my heartbeat started to normalize, I watched Feng Wu prepare himself for our upcoming spar. His movements were fluid and effortless, a stark contrast to the rigorous training I had put myself through.

Just watching him was a lesson in itself, his mastery of the Verdant Lotus Sect's Lotus Palm technique apparent in every gesture. His calm demeanor was the perfect testament to the tranquil life of a cultivator. Despite his formidable skills, there was a simplicity about him that was both intriguing and comforting.

The moonlight streamed down, casting a soft glow around us, and the air held a lingering scent of dewy grass and woodsmoke. My pulse quickened with anticipation as I squared off with Feng Wu.

Feng Wu took the first move. His form was like a ripple of water, as smooth and elusive as mist, as he deftly swirled around me. I tried my best to remember the essence of his movements to prepare myself mentally, but it was so hard to think in the midst of combat.

I attempted to parry his blows, using the techniques I'd learned from Elder Ming, yet they all fell short. It felt like my first time sparring with the old man. My attempts were met with the equivalent of batting at smoke; each strike was easily deflected, slipping away with an effortless fluidity. The ease with which he evaded my blows, moving as though in a dance, was both frustrating and fascinating. His movements were an intricate weave of defense and attack, his body moving in harmony with the rhythm of his breath.

My panic was on full display. It felt like there was a split-second delay between my body and mind. It felt disjointed and clumsy.

Feng Wu landed a gentle tap on my shoulder, his touch light and precise. It was enough to send me stumbling back, a clear sign of my inadequacy. My cheeks burned with embarrassment, yet he simply smiled. "Your moves are too rigid, Kai," he commented, his tone light, his eyes holding a soft glow under the moonlight. "Martial arts isn't just about strength or speed, but about flow and flexibility."

Despite the sting of his words, I didn't falter. I reminded myself that this was not a defeat, but a lesson. With newfound determination, I straightened up and faced him again. The sensation of Feng Wu's strikes, light as they were, reminded me of the gaps in my defense, and not painfully but humbling instead.

Elder Ming didn't teach me any style. He called it the basics. Punch, kick, block, parry. It was too early into my training to deviate. But here, I slowly learned how to put them all together into a cohesive art.

Motivated by this realization, I decided to press on, breaking away from my defensive stance and launching an offensive attack. Feng Wu's movements remained as smooth as ever, each of his movements as elegant and efficient as a swan gliding across a lake. I charged forward with a series of strikes, yet every attack was deflected as if it were nothing more than a leaf caught in a gentle breeze.

Though my frustrations mounted, a newfound respect for Feng Wu swelled within me. His skill and control were leagues above my own, and I was beginning to understand the extent of the gap between us. Yet, instead of discouraging me, this only served to fan the flames of my determination.

"Can I start using techniques?" I asked, panting slightly as I prepared for another round. This was my first time sparring with a high-level cultivator, and I wanted to see how I would fare with my full capabilities.

Feng Wu nodded, a knowing smile playing on his lips. "Very well, Kai. Show me what you've got."

Emboldened by his words, I went into my next attack. Drawing upon my qi, I executed a series of techniques, each move more powerful than the last. Yet, for every attack I launched, Feng Wu seemed to have an answer. My boost was minute. I was a little stronger than before, and my strikes were being launched at higher velocities, but I couldn't utilize the flow of qi throughout my body like he could.

At every step, Feng Wu was one move ahead, his counterattacks highlighting the weaknesses in my techniques. It was both amazing and frustrating. Even my most powerful strikes were met with grace and fluidity, his evasion and deflection as smooth and seamless as the flow of water. It was as though he was dancing around my attacks.

Despite the gap between us, there was no hint of arrogance in Feng Wu. His approach was patient and understanding, as if he was guiding me rather than competing with me. Each light tap from his palm was not a mark of defeat, but a lesson, a sign of where I needed to improve.

The differences between us were apparent, not just in our skill levels, but in our approach to martial arts. Where I was impatient and aggressive, Feng Wu was calm and controlled. Where I was rigid and forceful, he was fluid and gentle.

But I was learning. How he tended to shift left whenever he stepped backward. And whenever he did that, he'd draw himself back in and poke me in the chest as a reminder of the gap in my defense. I left it open, and watched him just as he leaped backward. I knew he would do it and left my guard open with the intent of luring him in.

"Rooted Banyan Stance!"

His knuckles brushed harmlessly off my chest as I activated the technique, hardening every inch of my body. Feng Wu wasn't expecting me to remain in my position, and I unleashed an upper cut from close proximity, knowing I had him.

For a moment, my heart pounded in my chest, the anticipation and exhilaration so strong it was almost tangible. But just as I was certain the blow would land, I felt it: the lightest brush against the skin of my knuckles.

Feng Wu had tilted his chin, the slightest movement that deflected the brunt of my attack. Instead of the satisfying impact I had been waiting for, my fist merely grazed the tip of his chin, the touch as soft as a feather. The shock of the near miss sent a jolt through me, leaving me standing there, my fist still raised and my breath caught in my chest.

I sighed, my shoulders dropping as I admitted defeat. The smirk on Feng Wu's face was both exasperating and amusing. But he remained quiet, his gaze thoughtful as he watched me.

"In the heart of a seed, an ancient tree lies," he murmured. I tilted my head but shook off my thoughts as I clasped my hands together and bowed.

"It was a good match. I learned well," Feng Wu said.

I responded the same, and we both sat down by the fire to recover. After a brief silence, I noticed that he entered a meditative state and had closed his eyes. As I placed a small bowl down and filled it with rice wine for Tianyi, I settled down across from the second-class disciple and began using the Crimson Lotus Purification Technique.

Even without bandit ambushes or spirit beast attacks, this journey would still hold incredible value for me, both as a martial artist and as an alchemist.

Under the moonlight's gaze, we each found solace in our cultivation. Two lone figures beneath the starlit sky, nurturing our potentials while waiting for dawn to arrive.

CHAPTER TWENTY-NINE

Unforeseen Developments

The initial discomfort of the previous day had given way to a rhythmic stride, Feng Wu leading the way with a natural grace that made the uneven terrain seem as smooth as a dance floor. There was a calmness in the monotony of the journey that reminded me of gardening. I used my iron staff as a walking stick, my other hand holding the reins to the horses.

"We're not likely to come across any major incidents," Feng Wu had said, yet a part of me was waiting for the sudden twist, the unexpected interruption that would remind me of the perilous path I'd chosen. But that moment never came, so we filled the silence with conversation.

Feng Wu proved to be a wellspring of knowledge about alchemy and herbalism. I knew he came from a family of herbalists, but it was still surprising. He held a calm demeanor as we traversed through the emerald and jade foliage, his green-and-white robes blending effortlessly with the surroundings.

Feng Wu paused, glancing at the wilderness around us, before saying, "Do you see these plants, Kai? An herbalist would take them as they are, utilize their inherent properties. But an alchemist . . . They seek to transform, to mold matter itself, to find new combinations of properties that nature alone couldn't conceive."

I furrowed my brows, trying to grasp the concepts. "So, it's like cooking? Salt, pepper, soy sauce . . ."

Feng Wu chuckled lightly at my analogy. "Well, in a way. But imagine your ingredients aren't just earthly but can also be celestial. And the flame you cook with becomes a pill furnace that channels spiritual energy instead."

He explained how an alchemist uses these pill furnaces, each one crafted from different materials, each material interacting differently with various ingredients. He talked about the Black Iron Furnace that could generate high heat for hardy, resistant materials, and a cauldron that can withstand the channeling of qi when creating pills. The numbers I heard were mind-boggling. Who would pay that much gold for glorified cooking utensils?

I hope the Verdant Lotus Sect won't mind me coming so empty-handed. All I brought with me were my knife, mortar and pestle, along with several dozen vials I prepared for fulfilling my contract with the Azure Silk Trading Company.

"You see, an alchemist isn't just scientific, but spiritual," he continued. "Your tool set extends beyond what you can physically touch. Your qi, your knowledge of the tools, and the environment itself will shape your product. That's the major difference that it has to herbalism, in my opinion."

Feng Wu's explanations about alchemy wove through my mind, absorbing each piece of information like a sponge to water. However, our intellectual exchange was soon interrupted by the hurried approach of a traveler.

A middle-aged man with a slight hunch in his posture, he held the air of a merchant accustomed to the roads. His eyes lingered on Feng Wu's green-and-white robes before he greeted us with a polite nod.

"Good day, sirs. Are you headed toward Qingmu Village by any chance?" he asked. His tone was casual, but the worried creases around his eyes suggested something more serious.

"We are," I replied, my eyes meeting Feng Wu's, catching a flicker of concern. He told me we'd have an opportunity to rest at a village nearby before we got to Crescent Bay City. I assumed that was the one he was talking about.

The man heaved a sigh, rubbing his weathered hands together. "Then you best be careful. There's a Wind Serpent prowling the area. Been attacking the locals for the past few nights."

My heart skipped a beat at his words. A Wind Serpent? I had only heard about them in *The Storm Sage Chronicles*. Beasts that could conjure gusts of wind, large enough to swallow a cow whole.

"I thought Wind Serpents were just myths," I admitted, turning to Feng Wu for answers.

Feng Wu gave a slight shake of his head, his gaze thoughtful. "They're extremely rare, but they exist. This is the first time I've heard of it appearing in the outskirts of the province, however."

The man nodded in agreement. "Just keep your wits about you. That beast isn't something regular folk can handle." His gaze lingered on Feng Wu, clearly reassured by the presence of a cultivator. He didn't even glance at me. Clearly, my ability to suppress my cultivation and hide my true abilities was at work.

"We will. Thank you for your warning," Feng Wu responded, his voice calm and composed.

"I heard the villagers sent out a plea for help to nearby sects, so one of them should be coming around to investigate."

With a final nod, the man continued on his journey, leaving Feng Wu and me in contemplative silence.

I wasn't exactly thrilled about the prospect of facing off against a Spirit Beast, especially one I barely knew anything about. My grip tightened around my iron staff, my mind running through the few combat forms I had managed to learn. I looked toward Feng Wu, trying to mask my apprehension. "Can . . . can we handle a Wind Serpent?"

Feng Wu looked at me, a reassuring smile gracing his face. "Let's hope we don't have to. But if it comes to it, I will do what I can."

From within his robe, he withdrew his arm, slowly unfolding his clenched fingers to reveal an object that glittered ominously in the harsh daylight. As if unfurling a forbidden secret, he allowed the hidden object to slide from its sheath and extend with an eerily harmonious sound—a bladed fan, a stunning weapon and tool of lethal elegance.

The fan, with its earthy green hue, immediately stood out against the background of dust and rugged terrain. It was a symbol of the Verdant Lotus Sect, with the gentle lotus patterns delicately inscribed along the blades, alternating between brighter and darker shades of green.

Each metal segment gleamed with a polished, silver edge that hinted at its sharpness, each blade designed for deadly precision. I could already imagine what it was capable of, a weapon that could unleash a whirlwind of deadly slices with every graceful swing. Feng Wu's light touch on the fan, twirling it effortlessly, displayed not just his mastery over this unique weapon, but also a signal of his preparedness to face whatever dangers awaited us. I let out a noise of awe.

"A bladed fan . . . just like Zhen Lu from *The Storm Sage Chronicles*! Wow! Can you make mighty gusts of wind and send people flying? Can you do it on me?"

But just as quick as he drew it, it dropped back into his sleeve as though it were all an illusion.

"Kai," he started, his voice firm but gentle, "this fan may look beautiful, almost harmless, but it's still a weapon. It's meant to protect, to attack, but never to be used carelessly, and certainly not against a friend."

I sighed. I supposed he was right. It was one of the main reasons why I went with a staff rather than a blade. It was dangerous. I only ever used my knife once, and that was to protect Tianyi from that damn crow. I felt embarrassed at being scolded, but my overeagerness got the best of me this time around. We continued on, and I continued to converse with Feng Wu about his weaponry. I always thought he was a hand-to-hand combatant, but he was more versatile than I assumed.

His show didn't completely dissolve my worries, however, but they did stoke a fire within me. That evening, when we stopped to rest, I decided to forego sleep for additional practice. As the moonlit shadows danced around me, I swung my iron staff with renewed determination.

As I swung my staff, I found my thoughts focusing not on the movements of my arms or the weight of the iron, but on the creature that might soon cross our path. A Wind Serpent. A beast of myth and legend, now a potential reality. I wondered how it might move, how it might attack. Would it truly control the wind, turning nature's calm breezes into deadly gusts?

I knew of these creatures through books and stories, where they were often depicted as benevolent beings, guardians of the wind element. Yet here they were, presented as a threat to people, a menace to be feared.

But then again, weren't we all capable of being both, depending on who's looking at us? Good, bad, hero, villain . . . Aren't these just labels we attach to ourselves and others based on our experiences and biases?

I halted my movements, the iron staff humming lightly from the sudden stillness. I glanced at the serene night sky, pondering this new insight. Yes, the world was no longer black-and-white, but rather a spectrum of grays where the line between right and wrong was often blurred.

The introduction of the Heavenly Interface had made this reality even more apparent. Previously unknown or mythical creatures, like the Wind Serpent, coming out the woodworks. The increased demand for weapons and armor from all over the province. It felt like the world was gearing up for something huge.

I still couldn't fully grasp the extent of the Interface's influence. But one thing was clear: It had opened doors to opportunities and risks that were previously unimaginable. Like the Grand Alchemy Gauntlet. I hadn't even considered it, a far-fetched dream . . . until the Heavenly Interface provided the means to turn it into reality. The ability to extract plant essence. The Memory Palace. All these techniques made me several times more capable than ever before.

But what was it that made the Verdant Lotus Sect so interested in me? I was a good herbalist, sure, but was I really that unique? Or was it something more . . . ?

These thoughts were not comforting, but I reminded myself that overthinking would not bring any solutions.

I resumed my training, channeling my energy through the iron staff. The cold night air whipped past me, my every movement creating a soft, rustling melody that seemed to echo my swirling thoughts. The rhythmic clash of the iron staff against the air served as a grounding anchor amid my anxieties, a reminder of the control I held over my own destiny.

As the night deepened, I found a sense of calm within the storm of my thoughts. The apprehension was still there, of course, but it no longer held the same crippling fear. A Wind Serpent . . . if we came across it, we would face it. And if the

Verdant Lotus Sect had ulterior motives . . . Well, I would cross that bridge when we came to it.

I trusted Feng Wu. He didn't seem like the kind of man with ulterior motives. But Elder Ming warned me of the dangers here in the Jianghu. And as I took my first steps into it, I would have to do my best not to fall.

My training finished, leaving me on the floor, gasping for air. I had strained myself, occupied by my worries for what tomorrow would bring. Feng Wu seemed to materialize out of thin air, handing me a bottle of water to satiate my thirst.

"You're a hard worker, Kai. I admire that. I wish my juniors could learn a thing or two," he said. I smiled confidently.

"I know my place in the world. How can I live up to being the genius of the Tranquil Breeze Coast without putting in some effort?"

The man rolled his eyes. "I don't recall your townspeople saying that. I remember a few, however, saying something else. Does 'Kowtow Kai' ring a bell?"

I groaned and put my hands on my head. Dammit! I bet it was Master Qiang who mentioned it to him. I'm giving that old coot an earful when I come back. Maybe even a few face-slaps as well to restore my honor.

As the sun rose, casting a warm glow on the landscape, Qingmu Village came into view on the horizon. I had expected a peaceful, quiet village, the type described in stories and paintings. But what met my eyes was a far cry from that idyllic image.

From afar, the village was a hive of activity. The rooftops were bustling, people moving back and forth, their motions hurried and anxious. And scattered amid the villagers were figures clad in ocean-blue attire. Their presence was like that of a falcon amid sparrows, their air of superiority impossible to ignore.

Cultivators.

"Feng Wu, those guys . . . They're not from the Verdant Lotus Sect, are they?" I asked, my eyes never leaving the blue-clad figures.

"No, they're from the Silent Moon Sect," he responded. I knew that the Silent Moon Sect was one of the most influential sects in the region. But what were they doing in a small village like Qingmu? Had they really answered the call for support?

"Do you think they're here because of the Wind Serpent?" I ventured to ask, my mind instantly recalling the warning we received from the merchant.

"That's a possibility," Feng Wu replied, a thoughtful look crossing his face.

We approached the village slowly, keeping our presence as low key as possible. As we came closer, the air felt heavy with tension. Villagers eyed us with a mix of suspicion and relief, their faces etched with lines of recent worries.

One of the Silent Moon Sect disciples spotted us. He was a young man, not much older than I was, but the look in his eyes was far too cold and cynical for his age.

"What brings you to Qingmu Village?" he asked, his tone carrying a subtle note of challenge. His gaze drifted to Feng Wu's green and white robes, and a flicker of understanding passed his eyes. But it quickly turned into something else . . . Contempt?

"We heard about the Wind Serpent . . ." Feng Wu started, but the Silent Moon disciple cut him off with a dismissive wave of his hand.

"That's been dealt with. There's nothing to see here," he responded, his tone brusque and condescending. His gaze then shifted to me, and for the first time, I felt a spark of hostility. It wasn't the open scorn he showed to Feng Wu, but rather an undercurrent of disdain, as though I was barely worth acknowledging.

"But . . ." I started, but Feng Wu gently touched my arm, signaling for me to stop.

"Thank you for your help," Feng Wu said, offering a polite smile that didn't quite reach his eyes.

The Silent Moon disciple merely huffed in response, turning away from us without another word. We watched him join his fellow disciples, their blue robes contrasting starkly against the rustic backdrop of the village. And I could see discussion among them. One of the disciples stood out to me: a man, his beard grizzled and eyes as sharp as daggers, who appeared to be a few years Feng Wu's senior.

His eyes were focused on my companion before landing on me. No, not on *me*. On my shoulder, where Tianyi sat.

The Azure Moonlight Flutter froze, just like the time she was attacked. My skin prickled.

This wasn't looking so good.

CHAPTER THIRTY

Silent Moon Sect

As we watched the Silent Moon Sect disciples from afar, the eldest among them broke away from the group. His stride was assertive, his eyes maintaining their cold, focused gaze on Tianyi and me. The murmurs of the villagers turned into hushed whispers as he approached us, and for a moment, the entire village seemed to hold its breath.

The man, decked in his cobalt-colored robe, a dagger-like glint in his eyes, and a smirk gracing his thin lips, walked up to us. He oozed a sense of haughtiness and condescension that made my stomach churn.

"You must be new here," he said, his voice as cold as his eyes. "I am Xu Ziqing, but the Jianghu knows me as the Azure Moon Marauder."

My eyebrows shot up at his nickname, yet my mind drew a blank. The Azure Moon Marauder? Was I supposed to know him?

His smirk widened at my silence. "Never heard of me, have you?"

"Honestly, no," I replied, my tone as calm as I could muster under his domineering gaze.

His eyes flashed momentarily with irritation, but he quickly masked it with a feigned chuckle. "Well, it doesn't matter. This place, Qingmu Village, is currently under the *protection* of the Silent Moon Sect," he said, emphasizing the word "protection" as if it held a greater meaning than I understood.

He looked at Feng Wu with a dismissive glance before his gaze returned to me. "We're handling the Wind Serpent situation. We don't need outsiders poking their noses in."

Feng Wu, who had been quiet, finally spoke up. "We have no intention of interfering," he said, his voice calm and collected, contrasting the hostile atmosphere. "We only stopped here to rest before continuing our journey. We'll be staying in Qingmu Village for the night, but that's it."

Xu Ziqing turned his gaze to Feng Wu. His icy eyes narrowed slightly, his smirk turning into a frown. "Is that so?" he asked, his voice dripping with skepticism.

"It is," Feng Wu replied, meeting Xu's gaze without flinching. "We respect the work that the Silent Moon Sect is doing here. We won't get in your way."

The horses under my control whinnied, sensing the tension in the air. Tianyi remained frozen still like she was doing her best not to catch the attention of anybody. Xu Ziqing turned his head and huffed in apparent annoyance.

"Very well," he said dismissively over his shoulder. "But remember, don't meddle in our affairs."

His eyes landed on me once more, lingering on the beautiful butterfly perched on my shoulder. I turned slightly to shield her from his gaze.

Leaving us by ourselves at the foot of the village, I turned to Feng Wu and whispered quietly.

"Those jerks! What the hell is up with them?"

The man seemed ineffable, although he had lost his smile and continued to keep his eyes on the Silent Moon Sect. "To think that Qingmu Village would become like this within a week . . . I advise you tread carefully, Kai. That man was a second-class disciple of their sect."

I gulped. Even without that information, I could see that Xu Ziqing fellow was a cut above the rest. Knowing he was the same rank as Feng Wu made me even more nervous. If such a person coveted Tianyi . . .

"Will it really be all right for us to stay here and replenish our supplies? I don't think it'll be safe."

"Regardless of their demeanor, the Silent Moon Sect still has a reputation to uphold. Attacking us would be tantamount to provoking the Verdant Lotus Sect. But it's clear that they're taking the situation into their own hands."

It didn't seem like it was for the sake of the villagers, however. The glum look on the Qingmu Village residents' faces bothered me. It was a stark contrast to the views I saw in Gentle Wind Village. They gave the disciples a wide berth, keeping their heads down and staying quiet as they went about securing the area. A dozen cultivators were more than enough to suppress a small village.

"But why, though? I've heard tales about how strong Wind Serpents are. They're one of the few Spirit Beasts that are native to our province! Why would they turn away our support so callously?"

Feng Wu kept his eyes sharp, walking through the village while we looked for an inn. "It's all about face, Kai."

"Face?" I echoed, confused.

He nodded, continuing to survey the area. "Yes. In the Jianghu, face is everything. One's reputation, honor, respect . . . These all boil down to one's face.

By handling the Wind Serpent situation on their own, the Silent Moon Sect can assert their dominance and strength. It tells others that they are a force to be reckoned with."

I scratched my chin, trying to process his explanation. "But . . . isn't it a bit risky? I mean, what if they fail?"

"Risk comes with every decision, Kai. However, they probably have calculated that the benefits outweigh the risks in this case." He pointed to the villagers working under the watchful eyes of the Silent Moon disciples. "If they successfully drive off the Wind Serpent, they'll gain the gratitude and respect of the villagers. This could translate into goodwill, tribute, and a stronger foothold in this region. It's a strategic move, aiming to secure resources and influence."

I looked at the villagers again, their faces etched with worry and fear. It all seemed so cold, so calculated.

Seeing my troubled expression, Feng Wu added, "Remember, we're in a world where power dictates everything, Kai. The Silent Moon Sect is just playing the game like everyone else."

The reality of it was a bit hard to swallow. As a child, I'd always imagined the Jianghu to be a place of honor and respect, where those with strength would protect the weak. The tales of chivalrous cultivators like Zhen Lu shone brightly and inspired all. But it seemed like it wasn't as simple as that. The mooks and grunts he dealt with weren't just caricatures or exaggerations, and noble cultivators like Feng Wu were more of an anomaly rather than the norm.

"Then what should we do, Feng Wu?" I asked, looking at him.

He took a deep breath, his eyes reflecting the determination within him. "We'll abide by their rules for now. We'll stay out of their way as planned. However, if they can't handle the Wind Serpent or if they put the villagers in danger, we won't stand idly by. The Verdant Lotus Sect may value neutrality, but we also value justice and protection of the innocent."

I felt a surge of admiration for Feng Wu. His words were a reminder of why I admired the Verdant Lotus Sect in the first place. We might have been outsiders in this village, but we wouldn't turn a blind eye to injustice.

"Yes, we'll do just that," I said, more to myself than to him. "For now, let's find an inn. I'm starving."

I checked over my interface. My stats have remained stagnant, leaving me in the mortal realm for my mind and body. But my qi was at the initiation stage. Did that mean my reserves were far ahead of my physical attributes? It was hard to imagine what I'd look or feel like with my mind and body at the first rank of the Qi Initiation stage.

If I had to deal with cultivators, having a large amount of qi wasn't enough. Being able to utilize it efficiently required a harmonious balance between all three areas.

"Feng Wu, on your interface . . . it also mentions what rank your mind, body, and qi are in, correct?"

He nodded as we tied the horses down to a post and entered the local inn. We were greeted by an employee who clamored nervously toward us, rubbing his hands.

"Hello, esteemed cultivators! Right this way!"

It was clear from how they treated Feng Wu that villagers were skittish around cultivators. Their treatment teetered between respect and fear. The second-class disciple from before appeared in my head. If they all looked like him, I'd be a bit nervous too.

Feng Wu turned to me and answered my question. "Yes, the interface does that. It's been a great way of tracking my cultivation and what I should focus on."

"Do you focus on harmony between all three? Or does it depend on the styles taught by individual sects?"

He paused, thinking about it deeply while the waiter handed us menus. "Although the methodology of sects affect it, the individual will also be an important factor that decides the style of their cultivation. I myself am predisposed toward the mind. My body refinement is lacking in comparison, but it is a personal preference of mine."

"What about having an equal distribution between all three? Wouldn't that be more . . ." I floundered, trying to find the proper word. ". . . Powerful?"

The waiter came back around and took our orders, before Feng Wu returned back to our conversation.

"I don't think so," he explained. "Think of it this way, Kai. Yes, being well-rounded can certainly be beneficial, especially when facing varied challenges. But to force equality between all three aspects would mean spreading your focus and resources thin."

Our food arrived within minutes. Plates of food aroused my appetite. But Feng Wu started, using his chopsticks to neatly divide a steamed bun into three parts.

"Imagine these three pieces are your mind, body, and qi." He motioned to the bun. "By trying to cultivate all of them equally, you'll have to divide your time, effort, and resources into thirds."

His eyes met mine, his expression calm but serious. "Now, consider this—what if you naturally excel in one aspect? What if, say, your mind cultivation could advance faster than your body or qi cultivation? By forcing equality, you might inadvertently slow down your mind cultivation, stifling your potential growth."

"But wouldn't having all aspects at the same level increase my overall power?" I asked, not entirely convinced.

"Not necessarily. In the world of cultivation, there are many paths to power. It's not always about balance. There are individuals who focus almost entirely on one aspect, either by choice or because their inherent talent lies there."

As I began to eat, my mind drifted back to Feng Wu's words. His perspective had thrown a wrench in my previous understanding of cultivation. I was left to ponder my potential path, what it meant for my future, and how it would shape me as a cultivator.

My gaze flickered over to Tianyi, the beautiful butterfly fluttering around aimlessly as she explored our surroundings. She returned to my side, taking a small drink of my herbal tea. Despite it being steaming hot, she didn't seem repulsed and continued her act.

I was reminded of the way my qi felt when I'd used it to infuse her. How it had worked alongside the energy of the Moonlit Grace Lily and saved her from the brink of death.

Could my talent lie in qi cultivation, then? I found the thought appealing, as I imagined myself controlling energy with such precision that I could heal or harm at will. The implications were enormous and it gave me a sense of power that I hadn't truly understood before.

However, that thought was quickly followed by another, the image of Xu Ziqing surfacing in my mind. He was strong, no doubt about it. The aura that he exuded, his confidence, his dismissive attitude . . . It was clear that he was no ordinary cultivator. I had to admit, the prospect of coming face-to-face with him in a battle made me shudder.

But if I wanted to stand against threats like him, or threats like a damn Wind Serpent! What did I need? A refined body? An enlightened mind? Or robust qi reserves?

I went through my various abilities. Memory Palace, qi manipulation, Rooted Banyan Stance, and Crimson Lotus Purification. What category did they fall under? Although they all used qi to an extent, did that mean focusing my efforts toward building powerful qi reserves was the right move?

I found myself circling back to the idea of a well-rounded cultivation. It was the safer choice, for sure. It would ensure that I didn't lack in any aspect, giving me a balanced set of abilities to rely on. But Feng Wu's words echoed in my mind—would it also limit me, hold me back from reaching my full potential?

Perhaps for now, it's best to stick with being an all-rounder, I concluded, taking a sip of my tea. *I am, after all, still figuring out my path. I don't even know where my strengths truly lie. And a rounded-out base wouldn't hurt, would it? It could provide a solid foundation upon which I can build, once I figure out my specialty.*

I found solace in that thought, the anxiety washing away as I came to a decision. Yes, the path of cultivation was long and daunting, but it was also filled with endless possibilities. For now, I would focus on honing all three aspects—my body, mind, and qi—simultaneously.

Once I discovered my true strengths, then perhaps I would choose a specialized path. But for now, I was content with the idea of being well-rounded, of growing evenly and harmoniously.

It might be slow, but it would be mighty.

My overexcitement led to the steamed bun in my mouth falling down the wrong hole. My chopsticks clattered onto the plate as I began suffocating.

Perhaps I should specialize in digesting food before I swallow first. That should be the primary goal. It would be embarrassing to become a cultivator and get felled by a half-eaten steamed bun.

CHAPTER THIRTY-ONE

Stir the Grass

Yes, and can we also have a room that has a view of the stables? That'd be appreciated, thank you."

The only inn available in the village also offered a stable for travelers to let their horses rest. Although they said it was secure, I didn't know if the claim could hold up against foul play from cultivators. The only guard there was a young boy who went around feeding the animals within. I wouldn't put it past them. Those Silent Moon folk were far from the chivalrous, taoist cultivators I knew from stories—they were like thugs.

"You do have to remember, Kai, not all sects are taoist. The Silent Moon is an unorthodox sect that follows the rule of might is right," Feng Wu said, listening to me rant about the disrespect shown by the disciples patrolling the village. "They don't respect those they deem as below them."

"That's not right! If we were the Whispering Wind Sect, they wouldn't be walking all over us! Judging someone based on background is . . ."

"What is out of your hands should not be in your worries. What can we do about their behavior? The important thing here is to avoid stooping to their level."

At what point do cultivators learn to speak only in metaphors and proverbs? Clearly Elder Ming and Feng Wu had reached that level. I sighed and leaned back into the bed, allowing the soft sheets to take some of the day's weariness.

"Feng Wu, there's something I don't get," I started. "The Verdant Lotus Sect, it's a taoist sect, isn't it? Then, why does it emphasize the pursuit of righteousness when others do not?"

Feng Wu eased back into his chair, his verdant eyes mirroring the soft flicker of the oil lamp that stood between us. "Well, taoist sects aren't all identical. For instance, orthodox sects, such as the Verdant Lotus, endorse values like balance, righteousness, and humility. They follow a moral code, striving for enlightenment and unity with the universe."

"And the unorthodox ones?" I asked, seeking more clarification.

Feng Wu's expression grew thoughtful. "Unorthodox sects adhere to the principle of survival of the fittest. They prioritize personal power and ambition above all else. For example, the Silent Moon Sect doesn't seek unity, but rather dominance, placing strength above all other virtues."

"Feng Wu, isn't the taoist way about balance? If all orthodox sects act as the Verdant Lotus does, and all unorthodox sects like the Silent Moon . . . where is the balance?"

Feng Wu's eyes shimmered in the dim light, reflecting the complexity of his thoughts. "Balance doesn't mean everyone acts the same, Kai. It means allowing for differences. The universe is a spectrum, not a uniform entity."

"But," I countered, leaning forward, "it seems to me that the unorthodox sects, like Silent Moon, are causing harm and disorder. They choose power and dominance over unity and harmony. Isn't that wrong?"

Feng Wu smiled, a hint of wistfulness in his expression. "Ah, the naivety of untouched lands. Wrong and right, Kai, are subjective terms. The Silent Moon Sect may seem chaotic and harmful from your perspective, but they see it as asserting their survival and strength. The universe thrives on duality, on the clash and blend of different forces."

"I can't agree with that," I asserted, the conviction in my voice surprising even me. "Causing harm, fostering fear . . . that can't be justified in the name of survival. There's a difference between survival and oppression."

"You're not entirely wrong," Feng Wu conceded. "But remember, our view is influenced by our experiences. You come from a sheltered village, nurtured by peace. Your perspective is invaluable, but it's not the complete reality of the Jianghu. It's a world filled with ambition, desperation, and strife, as well as peace and tranquility. The lines between right and wrong blur amid these complexities. It's about understanding, not merely judging."

I sat back, thoughts swirling in my head. The conversation had opened up a new perspective. Maybe the world wasn't as simple as it had seemed from the peaceful confines of my village. Still, the idea of causing harm for the sake of power . . . It left a sour taste in my mouth. Yet I knew I had a lot to learn, and Feng Wu, in all his taoist wisdom, was a beacon of guidance in this unfamiliar territory.

It was hard to believe we were close to the same age. Our experiences were worlds apart.

I took first watch and allowed Feng Wu to cultivate in peace while I watched over the stables, making sure none of the cultivators tried anything. But they rarely made their presence known, popping up in groups of two or three as they patrolled the village for any sign of the Wind Serpent. Despite their aloofness, they were quite diligent in their search.

The moon hung in the sky, casting its soft luminescence over the land. Tianyi was resting soundly on the corner of the windowsill. The words of Feng Wu still echoed in my mind, his wisdom challenging my seemingly naive worldview.

Feng Wu understood the human propensity for greed and conflict, far more intimately than I could. His experiences in the Jianghu, a world of martial arts and political, had given him perspectives that I, sheltered and nurtured by the serenity of my village, could hardly comprehend.

Yet I found myself unwilling to let go of my beliefs. They were immature, perhaps, when pitted against the realities of a world that thrived on ambition and power. But these beliefs were a part of me; they defined who I was; they were the rock against which the waves of change crashed but failed to erode.

I was reminded of my childhood dreams of becoming a cultivator. Many in the village had scoffed at my aspirations, ridiculing them as fantasies of a naive boy. But I held on, worked hard, and proved them wrong. I wanted to do the same now, with my ideals about right and wrong, about justice and oppression.

As I watched the shimmering stars, I felt a spark of determination ignite within me. No matter how complex the world, how ambiguous the definitions of good and evil, I knew what I couldn't tolerate: cruelty, manipulation, the strong preying on the weak. The very idea of judging someone based on their reputation or talent and then choosing to trample over them . . . It was repulsive.

In the silence of the night, I made a resolution. I might be stepping into a world where might often trumped right, where survival dictated actions. But I would not allow myself to become a part of such a cycle. I would hold onto my beliefs, stand for what I deemed right. No matter how many times I would be ridiculed, no matter how many obstacles I would face, I would stay true to myself.

That was my way.

"OVER THERE!"

A loud voice shook me from my contemplations, and Tianyi rose up in alarm. I peered out the window and tilted my head to see what was going on. The moonlight revealed a group of six Silent Moon disciples, all wielding their weapons and chasing after something.

Another shout alerted them, forcing the group to curse and move backward out of view. But just as they left, I saw it.

It was a brief glimpse of something extraordinary. My breath hitched as a creature glided across the wall. The Wind Serpent.

It was every bit as magnificent as the stories had described. Over one zhang long, with scales that shimmered like liquid silver under the moonlight, a being that seemed more at home among the stars than here on earth. It was so fast that it seemed almost as if it was a gust of wind itself.

I could hardly believe my eyes as the creature moved with the grace of a celestial dancer, its body twisting and turning with a fluidity that was truly mesmerizing. The serpent's scales reflected the moonlight in a way that made it seem almost invisible, camouflaged against the night sky. It was a creature of speed and beauty, an embodiment of the free, wild spirit of the wind.

I watched as the Wind Serpent disappeared into the night, the cultivators of the Silent Moon Sect oblivious to its presence. I grabbed my staff and gently alerted Feng Wu, making him rise from his seated position.

"The Wind Serpent! It's here! We have to go now!"

"Calm down, Kai." He put a reassuring hand on my shoulder. "We'll need to assess the situation before we dive in."

"Feng Wu, I saw it! The damn thing passed by the building next door and disappeared. We have to catch it before it's too late!"

There was no telling what it would do if it managed to find a way of entering a Qingmu Village resident's home. Even with that glimpse, I could tell it was massive. The girth of the Wind Serpent was equal to my torso. Maybe even bigger. It could easily swallow a child whole.

"Trust me, Kai. Breathe. Don't let your emotions control you, and assess the situation rationally."

Feng Wu's calm voice cut through the whirlwind of panic and anxiety I was feeling. His calm demeanor was like an anchor in a storm, helping me regain control over my escalating emotions.

"I just . . . I don't want anyone to get hurt, Feng Wu," I said, my voice hitching slightly.

"I understand, Kai. And neither do I. But that's precisely why we need to remain calm and make sure we're making the right decisions. We can't afford to rush in without a plan."

With a reluctant sigh, I nodded, recognizing the wisdom in his words. "All right, all right. What do you suggest we do?"

Feng Wu was silent for a moment, clearly deep in thought. "We need a better vantage point, somewhere we can see the entire village without being seen ourselves. Do you think you can climb to the rooftop?"

My stomach churned at the idea. Heights weren't exactly my forte, and we were on the third floor. But the urgency of the situation was a powerful motivator. I gave a shaky nod. "I can try."

Feng Wu gave me an encouraging smile. "That's all I ask, Kai. Follow me."

With a graceful agility that I could only envy, Feng Wu swung open the window, and before I could even process what was happening, he had pulled himself up onto the window ledge and then onto the roof of the inn—with a single arm.

I took a deep breath, trying to calm my racing heart, and then, mimicking Feng Wu, I clumsily managed to pull myself up onto the window ledge. But as I was about to hoist myself up onto the roof, a tile fell, and I felt a moment of stomach-dropping panic as I began to fall.

But then, in the next moment, a firm grip wrapped around my wrist, halting my painful path nearly three zhang below. I looked up to see Feng Wu, his arm outstretched, a small smile playing on his lips. "You're doing great, Kai. Just a little farther."

With Feng Wu's help, I managed to pull myself onto the roof, my heart pounding in my chest and embarrassment burning my face. The view from up here was nothing short of breathtaking. The moonlight cast an ethereal glow over the entire village, and from this vantage point, we could see everything.

"Look," Feng Wu said, pointing at a group of cultivators running past a house a few streets over, their lanterns bobbing like fireflies in the night. "They're still looking for the Wind Serpent."

"But they're going in the wrong direction," I observed, my eyes scanning the village. "The Wind Serpent went that way."

"That's our advantage, Kai. We know something they don't. Now we need to use that information wisely."

As we watched, another group of cultivators rushed past in the opposite direction, led astray by the misdirection of the Wind Serpent's wind trail. But I saw it again, and pointed it out to Feng Wu.

"Look! It's over there now! How the hell—?"

The speed it demonstrated was mind-boggling. Making its way from one end of the village to another made it look like it was teleporting. Was it possible for something to move that fast?

I watched in horror as it managed to slither through an opening in a window. It had managed to get in, almost as if it knew the other disciples would be out of reach.

Feng Wu narrowed his eyes. He took note of where we saw it and began to make his move, jumping lightly from rooftop to rooftop. Without much choice, I followed after him. I didn't even try to use qi to power my jump. I knew it was doable, but trying it now made me anxious. I jumped using the force of my legs alone, landing loudly onto another villager's rooftop with a fraction of the grace Feng Wu displayed. Inwardly, I hoped they would forgive me for the damage done to their tiles.

Just as I readied myself for the second leap, I saw something at the corner of my eye. Another brief flash of a tail. But this time, it was opposite to where I just spotted it a few seconds ago. It didn't make sense.

As it slithered away, I realized it was headed straight for the entrance of the stable where we placed our steeds. Within seconds, I began to hear screams.

The boy. The one who was feeding the horses!

Quest: Spirit Beast Subjugation
—Repel the Wind Serpents (0/2)

A pit formed in my stomach as realization hit. There's not just one.

With Feng Wu just out of reach and the Silent Moon Sect chasing another trail, I powered qi through my legs and leapt off the roof. It propelled me high into the air, and I began screaming.

"HEEEELP! IT'S OVER HERE!"

I landed on the floor, squatting deeply as my joints protested the amount of force it was put under. Despite my shouts of alarm, nobody came forward.

I would need to do this myself.

Armed with my iron staff, I rushed into the stables and hoped it wasn't too late.

CHAPTER THIRTY-TWO

Startle the Snake

I pushed through the aged wooden gates, and I was immediately met with the earthy scent of straw and horse sweat. Lanterns hung from the high ceiling beams, their dim light casting an unsettling shadow play on the neatly raked soil beneath. The murmurs of the horses in their bamboo stalls resonated through the cavernous space, accompanied by the occasional clatter of hooves and a soft sigh of equine breaths.

There, in the farthest corner of the stable, lay the monstrous Wind Serpent. It was a formidable sight, a living nightmare hewn from the darkest depths of folklore. Its scales shimmered with ethereal hues, flickering with the spectral light of the lanterns. It was immense, stretching almost two zhang in length—a sight that dwarfed the beasts in its presence.

As it slithered, its body created a soft rustling melody against the straw-covered floor. My heart hammered in my ribcage, an embodiment of the primal fear gripping me. Yet I was held captive in my spot.

My gaze followed the silhouette of the serpent, settling on its massive head. The depthless black of its eyes reflected the lantern's glow, its fangs threatening and razor-sharp. The very thought of being swallowed whole by such a creature, my life snuffed out in an instant, sent a chilling shudder through my spine.

A hasty movement in my peripheral vision caught my attention—the innkeeper's son, a young boy half my age. He was a small figure against the backdrop of terror, his face etched with raw fear. Clumsily, he tossed whatever he could reach the colossal beast—a tattered straw hat, a rusty pitchfork, even a worn-out wooden clog.

The stable was plunged into hysteria. My horses, their eyes wild with fright, kicked at the sturdy bamboo gates of their stalls, their neighs echoing through the structure. Geese, housed in the smaller aviary adjacent to the stable, added their frantic squawks to the chilling symphony of dread.

Despite the mayhem, the Wind Serpent was unnervingly calm. It ignored the horses, perhaps due to their size being too large for its consumption. It seemed to relish in the fear it invoked, its interest drawn more to the smaller critters that scurried in its periphery.

Even though my mind was flooded with terrible fear, I realized I had to act.

A wave of resolve crashed over me, the icy hands of fear momentarily receding. I knew what I had to do. My fingers tightened around the familiar grooves of my staff, the polished iron cool against my palm.

With a deep breath, I steeled myself. My battle cry cut through the air, a raw shout of determination that momentarily stilled the panicked cries of the horses. Then I was moving, sprinting toward the serpent with all the speed I could muster.

"HAAAAAAA!"

My mind played the scene in slow motion. I pictured the practice yard, the staff in my hands slicing the air in perfect arcs as I'd been taught. My footing faltered, my sandals skidding on loose straw. I wobbled, a sudden jolt of adrenaline saving me from a humiliating fall.

With a grunt, I regained my balance and continued my assault, my eyes locked on the colossal beast. My grip on the staff tightened, my muscles coiled, and I swung. My staff whistled through the air, meeting the serpent with a sickening thud.

But the serpent seemed barely affected. I could feel the shock of the impact reverberate up my arm, almost making me lose my grip. I realized then, training was one thing, but the reality of combat was entirely another. Even with hours of practice, the terror of the situation made every swing feel clumsy, every stance feel shaky.

I swallowed, my heart pounding as the Wind Serpent shifted its colossal body, its attention now focused on me. But I had to fight. Even if my swings felt like a child's against the monstrous serpent.

The air stirred, and the hairs on my skin stood up in response. It was going to attack.

Out of sheer panic, I turned to the only skill that could protect me in this situation. I slid my feet into position and tensed up my entire body. I drew qi to reinforce myself, feeling the stability and rigidity that came with completing the Rooted Banyan Stance.

I barely completed the stance before the Wind Serpent lunged.

BOOM!

An onslaught of wind and power. My ribs creaked under the immense pressure of a reptile slamming its entire body weight onto me, and I went flying through the wall of the stable and out to the clearing. I let out an ugly gasp as the air left my lungs. It was unlike anything I'd ever felt before.

I let out pitiful wheezing noises, trying to get back up, but it was near impossible. I dreaded thinking about what would've happened if I didn't protect myself with the Rooted Banyan Stance.

The hissing noise was followed by the snake's gaping maw ready to consume me whole. I screamed, hoping it would get anybody's attention before raising the staff and blocking the attempt on my life.

"FENG WU! HELP!"

There was no way I could defeat this on my own. Surviving that first attack took my all. My arms were rapidly giving out and my teeth nearly cracked as I fought desperately to stay alive.

SCHWING!

The snake flinched, before rearing its head back and hissing in agony. I scrambled upward and saw Tianyi, glowing brighter than ever. As the Wind Serpent turned and stared, I could see one eye had been sliced open as a result of her attack. I could feel her simmering anger through our connection as she circled around in the air. Her wings looked razor-sharp.

A figure leaped in from above, shielding me from view and taking the Spirit Beast's attention. Feng Wu. I nearly collapsed in relief. He was holding his bladed fan, fully extended. He held a severe expression on his face.

"No time to rest, Kai! Ready yourself. Watch your back."

"Wha—?"

From behind, I could see a second Wind Serpent going on a rampage as three Silent Moon disciples clung to its midsection. But due to the sheer speed, they were unable to hold and skidded onto the floor.

I threw myself to the side to avoid it, and it charged over to where the first one was.

Suddenly, the air around us charged with an energy so intense it made my hair stand on end. The two serpents intertwined, their scales flickering with an ethereal glow. Their bodies rose up like coiling towers, the symbols on their scales dancing and writhing in the lantern light. The wind whipped into a frenzy around them, stirring the straw and dust into a miniature whirlwind. The two beasts hissed and roared, their voices mingling into a haunting melody that echoed into the night.

My breath hitched as they spiraled around each other, their enormous bodies entwined in a complex dance. I could barely keep up with their movements. It was as if the serpents had melded into one, their bodies fusing in a beautiful but terrifying display. The power they radiated was almost tangible, a living, breathing force that made the ground beneath us tremble.

Then, with a deafening roar, the serpents released the energy they had built up. A shock wave of wind exploded outward, throwing everyone and everything away from them. The concussive blast flung me back, my body slamming into the ruins of the stable wall. A burst of pain exploded in my shoulder, but it was quickly forgotten as the world spun wildly around me.

My ears rang, the powerful roar of the Wind Serpents echoing inside my head. As I struggled to my feet, swaying unsteadily, I looked up to see the serpents had slithered off in different directions, hiding in the shadows as the rest of the cultivators arrived.

Xu Ziqing stomped toward me with a sword in his hand. He looked enraged and slightly worse for wear. The cocky smirk he wore when we first met was long gone, replaced by a volcanic expression as he picked me up by the collar.

"I thought I told you idiots not to interfere."

Was this guy serious?

"Interfere? That's what you're worried about?" I shot back. I tried to shove his arm off, but it was unrelenting. As a second-class disciple, there was no chance I could beat him in a physical contest. My arms trembled, already weakened from the battle. "There are two fucking Wind Serpents! One was about to eat the innkeeper's child!"

He threw me to the floor and scoffed. "You disregarded the Silent Moon Sect and put your nose in where you shouldn't have."

Although I knew I couldn't, I sorely wanted to punch him in the face. "How—?"

Feng Wu cut in between us. Several strands of hair fell down his head, showing he didn't come out unscathed from the massive attack the Wind Serpents performed. "I will not sit by and watch innocent people be attacked just to save your sect face. If you were truly competent, you'd know that this subjugation will require any help you can get."

Sparks flew between the two as they faced each other. The tension made it difficult for me to breathe as we were surrounded by the Silent Moon disciples. Some were paying attention to the conversation, but more than half had their backs facing each other, eyeing the shadows as they waited for the Wind Serpents to reappear.

"Enough!" I shouted. "Save this for when we're out of immediate danger. The Spirit Beasts could be anywhere!"

They both glanced at me, Feng Wu, with a measure of respect in his eyes, and Xu Ziqing, with disdain and irritation. After a few tense seconds, they turned away from each other and focused.

Xu Ziqing began barking orders, setting the cultivators into defensive positions, his anger turning into a focused intensity. "Zhou Li, Li Hu, cover the east side! Yu Han, Chen Wu, take the west! The rest, form a circle. And for heaven's sake, stay alert!"

Disciples hustled to their assigned places, their previous annoyance replaced with sharp, survival-driven alertness. This was no longer a mere power struggle, but a life-threatening situation. We were in the heart of the village now, surrounded by huts and outbuildings whose shadows concealed unseen dangers. The remnants of the day's life—empty carts, barrels, stacks of hay—all turned into potential hiding spots for the Wind Serpents.

Feng Wu, despite the animosity between him and Xu Ziqing, understood the gravity of our predicament. He positioned himself as part of the defensive ring, bladed fan at the ready. Its polished surface captured the feeble moonlight, reflecting an almost ghostly glimmer.

As I moved to join the formation, Xu Ziqing's stern voice stopped me. "You stay put. Do not act without orders. Cause no trouble."

His tone was condescending, and I clenched my teeth, biting back a retort. I didn't need him to tell me what to do. I knew my place in this battle. My role was to support Feng Wu and the others and to protect the villagers. But I also knew that I had to be careful. My eagerness to help had nearly cost me my life just moments ago.

Swallowing my pride, I nodded stiffly. Xu Ziqing huffed, turning his attention back to the darkness beyond. I tightened my grip on my staff, my senses heightened. Every rustle of leaves, every flutter of a bird's wings in the distant trees made me jumpy. I wanted to be useful, not just stand there waiting for something to happen.

The village was deathly quiet, every rustle, every creak seeming unnaturally loud. I stood, feeling helpless and frustrated but determined to do what I could. I might not be as powerful as the others, but I wasn't going to stand idle.

Then, from the direction of the old mill, we heard a faint rustling. It was a sound that could have easily been dismissed as the wind or a small animal. But we all knew better. It was them.

Feng Wu and Xu Ziqing seemed to have a silent communication of their own. With a curt nod, they sprang into action. Feng Wu's body glowed slightly as he took one side of the building. Xu Ziqing raised his blade and stood extremely still, before bursting into movement and slicing a deep gouge into the wall.

And then there it was—a deafening hiss, a dark, monstrous shape erupting from the confines of the old mill. The Wind Serpent was visibly disoriented, missing an eye. Its scales glistened eerily in the sporadic moonlight as it writhed in the air. Feng Wu seized the opportunity and charged forward, delivering lightning-fast strikes across its scales.

The second one struck at our group in that moment, forcing the third-class disciples backward as they fended off an errant tail whip that elicited a gust of wind.

Tianyi remained on my shoulder, her small body pulsating with a steady stream of qi, her eyes following the chaos unfolding before us. As I soaked in the healing energy, I couldn't help but agonize over my lack of ability to contribute. I was a burden in this situation, and the Silent Moon Sect would likely be more than happy to see me interfere and get killed so long as I didn't impede them.

How could I help them? How could I—?

An epiphany struck me at that moment. I looked to the stables where the horses were, past the hole my body had made, to the very end of the building where my cart sat. Potions.

My martial ability might not have been up to par, but that didn't mean I had to be useless.

As the battle raged in the middle of Qingmu Village, I began moving toward the stables with fiery determination.

CHAPTER THIRTY-THREE

Medicinal Might

I ran into the stables, rushing through the broken-down doors and past my skittish horses, looking half-ready to bolt. If it weren't for the absurdly tough bamboo doors holding them, it was likely they would've escaped and never looked back. Elder Wen wouldn't have been happy with that.

At the corner where my carriage lay, I hurriedly ran through the crates. My body moved faster than my head, sifting through the boxes and bags before I finally came upon the one I was looking for. It was a nondescript crate, but once opened, it was filled to the brim with slightly glowing vials of potions.

Then the sound of sniffling caught my attention.

In the dim light seeping through the slatted woodwork, my eyes adjusted to the dim stable interior, the sniffling growing louder. Pushed against a mound of hay and attempting to squeeze himself into the narrowest space between the wall and a hay bale was the innkeeper's son.

His eyes were overshadowed by fear, casting wary glances at the stable's cracked wooden door. His small body trembled each time a thunderous roar resonated from outside, a testament to the fierce battle between the cultivators and the Wind Serpents. He clutched a broken broom handle, his knuckles pale and strained from the tight grip.

Slowly, I closed the distance between us. "Hey, it's just me," I reassured him, keeping my tone low and soothing. At the sound of my voice, the boy's terrified gaze fixed onto me. It was almost as if he was seeing a ghost, or perhaps a man who'd been tossed around like a rag doll by a Wind Serpent not too long ago.

I held up my hands in a nonthreatening manner, hoping to ease his fear. "I need you to come with me. It's safer . . ." I trailed off as another monstrous roar shook the wooden walls of the stable.

The boy looked at me, his lip trembling. "But the . . . the monsters," he stammered, the words barely a whisper.

I couldn't blame him. The reality of our predicament was terrifying, even for me. But there was no choice. We needed to move to a safer place. His fear was real, as real as the colossal serpents wreaking havoc outside. However, I couldn't afford to let it paralyze him.

I let out a nervous chuckle, attempting to bring a little levity to the situation. "Those aren't monsters. They're . . . oversize reptiles!"

He blinked at me, a hint of incredulity washing over his fear-stricken face. It was enough to coax a smile from me.

"And do you know what the best part is?" I continued, my voice a soft murmur against the chaos outside. "Oversize reptiles are actually scared of humans. Little known fact."

"But . . . but I saw one fling you," the boy managed, a shaky finger pointing at me.

"Ah, well, you see . . ." I paused, feigning thoughtfulness. "That was . . . a game we cultivators like to play. 'Toss the Human.' Thrilling, isn't it?"

The boy stared at me, his expression wavering between disbelief and desperate hope. After what felt like an eternity, a faint giggle bubbled from his lips. "You're funny."

I extended my hand to him, a silent pledge. "Then let's make a run for it. Trust me, okay?"

Slowly, he untangled himself from his hiding place, his small hand slipping into mine. A gust of wind rattled the stable doors, the ongoing battle reminding us of the perils outside. We snuck back out, making sure to stay away from the thick of the battlefield. He refused to look in that direction, clinging to my hand as hard as he could. My other hand had an iron grip on my staff as I periodically checked over my shoulder to confirm none of the Wind Serpents locked onto us.

The battle was seemingly at a stalemate, but I knew it couldn't go on. Feng Wu and Xu Ziqing were faring better in their battle against the half-blind Wind Serpent, but the third-class disciples were being steadily worn down by the snake's evasive maneuvers and lightning-fast strikes. Death by a thousand cuts. They wouldn't last long against the Wind Serpent like this.

"Go back and stay with your family, all right? Don't go out until we say so."

The boy nodded. He thanked me quietly before scampering off into the inn we were staying at, far away from the dangers of battle. I turned on my heel and immediately ran back to the stables.

An impossibly loud noise occurred as scale met flesh, and I could see someone being flung into the building where my carriage resided. Wood splintered under the force, sending the person sprawling deep into the stable. I rushed forward and called out in concern.

"Hey! Are you all right?"

From the rubble, Xu Ziqing rose. His head was bleeding, but he looked more angry than hurt. Spitting blood from his mouth in a lackadaisical fashion, he turned his sharp eyes toward me but didn't say anything. His eyes gravitated toward the battle Feng Wu fought as he circled around the serpent.

"Oi! Azure Moon Marauder!" I rummaged through my pack, finding the bottle I needed. I threw it at him and he caught it with ease. A golden-yellow-and-orange liquid swirled around in the vial. "Drink! It'll recover your stamina."

He stared at me for a brief moment, opening the Invigorating Dawn Tonic and smelling it as if to confirm the item wasn't poisonous. How rude! If I truly wanted to, I could have him on the floor within seconds. Xu Ziqing drank after a moment's hesitation.

His initial reaction to the tonic wasn't immediately obvious. He continued to hold the vial to his lips, the liquid going down his throat in slow, purposeful gulps. Then a change swept over his countenance, subtle yet noticeable. His eyebrows knitted closer together, the tiny creases on his forehead smoothed, the sharpness in his gaze tempered into something less fierce.

It was as if a breath of spring had swept through his worn-out body, melting away the winter's ice. There was a slight rosiness to his pale cheeks now, and I could see his breathing gradually return to its regular pace. His shoulders, previously slumped from fatigue, seemed to rise as if a heavy weight had been lifted from them.

As he finished the last of the tonic, Xu Ziqing swirled the vial around, his eyes fixated on the final drops that clung to the glass. It was a curious look, the type of expression one had when they couldn't quite believe what they'd just experienced. A slight smirk pulled at the corners of his lips, but it faded as quickly as it had appeared.

He stood straighter, a renewed vitality radiating from him. The fatigue had washed away, replaced by an underlying strength that wasn't there before. It wasn't a miraculous transformation, but it was noticeable enough to make a difference in the upcoming fight.

Xu Ziqing looked at me, his icy eyes softening for a fleeting second. A nod, the tiniest dip of his head, was the only acknowledgment he gave me. He didn't say anything, but the look in his eyes spoke volumes. It was a look that acknowledged me, a look that no longer dismissed me as a mere alchemist in the middle of a cultivators' world.

I'll show them. I'm a cultivator, through and through.

Without another word, Xu Ziqing turned around, heading back toward the battle. The moonlight filtered through the debris of the destroyed stable. It made his silhouette seem larger, sturdier, a stark contrast to the wounded man who'd been flung into the building just moments ago.

As Xu Ziqing returned to the battlefield with a new vigor, I pivoted and made my way back into the rubble of the stables, my eyes scanning the rubble for the familiar glint of my potion vials. My staff was set aside for the moment; its familiar weight and balance replaced by the delicate coolness of glass and the promise of aid it held.

The Invigorating Dawn Tonic, with its soft glow of orange and gold, was easy to find. I gathered as many vials as I could hold. Alongside them, I gathered the Goji Clarity Potion, its deep red liquid swirling ominously, but the energy within held the promise of a sharpened mind.

They were meant to be for my shipment to the Azure Silk Trading Company, but no amount of gold would make me put others at risk.

Armed with my makeshift arsenal, I turned my gaze back to the battlefield. The scene was grim. The fight had split into two distinct factions with the serpents separated from each other. However, the twelve third-class disciples of the Silent Moon Sect were not faring well against their adversary. Their attempts to control and damage the Wind Serpent were failing, their movements becoming sluggish, and their coordination dwindling.

I approached them as quickly as I could, the clinking vials in my hands a lifeline I was desperate to throw. As I neared them, I held up a vial of the Invigorating Dawn Tonic and shouted over the chaos, "Take this! It will renew your strength!"

The desperation in their eyes reflected the dire state of the situation. One of them, a burly man whose robes were soaked with sweat and grime, snatched the vial from me without a word. He downed the liquid in one gulp, his eyes never leaving the Wind Serpent in front of him.

As the tonic took effect, I could see the change in him. His sagging shoulders straightened, the tiredness in his eyes replaced with a new spark, his movements became more fluid. The other disciples watched this transformation with wide eyes, their initial skepticism replaced with hope.

Knowing I couldn't afford to waste the remaining vials, I quickly assessed the other disciples. Relying on my knowledge of medicine and human physiology, I looked for signs of fatigue, injury, and stress. I singled out the ones who were most in need—the ones whose breathing was erratic, whose movements were stiff, and whose eyes held the glaze of exhaustion.

I passed them the Invigorating Dawn Tonic first. As they consumed it and their vitality visibly improved, I turned my attention to the Goji Clarity Potion. My experience with combat strategy told me that those in strategic roles or those whose abilities required precise control would benefit the most from increased focus. Selectively, I handed out the red elixir.

Their initial hesitation turned to gratitude as the effects of the potions kicked in. Rejuvenated and refocused, they readjusted their formation, making sure their newly regained strength was utilized effectively.

"Feng Wu!" I cried out, calling to the second-class disciple as he back stepped away from the Wind Serpent's attacks. His robe was torn in several places, and he looked determined as he held the bladed fan in his hand. His eyes turned for a fraction of a second to see the red potion sail through the air. It didn't take long for him to dash forward and catch it.

Opening the vial in one smooth motion and consuming it, he then stepped backward and parried powerful gusts of wind generated by the Spirit Beast. Xu Ziqing took its attention with a powerful blow to its tail, leaving a deep gouge and destroying several scales in the process.

Feng Wu dropped the vial onto the floor and moved forward, pressuring the Wind Serpent even more as it fought against the two renewed second-class disciples.

As the battle raged on, the effects of my potions became increasingly evident. The tide seemed to be turning in our favor. Where once stood tired and battered cultivators, now stood rejuvenated warriors. Their movements were quicker, more precise; their eyes held a renewed determination, their attacks coordinated and relentless. They moved as a unit, each member in tune with the other. The battle-field was filled with an unyielding spirit, and even the raging Wind Serpents were not immune to this shift.

Xu Ziqing and Feng Wu pressed on, their every strike a testament to the power of my potions. The Invigorating Dawn Tonic and Goji Clarity Potion worked won-ders in their bodies, boosting their physical stamina and enhancing their mental acuity respectively. Their attacks were relentless, pushing back the tiring Wind Serpent with every stroke.

Yet the Wind Serpents were not going down without a fight. They roared and hissed, their bodies coiling and uncoiling as they moved to strike at their tormen-tors. But even I could see that their movements were growing sluggish, their attacks less fierce. The strain of the prolonged battle was beginning to wear on them.

A flicker of hope bubbled up within me. Could we really turn this around? Could we drive these monstrosities away?

But we weren't there yet, and I knew better than to let my guard down. My gaze drifted back to my remaining supply of potions. There weren't many left, but if I allocated them properly, it might just be enough to see us through.

I analyzed the battlefield once more. There was still work to be done, and it was time for the second round of my potions. I'd need to—

"LOOK OUT!"

The warning cry, drenched in urgency, echoed through the din of the battle-field. But it was a fraction of a second too late. Before I could turn, an immense force blindsided me, catching me completely unprepared. It felt like being struck by a charging ox, and the impact lifted me off my feet.

The world spun as I was sent hurtling through the air, the violent expulsion tearing the breath from my lungs. The agony that exploded along my side was so intense, it bordered on numbing. I had no sense of direction, no control over my trajectory. I was acutely aware of a series of sharp cracks resounding within me— my ribs. Without the reinforcement from the Rooted Banyan Stance, I took on the full brunt of the Wind Serpent's attack.

My flight ended with an abrupt, jarring impact against a solid wall, the force strong enough to leave an imprint of my body in the weathered wood of the inn's exterior. The blow stole any remaining breath I had, and bright spots danced in my vision as pain erupted anew, sharper and more insistent than before.

I slumped to the ground, disoriented and gasping for breath. My hands moved instinctively to clutch my side, fingers probing tenderly around the epicenter of my pain. Even the slightest pressure elicited a wave of agony so intense it had me doubling over, a strangled gasp tearing from my throat.

Through the haze of pain, I heard the familiar hiss of the Wind Serpent, the ground trembling beneath its power. A collective shout went up from the disciples, the urgency in their voices echoing the pounding of my heart.

They were too far, too embroiled in their own battles to reach me in time. I was a sitting duck, and the serpent was closing in.

Would this be my final moment?

Ah, damn it all. Just when things were starting looking up for me . . .

Just as the inevitability of my fate began to settle in, two figures appeared in my blurred vision, their approach hurried and frantic. The innkeeper and his son, the same boy who I had saved minutes earlier, came charging at me.

Rough but gentle hands gripped my shoulders, pulling me back and away from the approaching danger. My vision swam as my body protested the sudden movement, but the urgency in their actions offered no room for reprieve.

As they dragged me to safety, I could hear the disciples engaging the Wind Serpent, their shouts and the clashing of their weapons a stark contrast to the pounding in my ears. Each breath was an uphill battle, a laborious task that did nothing to quell the fire burning in my side.

This was primal, a sort of pain that transcended the physical and seeped into the very marrow of my being. This was the kind of pain that could shatter one's spirit, and for a moment, I feared it might have done just that.

The world around me was a chaos of sounds and blurry sights. Shouts echoed in my ears, sometimes drowned by the roar of the Wind Serpents. The clash of metal against scales provided an uneven rhythm, the intensity of the fight ebbing and flowing. I was on the sidelines now, a mere observer watching the shadowy figures as they danced their deadly dance.

Hands worked on my battered body, but the sensations felt distant, muffled by the all-consuming agony. The innkeeper was trying his best, his brows furrowed in deep concentration. He was no healer, no cultivator, yet the urgency of the situation had thrust upon him the mantle of a caretaker.

His son held my hand, his grip tight. Fear was evident in his eyes, but there was determination there too. I could only offer him a weak smile, my throat too raw to form words of reassurance.

The world spun around me in a haze, reality and delusion blending seamlessly as my pain-addled mind struggled to hold onto consciousness. Shapes shifted and colors bled into one another, creating a surreal landscape that was both strange and eerily familiar.

It was then that my gaze landed on a splash of white decorating the interior of the inn: a small azalea.

I blinked, unsure if it was a hallucination or reality. But the flower remained, unyielding and radiant. A memory surfaced, slow and sweet like honey, dragging me back to a time far removed from the present calamity.

The white azaleas . . . we used to grow them in our home. Their vibrant blooms were a constant presence in our gardens, a sight that brought joy to my mother's eyes. But then, one day, they were gone.

I remember asking my father about it. He had looked at me, a twinkle in his eyes and a smile on his lips. I had eaten a few of the flowers, curious about their taste, and had ended up sick in bed for days. The azaleas were no longer welcome in our garden.

Azaleas . . . their sweet-smelling flowers, a source of medicinal components like anesthetics and sedatives and yet, if ingested raw, a poison.

In the fog of my mind, a spark of an idea emerged. It was faint and distant, but it held a potential that had me latching onto it like a lifeline. The azaleas, they could be the answer, the tool we needed to shift the balance in our favor.

CHAPTER THIRTY-FOUR

Unleashing the Azalea

To focus my thoughts, I closed my eyes and entered my Memory Palace. A visualization of my mindscape, a beautiful garden filled with vivid and thriving plants. The memory trees had grown larger since I last saw them. I brought myself closer to the largest memory tree in my garden, the one where I placed all my knowledge of plants.

Responding to my desires, the tree's gigantic branches unfurled toward me, as though extending a gentle hand. I placed my hand and sifted through the massive archive I had stored within my mind.

Camellia, daffodil, iris, lily . . . azalea! There it is!

Snow-white flowers and a delicate fragrance . . . contain grayanotoxins, natural toxins that can have harmful effects on organisms in significant amounts. These grayanotoxins are primarily found in the leaves, flowers, and nectar of the plant . . .

In significant amounts? It took a few to take me out of commission as a child. How much would I need to hurt a giant snake? There are several azaleas in the vase, but would it be enough? Do Spirit Beasts have a resistance to poison?

As I pondered over my dilemma, a wave of pain crashed through my mindscape and destabilized it temporarily, shaking the entire Memory Palace. I cursed and fell to the grass, fighting the urge to vomit. How could I vomit? I wasn't not even corporeal here!

There were no other compatible ingredients in my cart to make a stronger poison. All the other essences . . .

That's it!

Essence Extraction—You can extract the spiritual essence of plants for the creation of pills and elixirs.

If I used my skill, it would allow access to the purest form of the plant's essence, enhancing its natural properties. And if it did the same to the toxin within the azalea . . .

I opened my eyes, leaving my Memory Palace to look at the innkeeper tending to my wounds. I tried to speak, but a sharp pain in my chest caused me to let out a pitiful wheeze.

"Don't talk! It'll make your wounds worse," he said. A woman, who I assumed was his wife, approached from behind him, carrying more gauze. I raised my arm, using up all my strength to point at the white azalea. My finger trembled slightly as I did so.

The innkeeper glanced behind him, confusion etching lines onto his weather-beaten face. "What? What is it?" he asked, misunderstanding my silent plea. His gaze flitted between me and the direction I was pointing in.

I tried to speak again, to articulate what I needed, but my voice was a husky, breathless whisper, drowned out by the thunderous cacophony of the ongoing battle. My arm was growing heavier, the effort to keep it raised taxing my already-weakened body.

The innkeeper's wife stepped forward, her eyes wide with concern. She gently lowered my arm, her touch soft and soothing. "You need to rest," she said, shaking her head.

Rest. If only I could. But the battlefield was right outside, and I had a role to play.

The sound of small, scuffling feet echoed from the doorway, and a familiar face peeked in—the innkeeper's son. His eyes, once filled with terror, now held a hint of curiosity. He looked between his parents and me, catching sight of my pointed direction.

His gaze landed on the vase of azaleas. His brows knitted together, and then, like the first light of dawn, understanding flickered in his eyes. The child moved toward the azaleas, his small hands carefully lifting the vase.

"Dad, I think he wants this," he said, offering the vase to his father. His tone held a certain finality, a simple confidence that children often possess.

The innkeeper looked from his son to me, his confusion gradually melting away as he took the vase from his son's hands. "The azaleas? Do you want the azaleas?"

A nod was all I could manage. He looked uncertain, but as he handed me the vase filled with white azaleas, I couldn't help but feel a glimmer of hope. These flowers could very well be the key to our survival. Now it was up to me to unlock that potential.

Ever-present pain pulsed through my veins as I turned my attention to the white azaleas in the vase. The innkeeper's family watched me curiously from the corner, but I paid them no mind. It was time to test my extraction skill once more, this time on a plant much more complex than the humble mint.

Closing my eyes, I spread my hands above the white azaleas, letting them hover just an inch above the petals. I reached out with my senses, probing the flowers gently, seeking that singular point of extraction. The process was akin to searching for a tiny needle in a massive haystack, but my fingers tingled when I finally found it.

As if answering my silent call, a slender tendril of energy seeped out of the azaleas. It was a brilliant white, tinged with an ethereal blue hue, much like the azaleas themselves. It felt more volatile, more potent than the essence I had extracted from the mint.

The essence, despite its volatile nature, gradually formed a small, glowing orb above my palm. I realized, too late, that I had no vial, no receptacle to store the essence. With my right hand preoccupied with maintaining the extraction, I glanced around, searching desperately for something suitable.

Seeing my predicament, the innkeeper's son, perhaps hearing my silent plea, rushed to fetch a glass vial from a nearby shelf. With careful, quick steps, he brought it over and held it beneath the floating essence.

Releasing my hold on the essence, I watched it flow smoothly into the vial. It swirled around, a milky, white liquid in a confined space. Once the essence had settled, the boy swiftly corked it. His eyes were wide, filled with awe and a touch of fear at the mysterious procedure he'd just aided.

As I turned my attention back to the azaleas, I saw the immediate change. The once-vibrant petals had lost their luster, the leaves drooping listlessly, and the plant itself appeared drained, a ghostly image of its former glory. It was as if the very life had been pulled from it. I brought it closer to my face and took a whiff. There was still a faint scent, the unique, sweet aroma of azaleas, but it was greatly diminished, like a forgotten echo of its original fragrance.

"Feng . . . Wu . . ."

The boy leaned closer to hear what I was trying to say. Every word took a significant amount of energy. Was I going to die?

I don't think so, but I was hurt pretty badly. There might've been some permanent damage done to my body from all this. But I wouldn't rest until I delivered the vial to its intended target. How could I get this to the others? I could barely even speak as it was. As the family looked me over in concern, I saw a small blip of light from the door.

Fluttering wings descended onto my nose. Tianyi had found her way into the inn, sending waves of emotions with our telepathic bond—sadness, guilt, and shame.

A butterfly worrying about me. What has my life come to?

I tried to send her reassurance to confirm that I'd be all right, but it didn't seem to ease her tense and frightful body. A glow that threatened to blind me if I didn't close my eyes erupted from her.

The subtle floral aroma invaded my nose, eliciting a sigh of relief as my pain eased. I knew the damage done to my body was still immense. My cracked ribs had not magically healed. Tianyi's healing ability catered more to pain relief and illnesses, and the actual repairs to my body were minimal, but it helped regardless.

The blue aura around her had disappeared. She looked almost like a regular, mundane butterfly now. Tianyi had given me all the energy packed within her tiny body, trying her best to soothe my pain. Even when her qi was completely gone, I could feel the small attempts she made to try to squeeze out every last bit.

I slowly set her down, attempting to calm my shaking hand. Tianyi tried to stick herself onto me, but I gently coaxed her into the boy's palm and stood up.

"Mister . . . ! Your wounds are—"

"There's no time," I interrupted. I clenched my fist, looking down at the vial in my hand. It was a risky gamble, one that could end in my death. But if I didn't do it, the others would surely fall to the Wind Serpents. "Please take care of her."

Gritting my teeth at the stabbing pain in my side, I pushed open the door and stepped out into the conflict. The scene that unfolded before my eyes was a mix of devastation and resilience. Buildings bore deep gouges, and the cobblestone roads were pockmarked from the Wind Serpents' assaults. The air was electric with tension, the Wind Serpents hissing across the clearing.

From my location, I had a clear view of the skirmish. Feng Wu and Xu Ziqing were locked in a fierce battle with one of the Wind Serpents, while the twelve third-class disciples from the Verdant Lotus and Silent Moon Sects struggled against the other one.

Feng Wu, with his bladed fan dancing in his hand, was a picture of graceful fury. His movements were smooth and precise, each strike of his fan a brush making a wave of sparks as it clashed against the serpent's scales. Xu Ziqing, on the other hand, was a tempest, his sword whirling around him in a shimmering arc. His personality notwithstanding, he was a skilled fighter. They were clearly holding their own against the Wind Serpent, their opponent already missing an eye.

However, the same couldn't be said about the third-class disciples. They were putting up a brave fight, their weapons flashing in the fading light, but they were on the defensive. They were holding their own, yes, but barely. The Wind Serpent they faced was relentless, its tail whipping out again and again, constantly keeping them on their toes. The winds buffeting them tossed the formation off-balance and revealed vulnerabilities that the snake exploited with ruthless efficiency. It was clear that they wouldn't be able to last much longer.

"Almost there," I murmured, cradling the vial in my hand. It was warm, its contents pulsating with energy. If I could get it to Feng Wu and Xu Ziqing in time, they could finish off the Wind Serpent they were fighting, and the tide of battle could be turned.

I began picking my way through the chaotic streets, dodging fleeing townsfolk and fallen debris. The essence in the vial seemed to thrum in time with my heartbeat, filling me with a sense of purpose. I wasn't strong like Feng Wu or Xu Ziqing, but I wasn't helpless either.

The battlefield grew closer with each agonizing step. The Wind Serpents were massive, terrifying, and far more powerful than any of us. But they weren't unbeatable. The one Feng Wu and Xu Ziqing were fighting was already injured, its movements noticeably less fluid than before.

With renewed determination, I continued on, keeping my eyes fixed on Feng Wu. His verdant fan was a blur, meeting each of the Wind Serpent's attacks with a counterstrike of his own. He was tiring, that much was evident, but he wasn't beaten yet. He was still fighting, still standing. And as long as he was standing, there was hope.

"Just hold on, Feng Wu," I muttered, steeling myself against the pain that coursed through my body. "I'm coming."

With the vial in hand, I pressed on, driven by the urgency of the situation and the unshakable belief that we would prevail. We had to. For the town, for the people, and for ourselves. We just needed a little more time, a little more strength. And I was bringing exactly that.

The sharp tang of ozone filled the air as I finally made it to the edge of the battlefield. The pressure was thick around us, a physical weight pressing against my chest, making it harder to breathe. I staggered forward, my vision swaying as I fought against the agony racking my body.

"Feng Wu!" I called out, my voice barely more than a hoarse whisper. The ongoing clash between the disciples and the Wind Serpents was drowning out any other sound. I took a shallow breath, gathering my strength before again bellowing, "Feng Wu!"

At my second cry, Feng Wu's head whipped around, his eyes meeting mine across the chaotic battlefield. The look on his face was a mixture of surprise and relief, but mostly determination. He nodded, the corners of his lips pulling into a tight line.

As he broke away from the ongoing skirmish to approach me, the Wind Serpent capitalized on the opportunity. With a deafening roar, it reared back before unleashing a gust of wind powerful enough to send debris flying.

Xu Ziqing sprang into action, stepping in front of Feng Wu to deflect the brunt of the serpent's attack. His sword shimmered, a tangible force field that stalled the wind's advance, buying Feng Wu a few crucial seconds.

We met halfway, his breath ragged and his gaze focused. I extended my hand, the vial held tightly within. The pure, white essence within pulsed as if in response to our desperate situation. I saw his eyes dart to it, a hint of confusion marring his features.

"What's this?" he asked, his voice strained.

"An edge," I replied. "Throw this into the serpent's mouth."

His brows furrowed in confusion, but he didn't question me further. He took the vial from my hand, his grip firm, his fingers smudged with dirt and sweat. His trust in me, despite not fully understanding the situation, sparked a sense of pride and guilt within me: pride in having earned his trust and guilt over the dangerous gamble I had proposed.

With a sharp nod, Feng Wu turned back to the Wind Serpent. His posture was coiled like a spring, his fan clenched tightly in one hand and the vial in the other. He took a deep breath, his body visibly relaxing before he burst into a sprint, darting across the battlefield.

His movements were fluid, a stark contrast to the chaos around him. He danced through the battlefield, his fan providing him cover, while Xu Ziqing continued to keep the Wind Serpent occupied. It was as though time slowed, every detail starkly etched in my mind.

Feng Wu was close now, the Wind Serpent towering over him. With a final burst of speed, he leaped, his form silhouetted against the dusk light. The Wind Serpent roared, its mouth opening wide in an attempt to swallow him whole.

This was it.

Feng Wu's arm drew back before he threw the vial into the gaping maw of the Wind Serpent. It was a split second, an exchange of glances between prey and predator, before he twisted away from the Wind Serpent's jaw snapping shut. The vial disappeared into the abyss, swallowed by the monstrous beast.

The world seemed to fall silent then, the battlefield pausing as though in anticipation. Holding my breath, I watched as Feng Wu landed nimbly on the ground, the Wind Serpent's roars echoing ominously around us.

The serpent's head swung erratically as if it was dazed, its mighty body swaying like a tree in a storm. Its movements became uncoordinated, its tail lashing out aimlessly, its eyes glazed and unfocused.

Feng Wu and Xu Ziqing looked at each other before lunging in again, their weapons clashing against the serpent's scales with renewed vigor. The monster's movements, though still powerful, were sluggish and uncoordinated.

It was like a dream, the once-monstrous and terrifying Wind Serpent now reduced to a state of bewilderment. I felt a wave of relief wash over me, watching as Feng Wu and Xu Ziqing gradually gained the upper hand.

"Yes . . ." I muttered to myself, my voice barely audible over the roars and clanging of metal. I sagged against a nearby rock, my body wracked with tremors. "It worked."

As the poison seeped through the Wind Serpent's system, the disciples found an opening they could exploit. Every attack, every move they made seemed to strike true, causing the Wind Serpent to bellow in pain and confusion. Victory was within their grasp.

But as I watched, the edges of my vision began to blur. A wave of dizziness washed over me, my knees buckling beneath me. I could barely register the shouts from the battlefield or the frantic calls of my name as I crumpled to the ground. I could've sworn I saw the familiar blue of the Heavenly Interface messaging me, but the line between reality and hallucination was beginning to blur.

As the darkness claimed me, I couldn't help but wonder . . . what would I wake up to? If I even woke up at all.

Dear Interface, if you could reward me with a timely skill that saves my life, it would greatly be appreciated right now.

And then I knew nothing more.

CHAPTER THIRTY-FIVE

To the Victor Go the Spoils

The final Wind Serpent let out a dying hiss, its life cut short by Xu Ziqing's blade piercing through the roof of its mouth.

Despite their triumph, none of them could gather the energy to celebrate. Each of the third-class disciples of the Silent Moon Sect bore serious injuries, some falling to their knees after confirming the battle was over.

Xu Ziqing wiped at the side of his forehead as blood dripped down onto his robes. Small cuts and holes peppered his uniform, courtesy of the sharp winds that the Spirit Beasts buffeted them with. Even Feng Wu didn't come out unscathed, cradling his arm and wincing slightly with every move he made.

But they were alive.

". . . No casualties," Xu Ziqing muttered. His expression was in a state of suspended disbelief.

Feng Wu looked around. Several broken vials, containing what was once a valuable product meant for the Azure Silk Trading Company, littered the floor.

Would we have even won without him?

The question plagued Feng Wu's mind as he ran over to where Kai was. The boy, who was roughly the same age as the third-class disciples working under Xu Ziqing, was on the floor. For a brief moment the Verdant Lotus disciple feared he was dead but inwardly breathed a sigh of relief as his chest slowly rose and fell.

"We need some potions over here! You, go and . . ."

The Azure Moon Marauder barked orders at the group, forcing those who were able to move and distribute supplies and potions to those who were injured. His eyes drifted over to Feng Wu and the person he lay beside.

". . . give it to them as well."

Xu Ziqing huffed before noticing the Qingmu Village residents peeking out of their windows as the noises of battle faded.

With a last reserve of energy, he straightened his stance and faced the anxious villagers who had observed the perilous battle from a distance. Their eyes glimmered with hope and fear and even a sliver of awe for the group of warriors who had survived the brutal onslaught of the Wind Serpents.

"We have emerged victorious," Xu Ziqing declared, his voice weary but resonant. He raised his battered blade high, tainted by the essence of the slain Wind Serpents, a symbol of their triumph. "The Wind Serpents have been vanquished."

"But our task isn't over," he continued. He signaled the other disciples, who, despite their injuries, were slowly regaining their bearings.

Despite their exhaustion, the disciples of the Silent Moon Sect staggered toward the defeated creatures, ready to complete their grueling mission. The village folk watched, their expressions an odd mix of curiosity and repulsion as the warriors began their grim task.

"Praise the Silent Moon Sect!"

"The Verdant Lotus Sect as well! It was a joint effort to take down such terrible creatures!"

Whispers and praise spread through the crowd. The innkeeper and his son began spreading tales of the battle, pointing to the unconscious boy who had protected them.

"The boy in red! H-he saved me from the snake when it cornered me in the stable," the boy said, his eyes gleaming with gratitude. "He's the one who made it possible for them to win!"

Xu Ziqing gritted his teeth.

Fools. This village would've been destroyed without our presence. And they focus on that brat?

He glanced over at Feng Wu and the unconscious Kai. Despite the acrimony and resentment simmering beneath the surface, a grudging acknowledgment of their contribution hung heavy in the air. Still, the glory of the victory and its spoils belonged to the Silent Moon Sect. They accomplished their mission.

Amid the aftermath of their victory, Feng Wu cleared his throat, his voice cutting through the exhaustion that hung heavily in the air. "Brother Xu," he began diplomatically, "I believe we should discuss the distribution of the spoils."

Xu Ziqing's eyebrows knitted together. "Spoils? The bounty from the Wind Serpents is for the Silent Moon Sect."

"Indeed," Feng Wu agreed, casting a glance at the unconscious Kai. "But it seems you were not the only ones who took part in this mission." His eyes were filled with subtle meaning.

Xu Ziqing followed Feng Wu's gaze to the boy. The red garments Kai wore made him starkly stand out against the backdrop of chaos. His eyes narrowed, remembering the surprising strength that the young boy had displayed. He hadn't considered the possibility of the boy being a contributor to their subjugation. His own misunderstanding paired with Kai's gravely injured state could easily be mistaken for a heroic sacrifice, an interpretation that the crowd seemed to be accepting eagerly.

"The boy in red . . . He fought so bravely. He protected us all!" The innkeeper's son continued his tale to the crowd. The villagers nodded in agreement, their eyes filled with awe and admiration for the unconscious boy. Xu Ziqing felt a bitter taste crawl up his throat.

Realizing the unspoken challenge in Feng Wu's gaze, Xu Ziqing clenched his jaw. The Silent Moon Sect's reputation was on the line. Should they claim all the spoils, they'd risk seeming greedy, especially in the light of Kai's significant contribution.

"Very well," he finally conceded, the words leaving a sour taste in his mouth. "The spoils will be distributed fairly among the contributing parties. We will not ignore the assistance we've received."

A flicker of satisfaction passed over Feng Wu's face, but he merely inclined his head in a respectful nod. "A commendable decision. Fairness in victory honors the Silent Moon Sect greatly."

There were two Wind Serpent cores among the spoils. The Silent Moon Sect ultimately ceded one of the precious cores to them, along with a smaller portion of the scales and fangs. Though their share was smaller, securing one of the cores was a victory in itself.

A small, crystalline object, about half the size of his fist. It had a swirling pattern within it, reminiscent of gusting winds or coiling serpents, a reflection of the beast's nature or powers.

Feng Wu sighed.

The products originally meant for Kai's contract with the Azure Silk Trading Company were lost, but in their place, they'd gained something arguably more valuable.

A sense of awe filled Feng Wu as he held up a radiant core, pulsating with energy. It was well known that such a core held immense power, capable of catapulting a cultivator's skills and strength. Feng Wu could almost see the path it could carve out for him—a smoother journey through his cultivation, a jump in his standing within the Verdant Lotus Sect, respect from his peers . . .

But as he looked at the injured boy lying there, guilt gnawed at his conscience. Kai, despite not belonging to any sect, had fought as bravely, if not more, than any of them. His grave injuries were a testament to his contribution. Feng Wu found himself torn between the temptation of keeping the core and listening to his moral compass, which firmly pointed at giving it to Kai.

He looked back at the core in his hand, its glow reflecting in his eyes. It felt like a heavy stone, a test of his character. He remembered his sect's teachings about righteousness, about virtue being its own reward.

Sighing, Feng Wu made his decision. Holding the core carefully, he walked over Kai. He couldn't ignore the fact that the boy was the one truly deserving of this core, and he knew its healing properties could help his recovery.

As he placed the core into Kai's pocket, a sense of peace washed over him. He knew he had made the right choice. His own journey in cultivation could wait—for now, it was more important to uphold justice and honor. This victory, hard-earned as it was, wouldn't have been possible without Kai's contribution.

As Feng Wu watched Kai in quiet contemplation, he couldn't help but equate the boy's potential to the force of nature itself—quiet and subtle yet all-encompassing and undeniable. Just like the silent progression of seasons, Kai's growth seemed almost imperceptible in the day-to-day, but when viewed over months, it was nothing short of a grand transformation.

The Kai he'd initially met was barely above average—a small sapling struggling for survival amid towering trees. But the Kai who now lay unconscious before him was no longer that fragile sapling. He was a young tree that had weathered several storms and, with each one that passed, had grown sturdier and stronger.

His potential . . . It's like a river, Feng Wu mused, lost in his thoughts.

Even when compared to the third-class disciples of the Silent Moon Sect, Kai's rapid development was an anomaly. His ability to weather multiple attacks from a Spirit Beast and emerge alive—although gravely injured—suggested a capacity for growth that belied his apparent fragility.

Feng Wu was part of the Verdant Lotus Sect, renowned for its alchemy. They saw value in Kai's potential as an alchemist, but Feng Wu couldn't help but think that perhaps Kai's true potential lay elsewhere. His talent as a martial artist was unfolding each day, like a lotus blooming beneath the morning sun.

Could his growth as a martial artist even surpass his potential as an alchemist? The question lingered in Feng Wu's mind. He couldn't help but feel an exhilarating anticipation at the prospect of witnessing Kai's journey. There was an untamed energy within the boy, a raw power that hinted at a future filled with extraordinary accomplishments. His path as a cultivator was still a vast and unexplored territory, and Feng Wu found himself eager to see how far this path would go.

Feng Wu's sharp eyes caught the presence of another: Tianyi, the boy's loyal companion. An Azure Moonlight Flutter. She seemed to almost acknowledge the cultivator's presence, before making a beeline to where Kai was and resting on the tip of his nose.

The butterfly seemed like a shell of her former self, lacking the luster and glitter she always had. But despite it all, she continued to cycle qi through herself and into Kai. His expression seemed to soften as Tianyi pulled energy from their surroundings.

It was an ability he had never seen or heard of. Feng Wu couldn't help but admire Tianyi. Finding such a butterfly was a sign of good fortune, but to have one willingly stay by your side? Perhaps . . .

He shook his head.

I'm getting too ahead of myself.

Feng Wu examined his own injuries, assessing what healing could be done as he rested. His training as a cultivator had honed his ability to recover and continue fighting, even in the direst of circumstances. His thoughts, however, were interrupted by a soft knock on the door.

The innkeeper's son appeared, his face flushed with a mix of awe and nervousness. His eyes were drawn to the unconscious Kai on the floor before drifting to Feng Wu. "Do you need anything else?" he asked with a timid voice, a subtle shiver passing through him.

Despite the fatigue weighing him down, Feng Wu found the energy to smile at the young boy. "Some additional medical supplies would be appreciated. And clean water, if possible. Thank you."

The innkeeper's son nodded vigorously, his face lighting up at being given a task. He hurried away, only to return moments later bearing bandages, antiseptic, and a large bowl filled with clear water. He set them next to Feng Wu, his actions careful and deliberate. Yet, after fulfilling his task, he lingered, his gaze continually returning to the unconscious Kai.

He shuffled his feet, biting his lip as he gathered his courage. "Um . . . the boy who saved us . . . What's his name?" he blurted out. "I don't think I ever got it."

Feng Wu looked at the boy. In his eyes, he saw genuine admiration, curiosity, and gratitude. A small smile tugged at the corners of his mouth as he realized the immense impact Kai had made on these simple villagers. His gaze softened as he looked down at the boy who had fought bravely despite his age, who had impressed not just him, but an entire village with his strength and courage.

"His name," he said, his voice carrying a certain reverence and fondness, "is Kai Liu."

The innkeeper's son's eyes widened, the name rolling around in his mind as he savored both syllables. His face broke into a smile, one filled with deep reverence. "Kai Liu," he echoed, the name sounding like a chant, a whisper of a legend in the making. "A powerful name. It suits him."

With a final nod, the boy left the room, leaving Feng Wu alone with Kai. The room was steeped in silence once more, but it felt different now. It was as if the name had charged the air, filling the space with a sense of anticipation and promise.

Looking down at the unconscious Kai, Feng Wu couldn't help but agree with the boy's assessment. *Kai Liu . . . a name that carries the weight of an unfathomable future. Yes, a powerful name for a powerful soul.*

As he began tending to his wounds, Feng Wu breathed a sigh of relief. He knew the trials they faced were only the beginning, but he was also sure that they were witnessing the genesis of something great. A legend in the making, a story waiting to be told.

Kai Liu's story.

> *You have fulfilled the conditions for a hidden quest.*
> *Your mind is growing more powerful.*
> *You now have access to your own Memory Palace.*

CHAPTER THIRTY-SIX

Beast Core

I woke up feeling like I'd been trampled by a herd of oxen. My body was sore, my muscles crying out in protest with every breath I took. Memories of the battle were still fresh in my mind, and my chest tightened as I recalled the chaos of the fight.

I chastised myself.

The fight was over. We had won, hopefully.

My eyelids felt heavy as I tried to pry them open. The room was dark, save for the soft blue glow of the Heavenly Interface. I squinted at the projection, my mind spinning as I tried to decipher the text.

> *Quest: Spirit Beast Subjugation has been completed.*
> *You completed the quest with additional challenges.*
> *Your efforts do not go unnoticed.*

I snorted. I barely escaped with my life. I hoped it created a suitable reward for me.

The interface shimmered, and then, the unexpected happened. My mind was suddenly filled with detailed information about Wind Serpents. Everything from their dietary habits to their optimal environments for growth and even their abilities flooded into my head. It was as if I'd spent years studying these creatures, the knowledge was so extensive, so precise.

Confusion washed over me, quickly followed by a wave of understanding. This was my reward. For all the pain, for all the struggles, I was granted the knowledge of Wind Serpents. Was this the Interface's idea of a helpful tool for the future?

An image of a Wind Serpent, coiled and ready to strike, came to mind. With newfound understanding, I could tell it was a young one, the shimmering scales a clear sign of its youth. And those bright, venomous eyes; they were hungry, always on the lookout for the next meal. Small birds, rodents, and even insects were on its menu.

A shiver ran down my spine as I realized how they thrived in highly oxygenated areas, their metabolism adapting incredibly to such environments. And their abilities—lightning-fast reflexes, unparalleled flight speed, and the eerie capacity to control gusts of wind—make them formidable predators.

"Great. Just great," I muttered to myself. More danger. More challenges.

I fell back against my bed, letting the information sink in. There was so much to learn, to adapt to. But if this was what it took to survive in this twisted world, I would do it.

As the initial surprise wore off, a glimmer of excitement began to take its place. Yes, it was daunting, but also . . . intriguing. This was a chance to grow stronger, to become more than what I was.

I closed my eyes, the image of the Wind Serpent etched into my memory. I'd won today, and tomorrow I'd be ready for whatever came my way. I just had to keep pushing, keep learning. Perhaps I could incorporate this knowledge into my training somehow. Visualizing a Wind Serpent when I practice my swings, how it would coil and dodge . . .

The moment of silence was punctured by a rustling sound to my right. Startled, I shot up, wincing at the pain that ricocheted through my body. A figure detached itself from the shadows, walking over until it stood in the faint glow of the Heavenly Interface.

"F-Feng Wu?" I stuttered, squinting in the dim light. The familiar silhouette was a welcome sight, yet his uncharacteristic silence unnerved me.

"Yes, it's me, Kai." His voice was soft, as if he was trying not to startle me.

"I . . ." I croaked, the pain in my body momentarily forgotten. "Did we . . . did we really win? The Wind Serpent . . . ?"

A sigh, audible even in the quiet room. "Yes, we won. Thanks to you, there were no casualties."

His words lifted a weight off my chest. We had survived. All of us. I let out a sigh of relief.

"I . . . I'm sorry, Kai." Feng Wu's voice wavered in the darkness. "It was my responsibility to ensure your safety on the way to the Verdant Lotus Sect. I failed you."

The sincerity in his words hit me harder than any physical blow ever could. Feng Wu was a seasoned warrior, a protector. And here he was, blaming himself for my recklessness.

"Stop." My voice was firm, leaving no room for argument. "I knew what I was getting myself into. It wasn't your fault. I chose to take the risk, to fight. My foolishness led to this, not you."

Silence filled the room again, and I wondered if my words had made any impact.

"You're too hard on yourself," I said, breaking the silence. "We won, didn't we? No one died. That's all that matters to me."

Feng Wu remained silent for a while longer before finally responding, "You're a braver man than I gave you credit for, Kai."

His words held a note of respect, of admiration. It made the throbbing pain a little more bearable. I allowed myself a small smile, settling back into my bed. "Well, we can't all be cowards, can we?"

He told me I had been unconscious for a whole day, explaining how Tianyi never left my side. She was an iridescent glint in the bleakness, a beacon of hope. I could almost imagine the soft flutter of her wings against my hand, the comforting weight of her presence. At some point, Feng Wu had moved her to the windowsill, the moonlight spilling over her and offering her the sustenance she needed to recover.

Listening to Feng Wu, my heart was filled with warm gratitude for my steadfast companion. My eyelids feel heavy, the exhaustion creeping back into my bones. But I fought to stay awake, to hear more about Tianyi.

Feng Wu gave me the rundown of what happened after the battle. How the Silent Moon Sect went ahead with harvesting any and all materials they could gain from the Spirit Beast's bodies. They were quite large, so it didn't strike me as odd that the snakes would hold a lot of valued items within themselves.

"And your contribution in the battle was crucial. With that, I'd like for you to check your pocket."

I stumbled around, patting down my lower half. My upper body was covered in bandages and laid bare, but my clothes had been replaced with a clean pair of pants. I wondered who changed me while I was unconscious. Hopefully not Feng Wu. That'd have been humiliating.

As I felt through the deep pocket, the sensation of a round object brushed my fingertips. It was hard and cold, but from a simple touch I could feel an incredible amount of qi bearing down on me like a waterfall.

It looked like a crystal. An intricate, swirling pattern glowing dimly as I held it in my hand.

"What is this? Some kind of jewel?"

"It's a Beast Core. Specifically, the Wind Serpent's. The Silent Moon Sect deliberated . . . and ultimately decided one of it was what you merited for your valor in battle."

"A Beast Core?" My voice was a whisper as I grappled with the enormity of what Feng Wu just revealed. I could feel his gaze upon me, reading the shock that I was barely managing to hide.

As I held the core, I could feel the faint thrumming of power within it, almost like a heartbeat. A shiver of recognition passed through me. This was the same sensation I'd felt when my mind had been flooded with knowledge about Wind

Serpents. It was as if the essence of the Wind Serpent was held within this core, alive and humming with potential.

"Yes. The Silent Moon Sect saw fit to award it to you, considering the risk you took," Feng Wu explained.

"But this . . ." I trailed off. "Isn't this too valuable? Isn't it something the sect elders would covet for their own cultivation?"

Feng Wu seemed to understand my trepidation. His eyes softened, and his voice took on a firm, determined edge. "Yes, it is a valuable resource. But it is a sign of respect to grant you the Beast Core. I cannot in good conscience take it for myself."

He paused, considering. Then he spoke. "If you were to reject this, it would bring dishonor upon the sect and myself. This is your victory, your contribution. And it is fitting that you receive a reward in kind. It is not only valuable, Kai, but it will also greatly aid in your recovery and cultivation."

I was quiet for a moment, the weight of Feng Wu's words settling over me. The Beast Core felt heavy in my hand, the thrum of energy within it pulsating against my palm. It felt wrong, somehow, to accept it when Feng Wu was the one who had done the lion's share of the fighting.

"Feng Wu," I began, my voice wavering slightly. "This . . . It should be yours. You're the one who defeated the Wind Serpent, not me. I just . . . I just helped."

Feng Wu shook his head, his mouth a grim line. "No, Kai. You risked your life out there. You fought alongside me, not behind me. This Beast Core, this victory, it is yours as much as it is mine. Do not sell yourself short."

Tension filled the air between us, silence stretching on as I took it all in. I didn't want to dishonor Feng Wu or his sect, but the guilt gnawed at my insides. I was untrained and unprepared. Yet I was being handed a treasure that others would kill for.

The guilt was threatening to consume me when Feng Wu spoke again. "Kai," he started, quieter now. "In this world, strength is respected, courage is admired, and wisdom is sought after. You have displayed all three. Do not let guilt cloud your judgment. It is not a sign of weakness to accept a reward when it is deserved.'"

I turned the Beast Core in my hand, its heft substantial despite its small size. Part of me wondered if I really deserved this. But another part of me, the part that ached with the need to grow stronger, to not be a burden, clung desperately to this gift.

"I . . . I see," I finally managed, swallowing hard. "Thank you, Feng Wu. I . . . I don't know what to say."

I looked down at the core, considering the best course of action. A fitting reward. One that I've seen in multiple stories as a result of a daring victory against Spirit Beasts of legend.

"So, do I just . . . eat it?" I asked uncertainly.

The stories I read had some conflicting information on how cultivators used the cores of Spirit Beasts. In *Chronicles of Zhen Lu*, he just absorbed it into his body using mysterious magic. I had no clue on how to go about that. The other stories had the cultivators swallowing cores as they would pills.

Feng Wu blinked at me, the surprise etched on his face almost comical. "Well, yes, you could," he admitted. "Though it might be a bit hard on the stomach."

"Hard on the stomach?" I echoed, looking down at the Beast Core with apprehension. I didn't think my body had reached the level where it could digest crystals. The thought of it going out through the other end made me shudder.

Feng Wu chuckled, shaking his head. "I was joking, Kai. The process is slightly more refined than that. You absorb the energy within the Beast Core, using your cultivation technique to incorporate it into your body. Eating is not necessary."

"Understood," I said, relieved. My mind swirled with possibilities. "Might there be an optimal method for this? Could we, perhaps, incorporate it into a medicinal pill or concoction?"

Feng Wu looked thoughtful. "It's possible," he said slowly. "But such a procedure necessitates an in-depth understanding of alchemy and a precise concoction of ingredients. It's beyond our capabilities here."

"I'll hold out until we get to the Verdant Lotus Sect, then. My injuries . . . They're there, but it doesn't seem so bad. All thanks to Tianyi. I'll probably try to make something with what I have in my cart in the meantime."

Feng Wu nodded. "As you wish. You can rest for now, Kai. The Qingmu Village residents are holding a feast tomorrow. I'll be keeping watch tonight."

I nodded. My eyes were beginning to get heavy again. It seemed my body wasn't fully recovered after all.

"But . . . what about you, Feng Wu? Are you okay?"

The cultivator smiled. "Our battle with the Wind Serpents have allowed me to gain insight on a new ability. I have been taking this time to acclimate myself to its capabilities."

"Oh, what's it called?" I leaned in closer to hear. I was interested in what sort of ability Feng Wu gained as a result from his battle. Perhaps he unfolded a new technique while I was unconscious.

"Although it might be too complicated to explain in full, it's called a Memory Palace."

"Oh, I have that too!"

Feng Wu's soft expression turned to that of incredulity. It was the first time I'd seen the man caught so flat-footed.

"What?!"

His astonishment sent a brief chuckle rippling through me. I shrugged, a slow smile tugging at the corners of my mouth.

"Well, there's a lot you don't know about me, Feng Wu. But don't worry, I'll reveal my secrets one at a time."

Feng Wu floundered for a moment before closing his eyes and releasing a deep sigh. "You truly are an enigma, Kai."

His words hung in the air, a new understanding blossoming between us. I was an enigma, even to myself. A cool, mysterious and chivalrous cultivator who doesn't hesitate to put his body on the line to save civilians—that's me.

As Feng Wu moved to the other side of the room, taking up his watchful position, I reclined in my bed, the Beast Core cool and comforting in my hand.

The pain was still there, a constant, dull throb that was quickly becoming a familiar sensation. But despite the discomfort, despite the looming uncertainty, I felt a profound sense of peace. Giving one last glance to the resting butterfly on the windowsill, I closed my eyes, ready to face whatever the next day would bring.

CHAPTER THIRTY-SEVEN

Pillar of Gratitude

The village of Qingmu had come to life in a way that made the grim atmosphere I'd first encountered seem like a distant memory. Streets that once echoed with silence now buzzed with laughter and chatter. Children, once cooped up indoors, scampered about, their faces painted with joy. Stalls of vibrant colors lined the pathways, and the mouthwatering scent of roasted meats and aromatic spices wafted through the air. Gone were the hushed whispers and guarded tones; people now engaged in animated conversations, their faces lit with smiles.

Even their reaction to the cultivators, who they once seemed guarded and cautious toward, was grateful and enthusiastic. Silent Moon Sect disciples stood confidently as the festival took place, and I could see slight smiles on their faces as they were showered with praise.

"It's Kai Liu! The one who saved Hua Yin's boy!"

"I can't believe he's up and about after what he did. Did you hear about how he poisoned the Wind Serpent?"

"Look at that divine butterfly on his shoulder! He must be a warrior of renown! How have we never heard of him before?"

My ears turned red and I fought to keep an embarrassed smile off my face.

Ha ha, ha ha! It wasn't much. Just something any person would do. But I suppose if they're calling me a chivalrous, brave, handsome, and tall cultivator, then I'd have to graciously accept the compliment. I puffed my chest out slightly, standing up a bit straighter as more and more of the villagers noticed me.

Tianyi stood proudly on my shoulder, transmitting a feeling that I could almost translate into words. It was as if she was telling me, *They didn't compliment me to that extent*. But that was ridiculous. Likely a misinterpretation on my part. Perhaps when our bond grows deeper I'll be able to converse with her.

She hadn't regained the same glimmer in her wings as she did prior to the battle. I felt some semblance of guilt, but I'd hoped that the constant food and finest nectar would be enough to nurse her back to health. I had some idea on what to do with the Beast Core, but I'd have to wait until we got to the Verdant Lotus Sect to test out my theory . . .

"Elder Brother Kai! How're you feeling?"

The innkeeper's child. It was embarrassing how he knew my name but I didn't know his. I knelt to make eye contact, taking it easy so as to avoid aggravating the injury to my ribs.

"Hey. Looks like you're doing well. I don't think I ever caught your name . . . ?"

The boy's posture straightened before he bowed deeply and clasped his fists together. "Ah! How could I forget? My name is Hua Lingsheng!"

"Nice to meet you, Lingsheng. No need to be so formal. Just call me Kai, okay?"

"How could I, Elder Brother Kai!" he said loudly. "You saved my life! Anything less would bring shame to my family!"

Ugh. These kids were crazy. How could I make him calm down? I got that he was grateful, but I just wanted to relax.

"Come, Elder Brother Kai, you must see the preparations for the celebration!" he said, his eyes sparkling with excitement. He took my hand and pulled me toward the village square.

I followed Lingsheng through the festive streets, absorbing the transformation that Qingmu Village had undergone. The village that was once shrouded in fear was now radiant with hope. The joy in the air was palpable, and I couldn't help but feel a warmth in my heart. This was what a village was supposed to look like.

As we reached the village square, I noticed an enormous wooden structure in the center. It was a beautifully carved pillar, adorned with intricate designs and symbols, surrounded by a circle of colorful banners and lanterns. Villagers were adding the final touches, placing offerings of fruits, flowers, and incense around the base.

"What's this, Lingsheng?" I asked, intrigued by the mysterious structure.

He looked up at me, his eyes wide with excitement. "This, Elder Brother Kai, is the Pillar of Gratitude. It's an age-old tradition in Qingmu Village. We've not had the chance to perform this year, but now, with the Wind Serpents defeated, the village elder thought it the perfect time and host it earlier than usual."

"How does it work?" I asked, fascinated by the ritual.

Lingsheng's eyes sparkled as he explained, "The Pillar of Gratitude is a symbol of our village's unity and thankfulness. Tonight, during the celebration, the village elder will light a fire at the top. The fire represents our shared spirit and gratitude toward you, our saviors."

He gestured to the Feng Wu and Silent Moon Sect, who were greeted with bows and smiles by the villagers.

"Then every family will tie a red ribbon around the pillar," Lingsheng continued. "Each ribbon carries the wishes and thanks of the family. The more ribbons, the stronger our gratitude."

I was touched by the simplicity and profoundness of the ritual. It was a beautiful way to express thanks, a deeply spiritual gesture that connected the village to those who had helped them.

I saw Feng Wu poised in a group with the Silent Moon Sect, and he motioned me over. Lingsheng encouraged me to go, talking about how the festival would start now that everyone was present.

Soon, the village elder, a wise and venerable man with a kind smile, stood before the crowd, his eyes filled with emotion. He was different from Elder Ming. He was a lot more frail. But he still held himself in a manner befitting of a village elder. His hair was brown but turning gray at the roots.

"Today," he began, his voice trembling with gratitude, "we gather not just to celebrate our survival, but to honor those who made it possible."

He turned to us, standing in an informal line. A small murmur of cheers and applause rang throughout the crowd, and the village elder paused until they went silent.

"Members of the Verdant Lotus Sect and the Silent Moon Sect, we, the people of Qingmu Village, offer you our deepest thanks. Tonight, we honor you with our Pillar of Gratitude."

The crowd erupted into cheers, their voices carrying the love and respect they felt for their saviors. I could feel a lump in my throat as the village elder lit the fire atop the pillar, the flames dancing, reflecting the hope and joy in the eyes of the people.

It was one thing to read about the tales of heroes and how people celebrated and idolized them. But it was an entirely different matter of feeling it.

But Feng Wu and Xu Ziqing looked unfazed. They took the gratitude in stride. The Azure Moon Marauder observed the pillar and nodded his head in satisfaction, whereas Feng Wu dropped his head in a polite bow toward the village elder. Many of the third-class disciples held their posture and maintained the dignified aura of a cultivator, but from where I stood I could see some were unfamiliar with the praise.

Perhaps they weren't so far from where I was after all. Weren't the third-class disciples around my age? Admittedly, they've likely been training for over a decade, but the difference in experience showed between them and their leader, Xu Ziqing.

The village elder continued to talk for a few more minutes, sharing stories of the village's past, the bravery of its people, and the hope for a prosperous future.

He even brought up a basket of goods for both Feng Wu and Xu Ziqing as the representatives of both sects, and I clapped enthusiastically. Both second-class disciples shared a few words of celebration before giving the stage back to the village elder.

His words were filled with wisdom and kindness, bridging the gap between the old traditions and the newfound joy that filled Qingmu Village. As he concluded his speech, the villagers erupted into applause, and the celebration truly began.

People mingled around, their faces glowing in the warm lantern light, as they chatted and laughed. The aroma of the banquet filled the air, an inviting medley of flavors that made my stomach growl in anticipation. Long tables were laden with an assortment of dishes, all prepared with care and skill by the village's best cooks.

As the guests of honor, we were given the opportunity to check the dishes first and pick what pleased our palate. Feng Wu, with his green eyes sparkling in delight, led me to one of the tables, where a particularly succulent meat was attracting everyone's attention.

"Elder Brother Kai," he said in a playful tone, "I believe you must try this dish. It's rather special."

I groaned. This "Elder Brother" nonsense was going to be another point of ridicule, wasn't it? Hua Lingsheng was clearly being too loud. Oh well, I suppose it's better than Kowtow Kai.

I picked up a piece, savoring the aroma before taking a bite. It was tender, flavorful, and unlike anything I had ever tasted before. My eyes widened as I turned to Feng Wu.

"This is delicious! Is this pork? I've never had it taste like this before."

Feng Wu's eyes twinkled mischievously as he replied, "I think you would know. Most of the dishes here use the same meat, since they came across two large specimens not too long ago."

I nearly choked on my food, my eyes bulging in shock.

"What? The W-Wind Serpent?" I stammered, still trying to wrap my head around the idea. I was eating a Spirit Beast?

One of the villagers who had helped cook the dishes overheard our conversation and chimed in, "Yes, young hero. After the Silent Moon Sect finished harvesting all the valuable parts, we salted the meat to preserve it. We thought it fitting to use it all in this celebration, a symbol of our triumph over fear and a feast in honor of our saviors."

I stared at the meat, then back at Feng Wu, who was watching me with a knowing smile.

"Well," I finally said, taking another bite and savoring the taste, "it is quite delicious. A fitting way to commemorate our victory."

I've heard stories of cultivators consuming Spirit Beasts to absorb their powers, but I didn't feel anything like that. The food was to die for, though. Perhaps I should get into the habit of finding Spirit Beasts to hunt down and eat.

Although, I did wonder how Tianyi would taste, theoretically . . .

A wave of horror and betrayal flowed through me, and Tianyi slowly started to crawl away from my shoulder. I was joking. I was joking!

Feng Wu laughed, his chivalrous demeanor giving way to genuine warmth. "Indeed, Elder Brother Kai. It's a taste of victory, quite literally."

We continued to enjoy the feast, mingling with the villagers and other cultivators, sharing stories and laughter. The Pillar of Gratitude stood tall in the center of the square, a constant reminder of the unity and gratitude that had brought us all together.

As the feast went on, the village elder called forth the Silent Moon Sect to honor them. It made sense. After all, they were the ones who were requested to deal with it in the first place.

I gained respect for them. At first, I thought they were people who would exploit the village and intimidate them, but they were surprisingly diligent and only took an appropriate amount for their services.

They were a bit snobby, but I supposed I could live with that. It was wishful thinking to believe I could get along with everybody, but I'd try my best.

I was excitedly chatting with some villagers about the battles I'd witnessed when Xu Ziqing's piercing gaze met mine. I swallowed down my anxieties, although our interactions during the battle weren't the best, we had fought together. Showing any animosity during a celebration would be stupid. And I was anything but!

"Kai Liu," Xu Ziqing sneered, his eyes narrowing as he drawled my name. "It seems like the village elder didn't deign to honor your contributions. A shame, I suppose."

Feng Wu frowned beside me, a spark of anger in his eyes. But I didn't mind. It was a pretty easy misunderstanding to make that I was part of the Verdant Lotus Sect, even if I didn't wear the same uniform. No point adding me in when I was a small part of the battle.

Besides, who was I to demand recognition? The important thing here was that everybody was safe, and we had no casualties. Everything else was just adding flowers to a brocade at this point.

Taking a few seconds to respond, I opened my mouth with a plan of attack.

"Yes, Xu Ziqing," I said, keeping my voice steady and bowing politely. "I don't mind. Your sect put in most of the effort. I have no issue with you receiving all the credit, as it is rightfully yours."

I wouldn't give him the satisfaction. *Let's see how he likes a dose of over-the-top kindness.*

Xu Ziqing's eyes widened, and I could see the confusion on his face. This was clearly not the response he'd expected. Behind him, the third-class disciples exchanged glances, some looking slightly surprised at my comments.

"Indeed," Xu Ziqing said slowly, clearly trying to regain control of the conversation. "But surely, someone of your limited experience should understand that your contributions were but a small fraction of what was required to secure victory."

I grinned, feeling a surge of excitement. "Oh, absolutely! I'm fully aware that what I did was just a tiny part. Your group must have planned and strategized for days, even weeks! It was my first time seeing a sword formation in action. Do you guys train it as a unit? I'd love to know!"

Feng Wu's frown deepened slightly, but he remained quiet. From the corner of my eye, I could see him gauging me as I responded to their slight jabs with overwhelming positivity.

Xu Ziqing looked taken aback, his carefully crafted facade slipping for a moment. "I . . . Well, it's not something that a novice like you would understand easily."

"But surely you could explain it a little," I pressed, my eyes wide with fascination. "I saw how you took command of the disciples and got them into formation. You there"—I pointed at one of the third-class disciples—"the way you held your position whenever you blocked the Wind Serpent's attacks, it was simply marvelous! Can't believe you weathered so many strikes from it!"

The muscular disciple, who was the first one to take my Invigorating Dawn Tonic after Xu Ziqing, blushed and stammered, "Th-thank you, Kai Liu."

"Silence!" Xu Ziqing snapped, elbowing the disciple. He turned back to me, his face flushing with irritation. "This is not a matter to be discussed openly. Our techniques and strategies are not to be shared with outsiders."

"Oh, I understand," I said, nodding eagerly. "But perhaps you could share some general principles. I'm always looking to improve my skills and learning how to cooperate with other cultivators seems like a critical skill to learn for missions like these."

Xu Ziqing's face twitched, clearly at a loss for how to handle my enthusiasm and compliments. He glanced at Feng Wu, whose expression seemed to flatten out. The edges of his mouth were moving slightly, as though he were trying to fight off a smile.

". . . Your disciple is openly coveting our techniques. Is the Verdant Lotus Sect truly this destitute?"

"You misunderstand, Xu Ziqing," Feng Wu said with a smile. That was quite an insult to brush off, but the man didn't even flinch. "Kai isn't a disciple of the Verdant Lotus Sect. He's actually an herbalist who we're sponsoring for the Grand Alchemy Gauntlet. He's . . . quite passionate about martial arts. He isn't formally affiliated with us. Not yet, at least."

A wave of surprised murmurs spread across the disciples, as well as the villagers nearby who could hear our conversation. The third-class disciples started looking at me as though I grew an additional head.

"Enough of this," Xu Ziqing finally said, his voice dripping with annoyance. "Enjoy the celebration, Kai Liu, and leave the matters of cultivation to those who truly understand them. And one more thing," he added as he glanced at Tianyi, who froze up once more as his eyes narrowed in on her. "It would be wise to keep your beast close. You never know when someone might find it . . . useful."

I grinned at him. "Oh! Do you want a Spirit Beast like Tianyi? She's remarkable, isn't she? You know, if she ever lays eggs and is willing to part with her children, I'd be happy to sell them to you at a fair price! I'm thinking of writing a book on how to care for one since information about the Azure Moonlight Flutter is scarce; I could include it in the deal!"

The swordsman's face turned a shade of red I'd never seen before, his mouth agape at my response. The third-class disciples behind him looked equally stunned, and some were clearly holding back laughter.

"Wha—No! That's not what I meant at all!" Xu Ziqing stammered, clearly flustered.

"But it's a great idea!" I continued. "Tianyi's been such a wonderful companion, and I think anyone interested in martial arts would benefit from having a Spirit Beast. She's a really good companion and listens well. I think."

Xu Ziqing looked as though he were about to say something, but he stopped himself, his face contorting in a mixture of frustration and disbelief. He glanced at his disciples, who were all staring at him, some with amusement dancing in their eyes.

"Never mind," Xu Ziqing finally muttered, defeated. "Enjoy the celebration, Kai Liu. I see there's no use in provoking you."

"Provoking?" I asked. It was a bit harsh, but I didn't think he'd outright admit he was goading me. "I didn't think we were arguing. But thank you for the conversation! I learned a lot, and I'm really excited about the possibility of sharing Tianyi's offspring with you!"

Xu Ziqing merely shook his head, turning and walking away, his disciples following him, some of them casting bemused glances over their shoulders. *Ha! Kill 'em with kindness. That'll teach you. Did you think I was going to play along with your scheme?*

I learned it from the best. Lan-Yin was especially good at making others feel bad whenever they caused a ruckus at the teahouse.

I turned to Feng Wu, smirking slightly. "Did you see that, Feng Wu? Xu Ziqing might want a Spirit Beast like Tianyi! Isn't that great? Not to worry; if Tianyi lays eggs, I'll ask you first."

Feng Wu chuckled, shaking his head. "You truly are one of a kind, Kai. He didn't know what he was up against."

As the laughter and pleasantries of the celebration swirled around us, I looked out at the faces of the villagers, their smiles reflecting the triumph we all shared. There was a profound satisfaction in knowing that I played a part, however small, in their joy and safety.

This was awesome.

CHAPTER THIRTY-EIGHT

Quest Reward

There was copious amounts of alcohol during the celebration. It made me wonder how such a small village like Qingmu could possess that amount. Nevertheless, it made for a great time.

They had their own recipe using honey, rice, grapes, and hawthorn fruit. Whatever it was, Tianyi enjoyed it. She kept drinking from her own cup, and I swore that she consumed enough to get a refill or two while I wasn't looking.

Feng Wu, as well as Xu Ziqing, held themselves in a dignified manner throughout the entire celebration. The same couldn't be said for the third-class disciples, who were being somewhat rowdy during the celebration. Since they weren't taoists, I supposed they didn't need to abstain from alcohol like Feng Wu.

I had eaten my fill ten times over. Hua Lingsheng followed me around and acted as my servant for most of the night; whenever he noticed my plate was empty, he'd come back with another dish. If my cup wasn't full, he'd return carrying another jug. It was all too much, really. After two hours of that treatment, I quietly begged him to stop.

Now here I was, staring up at the ceiling with a pounding headache and a bloated stomach. Honestly, I didn't even know where that food went. My body felt much better, though. The constant ache that lingered around my upper body was now reduced to a negligible sensation. Getting all that food in me was a blessing in disguise. I should thank Hua Lingsheng later.

> *Reward calculation completed.*

Huh? The hell is this?

> *Your reward is marked by a yellow glowing orb, only visible to you.*

I got up out of bed and looked outside the window. There was no glowing orb in the vicinity.

But the system wouldn't lie to me. It had to be somewhere close by. I knew it. The system wouldn't just give me knowledge about the Wind Serpent for completing the quest. There had to be something more, like a martial technique. Or even a divine weapon. Oh, I could already imagine it; a blade imbued with the power of the wind, each swing capable of releasing gusts of devastating force. Or maybe a book filled with ancient martial techniques, passed down through generations, just waiting for someone like me to unlock its secrets.

My mind swirled with excitement, but I knew I needed to keep a level head. The reward was in the area, but it wasn't visible from my room. I would have to explore Qingmu Village to find it.

I hurriedly dressed, making sure not to disturb Tianyi who was still in a pleasant slumber, probably dreaming about more of that delightful brew she'd taken a liking to. I glanced at the butterfly one last time, assuring myself that she would be fine, then headed out into the crisp morning air.

The village was quiet, with only the faintest hints of movement as people began their daily routines. I made my way toward the inn's entrance, where the innkeeper was already up and about, tending to his tasks.

"Ah, Disciple Kai, you're up early!" he greeted me cheerfully. I didn't bother reminding him that I wasn't a disciple of the Verdant Lotus Sect. It was an easy mistake to make.

"Yes, I have some errands to run," I replied, trying not to betray my excitement. "Have you seen Feng Wu or Xu Ziqing and the Silent Moon Sect?"

The innkeeper's face brightened with recognition. "Ah yes, the Silent Moon Sect left early in the morning, before the first light. As for Feng Wu, I believe he mentioned himself to be meditating outside."

I thanked the innkeeper and made my way outside, but not before I felt a tug at my sleeve. I turned to see Hua Lingsheng, the innkeeper's child, looking up at me with curious eyes.

"Are you leaving, Elder Brother Kai?" he asked, a hint of sadness in his voice.

"Not yet, Lingsheng. I'm just looking for something," I assured him, patting his head gently. "Thank you for taking such good care of me last night."

His face lit up, and he nodded energetically. "It was my pleasure! If you need anything else, just ask."

With a warm smile, I continued to the garden, thoughts of the mysterious glowing orb fueling my anticipation.

Once I reached the outside, I found Feng Wu seated in a meditative pose, his face serene. I decided not to disturb him and instead focused on exploring the village.

As I wandered through the narrow streets, greeting the villagers who were slowly beginning their day, my eyes kept scanning for any sign of the yellow glowing orb. The reward had to be somewhere here, and I was determined to find it.

I passed the Pillar of Gratitude, its presence a comforting reminder of the unity and strength of the village. The faces of the villagers were filled with renewed hope, and I felt a connection with them, something deeper than just a fleeting encounter. Continuing on my path, I found myself moving away from the village and toward the perimeter where the landscape shifted to fields of tall grass, swaying gently in the breeze.

As I wandered through this untamed area, my mind kept returning to the mysterious reward. What could it possibly be? I was certain it had something to do with the Wind Serpents I had defeated. The Heavenly Interface wouldn't send me on a wild goose chase for something unrelated.

I recalled the battle, how two Wind Serpents had appeared together. That was unusual. Wind Serpents were known for their solitary nature, and to see two together was a rare occurrence. Even Feng Wu mentioned just how difficult it was to see one. Why were there two in the first place?

A thought struck me like a lightning bolt, causing me to pause in my tracks. Could it be that the Wind Serpents were a mating pair? If so, then that could mean . . .

I began to piece together the connections in my mind, excitement growing with each revelation. The Wind Serpents, the reward, the strange occurrence of two serpents together . . . It all made sense! My reward had to be—

As realization dawned, I stumbled through the tall grass, my eyes wide, my heart pounding. I could feel it; I was close. The yellow orb had to be nearby, marking the location of this incredible reward.

And then there it was.

The soft glow of the yellow orb caught my eye, nestled in the grass, leading me toward a hidden snake nest. My breath caught in my throat as I approached.

Inside the nest was a singular egg, its surface gleaming with an ethereal luster. It was unlike anything I had ever seen before, a treasure born from the essence of the Wind Serpents themselves.

I reached out, my hand trembling slightly, and carefully picked up the egg. It was warm to the touch, filled with pulsating energy that resonated with the beast core in my pocket.

The two Wind Serpents I had slain—they were not mere beasts acting out of malevolence. They were likely parents, desperately seeking food to nourish their young once it hatched.

My mind raced as I searched through the depot of knowledge I had received from the Heavenly Interface about Spirit Beasts. As the information flowed through my consciousness, my understanding deepened. The Wind Serpents were likely terrorizing the village in order to procure food for their young. It wasn't malice that drove them, but a primal need to provide for their offspring.

I looked down at the egg, now cradling it more gently. I had killed two creatures trying to survive and ensure the survival of their young. Yet, what could I have done differently? If I had not intervened, the Wind Serpents would have likely killed someone. Hua Lingsheng's face flashed briefly in my mind.

The world of cultivation was not as clear-cut as I had once believed, where monsters acted without rhyme or reason, and the arrogant cultivators were evil beyond redemption. It was a realm filled with complexities and contradictions, where right and wrong were not always easily discerned.

I sighed, clutching the egg and the Beast Core, feeling a profound connection to the Wind Serpents and the cycle of life they had been a part of. I understood now that every action, every decision, carried consequences and responsibilities that extended beyond myself.

This reward feels bittersweet.

The tall grass brushed against my legs, and the wind whispered through the trees, as if nature itself was sharing in my reflection.

The village of Qingmu, once a place of celebration and camaraderie, now felt like a stage where a complex drama had unfolded. I knew that I had grown and learned from my time here, but it was a growth accompanied by a painful realization.

As I approached the village, I spotted Hua Lingsheng playing near the entrance, his laughter ringing like a sweet melody. Suddenly conscious of the Wind Serpent's egg in my hand, I swiftly hid it in my pocket. The last thing I wanted was to stir up emotions among the villagers who had suffered from the Wind Serpent attacks. The fear of them trying to break the egg was too real.

"Hey, Hua Lingsheng!" I called out, waving and smiling as if I didn't have a care in the world.

"Kai!" the young boy cheered, running over to me with bright eyes. "You look different. Happier! Did you find what you were looking for?"

I chuckled, ruffling his hair. "Perhaps I did, little friend. Perhaps I did."

With a wink and a promise to see him again, I made my way to the inn.

Once inside my room, I carefully laid the egg on the bed, my hands trembling with a mixture of excitement and uncertainty. I began to draw on the knowledge I had gained from the Heavenly Interface, focusing my effort on creating a warm, nurturing environment for the egg. I wrapped it loosely in layers of the blanket before placing it between my legs and keeping firm hold on it. The egg twitched, responding to my efforts, and I felt a surge of connection.

That's when Tianyi, my trusty companion, fluttered awake, her wings shimmering in the sunlight. I believe the party had been an aid in her recovery, as the color in her wings seemed to return. She landed on my shoulder and turned her eyes toward the egg, tilting her head as if asking a silent question.

"It's the Wind Serpent's egg," I explained softly, feeling a sudden lump in my throat. "I found it, and . . . I want to take care of it. The parents tried to kill us and all, but this little thing shouldn't suffer from it."

Tianyi seemed to understand my intent. She floated down and landed softly on the egg, her wings gently caressing its surface. I watched in awe as she infused some of her energy into the egg. I couldn't directly explain the effects of her Qi Infusion skill on a snake egg, but I didn't think it could be a bad thing. Perhaps it would hasten the hatching.

We were so engrossed in this silent communion that we didn't notice Feng Wu, looking particularly refreshed, entering the room.

"Kai, are you ready to depart?" he began, then stopped short, his eyes widening as he spotted the egg. "What in the heavens is that?"

I was caught off guard but quickly regained my composure. I turned myself slightly, showing the egg wrapped in a bundle between my legs. "Oh, that? It's a Wind Serpent egg. Found it outside the village. I thought I'd take care of it, you know, raise it and all."

Feng Wu's face went through a series of expressions: shock, disbelief, confusion, and finally, resignation. He massaged his temple, letting out a deep sigh.

"Patience is a virtue," he muttered to himself, then looked at me with a forced smile. "Kai, why don't you start from the beginning? And please, take your time."

I grinned, launching into the quest completion, the glowing orb, and the egg itself. Feng Wu listened with a mixture of amusement and exasperation, his eyes occasionally drifting to Tianyi, who was still perched on the egg, infusing it with her gentle energy.

When I finished, Feng Wu shook his head, a bemused smile playing on his lips. "You never cease to amaze me, Kai. Just when I think I have you figured out, you surprise me with something like this."

I shrugged, my eyes twinkling with mischief. "Life would be boring if it were predictable, don't you think?"

The man chuckled, his stern demeanor softening. "Indeed. But taking care of a Wind Serpent's egg? That's a responsibility of a different magnitude. Are you sure you're ready for this?"

I looked at the egg, feeling the warmth and connection that had already begun to form between us. "I'm as ready as I'll ever be. The Heavenly Interface gave me in-depth knowledge about the species."

Feng Wu nodded, touching the egg and caressing it lightly. "Then let's get moving. Crescent Bay City awaits, and who knows what other surprises you have in store for us?"

I spent the entire time as we packed up guessing what sort of shenanigans I'd get up to in Crescent Bay City. If my hunch was right, I'd bet there was a chance of me meeting an arrogant young master in real life. Or perhaps a jade beauty would come and notice me hiding my true abilities and fall in love?

"BWA HA HA HA HA!" Feng Wu's raucous laughter seemed to shake the inn. It was the hardest I'd heard him laugh since I met him.

"You dare laugh at me? This humiliation will be repaid tenfold!"

The second-class disciple only laughed harder as we continued to pack up our goods and prepare for departure.

CHAPTER THIRTY-NINE

Recovery and Training

Our leave was marked by many farewells and gifts. We accepted the food and water but politely turned away any other luxuries. Feng Wu had a strong moral compass. Admittedly, refusing money hurt my heart slightly, but I knew that I gained more than enough from my experience here at Qingmu Village.

Hua Lingsheng seemed devastated but understood that it was necessary. I gave him a firm handshake and bade him farewell.

"Will I see you again?" he asked, his voice tinged with hope.

I snorted. "I'd hope so. I have to pass by Qingmu Village to return home."

It was odd having someone who idolized me so much. It was different from how the children back home looked up to me. I didn't know how to describe it. It felt more . . . genuine?

But throughout it all, I understood why taoists were able to refuse materialistic rewards. Feeling how sincere their gratitude was, how could I expect more? Although clearly the Silent Moon Sect took whatever they were given. They seemed like the type.

I'd probably see Xu Ziqing and his bunch again in no time. They were likely headed back to their sect, and from what Feng Wu told me, they were close to Crescent Bay City.

The horses seemed to recover from the battle which took place in their stables. I was glad. Although my potion stash had been reduced to a fraction of what I had originally brought, they weren't used in vain. Besides, the extracted essence of the Moonlit Grace Lily was still there. The potions I used could always be remade, but the same could not be said for a person's life. No regrets there.

"Farewell, heroes!"

"Bye, Kai! Make sure to visit soon!"

"Bring Tianyi with you!"

As we departed from the village, I waved back cheerfully, smiling brightly. Feng Wu gave them a small wave, but I continued until we were past the horizon. I turned to Feng Wu and asked him a question.

"How long till we reach Crescent Bay City?"

"At this speed, we should arrive by tomorrow."

"Is there anything I need to watch out for? Like avoiding conflict at a noodle shop?"

Feng Wu snorted. It seemed the longer we spent with each other, the more of his relaxed personality came out. Either that or I was slowly figuring out what his expressions meant.

"Why would you need to avoid conflict at a noodle shop?"

"Isn't that where most cultivator fights occur? I see it almost every time in all the books I read. Should I learn how to fight in an enclosed space?"

He paused for a moment, his eyes glazing over as if recounting the past. Then, slowly, his expression changed, eyebrows lifting in realization.

"Well, now that you mention it," he said, continuing to look forward, "I suppose a lot of conflicts have taken place in restaurants or teahouses. But that's hardly a rule. These are places where people gather; naturally, confrontations might occur."

He chuckled, and I joined in. It was a silly notion, but one that somehow rang true. Feng Wu continued to talk, and I sat and listened with Tianyi perched quietly on my shoulder. She seemed to be listening intently, facing her entire body toward Feng Wu.

"You know, I have engaged in battles in noodle shops, teahouses, and even a dumpling stall once," Feng Wu mused, a nostalgic smile on his lips. "But I've also fought in dense forests and beside raging rivers. The world of cultivation is vast, and conflicts can happen anywhere."

"Well, then, I guess I don't have to start practicing my noodle shop fighting techniques," I said, still chuckling.

"That might be for the best," Feng Wu replied, his tone teasing. "I'd hate to see you flinging soup and dumplings as your secret weapons."

We smiled, and as our laughter died down, a comfortable silence settled over us. The landscape gradually changed as we rode, with the dense greenery of the forest giving way to open plains. The horses maintained a steady pace, and our conversations, though sparse, were filled with humor and shared understanding. As the sun began to set, painting the sky with shades of pink and orange, the atmosphere was still lighthearted, our recent battle and the weight of our journey momentarily forgotten.

When night finally fell, we decided to set up camp in a secluded area, shielded by a few large rocks and a copse of trees. Feng Wu began to gather wood for a fire, his movements were efficient and practiced, while I took out the crate containing all the materials we'd brought with us. My mind drifted to the Wind Serpent egg, neatly tucked away and kept secure with layers of soft cloth. I carefully lifted the egg, feeling its smooth surface and the faint, mysterious pulse within.

The egg wasn't going to be warm during the night, and I felt a pang of concern. Digging into the knowledge gained from the Heavenly Interface, I realized that to help the egg hatch and develop safely, I must keep it warm. My current body temperature wouldn't be enough; I needed to raise my internal heat.

"I'm going to do some training," I told Feng Wu, setting the egg back into its cushioned resting place. I took off my robes and placed it around the egg while I rolled my shoulders and swung my arms.

I felt good. The phantom pains from the battle hadn't disappeared, but I couldn't delay my training. I was getting anxious after not having done so for the past few days. I dropped down into the horse stance, welcoming the strain on my muscles as I held the position in perfect form.

I moved a little distance away from the camp, finding a flat patch of ground. As I settled into my stance, I focused on my breathing, allowing the energy to flow through my meridians. The techniques I'd been practicing were not just about combat; they were about control and mastery over one's body. I pushed myself, feeling the warmth spreading through my limbs. Using qi to strengthen myself didn't come naturally, and the battle was proof of that.

The sounds of the night surrounded me—the soft rustling of leaves, the distant call of a night bird. I lost myself in the rhythm of my training, each movement deliberate and precise. Learning how to meditate while doing horse stance was one of the best things I could've done. I was training both my mind and body at the same time.

After thirty minutes, I paused, drenched in sweat. I could stop now, but I didn't want to. Getting back into training felt *good*.

With that in mind, I grabbed my iron staff and proceeded to swing.

It was bent slightly. Hopefully I could get someone to straighten it in the city. But it would do as a training aid. I swung with purpose. Downward swing, thrust, overhead strike.

I followed it with a small break. My body was fatigued but in a good way. It felt like all the excess energy I had was being put to good use. Nestling the egg between my legs while I rested, I watched as Feng Wu meditated quietly on his own.

I wondered how his cultivation technique differed from mine. Did it follow the same philosophy? I knew that I was probably slowing myself down with this insistence toward having pure qi, but it wasn't something I could compromise on. The Crimson Lotus Purification technique wouldn't allow me to purify my internal energy for no reason. There had to be a benefit for it. And if I pursued purity to the extreme, surely I'd see results.

The energy I had accumulated so far was still incredibly small. Compared to when I left the village, it had basically remained stagnant. The amount of qi I could take from the surroundings was minuscule, and I was making it even smaller by purifying what little I had. Even with Tianyi's support, raising my qi was difficult. I suppose it'd be best to focus on other aspects of my cultivation that could be readily improved.

"Ha, time to get back to work. Excuse me."

I set Tianyi down on top of the egg as I got ready to renew my martial arts training. This time, I'd be perfecting my hand-to-hand techniques.

Time slipped away as I trained, my body growing warmer, the energy within me more vibrant and alive. I felt connected to the world around me, each breath a part of the night's symphony. It was a peaceful, fulfilling sensation, and I knew that this was what cultivation was truly about. I felt refreshed. In fact, it was akin to pleasure. Why was I feeling this way?

> *Earthly Root Connection—When surrounded by nature,*
> *you can draw forth additional strength and utilize it as your own.*
> *Increases cultivation and recovery speed in areas of nature.*

Ah, that was probably why. We were in a forest, after all.

With that in mind, I intensified my training. My strikes got faster, and I began practicing how to chain my moves together in one fluid motion. I slowly incorporated qi into my attacks, feeling the wind blow past my hands and feet until—

"Grrghk!"

I watched in horror as my fist contorted into a painful position, bending in all the wrong ways, just short of dislocation. The dreaded Qi Deviation. Fortunately, the deviation occurred in my hand, not somewhere vital like my heart, but the pain and frustration were almost overwhelming.

Even after all these trials and tribulations, my body was still not exempt from Qi Deviation? Ah, this really hurt. I wanted to cry. Why was it turning like that? *Hey, stop! Damn you. Listen to me!*

I pressed down on my hand, preventing it from bending too far in a direction it shouldn't have been. The pain was immeasurable, and I had to keep myself in the fetal position, waiting for the pain to go down.

A wave of concern washed over me, as Tianyi fluttered over and landed on my head. Ah, my ever-so-beautiful butterfly companion. *You've come to save me!*

I nudged her toward my right arm, and she cautiously approached my hand as it continued to contort. A wave of qi passed from her through me, soothing the pain. The effects were immediate; my appendages weren't trying to twist themselves off, and the turbulent qi within began to settle down. I would kiss her if I could. *Tianyi's getting the finest wine as soon as we reach Crescent Bay City!*

"Are you all right, Kai?" Feng Wu asked.

"I'm all right, just a mild case of Qi Deviation," I managed to gasp out through gritted teeth. My voice must have sounded strained, and the pain in my hand was sharp, throbbing in time with my heartbeat.

"Mild?" Feng Wu questioned, his eyebrows furrowing. "Your hand looks like it's trying to solve a geometric puzzle on its own."

Despite the situation, I couldn't help but chuckle at his description. It hurt to laugh, but the humor was a welcome distraction from the pain.

"Are you able to fix it?" I asked, looking up at him with hopeful eyes. "Or not. I think Tianyi might be able to by herself . . ."

Feng Wu's expression became serious, his gaze fixed on my hand. "Yes, but it will be painful. Very painful. It's akin to putting a dislocated arm back into place. It would take a lot less time than what Tianyi is doing right now."

I grimaced at the thought, but I knew that leaving it untreated was not an option. I trusted Feng Wu, and I knew that he wouldn't suggest it if it wasn't necessary.

"Do it," I commanded, steeling myself for what was to come.

"Are you sure?" he asked, his eyes searching mine.

I nodded firmly. "Just get it over with."

Feng Wu took a deep breath and then placed his hands over my contorted hand. He closed his eyes, focusing his energy. I could feel the warmth of his qi enveloping my hand, and I knew that he was aligning my twisted meridians.

"Ready?" he asked, his voice soft.

"As I'll ever be," I replied, trying to keep my voice steady.

Without another word, Feng Wu began to manipulate the twisted qi within my hand, forcing it back into alignment. The sensation was akin to my arm's muscles cramping up as hard as they could. I couldn't help but let out a high-pitched scream, my entire body tensing as waves of agony washed over me.

The process felt like an eternity, but in reality, it was over in a matter of seconds. My hand was back to normal, the twisted fingers straight once more. The pain was still there but duller, a throbbing ache rather than a sharp, piercing sensation.

Feng Wu released my hand, and I could see the concern in his eyes. "How do you feel?"

I took a few shaky breaths, trying to steady myself. "Like I've just been run over by a herd of wild boars, but better. Thank you."

He gave me a small smile. "Rest now. You've had enough training for the night. Don't exacerbate your condition."

I couldn't have agreed more. My body was spent, and the ordeal had drained me both physically and emotionally. After moving Tianyi to an appropriate spot where she could rest, I crawled over to the Wind Serpent egg, cradling it in my arms as I lay down by the fire.

"You've got a lot of growing to do, little one," I whispered to the egg, feeling the warmth of its life energy. "And so do I."

CHAPTER FORTY

Arrival at Crescent Bay City

The journey to Crescent Bay City took considerably less time than our expedition to Qingmu Village.

There was a tranquility to travel that I hadn't anticipated. With Feng Wu at the reins, I sprawled out on the wagon, using a blanket as a makeshift cover for the egg. Tianyi perched on it, her silhouette pressing against the blanket. She instinctively seemed to recognize its importance, guarding it. I let the sun warm my skin, savoring the stillness.

Feng Wu's voice cut through my reverie. "We've arrived, Kai."

I stirred, carefully repositioning Tianyi and the egg in a secure nook of the wagon. The horizon unveiled Crescent Bay City.

The capital of Tranquil Breeze Coast sprawled before us, radiant like a gem caught in sunlight. My modest hometown on the province's fringe couldn't have prepared me for the grandeur of this metropolis. It felt almost sentient, pulsating with life, entirely surreal.

Drawing nearer, the city's intricacies emerged. Majestic spires and elaborate rooftops dominated the cityscape, reminiscent of tales I'd once dismissed as mere fantasy. The sun's reflection danced on the bay's waters, making the city walls gleam. It felt as if we approached a city of legend.

Yet it was the city's outskirts, teeming with life, that truly arrested my gaze. A continuous flow of humanity and vehicles surged in and out of the grand entrance. Laden merchants, horse-mounted travelers, nobility in lavish carriages; it was an intoxicating spectacle.

Trying to absorb every nuance, I marveled at how Crescent Bay City buzzed with activity, starkly contrasting the serenity of my hometown.

As we neared the city gate, our wagon became one with the multitude. A medley of aromas—fresh food, horses, and the briny hint of the sea—wafted around. Excitement, wonder, and a trace of nerves made my heart race.

"It's incredible," I remarked, almost out of breath. "Was this your experience on your first visit?"

Feng Wu considered it. "In a way. But it's grown since then. The city has thrived under the new magistrate."

I'd hardly been aware of the official overseeing Gentle Wind Village, much less the magistrate of Crescent Bay City.

While awaiting our turn at the entrance, we exchanged recommendations for sights and sounds of the city. But one thing was clear—our immediate destination was a dining establishment. My stomach demanded it.

Soon we reached the city's entrance where vigilant guards scrutinized incoming wagons, levied tolls, and occasionally frisked travelers. Feng Wu, foreseeing the delay, retrieved a finely crafted charm, bearing an intricate lotus design, and presented it to a guard.

Recognition flashed in the guard's eyes. He bowed deferentially. "Esteemed cultivator of the Verdant Lotus Sect, please forgive the inconvenience. Proceed unhindered."

Cool. I hope I can get something like that in the future. That'd be useful for when my garden shop expands into its own massive business.

Inside Crescent Bay City, a wave of vitality washed over me. The streets were animated with purposeful citizens. Stalls bustled, hawkers advertised their merchandise, and an array of culinary scents tantalized me. It felt like diving into a vibrant cultural mosaic.

"I'm craving noodles," I confessed, salivating at the surrounding aromas. "Do you think we might witness any cultivator duels?"

Feng Wu responded with a chuckle. "It's possible, but don't set your hopes too high. Most are here to dine, not duel."

A tinge of disappointment colored my excitement. We steered our wagon to a stable. Feng Wu expertly navigated the wagon, evident that he had been to this place many times before. After ensuring our belongings were safe, particularly Tianyi and the precious egg, I found myself pausing, eyes locked onto the Wind Serpent egg.

Such a priceless treasure would undoubtedly draw attention in a city brimming with unknowns. After a moment's deliberation, I felt it safest to keep it close. Carefully, I nestled it into my pouch, ensuring it was both concealed and protected.

With the egg safely nestled in my pouch, I strode deeper into Crescent Bay City, Tianyi flitting gracefully around us. Each flutter of her wings seemed to mirror the rhythm of the city: vibrant, unpredictable, and full of life.

The streets were a theater of human endeavor. Stalls showcased an array of goods, from rich spices whose scents made my mouth water to vivid fabrics that made even the dreariest day seem full of color. The street performers played instruments I had never seen before, with melodies that told tales of far-off lands.

Yet, amid all this vibrancy, it was the aroma of freshly cooked noodles that pulled me in. As we approached a particularly packed eatery, I couldn't help but chuckle at its sign. A whimsical illustration depicted two cultivators, swords in hand, dueling passionately amid a hailstorm of flying noodles.

"The Spirited Noodle," Feng Wu remarked with a knowing grin. "Quite the place. They say the noodles are so good, you'd duel for the last bowl."

"That's a catchy slogan," I mused, appreciating the humor. "Shall we?"

Before Feng Wu could answer, a loud clang echoed from within. Curious, I approached the entrance and was about to push the door open when a bowl narrowly missed my head, splattering its contents onto the street. I stepped back, startled.

Inside, the Spirited Noodle was a battlefield. Cultivators, with swords and staves, darted about, their faces intense but not truly malicious. Tables were flipped, serving as makeshift barricades, as they skillfully sparred, their weapons clanging and flashing. One cultivator deftly dodged a thrown dumpling, only to be met with a barrage of noodles from another opponent. In the corner, a pair seemed to be engaged in a fierce duel for the last spring roll.

Tianyi, ever the delicate butterfly, alighted on a nearby lantern, her wings reflecting the warm glow, watching the scene with what I imagined was bemused curiosity.

Feng Wu, clearly amused, leaned in. "You wanted to see a duel in a noodle shop. Here you go."

I chuckled. "I guess I did ask for this, didn't I?"

"Well, it's not every day you get dinner and a show," he replied. "Come on. Let's find a table that hasn't been turned into a fortress."

We settled into a corner table, relatively untouched by the raucous melee in the center of the room. The din of the ongoing clash was punctuated by shouts, taunts, and the occasional order for another bowl of noodles. Tianyi flitted onto a beam above us, giving her an overhead view of the skirmish, while I subtly adjusted the egg in my pouch to ensure it remained safe.

Watching the scene, I turned to Feng Wu, one eyebrow raised. "Is . . . this genuinely part of the dining experience?"

Feng Wu chuckled, taking a sip from a tea cup that had miraculously remained on our table. "Not intentionally, no. But over time, owners have learned to adapt. Some, seeing the entertainment value, let things run their course—as long as the cultivators foot the bill for the damages."

He paused, glancing at the rambunctious group. "Others hire muscle to deter unruly patrons. But hiring competent cultivators can be an expensive proposition. And even if you hire them, there's no guarantee they won't join the chaos themselves."

One particularly loud cultivator, wielding a glistening silver blade, bellowed at his opponent, "You dare disrespect me in this sacred house of noodles? You've tarnished my face!"

His adversary, a man armed with a staff and a sash of throwing darts, retorted, "It is you who started this! Over a spilled tea! You always were too prideful."

A third, apparently a neutral party until now, chimed in. "Both of you, enough! This is a disgrace. Let's settle this outside."

The two glared but continued their banter, seemingly more interested in exchanging words than actual blows.

I sighed, my earlier excitement replaced by a growing unease. "Shouldn't we intervene? This is getting out of hand."

Feng Wu's eyes scanned the room, assessing. "It's tempting, but remember, the dynamics in these situations are complex. For one, intervening might escalate things, making it worse for everyone. Moreover, we're outsiders. Jumping in might complicate matters for the local authorities. And besides . . ." He paused, eyes locking onto a group of children giggling at the scene from behind a flipped table. "They haven't targeted any civilians. If they do, that's a different matter."

I nodded, taking in his wisdom. It was a fine line between upholding justice and unnecessarily stirring the pot. Looking at the scene, I reconsidered my previous wish. "Maybe watching cultivators fight in noodle shops isn't as glamorous as I thought. It's hard to relax with the underlying threat of a bowl whacking me on the head."

Feng Wu clapped me on the back, chuckling softly. "Experience, Kai, is the best teacher. Come on, let's order some noodles before they run out or get thrown."

Just as the verbal jabs were reaching their peak, and the gleam in the fighters' eyes suggested a serious escalation, a low groan echoed from a distant table. The source was a man shrouded in a hooded robe, his head buried in his hands. "Would you two stop squawking already?" he muttered, voice thick with exasperation. "I've got a throbbing headache, and the last thing I need is to listen to third-class disciples bickering."

Both combatants froze, their faces a mask of shock and then indignation. The one with the blade spoke up, puffing out his chest. "Who dares to speak to a third-class disciple of the Rising Moon Sect in such a manner! Who are you to interrupt us, huh?"

His companion, clearly looking to rally support, added, "Indeed! And I'm a third-class disciple from the Sunlit Cloud Sect. State your name!"

The hooded man sighed, setting down his cup. "Honestly? My name's not worth mentioning. Just let me eat my noodles in peace."

Clearly offended, the blade-wielding fighter lunged at the hooded man, sword arcing with lethal intent. But in the blink of an eye, the robed figure vanished, only to reappear above the attacker, delivering a powerful and precise strike. The disciple crumpled like a sack of rice, unconscious before he hit the ground.

The second cultivator barely had time to process the event before the hooded man appeared in front of him, a whirlwind of movements, and with a single blow to the chest, sent him sprawling.

As suddenly as the storm had begun, calm returned. The hooded man glided back to his seat, his hood revealing disheveled gray hair, and resumed slurping his noodles, as if he hadn't just effortlessly dispatched two fighters. The restaurant's patrons, ever adaptable, resumed their meals and conversations, while a couple of workers began dragging the unconscious combatants out of the establishment.

While I stared in disbelief, the man's hood seemed to fly back into place.

I turned to Feng Wu, eyes wide, having noticed the gusts of wind that seemed to accompany the hooded man's movements. "Who is that guy?"

Feng Wu looked thoughtfully at the man, then shook his head. "I'm not sure. But judging by that brief display, he doesn't want to be bothered. It's best to leave him be."

The man's back was the only thing I could see from where I was sitting. His gray hair poked out from his hood, and several bowls showcasing his ravenous appetite lay empty in a stack beside him. His companion, who had a smaller frame and similar hood, barely acknowledged the battle, offering him a refill on his tea.

The world truly was a large place full of sleeping dragons and hidden tigers. I should've learned how to keep myself under the radar if I didn't want to attract attention to myself. Modesty benefits, and arrogance harms, as Elder Ming would've said.

With our orders being served in front of us, I poured out the alcohol I ordered into a wide-mouthed cup and beckoned Tianyi over from the beam she was standing on. It wasn't based on much evidence, but I swore she recovered faster from drinking alcohol.

I was barely a sip into my drink when my eyes caught the smaller figure next to the hooded man. Even under the hood, two piercing eyes staring directly into mine. There was something in that gaze, an intensity that sent shivers down my spine. I quickly looked away, hoping the brief connection hadn't been noticed. But a sudden movement from the corner of my eye made my heart sink.

The smaller, hooded figure stood up, their steps purposeful and direct. As they weaved through the tables, I could only pray. *Please don't come here, please don't come here . . .*

Stopping right in front of our table, the air around us grew a few degrees colder. The hood slightly tilted upward to reveal a pair of full lips. The voice that emerged was undeniably feminine, smooth, and as cold as an icy mountain stream. "How much for the Azure Moonlight Flutter?" she asked, her gaze fixed on Tianyi, who had nestled near my cup.

The table felt like a void of silence. Feng Wu looked just as surprised as I was, while Tianyi, seemingly unperturbed, flitted her wings casually.

This Spirit Beast is a trouble magnet. I swallowed nervously, making eye contact with the woman who continued to stare at my companion. Even if they offered me a million gold, I wou— Well, a million gold was quite the offer . . . I'd at least hesitate before I made the decision. But I knew that they wouldn't offer such a ludicrous amount for her.

Collecting my thoughts, I finally responded, "Tianyi isn't for sale. She's my friend, not an object."

"I can assure you, we can meet your desired price range. Our sect has extensive . . . resources."

I hated dealing with these kinds of guys. Those who though they could throw money at any problem and expect to solve it. There would be no selling taking place today. Unless it was for one of my potions.

Taking a deep breath, I replied with a bit more firmness in my voice, "I told you, Tianyi is not for sale."

A thin eyebrow arched beneath her hood, barely visible. "Surely, there's a price for everything," she pressed, her tone chillingly sweet. "You seem like a novice. Are you even aware of the many dangers that come with harboring such a rare creature? I can assure her safety."

The atmosphere around the table became so thick with tension it felt suffocating. Feng Wu's usually calm demeanor shifted, his eyes narrowing but maintaining the same posture he always had. Before the situation could escalate further, a shadow loomed over our table.

It was him, the gray-haired man who had effortlessly taken down the unruly cultivators. His presence was like an oncoming storm, casting a palpable sense of urgency and caution over us. A quick glance to Feng Wu and I could tell he recognized the looming danger.

But just before anything happened, he raised his voice and spoke in an even tone.

"Junior Sister," he said smoothly, hinting at amusement, but there was an undertone of authority. "Isn't it rude to pressure our fellow diners?"

The hooded woman, apparently the junior sister, pouted slightly. "But, Senior Brother, it's the Azure Moonlight Flutter . . ."

The hooded man, her senior brother, raised a hand, silencing her immediately. "Enough," he whispered, firm yet gentle.

Turning his attention to us, he bowed slightly, "Apologies for my junior's behavior." He then eyed Feng Wu with more scrutiny. "Ah, a fellow from the Verdant Lotus Sect, I see. It's an honor."

His hood shifted, revealing a youthful face framed with sharp, eagle-like eyes, a high nose, and a cheeky grin. The intense gaze was on Feng Wu for a moment longer than necessary, suggesting recognition, or maybe something deeper.

Feng Wu nodded curtly. "Thank you for your understanding. But may I know whom we have the pleasure of meeting?"

The hooded man chuckled. "Today, just a humble diner. But rest assured, our paths may cross again." And with that, he turned, leading his junior sister away from our table.

I watched as they left, putting down several coins on their table without a word. I tried to steady my heart, but it was quite difficult to do so.

That was nerve-racking. I stared at Tianyi, who seemed oblivious and uncaring to what had just transpired. She was content to unfurl her proboscis and drink the contents of the cup. Odd. She was quite sensitive to Xu Ziqing at Qingmu Village. I wondered what was so different now.

I really hoped our paths didn't cross again. *What a drag!*

CHAPTER FORTY-ONE

Tranquil Breeze Farm

N ow that's over with, we should go restock on ingredients for your potions," Feng Wu said as we left the noodle shop.

When the two hooded individuals trying to poach Tianyi left, we got to enjoy our meal. I could get used to eating like this. Although the entertainment was short-lived, I'm pretty sure an argument between two other cultivators was brewing by the time we exited, so the patrons would have another show to watch.

"That would be a good idea. I know this might sound shameful, but do you mind if I borrow some money to purchase them? I'll pay you back as soon as I'm able."

The second-class disciple gently shook his head. "You won't have to pay for a single thing. The Verdant Lotus Sect will reimburse you for all the damages."

"Ah, are you really sure about this? Although they're not from premium ingredients, it was a sizable sum. I'd feel bad if you guys paid for it all."

"Nonsense. You are our guest. I failed to protect you during our journey, and you were forced to use your potions as a critical component in our victory against the Wind Serpents."

I squirmed uncomfortably. It was my decision to do all that. It would've been nice if they paid for it partially, but the entire stock of ingredients? That was way too generous. Tianyi's wing grazed my cheek as she turned to see everything in our surroundings.

"Bu—"

"If we allowed you to pay, the sect would lose face," Feng Wu said, emphasizing the last word. Although his face looked perfectly inviting, he wasn't budging on this topic.

What a pain. In the best way possible. I sighed and relented.

"I know you have a good amount of money on you, but I don't want to run us broke from the amount I'm going to buy."

"Don't worry, our supplier bills the sect directly. There is no worry in that regard."

"Who is this supplier? I hate to be picky, but I do hold my ingredients to a certain quality!" I said with conviction. It was true. Regardless of me or the sect paying, I would've searched for quality ingredients. After several dozen uses of my essence extraction skill, I knew that fresher ingredients had a more potent turnout. "I can't in good conscience create mediocre potions."

Feng Wu patted me on the back. "I believe you'll be satisfied with the quality. Our supplier is the best in the province."

"What are we waiting for? Let's go!" I said with a grin.

Tranquil Breeze Farm was located away from the hustle and bustle of the city. The horizon was covered in crops. I grew most of these at home, but not even close to the scale at which they did it. The beaten path that led further toward the farm, giving me a proper view of the quality of their crops. It was high-quality. Better than the ones I grew. Even without touching them, it was clear that they were healthy and thriving.

It shouldn't have been a surprise, but I was far and away the best gardener in my village. I had my pride too.

The environment was rich with qi. I could feel it. My steps felt lighter. My back straightened. Even Tianyi seemed to go still, pulling energy toward herself and glowing slightly. Our connection twinged as she expressed feelings of satisfaction.

The main entrance was a grand, intricately carved wooden gate. A wide, square stone was situated right across the gate. It looked like it was missing something. Almost like a pedestal without a statue.

"Well, this is it. You'll see a few of our disciples working here as part of our agreement with Tranquil Breeze Farm," Feng Wu said, stopping at the large wooden gate.

"Have you worked here?"

"Not me, specifically. Many of our third-class disciples are assigned to Tranquil Breeze Farm as a way of learning more about cultivating plants, and to act as guards."

"Ah! I see," I nodded sagely. "This is a training opportunity for them, being low-risk and to establish a rapport with the supplier. Am I correct?"

The disciple flashed me a small smile. "Correct. Occasionally, our second-class disciples who joined the alchemy division would serve here for an extended period of time. There is much to learn from one of the largest farms in the province."

I looked around, curious. Nobody was tending to the fields. For a place of this size, I wouldn't be surprised if it took two dozen cultivators to maintain the crops here. But it was strangely empty. The farm was sprawling and full of life, with the crops looking lush and verdant. Yet there wasn't a single cultivator in sight tending to the fields. Nothing to suggest how these plants were being hydrated. For a farm that produced such a massive yield, this was unusual.

Perhaps there was some sort of sorcery at work here.

"Feng Wu, where is everybody?"

"Ah, you'll see. Most of the workers stay within the gates. We need to wait to be let in. They'll be here shortly."

"Who's they?"

Just as I said that, a rustle came from the grass. I stepped back and faced the source of the noise, but Feng Wu didn't seem to react. Perhaps it was the owner of the farm. He was likely—

WOOF!

A beast unlike any other I'd seen.

The creature was petite, but its presence was undeniable. It stood low to the ground with sturdy, muscular legs that belied its small stature. The most striking feature, however, was its face. It was like Elder Wen's dog. Instead of the familiar elongated muzzles of the village canine, this creature had a broad, almost-flattened snout. Its nostrils flared with each breath, and I could hear a soft wheezing.

Its eyes, large and round, were pools of curiosity. Framed by dark black fur, they seemed even more prominent on its face. The creature's coat was a marvel in itself. Like the hides of the cows that grazed in the Qingmu Village fields, its fur was a patchwork of black and white.

As it trotted around, the sunlight caught the creature's coat, revealing a soft sheen on its short, smooth fur. The dark fur around its eyes extended to its ears, which stood erect.

Feng Wu clasped his hands together and bowed. "With your permission, Venerable Guardian, I wish to tread upon these grounds."

This was the guardian of the farm?

I glanced over at Feng Wu, just to make sure he wasn't pulling my leg. But he wasn't; he dipped his head and kept a serene expression. I decided to follow suit behind him, clasping my hands together and bowing.

A few moments of silence passed before I felt something pressing on my leg. I opened my eyes to see the "guardian" sniffing my leg rigorously. It turned to look at me with its large, bulbous eyes, before letting out a small bark.

The massive wooden gate began to open. I watched as the rest of the farm was revealed before me.

"Many thanks, Venerable Guardian."

"Th-thank you!"

The guardian seemed content to sit on the pedestal at the front of the gate, staring at us as we went inside. As the gate slowly shut itself, I noticed nobody in the vicinity opening the gate. A few people milled about, but clearly uninvolved in the process of letting us in.

"Feng Wu, was that really the guardian of this place? How'd he manage to open the gate by himself?"

The animal wasn't quite what I expected for a gate guardian. It looked like a normal dog, albeit with a unique face and color. Maybe it was a lighthearted joke?

The man didn't even look at me while he replied, glancing as though he was searching for someone.

"You'd do well not to judge a book by its cover, Kai," Feng Wu said, walking slightly ahead of me. "Ma Xi has been the guardian of this farm for over a century. One of the oldest Spirit Beasts in the province. Even the elders of established sects would have to tread carefully here. None are allowed entry without his approval."

I balked. Spirit Beasts came in all shapes and sizes, so I should've expected that. I need to broaden my horizon! After all, who would expect Tianyi, a fragile and delicate butterfly, to be capable of gouging out a Wind Serpent's eye?

I could imagine it already. Ma Xi, the unassuming gate guardian is underestimated by a couple thieves. They attack him only to be met with spells, magic, and that laborious breathing. It was certainly enough to drive away skittish animals.

"Then was smelling me his way of checking if I'm worthy?"

"I don't think so. He likely found your scent interesting. He's never had to do that with me or other disciples."

I placed my forearm to my nose, taking a deep breath. I didn't smell anything particular.

"I don't smell bad, do I?"

Feng Wu's silence was deafening.

Before I could repeat the question, a man walked toward us, stopping the two of us in our tracks.

"Ah, Master Lian!" Feng Wu greeted warmly, bowing respectfully to the man approaching us. This man was tall and lithe, his movements graceful and calculated, reminiscent of a cat prowling in the night. His skin was sun-kissed, his hands rugged from work—a stark contrast to his polished green robes that flapped gently around his ankles.

"Greetings, disciple Feng Wu," the man said, his voice smooth and deep. His eyes, a rich shade of hazel, bore into mine with an intensity that sent shivers down my spine. "And who might this be?"

"This is Kai." Feng Wu placed a hand on my shoulder. "A gifted herbalist. He will be our sponsored participant in the Grand Alchemy Gauntlet. We need to restock on several ingredients for his potions."

Master Lian's gaze softened ever so slightly. "Ah, an herbalist! Welcome to Tranquil Breeze Farm. How can I be of service?"

I cleared my throat, trying to hide my nervousness under his intense gaze. "Thank you, Master Lian. I am in need of Morning Dew grass, ginger, and goji extract. And if possible, I'd like to see where these ingredients are cultivated."

Master Lian chuckled, the sound echoing like a soft chime in the air. "Of course! Right this way."

He led us past various patches, each brimming with unique flora, the air around them humming with the rich concentration of qi. But what truly captivated my attention were the specialized greenhouses dotted across the farm. These weren't your ordinary glasshouses. Made from a crystalline material; they refracted sunlight in such a manner that it painted rainbows across the ground, creating an ethereal ambiance.

"Ah, here we are." Master Lian gestured at a vast field, golden grass glistening under the sunlight. "Morning Dew grass. As for the ginger and goji extract, they're stored in our main storehouse. We just had a fresh batch extracted a week ago."

"That's fantastic!" I exclaimed, rushing over to touch the grass, feeling the coolness on my fingers. The potency of this grass was unparalleled. It made mine look subpar. Was it because of how rich the qi was in this area? Or something else?

I'd need to learn all I could and apply it to my garden at home.

Our tour led us to a massive wooden building, intricately carved, not unlike the main entrance. The storehouse was divided into several sections, each dedicated to various ingredients. The ginger was fresh, its spicy aroma tingling my nose, while the goji extract was stored in neatly labeled amber vials.

We were almost done gathering the ingredients when I couldn't contain my curiosity any longer.

"Master Lian," I began, trying to choose my words carefully, "earlier, when I arrived, I noticed the vast fields outside the main entrance. They seemed to be flourishing, yet I saw no water channels, sprinklers, or any form of irrigation. How do you tend to those crops?"

Master Lian's eyes sparkled with pride. "Ah, you have a keen eye, young herbalist. Follow me."

He led us to a patch of land just a little distance away from the storehouse. From afar, it looked like any other field, but as we approached, I noticed small mounds of earth between the plants.

Master Lian knelt down and began to brush away the dirt from one of the mounds, revealing a buried clay pot. "This," he began, with pride, "is a form of irrigation we use called the clay pot irrigation system."

I leaned in, intrigued. The pot seemed to be quite rudimentary—nothing more than a simple, unglazed clay pot with a lid. Yet I could feel the moist soil surrounding it.

Master Lian continued, "Water is poured into these buried pots, and since they're unglazed, the water seeps out gradually, providing consistent moisture directly to the roots of the plants. The soil draws out the water from the pot as needed, ensuring the plants get just the right amount."

I was astounded. "So, you're saying the crops take only the water they need, minimizing wastage?"

"Precisely." Master Lian nodded. "The pots need to be refilled every few days, depending on the crop and the climate. But compared to traditional methods, this technique saves an immense amount of water and ensures the plants are neither overwatered nor underwatered. The lid on top prevents evaporation and any unwanted critters from drinking from it."

I whistled in admiration. "It's simple yet incredibly effective . . . I've never seen such a method in action before. It's ingenious!"

Master Lian smiled. "This method has been passed down through generations. We've continued the practice, merging old wisdom with new techniques, ensuring that our crops get the best care possible."

I spent some time talking with Master Lian. He was forthcoming with the information, quite unlike what I expected. I suppose this information was readily available and not unique to Tranquil Breeze Farm. If I used this in my garden, I could expand it tenfold without having to hire someone to help me water the plants! It was nice talking with someone about the cultivation of plants. Feng Wu was knowledgeable, but it was clear his focus was on martial arts.

Tianyi wandered around, flattering between the plants in the storehouse and outside. I could only imagine how she felt. This was likely a paradise for her. I even got to talk about her with Master Lian, who took note of her qi-gathering abilities and gave her a coneflower to procure nectar from, free of charge.

Mid-conversation, I received a message from the Heavenly Interface.

> *Nature's Attunement has reached level 2.*

It seemed expanding my knowledge in all aspects of growing and cultivating plants raises my level for the newly evolved skills. Still, it was hard to believe that just one conversation was enough to tilt the scales. This trip would be an immense boon to all my skills. Soon, I'd be able to create powerful pills at home. And then I'd be able to rule the heavens. *Ha ha! Mua ha ha! HA HA HA—*

"Will this be all for today?" Master Lian asked. I snapped out of my stupor and nodded as Feng Wu came over to discuss how he'd pay.

After finalizing the details, workers came over and packed it up. Feng Wu explained it would be delivered to the sect.

The midday sun hung high, its rays spreading warmth over Tranquil Breeze Farm. We left the storehouse, stepping back into the picturesque scene that had welcomed us. I took a moment, inhaling deeply and feeling the vibrancy that surrounded us, a blend of nature and craftsmanship, old wisdom and new advancements. It felt as though the farm was a living, breathing entity, a place where time melded seamlessly with the essence of the earth.

Walking beside Feng Wu, my mind swirled with newfound knowledge and possibilities. The secrets I'd uncovered here had the potential to revolutionize my approach to herbalism and cultivation.

"Today has been quite enlightening," I said, finally breaking the comfortable silence that had settled between us. Feng Wu glanced at me, his eyes twinkling with a knowing smile.

"I knew you would appreciate this place, Kai," he responded. His words carried a weight of understanding, due to the depths of the friendship that was forming between us. Or had it formed already? I mean, we had gone through a battle together. It was safe to say we were comrades in arms.

We reached the entrance where our faithful, unassuming guardian Ma Xi awaited, his wise eyes seemingly knowing of all that transpired. Before we stepped out, I turned once more to behold the farm—a vibrant representation of what was possible when nature and nurture worked hand in hand.

I was jealous. Ma Xi seemed to have the best life, roaming the fields and enjoying fresh fruit whenever he pleased. If I had a chance to be reincarnated, I'd hope it was in a similar position to the gate guardian.

A gentle breeze swept through, carrying with it the sweet fragrances of blossoms and earth, whispering secrets and tales of the land. I felt a deep connection, an intertwining of my essence with the very heartbeat of the farm.

CHAPTER FORTY-TWO

Verdant Lotus Sect

Going back to pick up the horses and carriage, I was sad to leave Crescent Bay City without exploring the capital in its full glory. But perhaps it was for the best. I was carrying far too many valuables on me. I'd feel better knowing the egg tucked away in my pouch was lying secure in my room rather than on my person.

Feng Wu did mention I'd have opportunities to visit during my time here. That would be ideal. Visiting Tranquil Breeze Farm and the other shops were definitely on my list. I'd have to get souvenirs for my people back home. The second-class disciple recommended the city marketplace for trinkets to buy.

Our trek took us westward of the city, exiting into rolling hills and verdant forests that seemed to embrace travelers with a gentle, whispering welcome. As we progressed, Feng Wu shared tales of the sect's history, filling the journey with stories of legendary alchemists and martial artists who had once graced the very paths we trod. I soaked in every word, each tale weaving a rich tapestry of the grandeur and mystique that awaited us.

"You see, Kai, the alchemists who once graced this place were visionaries in their own right. Master Li Tao, for instance, was famed for concocting the Elixir of Prolonged Vitality using the most exquisite blend of herbs found in these very woods. His potions are still a vital part of our daily regimens, and . . ."

As the sun dipped lower, painting the sky with hues of orange and purple, we reached the outskirts of the Verdant Lotus Sect. Nestled at the junction where a tranquil river met a lush bamboo forest, the sect exuded a kind of ancient serenity. It was as if time itself had slowed, allowing nature and man to exist in harmonious symbiosis.

We crossed a narrow stone bridge adorned with delicate lotus motifs, the gurgling river below whispering secrets to those who listened. Feng Wu pointed out several disciples in the distance, engaged in fluid martial arts forms, their movements resembling a dance more than a fight. It seemed like the art of combat here was more about harmony and flow than brute force.

Tianyi fluttered happily, staying at a patch of beautiful flowers before hurriedly catching up with us on the cart.

Ah, this really was a breathtaking sight. I was going to be staying here for months? That was something I could get used to, indeed. It was quite a contrast to what I expected. It was cozier than I thought a sect could ever be. There were no arrogant young masters or snide remarks. It seemed as though everyone got along perfectly well. Perhaps Elder Ming was right; sects could be dangerous, and jealousy was a curse. But I suppose it depended on the sect. I wouldn't expect this sort of atmosphere from the Silent Moon Sect, if people like Xu Ziqing were running the place.

It was easy to see that this place was a sanctuary for those seeking knowledge in the ancient arts of alchemy and martial prowess. The scent of rare herbs mingled with the fresh bamboo, creating a fragrance that was as rejuvenating as it was invigorating. By Tianyi's glow, it seemed she agreed as well.

"I'll take you on a more in-depth tour later, but we should go greet Elder Zhu first. He's the head of the alchemy pavilion," Feng Wu said with a knowing smile. "He was the one that learned of your products and extended an invitation."

I puffed out my chest. "Well, I'll have to meet and thank Elder Zhu! It takes a keen eye to spot a talent like mine!"

The man put his hand to his mouth, stifling a laugh. Feng Wu was lucky. If I were a cultivator in the Essence Awakening stage, he'd be enduring several face-slaps for his impudence.

"Yes, Kowtow Kai. Whatever you say."

I waved my fist at him threateningly, looking around to see if anybody had heard. "Hey! Don't say that nickname out loud! I don't want it spreading here."

Feng Wu chuckled as we continued our journey to the alchemy pavilion. The path there was laden with vibrant greenery, a gentle reminder of the sect's intimate relationship with nature.

Soon we were greeted by the sight of the splendid alchemy pavilion. The structure was an architectural marvel, seamlessly blending the natural elements around it. It resembled a sanctuary of knowledge, where wisdom gathered from ages past was nurtured and bestowed upon eager learners.

As we entered, I was immediately struck by the atmosphere of intense concentration and scholarly pursuit. The pavilion was abuzz with disciples engaged in various activities; some hovered over ancient texts, while others were absorbed in the meticulous process of refining ingredients. My senses were enveloped in a myriad of scents emanating from rare herbs and concoctions simmering in rudimentary pill furnaces.

He pointed over at the center of the pavilion. "Elder Zhu's teaching the second-class disciples today. Let's join."

There, Elder Zhu, a figure of wisdom and grace, was engrossed in teaching a group of disciples. His voice carried a harmonious melody as he elucidated the nuances of handling a rare and delicate herb. The elder's hands moved with a fluidity that spoke of years of expertise, his fingers deftly manipulating the ingredients with an almost poetic grace.

I felt an overwhelming sense of wonderment as I observed the students attentively absorbing his teachings, their faces illuminated with the gentle glow of the burning cauldrons before them. They listened intently, occasionally jotting down notes with an air of serious commitment.

I found myself getting drawn into the intricate dance of alchemy that unfolded before my eyes. The technical terms being used were like a symphony of knowledge that sang a song of ancient wisdom. As I listened, I could feel the deep reservoirs of knowledge that lay within the sect, waiting to be explored. It was a stark contrast to the world of herbalism I was acquainted with.

I watched in awe as Elder Zhu masterfully illustrated the methods of extracting the essence of the herb, using a blend of techniques that befuddled me. I could feel my spirit being ignited with a fierce curiosity, a thirst to delve deeper and understand the profound secrets within the realm of alchemy.

Feng Wu leaned in, whispering, "Impressive, isn't it?"

"Do you think it's all right for me to listen in on the lecture? It'd be a shame to interrupt."

At the man's behest, I sat quietly at the back and listened. The elder seemed to notice our presence but continued on with his lecture as he handled a glowing yellow leaf.

Elder Zhu held up the leaf for everyone to see, his eyes twinkling with a kind of excitement that was contagious. He had a cheery aura. Although he was dignified, there was a certain energy to his movement that made him seem much younger than he looked.

I leaned in closer, my curiosity piqued. The leaf seemed somewhat familiar, but I couldn't place where I had seen it before.

"This, young ones, is the Sun Tea Leaf, a very rare and potent ingredient that is coveted by both alchemists and cultivators alike," the elder continued, his voice echoing softly in the tranquil space.

I racked my brain, trying to remember where I had encountered this leaf in my studies. It certainly sounded like a qi plant, but the specifics eluded me. I didn't know many qi plants existed outside of the Breezesong Fruit and the Moonlit Grace Lily.

Elder Zhu began to detail the plant's properties. "The Sun Tea Leaf possesses a delicate balance of yin and yang energies. When prepared correctly, it can harmonize the internal energies, promote vitality, and even enhance one's spiritual connection with the natural elements."

My eyes widened as I realized the significance of what he was saying. This plant was a treasure trove of potential benefits, an herbalist's dream!

The elder placed the leaf on a clean surface and proceeded to show the method of preparation. "To unlock its full potential, one must be delicate in the preparation phase. A hurried hand can easily ruin its delicate properties."

I watched with rapt attention as the elder meticulously separated the veins from the leaf, his hands moving with a grace that was almost hypnotic.

Once the leaf was prepared, Elder Zhu retrieved a small pill furnace from the table beside him. It was a beautiful piece of craftsmanship, adorned with intricate patterns, symbols of power and transformation.

I was excited to realize I was about to witness a true master at work, an artist in his element.

Elder Zhu began to explain the art of pill-making as he worked, his voice a soothing melody that accompanied the rhythmic movements of his hands.

He placed the prepared leaf inside the furnace, adding a few other ingredients which I recognized as common elements in alchemical concoctions. The mixture was heated to a specific temperature, as the elder controlled the flames with a focus that was both fierce and gentle.

As the concoction simmered, a fragrant aroma began to permeate the room, a scent that was both refreshing and invigorating. I could feel a subtle change in the energy around me, a gentle pulsating that seemed to resonate with my own internal rhythms.

"The Sun Tea Leaf, when combined with these ingredients, creates a simple but potent pill that can harmonize the body's energies, promoting both physical and mental well-being," the elder explained, his face glowing with a serene light as he spoke.

I could feel my heart pounding in my chest as I watched the liquid in the furnace transform, bubbling gently before solidifying into a powder. With a strange technique, he formed the powder into pills, all without laying a single finger on them.

Elder Zhu retrieved the pill with a pair of silver tongs, holding it up for everyone to see. "This, young ones, is the Sun Harmony Pill. A pill that can be a boon to both cultivators and regular people alike, aiding in meditation, enhancing vitality, and promoting a deep sense of peace and harmony."

I felt a sense of awe wash over me as I gazed at the pill.

As Elder Zhu concluded his lecture, the students gathered around him, eager to ask questions and gain further insights into the lesson. Feng Wu and I seized this opportunity to move closer, exchanging respectful bows with the venerable elder.

"Elder Zhu, it's an honor to be in your presence," I said, my voice brimming with genuine admiration and reverence. The elder's gaze settled upon me, a warm and welcoming smile gracing his features. "This one's name is Kai Liu."

"The honor is mine, young one. I've heard much about your exceptional talent," Elder Zhu said, his eyes twinkling as he nodded at Tianyi's direction. "Your creations, especially the Invigorating Dawn Tonic, are indeed ingenious. We hope you find our sect to be a place to explore your potential."

Pride and joy rushed through me at hearing such words from a master of his stature. I could feel my cheeks warming, a shy smile forming as I replied, "Thank you, Elder Zhu. Your words mean a lot to me. I've always sought to understand and harness the true essence of herbs in my creations. To bring healing and wellness to others."

Elder Zhu nodded approvingly, his gaze lingering on me for a moment longer, as if assessing the depths of my potential. "I can see a strong affinity within you toward the elements of nature. Your path is a promising one, young Kai."

Feng Wu excused himself shortly, leaving me and the elder to introduce ourselves to each other. I thought it'd be awkward, but the elder felt like a kindred spirit. Someone who had a thirst for knowledge like I did.

"I believe you'll be spending most of your time here at the alchemy pavilion, so it's best if I show you around. Follow me," Elder Zhu said, giving me a tour of the building.

Elder Zhu led me through an intricate maze of corridors, each one seemingly more fascinating than the last. We passed by laboratories where disciples were intently focused on their work, experimenting with various concoctions and substances, their faces glowing in the soft light cast by the flickering flames of their furnaces.

As we moved further, the fragrance of different herbs melded in the air, forming a rich tapestry of scents that was both invigorating and calming. Here, a garden bloomed with plants I had only ever read about in books, plants whose properties held the secrets to potent brews and remedies. I could barely contain my awe and curiosity, my mind buzzing with questions and possibilities.

Elder Zhu seemed to sense my bubbling excitement, for he chuckled softly, his voice carrying the richness of a gentle stream flowing over time-worn rocks. "This is just the beginning, young one," he said, his eyes twinkling with an ageless wisdom. "In time, you will learn to navigate this world of wonders, to unlock the secrets held within these plants and elements."

As our tour came to an end, we stood in a serene courtyard where a gentle breeze played with the leaves of ancient trees, their branches stretching toward the sky in a silent prayer. The setting sun cast a golden hue on everything, painting the scene with the warm tones of an ending day.

Elder Zhu turned toward me, his face bathed in the soft glow of the fading light. "It has been a long day, young Kai. You must be tired. It would be best for you to rest and gather your energies for the days to come. Preparing for the Grand Alchemy Gauntlet will be no easy task."

But as I stood there, amid the captivating beauty that thrummed around me, I found that rest was the farthest thing from my mind. Instead, a fervent desire had ignited within me, a burning need to immerse myself in the art that beckoned me with open arms.

Just learning about the clay pots in Tranquil Breeze Farm raised my Nature's Attunement to the next level after I had plateaued. If I were to learn about alchemy, I could only wonder how it would impact my Spiritual Herbalism technique. Or maybe even create an entirely new set of skills? I wouldn't be able to rest until I got my first lesson.

Taking a deep breath to steady my racing heart, I turned toward Elder Zhu, clenching my fist. "Elder Zhu, I know it's been a long day, but I find myself restless amid all this wonder. Would it be possible for me to start learning right away, perhaps make some simple potions? I promise I won't overdo it."

Elder Zhu studied me for a long moment, his eyes seeming to peer into the very depths of my soul. And then, with a gentle smile that held the warmth of a thousand suns, he nodded. "I suppose I can spare some time to host a quick lesson. I admire your spirit. Very well."

As we walked toward one of the laboratories, I could feel a rush of exhilaration coursing through me, a tingle of anticipation that danced upon my skin.

CHAPTER FORTY-THREE

Initiation into Alchemy

Elder Zhu stood a few paces away, explaining how a pill furnace worked to me. It was hard to reconcile how . . . ordinary it looked. Whenever they described it in books, they made it sound like a contraption beyond human comprehension, fraught with profundities that a mortal's mind couldn't understand.

Sure it didn't look easy to handle, but my mind wasn't turned to mush by the sheer complexities of the pill furnace. It reminded me of the forges in Master Qiang's smithy, just much smaller and intricate.

"Think of this pill furnace, Kai, as a sophisticated cooking pot," Elder Zhu began, his voice clear and grounded in simplicity. "But instead of preparing food, we are refining and combining various herbs and minerals to create medicinal pills."

Ah, I remembered having this conversation with Feng Wu before.

"Inside the furnace, we place our ingredients. The furnace's job is to evenly distribute heat, which we control not just with fire, but with our own qi. This ensures that the ingredients don't burn but slowly blend together."

He tapped on the furnace, before moving onto the beetle shells preserved neatly in a jar. Elder Zhu turned them into dust with his skillful usage of the mortar and pestle.

On my own desk, I mimicked the action, listening to his explanation as the careful sound of grinding echoed throughout the room.

"Imagine you're steeping tea," he continued. "The water's heat extracts the tea's essence, right? Similarly, the furnace's controlled heat extracts and merges the essences of our ingredients, transforming them into something much more potent."

"So, it's all about controlling the heat and knowing your ingredients," I ventured. Elder Zhu's explanation was so simple that I felt that the kids from back home could understand what he was saying!

Although I must admit, comparing the pill furnaces I had envisioned as heaven-defying treasures to a teapot made me sigh. It wasn't as cool as I had made it out to be.

"Exactly," Elder Zhu confirmed with a nod. "And your qi is the key to that control. It's like turning the knob on a stove, but using your inner energy. Master that, and you master the heart of alchemy."

That was easier said than done, that was for sure.

I glanced at Tianyi, who was fluttering around the workspace, her antennae twitching as she inspected the array of ingredients with a curious and discerning gaze. Every so often, she would flit toward me, offering silent encouragement or perhaps sharing her own insights from her own vantage point. It was nice having someone familiar with me here.

Elder Zhu, with a subtle gesture, turned his attention to the pill furnace. "Now that the ingredients are prepared, we approach the crux of our endeavor—the pill furnace. This is where the true alchemist emerges, through attention to detail and the passage of time. The furnace does not forgive haste nor ignorance."

I nodded. I was ready, all my years of reading novels have culminated to this point.

This was it, the moment where raw materials would transcend their mundane origins to become something . . . divine. I couldn't help but be swept up in the moment, my thoughts echoing the grandiloquent style of Liang Feng, the author of my favorite works!

Behold, as the gates of alchemical mastery beckon, I stand on the threshold, ready to meld the essence of heaven and earth with the fervor of my spirit. The furnace, this celestial cauldron, awaits the touch of a true alchemist to awaken its dormant might!

As I focused on the task at hand, the measured addition of ingredients, the careful modulation of qi to stoke the furnace's flame, the grandiosity of my thoughts felt increasingly out of place.

This was more similar to cooking than I'd thought.

The furnace, for all its mystical significance, responded not to the poetry of my inner monologue but to the precision of my actions.

Eh, I don't get it. Let's just focus on what's happening here. I'm not getting any of the enlightenment those novels talk about.

The profound transformations and mystical insights I had expected, the ones so vividly painted in the pages of my beloved novels, seemed absent.

With a mental shrug, I redirected my focus to the tangible, the real. The heat of the furnace against my skin, the subtle changes in the color and consistency of the mixture within, these were the signs of alchemical progress, not the flowery language of my internal narrative.

I snuck a glance at the mixture in my furnace and the one inside of Elder Zhu's. The difference was like night and day.

His mixture had a consistency that was smooth and even, glowing with a subtle inner light that seemed to pulsate in rhythm with the gentle hum of the furnace. Mine, on the other hand, was less inspiring. The realization hit me; perhaps emulating Elder Zhu's movements, his subtle manipulations of qi and ingredients, could bridge the gap between my crude attempts and his masterful precision.

With renewed determination, I tried to mirror his every move, the way his hands seemed to dance with an almost imperceptible grace around the pill furnace, the slight tilts and turns that suggested a deep, unspoken communion with the elements at play. Yet, try as I might, my movements felt hollow, lacking the depth and intuition that Elder Zhu's possessed. It was like trying to capture a shadow; the form might've been similar, but the essence was worlds apart.

I couldn't sense the qi in the same way he did, couldn't feel the subtle shifts in temperature and energy that dictated the precise moments to add, to stir, to infuse. My hands moved, but they were like a puppet's—lacking the soul that animated Elder Zhu's artistry.

As I stood before the esteemed furnace, envisioned as the crucible of the dao, where elements danced to the tune of ancient cultivators, I couldn't help but reminisce about the tales of immortal alchemists. These were beings who, with a mere gesture, could coax the heavens and earth into their cauldrons, their concoctions capable of defying the very cycle of reincarnation. Each ingredient was not merely a plant or mineral but a treasure bathed in the essence of the universe, each pill a convergence of yin and yang, a microcosm of the dao itself.

Yet here I was, grinding beetle shells as one might do to season a particularly stubborn stew, the grandiose symphony of creation reduced to the culinary equivalent of following a slightly burnt recipe. The pill furnace before me, far from the cosmic cauldron I had envisioned, seemed more akin to an ornate teapot, albeit one that demanded a peculiar blend of finesse and internal energy rather than loose leaves and boiling water.

I had dreamed of standing amid the swirling energies of creation, a conduit for the profound laws of nature.

Instead, I was a humble apprentice, sweating over the alchemical equivalent of not burning the rice.

It appeared the true essence of alchemy wasn't found in the dramatic manipulation of qi and essence but in the quiet dedication to perfecting one's craft—less a battle against the heavens, more a patient courtship of the natural order.

That was no problem. I, Kai Liu, would embrace the true spirit of alchemy, with missteps and all to bring my image of alchemy to life.

In my focused mimicry and monologue, I barely registered Elder Zhu's voice, calm and steady, cutting through my concentration. "You may want to reduce the qi input. You're pushing too hard."

Startled, I glanced at my furnace. The mixture had begun to clump, a sure sign of overheating, of qi infused with too much haste and not enough finesse. Panic fluttered in my chest as I hastened to adjust, to salvage what I could of the process. I reduced my qi flow, but the damage was done. The once-promising blend of ingredients had suffered under my heavy-handed attempt at control.

With a hesitant hand, I opened the furnace, bracing myself for the sight. The powder lay there, clumped and sullen, a stark testament to my failure. It was a far cry from the vibrant, potent concoctions I had read about, the ones that seemed to leap off the pages of my novels with their promise of power and enlightenment.

Elder Zhu, his attention still on his own work, spoke without looking up. "Alchemy is not just about following motions, Kai. It's about understanding the why behind each movement, the how behind each adjustment of qi. It's a language of its own, one you must learn to speak with your heart, not just your hands."

His words hung heavy in the air, a gentle yet firm reminder of the gap between rote imitation and genuine understanding. I stared at the disappointing result of my efforts, a lump of misshapen intentions and misguided execution. It was a hard pill to swallow, realizing that my eager attempts to replicate Elder Zhu's graceful mastery were akin to a child mimicking the brush strokes of a master calligrapher without grasping the essence of the art.

As I sifted through the process in my mind, reviewing each step and trying to pinpoint where my understanding had faltered, Elder Zhu turned to me, his expression softening. "Do not fear failure, Kai. We did not bring you to the Verdant Lotus Sect for your expertise in alchemy, but for the potential we see in you to become a true alchemist."

His words, meant to comfort, only served to deepen my resolve. "May I try again?" I asked, my voice steady despite the turmoil within. "I have . . . a different approach in mind. Something that might align more closely with my understanding of herbalism."

Elder Zhu regarded me for a moment, his gaze piercing yet not unkind. "Altering the recipe increases the volatility of the process. There are countless ways to achieve similar ends in alchemy, but the method we've been using is the most stable."

I nodded, understanding the gravity of his caution. "I'm aware of the risks. But I believe this could work. I want to show the sect that their decision to sponsor me was the right one."

Elder Zhu's smile was a mix of admiration and apprehension. "Very well, Kai. Show me your path."

Turning back to the task at hand, I poured over the recipe once more, my mind racing. The plants, the heart of the concoction, seemed to whisper their secrets to me, their potential begging to be unleashed in ways the traditional recipe did not account for. The ginger root, in particular, called to me. If the goal was to enhance vitality and yang energy, then surely the fiery essence of ginger could be harnessed more directly, more potently.

I had the skill just for the occasion.

For a moment, the thought crossed my mind. Should I reveal this right here, right now?

But I knew that there were times when one had to show what they were capable of. This was one of them.

With a deep breath, I reached for a fresh ginger root, my fingers tingling with anticipation. I closed my eyes, focusing on the dense, vibrant life force within the plant. Slowly, carefully, I coaxed the pure essence of the ginger root into my palm, where it shimmered like a captured star.

The gasp that escaped Elder Zhu's lips was so uncharacteristic of the composed elder that it jolted me from my concentration. His wide eyes met mine, and for a moment, I saw a flicker of something like disbelief—or was it recognition?—in their depths.

Shaking off the momentary distraction, I focused on the pill furnace. The introduction of the ginger essence seemed to calm the tumultuous mixture, lending it a stability that had been absent before. It was as if the essence acted as a mediator, smoothing over the rough edges of the other ingredients' interactions.

Yet, as I worked, I could feel my control over my qi beginning to wane, the delicate balance I had maintained starting to slip through my fingers like grains of sand. Just as I began to despair, a gentle fluttering by my ear heralded Tianyi's arrival. The qi flowing from the meridian on my like a breath of fresh air, rekindling my flagging spirits and bolstering my control.

With Tianyi's support, I dove back into the process, my movements more assured, my focus sharper. The pill furnace, albeit a far cry from Elder Zhu's operation of it, ebbed and flowed according to my will.

As the final moments of the process approached, I held my breath, my entire being focused on the furnace before me. The anticipation was palpable, a tangible force that seemed to fill the chamber.

And then, as I gently withdrew my qi, the furnace's glow subsided, revealing the fruits of my labor. The powder that lay within was unlike any I had seen before—vibrant, pulsating with energy, and imbued with the unmistakable essence of ginger. The consistency was far from perfect, but a marked improvement to my terrible first attempt. It was a bold departure from tradition, a testament to the synergy between herbalism and alchemy, and a clear indication of my unique path in this ancient art.

Elder Zhu approached, his expression inscrutable. He studied the powder for a long moment before turning to me, a myriad of emotions playing across his features. "Kai," he began, sounding steady with an undercurrent of excitement, "this is remarkable. Truly remarkable."

Elder Zhu's fingers gingerly scooped a pinch of the radiant powder, bringing it close to his lips. His eyes, usually so revealing of his thoughts, now masked his anticipation. With a delicate motion, he tasted the powder, his expression unreadable as he savored the concoction.

After a moment, his face relaxed into a smile, nodding in approval. "Almost as potent as the original recipe, despite the imperfections," he mused aloud, his gaze now fixed on me with renewed interest.

The acknowledgment from Elder Zhu sent a wave of relief through me, mingling with a burgeoning pride. But before I could bask in the glow of success, his demeanor shifted to one of curiosity, almost analytical. He picked up the ginger which had its essence taken. "That skill . . . You took the ginger's energy. Tell me, Kai, how did you achieve this?"

I hesitated, his question hanging between us. "It's from the Heavenly Interface," I began cautiously. "A reward, I suppose, after my Herbalism skill reached its maximum level."

Elder Zhu's brow furrowed slightly, his interest piqued. "And how do you use it, exactly? What effects does it have on the plants you apply it to?"

I explained as best I could, detailing the delicate process of coaxing the essence from the plants, how it seemed to distill their very life force into a purer form.

"Have you tried it on other ingredients? Metals or minerals, perhaps?" he pressed further, his questions flowing like a stream, each one probing deeper into the nature of my skill.

I shook my head, a frown creasing my brow. "No, I haven't. I'm not sure it would work the same way. My connection has always been strongest with plants."

Elder Zhu nodded, seemingly lost in thought for a moment. "And the essences you extract, have you used them in any of your other products?"

I recounted the few experiments I had conducted, the tentative steps I had taken in integrating the essences into my concoctions, each one a journey of discovery and learning.

With each answer I provided, Elder Zhu's expression grew more thoughtful, his gaze drifting away as if piecing together a puzzle only he could see. Finally, he spoke, his voice carrying a weight of consideration. "I need to do some research. There might be something in the sect's library that references a skill like yours. It's eerily similar to something I encountered in my youth."

His words sparked a curiosity within me, a hunger for knowledge about this connection to Elder Zhu's past. "What was it?" I ventured, eager for any insight he might offer.

But Elder Zhu was cryptic, his usual openness replaced by what seemed to be nostalgia. I saw that expression on Elder Ming's face more times than I could count. "It's something I hadn't seen or thought would resurface again," he said, his tone final, leaving no room for further inquiry.

As he turned away, his steps hurried as if driven by a newfound urgency, I was left standing amid the remnants of my experiment, Tianyi fluttering by my side.

"Come on, let's get going," I called out to her. Her wings glimmered as we left the area and headed down into the lobby of the alchemy pavilion. A couple hours had passed, and there were only a few people left inside. Most of them were engrossed in whatever they were doing, but a couple sneaked curious glances at me and Tianyi.

I left the pavilion and closed the door behind me, taking a deep breath and enjoying fresh air. I looked over the horizon with a small smile. Several disciples roamed freely, but Feng Wu was nowhere to be seen.

"Where the hell am I supposed to go?"

Dammit, Feng Wu. You were supposed to give me a tour of the sect.

CHAPTER FORTY-FOUR

Blissful Rest

Oh, Feng Wu? He passed by an hour ago, said he was going to the mission chamber. Let me show you."

It seemed Feng Wu was a person of significance in the sect, considering how the disciple I approached knew immediately where to look. That led me to wonder just how many second-class disciples there were. Aside from training and getting stronger, disciples were handling many tasks and errands for the sect.

The disciple directed me to the mission chamber, east of the alchemy pavilion and a short walk away. I gave him my thanks and headed off. I noted that the sect was used to having guests come in and out, judging by how lax it was. I was expecting suspicious stares and interrogations for wandering on my lonesome, but everybody minded their business. With the night encroaching, I hastened my strides to get there faster.

The structure stood imposing, bordered with simple wooden pillars. The evening sun cast elongated shadows, gently revealing the quiet exterior. Not as vast as the training grounds, but it was larger than Lan-Yin's family teahouse back home. Stepping inside, I noticed rows of secluded booths, shielded with wooden partitions for disciples to pen down their mission details privately. There were fewer than a dozen people in the main hall.

Ah, this was awkward. Doesn't seem like a place for me to go. I flinched as I heard a voice come from my flank.

"Sir, I'm afraid guests are not permitted beyond this point," it said, breaking my inward stream of thoughts. I turned my head to face a disciple who seemed barely older than me, with an earnest and slightly stern expression adorning his face.

"I apologize," I began, bowing slightly in a gesture of respect. I felt a little foolish, walking into an area where I clearly did not belong, carried away by my eagerness to reunite with Feng Wu. "I was looking for Feng Wu. Is he here?" I asked.

The disciple's features softened a bit as he recognized the name. "Senior Brother Feng Wu, you say? He is actually with the elder right now, finishing up his report. It shouldn't be much longer." The disciple glanced back toward the private chambers before turning his gaze back to me, his eyes holding a hint of understanding.

"I see . . ." I muttered. At least I was in the right place. "Would it be possible to ask him to meet me outside once he's done?"

The disciple nodded, offering a small smile in return, his demeanor transforming from stern to somewhat friendly. "Certainly, I'll let him know. Please wait outside; he should be with you shortly."

I sat outside of the building, taking the time to decompress and calm myself. Today was an exhausting, but fulfilling venture. My mind was brimming with new ideas. The pill furnace was a complex item, so the more I learned about its intricacies, the better my products would be. The sect had several lying around. Perhaps I could negotiate the purchase of one. I'd heard from Feng Wu already about how much they cost, so I'd need to save up from the results of my contract with the Azure Silk Trading Company.

So, aside from learning alchemy, I'd need to make my potions for my contract, keep up with my conditioning, and cultivating.

"Tianyi, it's gonna be busy over the next few months," I said with a sigh. "But it's not so bad. In fact, I look forward to it. This place is beautiful. What about you?"

The butterfly let out a feeling of contentment. The environment here was probably doing wonders for her. She was exuding qi constantly back at home, creating pockets of a qi-rich environment in areas she frequented. But here? Her wings had returned to its full glory, maybe even surpassing it. I wondered if it was because she could focus fully on drawing the energy from around us without worry.

It'd be a crime to waste my time here. If my name were to match my reality, I'd have to work harder than anybody else.

"Kai, sorry to keep you waiting."

I spun around to face Feng Wu, an apologetic smile on his face. He looked a little tired but kept himself upright.

"No problem. Were you at the mission chamber penning down the details of the escort mission assigned to you?" I queried, curious. The entire concept of missions and the dynamics of sects was new to me, every piece of information a treasure to hoard.

Feng Wu nodded, his countenance displaying an open book of experiences and learnings. "Yes, it's also where I handed over the materials I gained from the Wind Serpent we took down in Qingmu Village to the elder in charge of the mission chamber."

I blinked, absorbing the information. It seemed like a lot of things were handled meticulously here, a trait I found respectable. A creeping thought entered my mind, causing an uneasy churn in my stomach. "So, do I also need to hand over the materials I received from the serpent?" I was uncertain, questioning the dynamics of my stand in this transaction.

He did say it was mine, but I'd be pretty sad parting with the egg tucked away in my pouch.

Feng Wu, seeing the quick glance I made at the Wind Serpent egg, gently placed a finger on his lips, his eyes twinkling with mischief and assurance combined. "It's handled," was all he said, but in that simple phrase lay a depth of trust and understanding.

A chuckle escaped me, resonating with the trust woven in his words. My heart felt lighter, the worries momentarily dissipating, and I found myself grinning in response. "I guess I owe you one, Feng Wu."

Feng Wu shook his head, his smile remaining. "You owe me nothing. Now, let me show you to the guest quarters."

As we walked, the intricacies of the sect became even more apparent. Feng Wu led me through paths adorned with cobblestones, where the whispers of the leaves and the soft murmur of distant waterfalls seemed to sing a gentle lullaby to the coming night. The architectural symmetry of the buildings that we passed was nothing short of an art form, a perfect marriage of elegance and function.

I couldn't help but remark, "This place is incredible. It feels straight out of a fairy tale."

Feng Wu nodded, pride in his eyes. "Indeed, every structure here is designed to integrate seamlessly with the natural surroundings. It's a place where one can cultivate both the mind and the spirit."

As the sky wore a cloak of stars, Feng Wu continued, "I've received word that your ingredients from Tranquil Breeze Farm have arrived. And if you're interested, I can give you an in-depth tour of the sect early in the morning tomorrow."

I paused, a ripple of excitement coursing through me. This was a golden opportunity, not just to familiarize myself with the sect but to forge deeper connections here. I could probably find a place to train as well. I'd absorb as much as I could while I was here. "I'd like that," I said, my enthusiasm unmistakable.

Feng Wu nodded again. "We can start at dawn, if that suits you?"

I nodded eagerly back, my curiosity about this place mounting with every passing second. "Absolutely. I'm looking forward to it. By the way, when do the classes for alchemy start?"

Understanding flickered in Feng Wu's eyes as he said, "The alchemy pavilion elder will be overseeing that. You can meet him tomorrow morning to discuss your schedule and other particulars."

I took note of this, a new chapter in my journey about to unfold. "Sounds good. I appreciate the guidance, Feng Wu."

It was hard to think we met by chance, trying to showcase my talents to the Azure Silk Trading Company just a couple months ago. It was hard to tell where life takes you.

After a few moments, we reached the guest quarters. The building had a humble facade but carried a silent dignity that was echoed in the simple but refined interior. Feng Wu opened the door to a room adorned with delicate silk curtains and a bed that promised serene dreams. A gentle lantern cast warm light, creating a soothing ambiance.

"Rest well, we have an early start tomorrow."

After his departure, I dropped my pouch and revealed the egg, which had been secured comfortably. I inspected it for any cracks and deficiencies, but found it unscathed. I kept it by the lantern, giving it a source of warmth and light while I eased myself onto the bed. For the first time in a while, I could just sit back and truly rest.

This bed was so comfy . . .

But sleep evaded me, as if teasing my exhausted limbs and urging my mind to wade deeper into a tumultuous sea of creativity and innovation. There was a relentless buzz in my head, the unfettered cogs of imagination tirelessly turning, concocting formulas and untested alchemic theories. Even as I nestled deeper into the softness of the bed, trying to drown out the noise, the calling was too strong, the pull of potential discoveries too enticing.

As the ideas kept flooding in, a part of me yearned for the blissful ignorance of sleep, for a momentary respite from the relentless pursuit of knowledge. Yet a deeper, insatiable part couldn't bear to let these fleeting glimpses of innovation pass unrecorded.

Was this what it felt like to be on the cusp of something truly revolutionary, I wondered, feeling like a lone explorer on the brink of a new frontier.

Ha, being a genius unrivaled throughout the heavens has some drawbacks, I suppose.

In the stillness of the night, I found myself sitting up, my eyes staring at the dancing flame of the lantern, but my mind was light years away. I contemplated new combinations of herbs, innovative brewing techniques, and the fantastical creations that awaited in the yet uncharted territory of alchemy. The veil of fatigue seemed to lift, replaced by a fervent desire to explore and understand, to forge new paths where no one had ventured before.

I slipped out of bed, the cool breeze from the open window caressing my face, grounding me yet also encouraging the flames of curiosity to burn brighter. A notebook lay on the small table by the window, beckoning me to pen down the whirlpool of thoughts that threatened to consume me. As I began to write, my hand moved with a life of its own, dancing across the paper in an unrestrained ballet of knowledge and inspiration.

But I knew I couldn't just rely on notes; I needed a place where these ideas could solidify and take form, an inner sanctum where the chaos of creativity could find order and purpose. My mind drifted into the Memory Palace, a labyrinthine repository where each idea could find a home, a place to grow and evolve.

As the night advanced, I found myself entering this mental space, walking down the sprawling forest that represented my mindscape. Among them was a budding sapling, the one that represented my knowledge of alchemy.

I approached it, watching as it reached toward the stars, each leaf a concept, a fragment of understanding. The time had come to nurture this sapling into a tree, to foster its growth with the fertile soil of information and knowledge.

The intricacies of herbalism sprawled out before me in a vibrant tapestry of interweaving concepts. Each herb held a story, a potential to heal or harm, to nourish or weaken. It was up to me to unlock those secrets, to coax forth the true potential lurking within each leaf and root.

I paused, closing my eyes to let the pulsing energies of the natural elements infuse my understanding. My fingertips tingled with the sensation of vibrant leaves and tender petals, the earthy scent of roots filling my senses. Here, in the quiet cradle of my mind, I sifted through each fragment of knowledge I had acquired, connecting the dots, forming a more cohesive picture.

I delved deeper, losing myself in the intricate dance of compounds and their effects on the human body. Antioxidants that could heal and rejuvenate, alkaloids that might wield both danger and medicinal properties, saponins that could cleanse and purify. The labyrinthine pathways of herbal interactions unfolded before me, a grand yet delicate ballet of nature's wonders.

Each new revelation was like a gentle rain, nurturing the growing tree within my mind, encouraging it to reach higher, to expand its branches and deepen its roots. I could feel it maturing, strengthening, becoming a repository of wisdom and insight.

The hours dwindled away as I wandered deeper into my own consciousness, immersing myself in an ocean of potential, where every droplet held a universe of possibilities. I sensed that I was standing at the threshold of something great, my pulse quickened, beating in harmony with the rhythmic song of the universe.

But amid this profound journey, a gentle chime echoed, pulling me back to the surface, back to the tangible reality of the room I inhabited. It was the Heavenly Interface.

Spiritual Herbalism has reached level 2.

With that, I meditated peacefully through the night, enjoying the presence of Tianyi and the Wind Serpent Egg. I hummed quietly during my contemplations; the lullaby my mother sang about the Moonlit Grace Lily.

Sleep, my dear, and worry not for Moonlit Grace will soothe your thoughts. Wrapped in lily's tender hold, you'll awaken strong and bold.

CHAPTER FORTY-FIVE

Tales of Tianyi

The garden was more than just thriving. With our combined effort, every plant, be it the mystical ginseng, the rejuvenating goji berry, or the invigorating ginger, blossomed with an unparalleled qi. The scents they exhaled were heady, almost intoxicating, promising healing and power. It was paradise, and I felt blessed every time I fluttered amid these living treasures.

But, as with all things precious, our haven attracted unwanted attention.

At first, it was just the occasional "beetle" or "aphid," as Kai would name them. But before we knew it, our sanctuary was under siege. The invaders weren't just content with the typical green foliage; they were after the qi-rich essence of the most treasured plants in the garden. The goji berries, usually glowing with a faint luminescence, now had tiny bite marks. The ginseng's leaves, which once stood tall and proud, were pockmarked and wilted under the onslaught.

Each day was a new challenge. The "whiteflies" seemed particularly fond of the aromatic ginger leaves, clouding around them in swirling masses, drawing their essence and leaving them sapped of vitality. The "caterpillars," on the other hand, had an insatiable appetite for the goji berry vines, wrapping around them in a devastating embrace.

With so many enemies, I was forced to optimize the usage of my qi. Using the bare minimum to cut through their exoskeletons. Making my wings sharper with less qi, refining it to the point of zero waste.

> *Wing Blade: Your wings become razor-sharp with the infusion of qi.*

A reward for my efforts as the guardian of the garden. From there, my Wing Blade became more refined and solidified.

Kai had the foresight to apply some sort of essence on the most sought-after plants, explicitly warning me several times not to touch it through our bond.

Seeing the unfortunate souls land on the plants coated in that essence he created becoming paralyzed and dying was more than enough to make me give these plants a wide berth.

Thankfully, not every plant received this treatment. The lily that glowed under the moonlight repelled most by itself, leaving me to absorb the essence freely and recover. Several others I frequented were free of the essence, which I understood as my responsibility to care for and defend.

The battle wasn't just about warding them off. It was about understanding them, and predicting their patterns. Every time I zipped past a plant, shooing away a group of "locusts" or diving at a cluster of "mites," I'd remember Kai's words, naming them, trying to understand their nature. It was essential, not just to defeat them but to restore balance.

One early dawn, as I rested on a ginseng root, Kai approached. His brows were furrowed, reflecting the same concern I felt. "The grasshoppers are multiplying faster," he whispered, as if saying it louder would make it more real.

I nodded, my wings drooping slightly with fatigue.

However, amid this turmoil, the resilience of our garden was evident. Some ginseng plants, after being nearly consumed, drew deep from the earth's qi and sprouted anew, even more robust and full of vitality. Their undying spirit and refusal to be defeated were sources of inspiration.

Our resolve hardened. This was more than just a garden; it was my home. The likes of beetles and whiteflies would not diminish its glory. Not while I remained alive.

Every day felt like an endless whirlwind of activity, a perpetual dance of evasion and attack. My desire to become faster, stronger, and more resilient seemed to fall short when faced with the overwhelming flood of pests that threatened our garden.

One twilight, while patrolling the dense foliage, I discovered an unusual scene. A secluded clearing amid the dense plant life was scattered with spider carcasses. These were the spiders I dreaded. Their predatory aura always presented a challenge. To see them lifeless, devoid of their menacing essence, was shocking.

But the real surprise was at the center of this eerie tableau. A smaller spider, with intricate patterns adorning its body, stood amid the larger, now lifeless ones. Its deliberate, almost-methodical movements showed it was feasting on the fallen. I hovered silently, concealed by a nearby leaf, my attention entirely captivated by this unexpected sight.

As I observed this peculiar arachnid, another spider, larger and seemingly more formidable, emerged from the dense undergrowth, sensing an opportunity for a meal. The smaller spider, seemingly oblivious to the impending danger, continued its meal.

Suddenly, the larger spider lunged, but not at the smaller spider's body—it targeted one of its legs. It was a tactical move, aiming to cripple its adversary, rendering it defenseless. But the smaller spider was not to be underestimated.

It moved with an agility and foresight I had not seen in any other creature in our garden. As the larger spider lunged repeatedly, the unique spider dodged and evaded, calculating its moves as it went. There was a clear demonstration of intelligence in its actions, a methodical approach to combat that took into account its opponent's abilities and strategy.

Compared to my feathered adversaries, these pests rarely demonstrated anything more than instinct. Every move was driven by survival, wired into their very being. But this one seemed to show more than just self-preservation.

The dance between the two continued, each trying to outwit the other. The larger spider's strength and size seemed to give it an advantage, but the smaller spider's agility and cunning made the battle evenly matched. At one point, it seemed cornered, with the larger spider having successfully grabbed onto one of its legs, ready to deliver the final blow.

But in a startling display of strategy and sacrifice, the smaller spider released its ensnared leg, leaving it behind in its attacker's grasp. Using this momentary distraction, it lunged at its adversary's main body, its fangs sinking into a vital spot. The larger spider writhed for a few moments before becoming still, its life force extinguished.

As the victor resumed its feast, it occasionally glanced at the leg it had lost, almost as if contemplating its own sacrifice. The battle I had just witnessed was unlike any other. It was not just a showcase of strength but of intelligence, problem-solving, and strategic sacrifice.

Perhaps . . . ?

The garden's pests had always been a formidable challenge, but now, with the discovery of this spider and its unique intelligence, there was hope. Perhaps nature, in its infinite wisdom, had presented a solution to the imbalance. A new ally in our never-ending battle to protect our sanctuary and preserve the ancient knowledge it held.

I continued to hover, hidden, watching the spider for a while longer. Its movements, its calculated decisions, and its apparent understanding of its surroundings fascinated me. Here was a creature, small and seemingly insignificant, yet wielding such intelligence and strategy that it could defeat adversaries much larger than itself.

Suddenly, my curiosity got the better of me, and I felt an urging need to make contact with this unique creature. Taking a deep breath, I summon my courage and gently fluttered out of my hiding spot, positioning myself a safe distance away from the spider.

It froze, its multitude of eyes looking into mine with unnerving intensity. The stillness of the moment hung heavy, like the stillness just before a storm. It didn't scuttle away or act in fear. Instead, it tensed, its legs shifting minutely as if pre-paring for battle. I found myself unexpectedly impressed. Despite its small size compared to me, it had no hesitation, no fear, and seemed ready to face whatever threat I might pose.

However, in a twist I hadn't seen coming, after a few heartbeats of our stand-off, it did something entirely unexpected: It turned and bolted.

I fluttered in place, taken aback. The little creature was clever, realizing that perhaps in a direct confrontation, it was outmatched. Its earlier battle had already taken a toll, and with its missing leg, the odds were against it.

Without missing a beat, I pursued. Darting over the undergrowth, we engaged in a high-speed chase. With each zig and zag, the spider threw at me, I matched, anticipating its moves with my heightened senses. Finally, I cornered it against a moss-covered rock. It turned to face me, fangs bared, the glint in its multiple eyes showing defiance.

But I did not want a fight. I slowly approached it, infusing a small stream of my qi into the spider's body, focusing on the area where its leg had been torn off. The creature stiffened momentarily, then relaxed as my healing energy sealed its wound, stemming the bleeding.

Now, the challenge was to communicate. Unlike Kai, with whom I shared a deep, unspoken bond, I had no such connection with this being. But sometimes, actions spoke louder than words. I settled down a short distance away from the spider, wings fluttering gently, showing no intent to harm. The creature seemed to watch, cautious but no longer openly hostile.

I hope you understand, I thought, pouring all my sincerity into the sentiment, hoping the emotion would somehow transcend the barrier between our species. *I mean you no harm. You have a gift, a unique intelligence that sets you apart. Let us not be adversaries, but allies.*

As moments ticked by, the spider seemed to size me up, processing our encounter. It seemed to be understanding, perhaps on some primal level, my intent. Slowly, almost cautiously, it approached, stopping just a whisker's width from me.

Then it turned away, leaving me to my own devices.

An unbidden memory came up in my mind. Faint and fleeting. Being chased by a pesky human through a forest, finding solace in a waterfall, and being awo-ken with a spark that made me what I am today.

In the same way Kai and I became steadfast partners, perhaps this intelligent creature may prove to be a useful ally in our battles to come.

I watched as Tianyi gracefully fluttered over from the dense foliage, her vibrant wings catching the last rays of twilight. She alighted on a stone beside me, and I couldn't help but admire her grace. For a creature who had bisected a bird when it encroached upon the garden, she looked deceptively delicate.

"How have you been?" I asked her.

Instead of words, a warm rush of positive emotions flowed through our bond. Relief, contentment, and a touch of amusement. It always amazed me how Tianyi, despite her lack of spoken language, could communicate her feelings so vividly.

I chuckled, letting the emotional wave wash over me. "You're doing an incredible job, you know? The garden's never been safer. Keep up the work!"

Tianyi emitted a burst of pride through our bond, her wings fluttering in response.

But then, my expression turned pensive. "However, I can't help but notice that the bugs are getting . . . stronger. And there's more of them than before. The chrysanthemum essence I applied on the plants worked, but I could see a few were resistant to it. I suppose I'll have to see other ways of keeping them under control."

When I was a child, my parents spoke of the spirit of the land. Of how it communicates, nurtures, and sometimes challenges. These creatures, these challenges, are they tests the land imposes upon us? Perhaps the garden is testing our worthiness. To see if I can protect what I'm cultivating in this little space of mine?

"Do you think it's the garden?" I mused aloud. "Its high concentration of qi drawing these creatures in? Or maybe . . . the ambient qi in this region is . . . evolving the fauna."

There was an unsettling pause. The implications of that idea hung heavy. This wasn't just about defending a garden anymore; the land's creatures evolving due to an abundance of qi could change everything we knew.

What if Tianyi's powers grew stronger and spread to the village? What would happen to the livestock?

What would happen to the humans?

We both shared a look, our bond resonating with mutual unease. The silence that settled was thick, a stark contrast to the usually harmonious backdrop of our garden's ambiance.

I laughed, albeit a bit shakily. "Ah, I'm probably overthinking things. Just the musings of a tired cultivator. The fumes inside the house are probably getting to me."

Tianyi emitted a gentle feeling of reassurance through our bond, which did wonders to lift my spirits.

"I suppose I should get up and train," I said, trying to sound more cheerful than I felt. With a final glance at the sprawling garden, I concluded, "Tomorrow is another day, after all."

I stood, feeling the coolness of the stone bench for a moment before turning to face the garden in its entirety. Whatever the future held for me, I knew that this little garden would be, forever always, my home. And I'd protect it at all costs.

CHAPTER FORTY-SIX

Alchemy for Dummies

Waking up before the roosters crowed wasn't something I experienced in some time. Being on the road, our sleep schedule became more lax compared to when I was running the shop back home.

Traversing the sect's surrounding areas kept me active and chipper, despite the slight mental fatigue from reviewing my knowledge and trying to gain every fragment of understanding I could from my lesson with Elder Zhu.

"Over there is the training grounds. The third-class disciples are doing their morning drills, as you can see." Feng Wu pointed from the distance.

Following his finger, I stared at the clearing filled with a few dozen disciples, my age or younger, following along an intricate dance of palm strikes and sweeping kicks. It was similar to Feng Wu's strikes, the first stance of the Lotus Palm. It looked like they were here for a substantial amount of time already. That was true dedication.

At the forefront, an older man was leading the group and shouting the moves they performed. Compared to Feng Wu's, the disciples couldn't hold a candle in terms of speed and precision. Although that didn't mean I could beat them in a fight. They were far more agile than I was, that was for sure.

"Do they train like this every day? That's incredible!"

Feng Wu dipped his head. "Of course. Although our combat prowess falls short of the Silent Moon and Whispering Wind Sects, we are diligent. One cannot be at their mental peak without some form of martial training."

Feng Wu then led me farther into the sect's serene landscape, and the shouts of the working disciples grew fainter as we walked away.

"As you already know, the alchemy pavilions are to the east, and the administrative buildings are to the north. As a guest, you won't need to venture to those places often," Feng Wu mentioned casually, his words floating by like the gentle wind.

We then approached what appeared to be a breathtaking structure—a vast, shimmering greenhouse. The sunlight reflected off the crystalline material, scattering rainbow hues in every direction. It was awe-inspiring and reminded me of the greenhouses from Tranquil Breeze Farm. Smaller, and more compact, but still eye-catching in its own right.

"This is our sect's prize possession, the Crystal Alchemy Greenhouse," Feng Wu said, proud.

I couldn't help but get closer, my fingers lightly grazing the crystalline glass. "This . . . It's just like the greenhouses from Tranquil Breeze Farm. This isn't regular glass, is it?"

Feng Wu chuckled. "Good eye. The process might be similar, but the crystals we use are specially treated with alchemical methods, enhancing its properties and making it the perfect environment for the more uncommon herbs grown here."

The greenhouse was divided into several sections, each dedicated to a particular herb or plant vital for alchemy. Walking inside, I felt an immediate change in the atmosphere. It was warm, humid, and charged with a soothing energy. My senses tingled with every step, drawn to the various fragrances that filled the air. The beauty of the blooming flora, the shimmering leaves, and the vibrant colors all around was a sight to behold.

"Each section has a dedicated caretaker, ensuring the perfect growth conditions for the herbs. Our sect might be smaller, but we take pride in the quality of our alchemy ingredients," Feng Wu continued, leading me deeper inside.

I saw various plants, most of which I wouldn't have seen in my lifetime without traversing to Crescent Bay City. I spotted a vine of Breezesong Fruits, small in number but an attractive addition to the greenhouse. Even the Moonlit Grace Lilies were being cultivated in a small patch. They were still in an immature state, but clearly thriving under the conditions set by the Verdant Lotus Sect.

Every few steps, he would pause, allowing me to appreciate the unique plants and explaining their uses and importance in the world of alchemy. I was lost in a trance, captivated by the harmony of nature and alchemy. Tianyi had wandered off from sight, but through our bond I could feel her contentment and knew she was safe.

Several plants glowed in soft, luminescent colors, and water features were artfully placed around, adding to the serenity. In the heart of the greenhouse, a tranquil pond, surrounded by exotic plants and filled with koi of myriad colors, stole my breath away. Their graceful movements, combined with the gentle trickling of water, created an ambiance of peace.

"It's beautiful," I whispered, not wanting to disturb the tranquility.

Feng Wu smiled. "It's the pride and joy of our sect. Our founder believed that being close to nature and understanding its rhythm was essential for alchemy."

Time seemed to stand still as we continued our walk. Each plant, each sound, and each scent only deepened my admiration for the sect and its dedication to the art of alchemy. Before I knew it, we had reached the exit.

"It seems we ended up spending too much time here. Come find me after your class, and I'll show you where your ingredients are, all right?" Feng Wu said. "I'll be in the training compound around the time you finish so look for me there."

I entered the alchemy pavilion, the familiar aroma of herbs and elixirs filled my nostrils, a blend of comfort and excitement. Disciples moved with purpose, and I immediately noticed the uniformity of their attire. Third-class disciples, judging by the sheer number, donned pristine white robes, accentuated with delicate green trims that seemed to reflect the very essence of the Verdant Lotus Sect.

Compared to them, I stuck out awkwardly in my maroon robe, a far cry from the calming colors that surrounded me.

Reaching the chamber, I was met with rows of long tables. Students were already there, laying out their tools with practiced ease. A sinking feeling began to envelop me. I had already been to this pavilion, and yet, engrossed in the wonders of the sect and my earlier lessons, I had forgotten to prepare for this class. My tools were still snugly packed away.

Noticing my evident disarray, a few third-class disciples approached. "New here?" asked a girl with a braid that cascaded down her back. The stark difference in our attires made me feel even more out of place.

"Actually, I've been here before," I started, feeling my cheeks burn, "but I, uh, forgot my tools. They're still in my pack."

A young man with his hair pulled back into a neat bun smirked. "Already visited and still forgot? You're quite the klutz. When did you arrive?"

I scratched my head, embarrassed. "Well, technically, I'm not a new disciple. I'm a sponsored participant for the Grand Alchemy Gauntlet."

Their eyes widened in surprise. "The Grand Alchemy Gauntlet?" the girl with the braid exclaimed, "You're going? But still, forgetting your tools? You might be the first Gauntlet participant to do that."

The playful teasing made me laugh, easing the tension. "Seems like it. Do you guys have any spares?"

She chuckled. "Of course. We can't have the sect's guest stumbling on his first day."

As they generously offered their spare tools, my eyes landed on a first-class disciple at the head of the chamber. His robe, similar to those of the third-class, was lengthier, more refined, bearing detailed green patterns. It brought to mind Feng Wu's attire, the deep forest green robe that flowed with authority and grace. It clicked then—the variation in the shades of green was likely a representation of one's seniority in the sect.

Amid the different shades of green and the disciplined atmosphere of the Verdant Lotus Sect, my mind drifted back to the Gentle Wind Village. The days spent under the tutelage of my parents, the painstaking precision required in handling delicate herbs, and the gentle guidance received in the quaint, earth-scented shop were far removed from the regal discipline of the Verdant Lotus Sect.

The memories, tender and resilient, made me smile despite my initial nervousness and I steeled my nerves.

The man's gaze, sharper than any blade, scanned the room, taking in every detail. His dark eyes seemed to hold secrets, and his hooked nose gave him a hawkish appearance. His hair, peppered with streaks of gray, was pulled back into a tight ponytail. Compared to the cheery and enthusiastic nature of Elder Zhu, this man was quite severe.

"Looks like you've spotted the first-class disciple who'll be overseeing our class," the young man whispered, his voice laced with a hint of apprehension. "He's Instructor Xiao-Hu."

"And?" I asked, trying to match their subdued tones.

"He's . . . strict," the girl with the braid murmured, glancing uneasily at the stern figure. "I've had the, er, pleasure of being in his class before. He expects nothing less than perfection."

"He teaches the basics, you see," the young man added, "like preparation, theoretical knowledge, and safety. All fundamental for us. His methods might seem militaristic, but he's thorough, and there's no doubt you'll learn."

I recalled the manuscripts I'd read last night. The basics of alchemy had parallels to the foundations of herbalism. Preparation and safety were paramount, as one small mistake could spell disaster. "Sounds like someone who'll keep us on our toes," I murmured, grateful for the study session I'd indulged in.

Before I could contemplate further, the stern disciple cleared his throat, the room falling silent. "Settle down. We begin," his voice commanded attention, every word precise and dripping with authority.

Disciples scrambled to get to their stations. They began their preparations, the room a flurry of motion as they chopped, measured, and analyzed ingredients. I did my best to follow, the maneuvers surprisingly familiar due to the similarity with herbalism.

The first-class disciple began his rounds, observing and correcting. "Too much force! Do you wish to ruin the herb?" he snapped at a student who chopped a little too vigorously. At another table, he quirked an eyebrow at a pupil's uneven piles. "Precision, disciple! This isn't a game."

My anxiety grew with every step he took toward my table. I tried to focus, my hands steady as I went through the process, reminiscing about the times I had prepared herbs back at home.

"And you are?" His voice, cool and cutting, made me jolt.

"Kai Liu, an herbalist from Gentle Wind Village," I responded, trying to keep my speech even.

The first-class disciple's eyes narrowed in recognition, assessing me. "I see. Show me."

I hesitated for a moment, then took a deep breath. My fingers began to move, handling the herbs and tools with practiced ease. The repetitive motions of grinding and measuring that I had done countless times at my shop now came to my rescue. The room felt silent except for the occasional rustle and scrape of tools.

He observed silently, his face betraying no emotion. After what felt like an eternity, he straightened up and looked around the room. "This is how it's done," he declared, pointing at my table. "Mimic his precision, his technique. That's the foundation of alchemy."

I could feel my face heat up with both pride and embarrassment. The weight of dozens of pairs of eyes was heavy upon me, yet the small nod of appreciation from the first-class disciple made all the anxiety worthwhile. The foundation laid by my years of herbalism had somehow, unexpectedly, set me on the path of alchemy with a strong footing.

The rest of the lesson was unexpectedly informative. Instructor Xiao-Hu delved into topics and methods of alchemy that I had never even considered. With each explanation, I found myself understanding why he was so severe. The foundations of alchemy were delicate, and a small slip in the process could result in an inferior product. He wasn't being overly strict; he was teaching us the importance of precision and the cost of carelessness.

Once the class ended, I was approached by a few third-class disciples, including the duo who had earlier lent me their tools.

"That was some impressive skill you showcased earlier," the girl with the braid said, a genuine smile on her face. "Is that why you were brought in from the outside?"

I chuckled, "Actually, it's my experience as an herbalist that probably gave me an edge. Alchemy and herbalism share some foundational principles."

The young man with the bun added, "I guess that makes sense. Among us third-class disciples, not many have a strong talent for alchemy. Most of us gravitate toward martial arts or other departments."

"You're saying none of you are alchemists?" I asked in surprise.

He laughed. "Well, some of us try, but we've never seen someone so young handle herbs with the finesse you showcased today. You remind me of the second-class disciples with the way you were doing it!"

The girl added, "Many of us are still finding our footing. It's said that one's path in the sect often finds them, rather than the other way around."

Our conversation flowed naturally as we introduced ourselves. The girl with the braid was named Li Na, and the young man was called Han Wei. They were both disciples who were trying to harness their talents and were part of a close-knit group within the third-class disciples. It turned out they were younger than me, by almost half a decade. That was hard to believe, seeing them so young yet so capable. I wouldn't hold a candle to these disciples when I was their age. I felt old . . .

As we continued talking, Instructor Xiao-Hu approached. My heart rate picked up a bit, recalling the stern gaze he'd fixed me with earlier.

"Kai Liu," he said. I straightened up immediately.

"Yes, Instructor?"

"Meet Elder Zhu at his office after this. He wishes to speak with you."

I nodded in understanding. "Of course."

Before turning away, Xiao-Hu added, "Oh, and in future classes, your butterfly companion should not be present. It's too . . . sparkly. It could be a distraction for the others."

I glanced over to where Tianyi was hovering, her wings giving off a soft luminescence. Suppressing an embarrassed smile, I replied, "Understood, Instructor."

As Xiao-Hu walked away, Li Na and Han Wei exchanged amused glances.

"It looks like you're making quite an impression already," Han Wei said with a playful smirk.

Li Na nudged him gently. "Leave him be. At least he didn't get reprimanded for forgetting his tools."

I laughed. "Thank you both, really. Hopefully, we'll have more opportunities to learn together."

They nodded, and with that, I made my way to Elder Zhu's office, wondering what the esteemed elder wanted to discuss.

CHAPTER FORTY-SEVEN

Conditioning & Grit

Elder Zhu? You wanted to see me?"

The rich aroma of aged parchment wafted through the air as I stepped into the chamber. Elder Zhu's office was a veritable labyrinth of wisdom. Tall mahogany shelves, packed edge to edge with scrolls, flanked the walls. Delicate ink brushes and meticulously inked papers lay scattered across the wooden surface, evidence of a mind forever at work. In the soft, dim glow of the room, the intricate shadows of numerous curios—some jade statues, bronze instruments, and other indecipherable trinkets—played on the walls, each silently narrating tales of ancient traditions and forgotten lore.

Amid the expansive display of artifacts and scrolls, the centerpiece of the room was an opulent desk, made of dark, polished wood and engraved with symbols that resonated with profound energy. On it lay a vast spread of papers, sketches, and manuscripts, but what caught my attention the most was a lone journal, its leather-bound spine slightly worn, placed meticulously at the center.

"Ah, Kai! How was your first class?"

The Elder's voice snapped me out of my reverie. "It wasn't too much trouble," I said, scratching my head. "Instructor Xiao-Hu is very thorough. Reinforcing the basics."

Elder Zhu chuckled warmly, his eyes twinkling with amusement. "If only the other disciples could see things as you do. They often look at the sky from the bottom of a well, fixated on a small patch of blue and unaware of the vastness above. But enough of that; there's another matter I wish to discuss."

He gestured to the journal, its untouched pages seeming to beckon with a subtle allure. The absence of any title made it even more intriguing. Void of any ostentatious ornamentation, it seemed simple, but there was an unmistakable weight to its presence. I tilted my head, my curiosity piqued.

"Have you heard of Master Li Tao?" Elder Zhu's question caught me off guard.

My mind thought back to my journey with Feng Wu. "Yes, he was mentioned by Feng Wu. Master Li Tao is credited for the creation of the Elixir of Prolonged Vitality, right?" I replied, trying to piece together the fragments of information I had gathered.

Elder Zhu nodded, his fingers lightly drumming the cover of the journal. "That is accurate. However, there is more to Master Li Tao than just the creation of that elixir."

He paused, looking deep into my eyes, seemingly gauging my reaction. "Master Li Tao had a talent, similar to yours—the essence extraction skill. But unlike you, his talents extended beyond just plants."

A mixture of surprise and curiosity welled up inside me. Tianyi twitched upon feeling my anticipation through our emotional bond.

Elder Zhu continued, "Master Li Tao was an ancestor of our sect, the alchemy pavilion elder two generations ago. He was instrumental in shaping the pavilion into what it is today. His unparalleled ability to extract essences from various ingredients—minerals, metals, and animals—elevated our sect's alchemy techniques. But his unique gift was not hereditary, making it a challenge to find a worthy successor when he passed on."

I glanced again at the journal, its significance now clearer. "Is that," I began, pointing at the book, "his journal?"

Elder Zhu nodded. "Indeed. It contains Master Li Tao's teachings, his observations, and detailed notes on the essence extraction skill. He penned down his experiences, hoping that someone in future generations might resonate with his ability and further the art."

The weight of the revelation settled on me. My essence extraction skill with plants had already opened up possibilities I hadn't imagined. But the idea of extracting essence from a wider range of ingredients was . . . staggering.

"And you believe," I hesitated, trying to wrap my head around the thought, "that I could do this as well?"

Elder Zhu's expression softened, and he leaned back in his chair. "It's a possibility. Your ability with plants is already exceptional. Whether you can extend it further, that remains to be seen. But in this journal"—he gently tapped its cover—"lies the potential path for you to walk."

My mind raced. Holding this journal felt like a monumental gift, an honor. Yet with it came an unease, a shadow of doubt. I clutched the journal closer, feeling its weight both physically and metaphorically. "Elder Zhu," I said, hesitant, "I'm truly honored by this gesture, but I must ask . . . what price is attached to such a gift?"

Elder Zhu studied me, his eyes piercing yet patient. "Your skepticism is understandable. In the Jianghu, nothing is given without expectation." He paused, his fingers interlacing thoughtfully. "As a taoist sect, our primary goal is the betterment of the world. We have a duty, almost a sacred commitment, to nurture potential when we recognize it. Not to hoard it but to let it blossom, enriching the world with its gifts."

Elder Zhu's calm demeanor radiated wisdom. "Kai, in you, we see the budding promise of a talent that could redefine alchemy. And as custodians of knowledge and tradition, if we didn't extend our resources to cultivate that talent, we'd be doing a disservice not just to the sect, but to the entire province."

He leaned forward, his gaze unwavering. "Over the years, we've sponsored numerous talents—many of whom had the skill, but lacked the backing or reputation. They've moved on, contributing to the world in their unique ways, bearing no direct allegiance to our sect."

Drawing a deep breath, he added, "That being said, while we do this with altruistic intentions, we aren't naive. The hope is, of course, that after the Grand Alchemy Gauntlet, should you see the benefits of this relationship, you might consider deepening your association with the Verdant Lotus Sect."

I contemplated his words, their meaning. While the offer seemed genuine, without any overt strings attached, the unspoken implication was clear. This act of goodwill wasn't a debt per se, but it was certainly an investment in a potential future relationship.

Sensing my thoughts, Elder Zhu offered a knowing smile. "It's a testament to your character, Kai, that you don't accept gifts without understanding their implications. We ask nothing of you now, but the door to future collaborations remains open. Think of this journal not as a shackle, but as a bridge—one that you can choose to cross when you're ready."

I held the journal in my hands, its pages filled with ancient wisdom waiting to be unlocked. "Thank you, Elder Zhu," I finally said, my voice filled with gratitude. "I'll treasure this knowledge and ensure it's put to good use."

Elder Zhu nodded, the hint of a smile playing on his lips. "In the world of alchemy and martial arts, potential is nothing without perseverance. I believe you have both. Use them wisely."

With those parting words, I took my leave, the journal safely tucked under my arm, feeling both the weight of responsibility and the thrill of the journey ahead.

The Verdant Lotus Sect sprawled across a vast expanse of scenic beauty, with lush meadows and serene water bodies punctuating the tranquil landscape. As I walked, gentle breezes caressed my face, carrying with them the fragrant scent of lotuses in full bloom. Every corner of this sect was like a painting come to life.

"This truly is a beautiful place, isn't it, Tianyi? Hard to believe it belonged to a cultivator sect."

If I recalled correctly, the training compound was supposed to be here. Feng Wu should've been here, I hoped.

My silent reverie with Tianyi ended when we came across a large open field. Here, third-class disciples were now engrossed in what appeared to be practice sparring. Their movements were fluid, a beautiful and intricate dance of feints, dodges, and strikes. Though no physical contact was made, it was clear they were mirroring each other's moves, predicting and countering them in a harmonious rhythm.

Even if it was sparring, I couldn't be confident in being able to stay in front of the third-class disciples. They were going quite fast.

Moving past this breathtaking display, I approached a more secluded compound where the rhythmic thudding from earlier grew louder. Entering, I was met with a starkly different scene. Disciples were engaged in intense training. Some struck wooden logs, while others kicked against sandbags or ground their shins against bamboo poles. Their faces were etched with determination, and every grunt echoed their unwavering commitment. Some had bloodied knuckles or bruises along their extremities.

In the midst of this, Feng Wu stood out in the corner quietly performing a similar exercise. Shirtless, with sweat glistening on his lean torso, he was hammering his knuckles against a rugged stone with singular focus. Every strike seemed to resonate with an inner strength that was awe-inspiring.

Before I could approach Feng Wu, a shorter woman with flowing raven-black hair and wearing the distinct robes of a first-class disciple intercepted me. Her sharp eyes held an intensity that seemed to dissect everything in their gaze.

"You must be Kai Liu," she said authoritatively. "I am Xia Ji, the instructor overseeing this training ground. I suppose you haven't seen conditioning before. It is a grisly sight for those who aren't familiar with martial arts."

I clasped my hands and bowed respectfully, observing a disciple striking a wooden log with fervor. "I've read about conditioning, but witnessing it first-hand . . . It's intense."

Xia Ji's eyes followed the disciplined actions of the trainees. "Conditioning is about forging the body. Qi is powerful, yes, but the physical body remains our foundation. We strengthen it so that every muscle, bone, and sinew is honed."

"But the pain . . ." I trailed off, watching as another disciple's knuckles turned raw against a sandbag.

She nodded curtly. "Pain is part of the process. It teaches us our limits and how to push past them. In battle, a conditioned body can withstand blows that might otherwise incapacitate. It's preparation, ensuring every part of us is ready for any challenge."

Although it was talked about in some of the books I had read, they never went in-depth about the topic. Seeing it in person was different from hearing someone say they struck a wooden pole for hours on end until they bled.

I nodded in acknowledgment. "This training . . . It's unlike anything I've ever seen. Especially when one can reinforce their body with qi."

Xia Ji looked over the disciples and then back to me. "Qi reinforcement is a formidable technique, but it's only one layer of a martial artist's defense. Imagine going into battle with only one strategy, one line of defense. No matter how strong it is, once it's breached, you're vulnerable."

She gestured toward a disciple, his fists bloodied but unyielding. "This training is about forging the body and mind, ensuring that beneath the shield of qi lies a fortress of resilience. In the most grueling battles, when qi wanes and exhaustion sets in, it's this raw, physical toughness, honed through relentless conditioning, that keeps a warrior standing."

My gaze returned to Feng Wu, his hands showing the testament of years of dedication. "It's about preparation," Xia Ji continued. "Qi is our spiritual armor, but this"—she clenched her fist—"is our innate armor. Combine the two, and you give yourself another edge, one you may need for victory."

She smiled, a rare occurrence I assumed, which softened her stern features. "Qi is the sky, vast and boundless, but even the sky needs the earth to be revered. This conditioning? It's our earth."

I took a moment to let her words sink in, a profound realization dawning upon me. "Thank you, Instructor Xia Ji, for this insight. May I try it for myself?"

She hesitated, her sharp eyes scanning me from head to toe. "You? An alchemist wants to try martial conditioning?" There was an undercurrent of disdain in her voice.

"I am a beginner alchemist, true," I began, sensing the skepticism in her voice, "but I also have some foundation in martial arts." I held out my hand, revealing the calluses that had formed over the months of gripping my iron staff. "These aren't just from handling pestles and beakers."

To be fair, I'd say some of them were from working in the garden for years. Running the shop back home hadn't made me weak by any means.

Xia Ji observed my hands closely, her gaze thoughtful. "Hm. Calluses from an iron staff, correct?"

I nodded, questioning internally how she could tell from a glance. "Yes, I've been training with it for a while now. I understand the importance of discipline and perseverance. I believe I can handle the rudiments of conditioning."

She leaned back, her arms crossed, still looking unsure. "Conditioning one's body for martial arts isn't just about withstanding pain or having calluses, young alchemist. It's about pushing your limits, mentally and physically. The rope-wrapped poles might seem like a simple training tool, but striking them repeatedly can be excruciating for beginners."

I met her gaze determinedly. "Every discipline has its trials, Instructor Xia Ji. In herbalism, we endure hours of painstaking precision, moments where a slight miscalculation could lead to disaster. I believe the principles are the same—dedication, patience, and resilience."

Xia Ji regarded me for a moment longer, her expression inscrutable. Then, she exhaled slowly, her stern demeanor relaxing slightly. "Very well, Kai Liu. Your determination is clear, and your argument holds weight. Let's see what you've got."

Walking over to Feng Wu, she instructed, "Feng Wu, guide him through the basics with the rope-wrapped poles."

Feng Wu nodded, his expression a mix of surprise and intrigue. I noticed he paused from the corner of my eye. "Of course, Instructor Xia Ji."

He led me to a tall pole, tightly wrapped in coarse rope. "The rope gives some cushion," Feng Wu explained, "but don't be fooled. Striking it consistently will test you."

Following his lead, I assumed the correct stance, channeling my energy to my fists. "Start with gentle strikes," he advised. I tapped the pole, the rough texture of the rope scratching against my knuckles. "The line between injury and progress is very thin."

Every subsequent hit was a challenge as I pushed past the initial discomfort. Feng Wu's voice guided me, encouraging and correcting as needed. The rhythmic thudding became a kind of meditation, each strike a blend of pain and purpose.

After some time, he left me to my own devices to finish his own training. I continued, the discomfort giving way to pain as the skin on my knuckles turned raw. Tianyi seemed confused and concerned while fluttering her wings on top of the pole, feeling the pain through our bond. But I reassured her, continuing the exercise without pause.

This was all about resilience, wasn't it? It would be a disservice to stop just when things got rough.

Sweat poured down my face, and the pain in my hands intensified with each successive strike. The coarse rope seemed to bite into my flesh, a stinging reminder of the commitment I'd made. It was almost as if the pole was a sentient being, testing my resolve.

Breathe in, strike. Breathe out, retract. Each movement was deliberate. My focus tightened, trying to ensure that every blow landed accurately, efficiently, even as the pain became nearly unbearable. The rhythmic sound of my knuckles connecting with the pole was interspersed with my heavy breathing. The world around me blurred, and there was only the pole, my hands, and the cycle of breath and motion.

I switched hands when I felt the searing pain becoming too intense, worried that I might permanently damage myself. I had almost lost track of time when a firm hand grabbed my wrist, stopping the motion.

"That's enough, Kai Liu!" Xia Ji's voice broke through my trance-like state. Her grip was unyielding, and her gaze bore into mine with a mix of concern and surprise.

I looked down at my hands and recoiled. My knuckles were raw and bleeding, a gruesome testament to my determination—or perhaps my stubbornness. The stark contrast of my blood on the pale rope was a jarring sight.

"You've pushed yourself too far," she chastised. "This isn't about proving a point. Conditioning is a journey, not a one-time event. Your hands . . ." She trailed off, shaking her head.

Feng Wu, having finished his routine, hurried over. His face held a look of genuine concern. "Kai, do you need to go to the infirmary?"

I clenched my fists, wincing slightly. "No, it's all right. Tianyi can help with the healing." I glanced at the little butterfly, her wings flapping anxiously. "But I might need some gauze to wrap them."

Xia Ji sighed, her stern demeanor softening. "You certainly have spirit, alchemist. But remember: There's a difference between tenacity and recklessness. Learn your limits."

I kneeled there, being scolded by the shorter woman alongside Feng Wu for not supervising me properly.

CHAPTER FORTY-EIGHT

Essence of Extraction

With Tianyi resting on my shoulder, gently radiating a soothing warmth to aid in the healing, I followed Feng Wu out of the compound, bidding Instructor Xia farewell. I heard her muttering quietly to herself, something about Elder Zhu wringing her neck, but I wouldn't tell. It wasn't her fault, after all. The verdant landscape of the sect felt calming after the intensity of the training session. The touch of the cool air made me glad that my knuckles were secured in gauze.

"You really are an odd one," Feng Wu remarked with a bemused smile. "Most newcomers wouldn't push themselves to such extremes, especially on their first attempt."

Grinning sheepishly, I responded, "I wanted to experience what you all go through, to truly understand. And in a strange way, I enjoyed it. Sorry for getting you in trouble, by the way."

Shaking his head in exasperation, Feng Wu led me to a storage area. "Here are the ingredients you ordered from Tranquil Breeze Farm." He handed over bundles containing Morning Dew grass, ginger, and vials of goji berry extract. "Remember to manage your time wisely."

Taking the bundles gratefully, I nodded. "Thank you, Feng Wu. I'll get started right away."

The carriage containing all my goods was also there, and I picked up a dozen vials along with the tools I had brought to get my work done.

As we walked back, the sun now dipping low in the sky, Feng Wu turned to me with a smirk. "Try not to work yourself to the bone, all right?"

"I think it's already too late for that." I laughed, waving my injured knuckles with a grin. "But is this your daily routine? I know you don't really use your fists in combat. You seem more of a dexterous type."

Feng Wu paused, gazing out to the horizon, deep in thought. His dark pony-tail fluttered slightly in the breeze, revealing that familiar glint of determination in his eye. "Kai, I've not mentioned this to many, but after our encounter with the Wind Serpents, I was bestowed with the gift of the Memory Palace technique. And since you have it too, I've been curious. How have you been utilizing it?"

I tried to hide my surprise, but a hint of it crept into my voice. "I've mainly used it as a repository for knowledge, a tool for efficient studying and reviewing. But you've applied it to cultivate your mind?"

A rare grin formed on Feng Wu's face. "Indeed. Instead of merely storing infor-mation, I use it as a mental dojo. Each room, each corridor doesn't just hold a memory or knowledge but embodies the essence of experiences. It allows me to relive moments, analyze outcomes, and refine my decisions. Through this, I've advanced rapidly in my mental cultivation, thus freeing more time to perfect my body."

I nodded slowly, absorbing his words. "Using it as a mental training ground . . . No wonder you've progressed leaps and bounds."

Feng Wu chuckled, looking at me with appreciation. "Thank you, Kai. And with your intellect, imagine what you could achieve if you harnessed the Memory Palace in a similar manner."

Eager to learn more, I asked, "Could you guide me more on how to use my Memory Palace?"

He nodded with enthusiasm. "Certainly! The key isn't to just remember, but to immerse. Relive each experience, evaluate outcomes, and imagine alternate sce-narios. This iterative mental exercise will refine your skills and decisions."

We approached the sect's main entrance, the setting sun painting the sky with vibrant shades of orange and purple.

As we parted ways, Tianyi fluttered her wings, conveying a sense of wonder. Alone with my thoughts, I looked up at the evening sky, contemplating the vast expanse. The Heavenly Interface, a phenomenon I had helped birth, reshaped the world in ways I couldn't have guessed. How many others had been granted new abilities? How would it change the dynamics of the province?

In some ways, it made me stronger than I imagined. But I supposed that meant the same for everybody else. Including those participating in the Grand Alchemy Gauntlet. I needed to work harder than ever to catch up with the others.

The Memory Palace technique was just the tip of the iceberg. Perhaps I'd need to find a way to evolve it like I did with the other skills.

Argh, too many tasks, so little time! If I wanted to make the most of my time here, I couldn't afford to keep planning. I'd need to start *doing.*

I walked back to the guest quarters. It was a sizable building reminiscent of a small inn. I hadn't seen the guests staying in the other rooms, if there were any. The door to my room opened to reveal it as I had left it this morning. I took care not to move my hands too much; the skin on my knuckles were sensitive to the touch, and jostling it resulted in discomfort.

As I carefully placed down the ingredients, I greeted the Wind Serpent egg. It was nestled in the blanket beside the oil lantern, giving it a semblance of warmth.

"Ah, my silent companion, what tales you could tell if only you could speak!" I mused aloud, my voice playful with mock grandeur.

Drawing upon my vast knowledge of Wind Serpent lore, I began inspecting the egg meticulously. "You see, dear egg," I began, the room filled with the weight of my words, "for you to truly flourish, your shell should be smooth to the touch, not mottled or pocked." I gently ran a finger over its surface, feeling the cool texture beneath my touch. "A fine specimen indeed. You, my precious, shall grow up to be the envy of the skies!"

Leaning in closer, my eyes scanned for the subtle hue shifts that would indicate a healthy embryo within. "Ah! The gentle shift from azure to teal; a most promising sign!" I exclaimed, unable to contain my excitement.

Then, with a teasing flourish, I said, "Under my tutelage, you shall ascend to unparalleled heights! Why, with me, Kai Liu, genius of the ages, as your guiding light, how could you not?" I chuckled, imagining the mighty creature this egg would one day become. If it grew to even half the size of the Wind Serpents we fought, I'd have my work cut out for me. Feeding a Spirit Beast was no easy task. Tianyi was a blessing in that regard.

From my shoulder, Tianyi gave a gentle flutter, the sensation through our bond clearly suggesting, *Here he goes again*. It was almost as if she was rolling her eyes at me. But I was undeterred. After all, one needed a touch of drama in their life to keep things interesting.

Inspecting the base of the egg, I noticed the fine veins, an intricate network pulsating with life. "Ah, the lifelines," I mused. "Bright and vivid, just as they should be. This means you're receiving all the nourishment you need."

Lifting my gaze to the unresponsive egg, my tone grew more earnest. "Understand this, little one. Our journey together will be filled with trials and tribulations. But fear not! For I shall be by your side, guiding, nurturing, and ensuring you grow strong and proud."

Tianyi gave a gentle sigh through our bond, a hint of affectionate exasperation tinged with amusement. But I could sense her quiet agreement: this egg had potential, and under our care, it would undoubtedly thrive.

Settling down next to the egg, I murmured, "Rest now, for the morrow brings new adventures. And remember, you have the unwavering support of Kai Liu, unparalleled caretaker and your soon-to-be best friend." I ended with a wink, even though the egg couldn't see it. But it was all in good fun, and deep down, I genuinely believed in the bright future we'd share.

I set it aside, preparing the ingredients for my potions. I suppose I should start off with my bestsellers, the Invigorating Dawn Tonic. So that would mean I'd need Morning Dew and ginger. There were a few other ingredients I'd need, but those were the critical components.

As I organized and prepared the ingredients, I couldn't help but think on whether or not I should adjust my recipe. Although it was early, there were some potential refinements I could make that would make it even stronger.

With the thoughts of enhancing the potion swirling in my mind, I laid out the ingredients meticulously in front of me. The scent of the Morning Dew grass wafted in the air, a fresh, invigorating aroma that was a natural stimulant. The ginger, with its pungent and spicy scent, was waiting to be extracted.

However, the thought of changing the recipe was tempting. If I could improve the potency, it could give me an edge. But then, there was also the risk of introducing unforeseen side effects, especially when combined with the other ingredients. In the end, quality assurance was paramount; delivering a polished product without defects was my brand's promise. The thought of renegotiating for better prices using the additional enhancements was put away for later. I needed to create.

Rolling up my sleeves, I focused on the ginger. It used to be a tricky ingredient to work with. Ginger's essence lay deep within its fibers, and a crude extraction wouldn't capture its full potency. But now, extracting its pure, unadulterated essence required only my will. Holding a piece gingerly, I placed my hand, searching for an extraction point. I began to pull, feeling the familiar sensation as energy left the ginger's form and coalesced into a sphere in my hand.

As I worked, I began to reminisce about the alchemy techniques I had learned and how they were closely related to the art of potion-making. A pill furnace, for instance, employed control over heat and the ability to distill the essence of ingredients. I wondered if there was a way to infuse such a method into my potion-making process. The furnace's controlled environment could perhaps allow for an even purer essence to be refined. But I'd need to do some more research.

Next was the Morning Dew grass. Unlike the ginger, this ingredient required a cold-infusion method. I took the fresh stalks and crushed them gently, ensuring the dew trapped within was released. Mixing it with a base solution, I allowed it to infuse overnight. The resulting liquid would be cool, refreshing, and brimming with vitality.

With the two main components prepared, I moved on to combining them with the other ingredients. As I meticulously mixed, measured, and brewed, I kept reflecting on the potential of alchemy to enhance my craft. Even with my injured hands, creating the potion was as easy as breathing to me. I had done it too many times, both in theory and in practice to make a misstep.

Thinking about the pill furnace, an idea struck me. What if I could combine the two crafts? If I could use a pill furnace to help refine the ingredients further, ensuring an even higher level of purity and potency, then the Invigorating Dawn Tonic would indeed be unparalleled.

But first, I had a promise to keep, a reputation to uphold. The current batch would remain as it was. However, future batches? Those held promise, an exciting frontier of innovation waiting to be explored.

The only thing left now was to wait. But I wouldn't remain idle. It was time to read the journal left behind by Master Li Tao. I had put it off despite my initial temptations, but I wanted to do things in the proper order. A cultivator of renown that advanced alchemy in the Verdant Lotus Sect more than any other alchemist before him.

I plotted myself down on the ground in a cross-legged position, and opened the page.

The first page stared back at me, each character meticulously crafted, displaying a quiet authority.

If you are reading this, you possess the ability of essence extraction. This sacred art, passed through generations, is not just a gift but a responsibility. One must wield it with knowledge and wisdom.

I paused, intrigued and compelled to read further. The journal continued:

My journey began in the prime of my forties, at a time when most men settle into the routines of their life. Essence extraction revealed itself to me not as a sudden awakening but as a slow, patient realization. Initially, my power was limited. Metals whispered their secrets to me. The iron, the gold, the silver, they all yielded their essence to my touch. But over time, with rigorous practice and countless failures, I expanded my realm.

I could sense the gravity and weight of Master Li Tao's words. His journey of discovering this art was fraught with trials and tribulations, yet he persevered. As I delved deeper into his writing, the master described his forays into manipulating other elements.

Plants came next. Their energy, I found, was more elusive. They did not possess the stubbornness of metals but carried a gentle fragility. Extracting their essence required finesse, not force. My first success was with the Wolfsbane. From there, it was a cascade of discoveries.

I thought of the ginger and Morning Dew grass, comparing my method with the techniques he described, seeing the parallels and understanding the deviations.

Beasts were the final frontier. Their essences were complex, a combination of the elements they consumed and the environments they inhabited. One requires a deep knowledge of the animal they are extracting an essence from to maximize their gains.

It was a revelation. The distinction between the essences of inanimate ingredients and those of living entities was empathy. Suddenly, my gaze shifted to the Wind Serpent egg beside me. If Master Li Tao had learned to extract the essences of beasts, what stopped me from extracting the life force of living beings like this egg?

But the thought was jarring. The idea of extracting the life essence of a living entity felt deeply wrong. Would doing so end the life of the hatchling within? Was I willing to cross that line?

I shook my head, dispelling the dark contemplation. No, I wouldn't, and it wasn't the path I wished to walk. That could be the gateway into a darker, demonic path. What would stop me from burning such powers against people? My friends? My family? I've read enough stories to learn that overwhelmingly powerful abilities like that would come at a price too heavy to bear. I'd learn, adapt, and evolve, but my moral compass would guide me.

The journal's next line drew me in again.

In this journey, I will teach you the art of extracting essences from metals, plants, and beasts. Practice the exercises, understand the theory, and advance the art of alchemy.

My heart raced with excitement. This was a treasure trove of knowledge that could reshape my alchemical pursuits. With this, I could redefine what was possible.

But first, practice.

Time flowed like water as I thoroughly absorbed Master Li Tao's teachings.

CHAPTER FORTY-NINE

Homework

The pages smelled of old parchment and were interspersed with ink sketches. The first illustration showed a hand placed over a block of metal, fingers spread wide with lines of force emanating outward.

Understanding Metal's Nature: Before one can extract from metal, they must understand its nature. Place your hand upon a piece of metal and attempt to sense its core. Do not extract. Instead, attune yourself. Feel its solidity, its weight, and its resistance.

I looked around for any metal item within my vicinity. But the closest one I had was my iron staff from Wang Jun. I left it underneath the bed, as I hadn't found the opportunity to train yet.

Placing it by my legs, I reached out and searched for an extraction point, like how I do with plants. But all I felt was an unyielding wall. I had never attempted to extract anything else with my powers aside from plant matter. It didn't occur to me to attempt it on anything else. After all, the Heavenly Interface told me it was supposed to be used for plants only.

Where I would try to feel out gently and coax out the extraction point, my qi seemed to bounce off any attempts at extracting the metal. I kept testing different spots, brushing my fingertips along the iron staff to find the point of extraction.

After several minutes of failure, I opened my eyes and let out a small exhale.

I was pushing my essence and qi against the iron. It was like trying to push my hand through a wall. It didn't budge, it didn't yield.

That clearly wasn't going to work. What did Master Li Tao say to do afterward?

If your initial attempt is not successful, do not fret. The will is a tool when dealing with metal. Strengthen yours. Sit in meditation, envisioning a wall. With each breath, see this wall become taller, thicker, and more impregnable. Your will must be strong enough to climb and then break down this wall.

A matter of will, huh?

That didn't seem right. I was made of pure, concentrated power and will. At least 15 percent.

I put down the staff and tried again but with an intensity unlike anything before. I gritted my teeth, remembering how I had to push through against the rope-wrapped poles during my conditioning exercise.

After finding a good spot to hold, I began to *push*.

The metal refused to yield. My grip tightened on the staff as I pushed harder and harder, trying to make it bend to my will.

Suddenly, a sharp, splintering pain pierced through my mind, making me recoil in agony. It felt as if a thousand needles were being thrust into my head, each one more painful than the last. My vision blurred, and the room around me spun. Dropping the iron staff, I grabbed my head in my hands, trying to control the surging pain.

Amid the haze, I felt a burning sensation seeping from my palm. Looking down, I noticed the muscles on my palm had twisted and turned a darkish purple. My thumb contorted into a painful position. Panic welled up inside me. *Qi Deviation*, a voice echoed in my mind.

I tried to focus my internal energies to stabilize my qi, but the pain was overwhelming. The surge had disrupted my internal pathways, and now my qi was running wild, unchecked. Each attempt to control it only led to more pain.

Despite my eyes being closed, I felt a white flash of light close by and a soft touch on my shoulder. Tianyi.

Almost immediately, the pain subsided. It was still debilitating, but I no longer feared for my life. I released a sharp intake of breath, internally thanking my steadfast companion for her swift intervention. I truly would be dead several times over without her help. She's getting some alcohol as a treat after this is all settled and over with.

Hours or perhaps minutes later, the worst of the pain subsided, leaving me drenched in sweat and panting heavily. My hand throbbed, and a few bruises remained, a stark reminder of my foolishness.

Laying on the ground, I took stock of the situation. My body felt drained, my mind foggy. Muttering out my thanks to Tianyi, she fluttered over to her corner by the windowsill, resting amicably.

It was then that Master Li Tao's words resonated even more profoundly.

Your will must be strong enough to climb and then break down this wall.

My will had faltered because it had never truly been tested in this way. It wasn't about sheer force or trying harder, but about understanding and then dominating. Ha, where was Wang Jun when I needed him? As a master of the forge, surely he could've helped me with this.

Lifting myself up slowly, I made a decision. If it was my will that needed strengthening, then I would push my body and mind to its limits.

I looked at my knuckles. They were still tender from the conditioning drill, although the skin was beginning to heal. Even though I knew honing my resilience and will be done through the drill, Instructor Xia Ji's words crossed my mind.

Conditioning is a journey, not a one-time event.

Pushing myself in overeagerness would result in permanent damage. As much as I wanted to get all these done, I couldn't screw myself over. These hands were worth hundreds of gold! Recovery meant losing out on time to improve my alchemy, herbal, and combat skills.

My spirit sank at the realization that I might not be ready for the Grand Alchemy Gauntlet in time. What could I do to heal faster?

Could I possibly create an elixir to expedite the healing of my hands? I could potentially use my expertise in extracting plant essence to create a potion, but this was a step up from what I usually made. Even with all my breakthroughs so far, my potions were aids in day-to-day life, not a panacea that could cure one of everything. Even though I used them to help win the battle against the Wind Serpents, I only kept them in mind to help regular people. Those with back pain, or struggled to get a full night's rest.

They weren't the sort that cultivators would use to aid themselves in battle against powerful spirit beasts. The ingredients I used were just too . . . *mundane.*

But now I had access to an entire sect's resources. They even had rare plants that boasted unique properties I never dealt with before. As I dove deeper into alchemy, I'd learn how to refine them into more powerful products.

This would be my personal project. I'd need some ginseng, although the age of the rootlets wouldn't matter.

I delved into my Memory Palace, reviewing my wide knowledge of plants to see the ingredients I needed for my purposes. As I continued to think, a prototype of sorts began to unfurl in my mind. I think forming it as a hydrosol would be a good idea. The effect would be mild, and I could make it in large quantities for dipping gauze into. That gauze would not only keep my fists secure after conditioning drills, they would also speed up the healing process and hopefully numb the area to help me continue working when I wasn't doing physical training.

The thought was enticing. With a properly made hydrosol, I could push my limits without the fear of lasting injury. It could support faster recovery and even strengthen my qi pathways. Constant use would strengthen them, so long as I didn't get Qi Deviation again. I'm thankful that the strengthening of my body made it less and less likely to happen.

Best of all, I wouldn't have to tire out Tianyi. If it was effective, I could see it being used in the sect as well. People like Feng Wu would be able to do these conditioning drills without worrying about the recovery process.

If I completed this, it might just be the key to *everything.*

I exited the Memory Palace technique, keeping the template for my new product unfinished. I'd need to do some more reading tomorrow to find the best possible way to go about this. I didn't make hydrosols often back in my village, after all.

My eyes flitted to the array of vials and beakers on the table. The Invigorating Dawn Tonic potions I had left overnight to infuse were finally ready. I examined the amber liquid, swirling it in the light. If I could make this, creating a more specialized potion for my needs wasn't an insurmountable task.

Picking up an empty vial, I began to think of what components I would need. Certain roots for their anti-inflammatory properties, a bit of spirit moss to boost qi flow to the area, and perhaps some sort of reed for the cooling and numbing effect. The potential combination of ingredients seemed limitless.

While lost in my musings, a delicate fluttering caught my attention. Tianyi, her wings like opalescent gemstones, flew in circles. She tilted her head as if to inquire about my train of thought. I couldn't help but chuckle at her inquisitiveness. "Thinking of brewing something new, Tianyi. Something to mend these battered hands of mine."

She fluttered up, her wings catching the sunlight and producing a dazzling display of colors, before landing gracefully on one of the potion vials, inspecting it. I took that as a sign of encouragement.

"But . . ." I paused for a moment, feeling a sudden wave of vulnerability. "What if I fail? What if I can't make it in time?" The significance of the upcoming Gauntlet and the uncertainty of my plan pressed heavily on my mind. This all rode on one main factor: me actually making the potion.

Tianyi sensed my hesitance. With a gentle flutter, she landed back on my shoulder, her delicate legs lightly touching my skin as if to comfort me. Her action reminded me of the countless times she had been my pillar, both in spirit and in action.

I couldn't fail. I *wouldn't*.

With renewed determination, I said, "Let's do this, Tianyi. Time to concoct the best healing elixir the world has ever seen!"

But in all honesty, I need to rest. I could see dawn breaking. I wouldn't want to mess up in front of Instructor Xiao-Hu tomorrow. Li Na and Han Wei would definitely poke fun of me if I were to.

And just like that, a quest appeared.

Quest: Creation of Healing Hydrosol
—Study ancient alchemical texts from the Verdant Lotus Sect's library to uncover the secrets of hydrosol creation. (0/3)
—Harvest fresh tienchi ginseng, spirit moss, common reed, and hyacinth orchid and deepen your understanding of each ingredient. (0/4)
—Extract the pure essence of spirit moss and find its hidden properties. (0/1)
—Learn the method to create purified water using alchemy.

I gave myself a minute to digest the quest fully. I went to my freshly made batch of Invigorating Dawn Tonic and chugged one down. Energy washed over my body, soothing my physical and mental fatigue.

I supposed I wasn't sleeping tonight.

My vision blurred, a throbbing sensation originating from my temples. The last thing I remembered was being completely engrossed within my Memory Palace, and now . . .

I was seated at a wooden bench, surrounded by students. Each was engrossed in preparing various ingredients, carefully following instructions from an imposing figure at the head of the room. The realization hit me suddenly: I was in class.

Li Na was waving her hand over my face, a concerned look etched on her features. "Kai? Are you all right? You seem . . . elsewhere."

Pushing away the fatigue clouding my mind, I forced a smile. "I'm fine, Li Na. Just a bit distracted. Thanks for checking on me."

She gave me a pointed look but didn't press the matter. Turning back to the task at hand, I tried to follow the instructions being shared.

"Our focus today," Instructor Xiao-Hu began, "is on prepping ingredients with efficiency. Remember, your diligence here affects the final product. Do not rush. Instead, be methodical and precise."

My fingers shook as I picked up an herb. Fatigue clung to me, weighing down every movement. Each snip of the herb seemed to drain me further, making me acutely aware of the long hours spent in experimentation the previous night.

Amid my struggle, memories of Master Li Tao's exercises resurfaced. *Strengthen your will.* That phrase echoed in my mind. Wasn't this just another wall to climb?

With a deep breath, I focused. My knife moved with a newfound purpose, quickly and efficiently prepping the herb in front of me. I tuned out the rest of the world, focusing only on the task. The herbs, the knife, and me.

Li Na, seemingly impressed, nudged me with her elbow. "Looks like someone finally woke up. Keep this up, and you might just get moved to the advanced classes."

I chuckled, not breaking my rhythm. "Let's not get ahead of ourselves."

"Quiet!" Instructor Xiao-Hu scolded, turning to our corner of the class. I muttered out an apology and kept my head down, too tired to even feel embarrassed.

However, as the class continued, the fatigue came back in waves, stronger each time. I found my grip slipping, my focus waning. But every time I felt like giving in, I remembered Master Li Tao's words. The metal. The wall. This was just another challenge to overcome.

When the instructor finally called an end to the session, I exhaled in relief, my fingers aching, my mind exhausted but proud of the work I'd done. Li Na smirked at me, her playful demeanor returning. "You did well today, despite your zombie-like state at the start. Got any secret potions you're hiding?"

Grinning, I responded, "Maybe, but a cultivator never reveals all his secrets."

CHAPTER FIFTY

Impressions

After a short break from class, Li Na and Han Wei went back to their seats in class. I looked down at my workstation—neatly arranged bamboo mats, a basic mortar and pestle, and a set of steel knives designed for precise herb-cutting.

As the class delved into the meticulous process of herb-grinding and equipment cleaning, my hands worked almost on autopilot. I sliced the roots and leaves with practiced ease, all the while stewing in my thoughts.

If I get through this class quickly, maybe I can sneak in a quick nap before physical training. Heaven knows I'll need all the energy I can muster for the martial drills later. Balancing the physical and the alchemical—now there's the challenge.

"Kai, please stay after class." Instructor Xiao-Hu's voice snapped me out of my reverie. I looked up to find his eyes on me, serious but otherwise unreadable.

The pit of my stomach tightened. Why would he want me to stay behind? My eyes darted toward my classmates, each engrossed in their own tasks, oblivious to my small crisis.

As the lesson wound down, I followed the protocols for cleaning and storing each tool. I wiped down the table, ensuring not a speck of residue remained. My classmates started to pack up, leaving the classroom one by one, their chatter receding like a fading storm.

Li Na and Han Wei lingered, glancing in my direction as they passed.

"Hope everything's okay," Li Na said softly, concern flickering in her eyes. Han Wei patted my shoulder, a look of sympathy on his face, and then they were gone, leaving me alone with Instructor Xiao-Hu.

The room fell silent except for the subtle creaking of bamboo and the distant chatter from outside. I waited, my heartbeat drumming a rapid rhythm in my ears.

"Your basic skills are solid, Kai," Instructor Xiao-Hu began, "but remember, even the simplest techniques can be elevated to an art form. It's the subtleties, the nuances that set the true alchemists apart."

Is he leading up to something? Some advanced lesson or secret tip, perhaps? I waited for him to continue, a jumble of hope and apprehension swirling within me.

"Instructor Xiao-Hu, does this mean there are still areas I need to improve on?" I asked cautiously, careful not to sound too eager or defensive.

"Actually"—he looked me squarely in the eye—"your fundamentals are already up to par. You're ready to take the exam to accelerate your curriculum."

A rush of pride swelled within me. *Finally, recognition!*

"When can I take this exam?" I managed to ask, pushing my concerns to the back of my mind.

"We can have it prepared by tomorrow," Instructor Xiao-Hu said. "In the meantime, visit Elder Zhu's office to discuss how we will proceed with your advanced classes."

I nodded, a mixture of elation and anticipation filling me. "Thank you, Instructor Xiao-Hu. I'll prepare myself accordingly."

"Very well. Remember, the path of an alchemist is ever-changing and challenging. Do not become complacent."

"Understood," I replied as I took my leave.

Walking through the tranquil halls of the Verdant Lotus Sect, my thoughts bounced between pride in my accomplishment and the emotional tug of having left Tianyi alone. I had left her in my room, with the window ajar for her to leave if needed. Was she all right? I was anxious but quickly suppressed it. The Verdant Lotus Sect was a safe space, filled with disciplined disciples and powerful barriers. Still, the parent in me worried.

Before I knew it, I found myself standing before the elegantly carved doors of Elder Zhu's office. Taking a deep breath, I knocked softly, my knuckles barely grazing the ornate woodwork. I winced, my hands still sensitive but no longer painful. Making the hydrosol was going to be a top priority of mine.

"Come in," Elder Zhu beckoned from within.

As I stepped into the room, I felt a sense of anticipation knotting my stomach. Advanced classes. Accelerated curriculum. The thought tantalized me like a rare elixir, but there was also a gravity to it.

Elder Zhu looked up from the scrolls sprawled across his desk, his eyes sharp yet comforting. "Ah, Kai. I've heard about Instructor Xiao-Hu's recommendation to have you go into advanced classes. Quite the achievement, I must say."

I scratched my nose. Instructor Xiao-Hu was so nice. I'd have to get him something as thanks.

"Thank you, Elder Zhu. I've been told to discuss the accelerated curriculum with you?"

"Yes, you have," he said, smiling warmly. "But before we delve into that, tell me, how are you finding life here at the Verdant Lotus Sect? Especially with your unique companion?"

Ah, Tianyi. Even here, away from her, she was still with me. "It's been fulfilling, Elder. As for Tianyi, she's adjusting. I was actually a bit worried leaving her alone today."

Elder Zhu chuckled. "Ah, the responsibilities of a guardian. But you're right to keep her in mind. Spirit Beasts are not just pets, they require far more care and consideration."

"Indeed they are."

"Well, then," Elder Zhu continued, unrolling a fresh scroll from his desk, "let's discuss your future here, shall we?"

Taking classes, learning about new topics and concepts . . . It was incredibly refreshing for me. The way they taught things here was so structured compared to what we had in Gentle Wind Village, where several of the elders were rounded up to teach us how to do basic things. I suppose if I had the opportunity, I could've gone into the school system in Crescent Bay City, taken the exam to get into the Imperial College and become an official. I would've gone into classes like this, although catered toward philosophy, calligraphy, and whatnot. It would've been a trivial thing for me, a genius of the ages, to get into somewhere like the Imperial College.

But alas, I took the more daring opportunity as a country bumpkin, learning the art of herbalism and martial arts to forge my own path in the world.

We ran through the selected courses that the alchemy pavilion offered. They were taught by several first-class disciples. I could see that Instructor Xiao-Hu taught many of the more advanced branches of alchemy himself.

Advanced Herbology seemed like a logical step for me to take in my progression through alchemy. I could hardly say I knew a lot about the rarer and esoteric plants found in the province. I also confirmed with Elder Zhu that this class was very hands-on, which made me even more excited. I would be able to harvest rare ingredients on my own. I couldn't wait.

Elixir Synthesis, Qi Infusion in Alchemy, Pill Concoction, and Toxicology and Antidotes were all fascinating topics that would bolster my foundation in alchemy. If I wanted to get to an acceptable level before the Grand Alchemy Gauntlet, I'd need to work my tailbone off. There, I'd learn how to use more tools like the alchemical still, and even how to create purified water. I'd be able to shore up my weaknesses and fortify my strengths over the coming months while completing portions of my quest.

But the most interesting one I learned about was Alchemy Array Crafting. In this class, students would learn how to create alchemical arrays that can automate some aspects of the alchemical process, increase the efficacy of the ingredients, or even produce new, unique effects. Elder Zhu emphasized its importance, declaring how knowing the basics would be enough to take me far into the Grand Alchemy Gauntlet, so I enrolled in the class as well. My schedule was going to be packed.

As we delved into the complexities of the advanced courses and what the accelerated path entailed, I felt as if a new chapter was opening in my life. But amid all this talk of progress and growth, my thoughts still drifted back to Tianyi. Our paths were entwined, after all. If I were to ascend, she would be right there with me, soaring on delicate wings into our uncertain but promising future.

I wanted to create a pill just for her. It wouldn't be fair for her to receive nothing after all the help she has given me. And considering her affinity for the Moonlit Grace Lily, I would make it with its essence. Once I was confident in my skills, I'd make one for Tianyi.

But she couldn't consume one like I could, so I'd likely have to make it in the form of a liquid. Or even alcohol. Who said cultivation pills couldn't taste good?

Elder Zhu paused, his quill suspended over the parchment, and looked up at me with a twinkle in his eye. "Ah, yes, I almost forgot. I wanted to talk about your skill, Essence Extraction."

I blinked at the change in topic. "Yes, Elder. I acquired that skill after maxing out my Herbalism skill. It allows me to extract the essence from plants, concentrating their properties. It differs from Master Li Tao's ability, in the sense that mine only allows me to extract the essence of plants only."

"And what else?" Elder Zhu leaned in, an unspoken excitement in his eyes. "There was mention of a skill evolution, yes?"

"Ah, yes. The skill evolved into something called Spiritual Herbalism. Not only can I extract essences, but it also grants me the ability to infuse plants with qi, enhancing their qualities," I elaborated, keenly aware of my words. After all, I didn't know the full extent of the Heavenly Interface, and the extent of the Interface Manipulator perk. I hadn't recalled anybody else mentioning any perks in all my conversations either.

As much as I trusted the Verdant Lotus Sect, there were some things I felt should be better kept as secrets.

Elder Zhu's eyes widened as he eagerly reached for a new scroll, unrolled it, and started jotting down notes. "Infusing plants with qi, you say? That's remarkable, Kai. Since the Day of Awakening, the sect has been trying to compile all the skills and their branching paths. It's all to understand how this new system, this Heavenly Interface, is affecting our traditional methods and practices. And yet I've never come across a skill named Spiritual Herbalism."

I found myself leaning in, captivated. "So, you're saying my skill branch is unique?"

"Seemingly so," Elder Zhu replied, capping his ink bottle. "This leads me to believe that the path one's skills take is influenced by individual factors. You've practiced herbalism for most of your life, yes?"

I nodded, the realization dawning on me. "Are you suggesting that my background could have affected the direction of my skill evolution?"

"Precisely. It appears that the system is more dynamic and personalized than we initially thought. Your unique path could be invaluable knowledge for the sect, and I would appreciate your contribution to our archives."

An odd sense of pride filled me. My skills, honed over a lifetime of trial and error, had finally led me somewhere unexpected and crucial. My contribution could actually matter. And unlike my previous worries, my ability couldn't be replicated so easily.

Elder Zhu broke the silence. "You mentioned being able to infuse plants with qi. Could you perhaps give a demonstration at some point? It would be educational not only for our records but also for you to understand the limits and potentials of your skill."

"Of course, Elder Zhu. I'd be honored to share what I've learned," I replied, feeling an uplifting sense of responsibility and excitement flood through me.

As I prepared to rise from my seat, Elder Zhu spoke again, this time with a more solemn tone. "There's another matter we need to discuss, Kai."

I settled back down, my curiosity piqued. "Yes, Elder Zhu?"

"First, I want to thank you for contributing to the archives with your unique skill," Elder Zhu began, locking eyes with me. "It may seem trivial to you, but this is part of a larger discourse among the elders of the Verdant Lotus Sect. Not everyone is comfortable embracing the Heavenly Interface."

"Why is that?" I asked, unable to suppress my astonishment.

"Some among the elders feel that traditional teaching methods should be preserved. They worry that the Heavenly Interface might dilute the centuries-old wisdom passed down through the generations," he explained, and I detected melancholy in his voice. "I, however, see it differently. As a scholar on the path of learning, I believe the Heavenly Interface has the potential to accelerate our understanding and capabilities."

"What makes you so certain, Elder?"

He sighed, his face creasing with concern. "Do you recall the Silent Moon Sect and the Whispering Wind Sect?"

I nodded. Those two sects, after all, were the most powerful in Crescent Bay City, where the Verdant Lotus Sect also resided. The politics among the sects were complicated, to say the least.

"Recently, the Silent Moon Sect has been making aggressive moves to expand their territory. Their ambitions seem to know no bounds, and it's only a matter of time before this turns into skirmishes or even all-out fights between sects," Elder Zhu confided, the weight of his words settling around us like a dense fog.

"So, you're saying the Heavenly Interface could be a game-changer in defending yourselves?"

"Exactly. We need to amass our own power. We can't afford to fall behind, especially not when the stakes are so high. It's crucial for the Verdant Lotus Sect to utilize every advantage we have, including the Heavenly Interface," he stressed, his eyes locked onto mine, filled with an intensity I had not seen before.

I felt the gravity of his words pull me back to reality. Beyond the walls of the Verdant Lotus Sect lay a world teeming with unpredictable dangers. It made me worry for those who couldn't protect themselves. What would happen to villages like Qingmu during such skirmishes?

"The path you're treading, Kai, might very well be critical to our sect's continued prosperity and survival. It is essential that we embrace innovation while honoring tradition. That's how we grow. That's how we survive," Elder Zhu concluded, his eyes burning with a fire that could only be fueled by a lifetime of wisdom and a dash of hope.

For a moment, I was speechless. The responsibility, the possibilities, and the urgent need for action all descended upon me, heavy but not crushing. I felt a renewed sense of purpose, fortified by Elder Zhu's words.

"I understand, Elder Zhu," I finally said, my voice steady. "I'll do my best to contribute in any way I can, not just for my sake, but for the Verdant Lotus Sect as well."

Elder Zhu nodded, a smile spreading across his wise face. "I had no doubt you would, Kai."

I left Elder Zhu's office with my head swirling with new thoughts and a syllabus containing all my advanced classes. With classes done for the day, it was time for me to continue training on my own.

CHAPTER FIFTY-ONE

Uncertainty and Insecurity

My feet lead me to a secluded clearing, far enough from prying eyes. The grunts and echoes of clanging weapons from the third-class disciples still resonated faintly in my ears. They were young—far younger than me—but their strength, their skill, outclassed my own.

I shouldn't neglect my physical training, even if I wanted to improve my skills in alchemy as much as I could. A well-rounded approach suited me best. I brought up my status, to check the progression of my skills.

Heavenly Interface: Kai Liu
Perk(s):
Interface Manipulator—Allows manipulation of the
Heavenly Interface and access to special features.
Race: Human
Vitality: Sufficient
Primary
Affinity—Wood
Cultivation Rank: Mortal Realm—Rank 3
Qi: Qi Initiation Stage—Rank 1
Mind: Mortal Realm—Rank 2
Body: Mortal Realm—Rank 2
Skills
Spiritual Herbalism—Level 2 (. . .)
Nature's Attunement—Level 2 (. . .)
Reading—Level 4 (. . .)
Cultivation Techniques:
Rooted Banyan Stance—Level 1 (. . .)
Crimson Lotus Purification—Level 1 (. . .)

I bit my tongue, unhappy with the lack of progress. Even after all I've gone through, my cultivation rank was still at the mortal realm. I couldn't even be classified as a true cultivator. At what point could I consider myself at the level of the third-class disciples, who were years younger than I was?

The forest's embrace was tightening around me as I took off my robe and placed it neatly on a flat stone. My breath felt lighter as I inhaled the scent of the grass. I stood in the center of the clearing, my feet shoulder-width apart, sinking into the horse stance. My muscles tensed as I lowered my body, thighs parallel to the ground, calves vertical, back straight as a rod.

"Deeper stance, hold it longer," I muttered to myself, tightening my core. The familiar burn in my thighs intensified, but today it felt like a comforting embrace compared to the inferno of insecurities boiling in my mind. I could see those third-class disciples pushing themselves harder, defying their limits, making breakthroughs. And here I was, stuck in this ancient stance. Could I afford to slack?

It was selfish of me to request more resources from the sect. They were gracious enough to give me their alchemical texts despite not being a disciple, but asking them to teach me martial arts was the height of ungratefulness.

No. I had to push myself—raise the intensity, shorten the training time. Every second was precious. With Elder Ming's guidance and the support of the Heavenly Interface, I'd pave my own path.

My muscles trembled as I forced myself into a deeper stance, my fists clenched so tight they turned white. Minutes felt like hours, but eventually, I let myself rise. No time to catch my breath; I transitioned into a series of strikes, punches, and kicks, each movement more forceful than the last. I tried to remember what I learned from Feng Wu, and even that dastardly second-class disciple from the Silent Moon Sect. But all I could do was a pitiful mimicry.

I remembered the elegance of Feng Wu's bladed fan, how it danced gracefully in his hands like a petal caught in the wind; the sharpness, the unpredictability of his moves. I tried to emulate the fluidity, but my iron staff's weight clashed with the delicate nature of the fan. The fan moved with the wind; my staff sought to break it. I felt heavy, clumsy.

I took a deep breath, shaking away the sweat trickling down my temple. "Focus," I whispered to myself.

Next, I tried to recreate Xu Ziqing's swift swordplay—sharp, lethal, and utterly captivating. His sword cut through the air like a silken ribbon, every motion masterful and deliberate. As I tried to mirror him, my staff movements felt unnatural, rigid, trying to fit a square peg into a round hole. Xu's technique was catered for swift slashes, while my staff was made for sweeping arcs and quick thrusts. The contrast was too much; I felt torn between two worlds.

I grunted in frustration, whirling my staff with more vigor, desperately attempting to fuse the two contrasting styles together. But the more I pushed myself, the more the techniques resisted, as though they were water and oil, refusing to blend.

"It's no use," I huffed, feeling defeated. Why did I think I could mimic such unique techniques with my staff? Perhaps I was a fool for thinking so.

My heart ached, longing to be as graceful as Feng Wu or as swift as Xu Ziqing. But the truth stared at me squarely in the face—I was neither of them. The bitter pill was hard to swallow. I gazed at my staff, its solid iron form reflecting the dappled sunlight from the canopy above. It was an extension of me, and I of it.

Finally, my body screamed for a halt, every muscle fiber begging for respite. I sat down, cross-legged, and closed my eyes. It was time for the Crimson Lotus Purification Technique.

I felt a phantom touch on my shoulder and momentarily opened my eyes to see nothing there. I sighed. It had been quite some time since I trained without Tianyi's company. I hope she's resting well. It was much lonelier than I expected, not having her by my side for such a long period of time. With only my own thoughts as company.

I began to circulate my qi, drawing in the ambient energy from the surrounding forest as my worries and anxieties faded away into the background. The influx was like a stream, gently trickling into my dantian. But before it could merge with my core, I ignited it with my internal fire, burning away the filth, the impurities. The technique was like a crucible, purging everything unnecessary, leaving behind only the essence, a purer form of qi that would empower me.

The purification aspect was the most important, but arduous portion of my technique.

As Elder Ming said, my body was a vessel to hold qi. And compared to regular cultivators, mine was only the size of a small cup. I could only fill it with the purest energy, to make the most of what I had.

I don't know how much time passed, but after gathering what energy I could and shedding away all but the purest, I was left with a marble-sized ball of qi, which I promptly added to my dantian.

In contrast to the first time I attempted this, no black sludge appeared. My body felt revitalized and further cleansed, as though I had just come out of a nice, long bath. I breathed out a sigh of relief. It was minuscule, but I could feel the growth established within my reserves.

As I opened my eyes, I was met with another pair of deep green eyes.

"AAAAACK!"

I scrambled backward, realizing that it was Feng Wu. I could see the ghost of a smile on his face. It was clear to me he was holding in a laugh from the clenching of his jaw.

"How long have you been here? That's not funny, Feng Wu!" I waved my fist at him angrily, trying to soothe my rapidly beating heart. It seemed my cultivation took longer than expected, judging by the sun setting on the horizon. "I could've gotten Qi Deviation!"

Feng Wu chuckled, his green eyes twinkling with amusement. "I apologize for startling you. I didn't intend to, I promise."

"Yeah, well," I retorted, still trying to collect myself, "you've got a talent for creeping up on people."

Feng Wu sobered up and took a step closer. "You're quite engrossed in your training. I didn't wish to disturb you. I came to ask if you'd like to join me for dinner in the dining hall."

I opened my mouth to say yes, grateful for the chance to eat a good meal and socialize for a bit. But then my eyes fell on the setting sun, and my thoughts went back to the third-class disciples I saw earlier. My hand unconsciously clenched.

"No thank you," I said, the words heavy as they left my mouth. "I think I'll continue my training here."

A hint of concern washed over Feng Wu's face. "Is something bothering you? You seem . . . uneasy."

I shrugged it off with a grin. "Ah, you see, I'm just too much of a genius to waste time eating. I've got this immense talent to cultivate, you know?"

He stared at me as if contemplating the sincerity of my words. "Kai," he finally said, serious, "is something truly bothering you?"

His words broke through my facade. My shoulders slumped as I sighed, letting the weariness take over.

"It's just . . . I can't help but feel so far behind," I confessed. "I see these younger disciples, already making so much progress, and here I am struggling to keep up. The thought of going to dinner, and taking time away from training, makes me feel like I'm falling even further behind. I'm afraid of seeming weak, of disappointing everyone, and myself."

Feng Wu's expression softened. "You've been working incredibly hard, and you're improving quickly. Don't forget, you started with practically no martial arts background. In less than a year, you've managed to survive an encounter against a Wind Serpent, and can even utilize the Rooted Banyan Stance. Do you know how extraordinary that is?"

"But it doesn't feel like enough," I whispered, my insecurities laid bare. "There's so many incredible people out there. It feels like I'm an impostor wearing someone's skin at times. Am I really capable of standing up there, participating in the Grand Alchemy Gauntlet?"

"Progress isn't only measured by how quickly you reach a milestone. It's about the journey, the persistence, and the effort you put in. Stop comparing yourself to others. You are your own person, with your own unique path," Feng Wu said.

I looked at him, taking in his earnest expression. Maybe I had been too hard on myself.

I pondered his words, letting them sink in. For the first time, I allowed myself to consider the weight of my own achievements. "I guess you have a point," I finally conceded, a reluctant smile tugging at the corners of my mouth.

Feng Wu's eyes brightened. "That's the spirit! Besides, you're talented in herbalism and alchemy. I dare say you're leagues ahead of anyone in that domain. You have a unique set of skills that will serve you well in the future."

"Thank you, Feng Wu," I said quietly, feeling a weight lift off my shoulders.

His green eyes sparkled as a warm smile spread across his face. "Now, will you join me for dinner? I'll trade pointers with you after if you'd like."

I chuckled, feeling lighter. "Yeah, I think I'll take you up on that offer."

As we made our way back toward the sect, I took one last glance at my secluded training spot, almost as if bidding it goodbye for the evening. I felt a mixture of guilt and relief. Yes, training was essential, but so was learning to appreciate myself and my own journey. I had almost forgotten Elder Ming's words, which emphasized the importance of rest. If I wanted to maximize my gains, I'd have to rest just as hard as I worked.

I opened the blue window, displaying my skills and stats. I looked at them with a newfound respect, acknowledging the effort that got me to this point. Sure, there was a long road ahead, but for the first time in a while, the journey didn't seem so daunting.

I closed the interface, catching up to Feng Wu who had slowed his pace to wait for me. As we walked, I thought about what Feng Wu had said. The third-class disciples had their journey, but I had mine. Mine was unconventional, filled with the scent of herbs and the texture of ancient alchemical tomes. It was lined with the wisdom of Elder Ming and peppered with the concern and camaraderie of Feng Wu and others who had come into my life.

I was a cultivator, but I was also an alchemist, a student of the natural world, and an ever-growing pool of untapped potential. Perhaps these roles were not as separate as I had thought; maybe they were threads in the intricate tapestry that was my own, unique path.

As we strolled toward the sect, a sudden epiphany began to crystallize within me. I paused, letting the moment linger, my mind wandering to the image of a sprawling banyan tree. This magnificent tree didn't reach its towering height and grandeur overnight. It took time, its roots expanding slowly, intertwining with the very essence of the earth.

Similarly, my dao, I realized, wasn't merely about relentless cultivation or proving myself to be more resilient than the next cultivator. It was about understanding when to push and when to allow myself rest and nourishment. Just as the banyan tree absorbed nutrients and relied on the symbiotic relationships with its environment, I, too, should understand the significance of leaning on those around me. For what is a tree without the soil that feeds it, the rains that quench its thirst, or the creatures that find sanctuary in its branches?

> *Your understanding of the dao has deepened.*
> *Your mind has reached Mortal Realm—Rank 3.*

The tension between pushing hard and letting go, the struggle to force outcomes versus allowing them to flow naturally, all seemed to click into place. My breathing deepened, drawing in the evening's crisp air, and with it came a sense of contentment, an understanding I hadn't fully grasped before.

A soft chuckle escaped my lips. The interface had a way of making moments like this slightly comical. Yet, beneath its unexpected timing, lay a deep truth.

We often pushed ourselves to the limit, trying to harness the power within and around us. Yet, perhaps sometimes, the true strength lay not in the push but in the pull—allowing the universe to guide us, to accept its rhythm and dance with it rather than against.

As we entered the dining hall, greeted by the rich aroma of cooking and the ambient chatter of disciples, I felt like a regular person again. And, for the first time in a long time, that was more than enough.

CHAPTER FIFTY-TWO

It's Okay to Have Fun, Right?

Wrapping up my Azure Silk Trading Company orders early had its advantages, freeing my schedule for more challenging pursuits.

Advancement exams under Instructor Xiao-Hu went perfectly. I now found myself amid the brainier echelon where the second-class disciples dwelt. It was clear to me: The sharpening of my mind and spirit had just begun.

Advanced Herbology taught me more about the esoteric plants available in the province, and what their properties were. It had us in the garden often, discussing how to grow and harvest the plants without damaging them. With Plant Whisperer, I had an instinctual feel on how to do this, even with plants I hadn't seen before. I could even tell when they weren't ready to harvest yet. My instructors were quite impressed, saying I had a rare talent when it came to herbs and plants.

And the prophecy of Kai Liu—heralded as peerless under the heaven's expanse—was becoming ever more tangible.

I think the biggest thing I learned was the concept of environmental alchemy; crafting unique environments that would enhance or alter the properties of certain plants. The secondary ability I gained from Spiritual Herbalism, Spiritual Plant Cultivation, seemed to do the same thing.

> *Spiritual Plant Cultivation—You can infuse plants with your qi,*
> *increasing their potency or imbuing them with new properties.*

However, I haven't been able to do anything like imbue them with new properties. Whenever I infused them with my qi, it became more potent, but it didn't get an entirely new property. Although I had a feeling this class would provide me with insights on how to do that.

Elixir Synthesis, Toxicology, Antidotes, and Pill Concoction—domains under Instructor Xiao-Hu's meticulous guidance—sharpened my alchemical foundations. I learned that to him, precision was not just practice, but reverence for the craft.

The hardest one, however, was Alchemy Array Crafting taught by Instructor Fei Ni. It was unlike anything I had ever done before. It was the closest thing I've seen to magic thus far, aside from the Wind Serpents conjuring gusts of wind.

Alchemy Array Crafting was the art of imposing order on chaos, a structured dance of qi, elements, and intent. I was no stranger to qi manipulation, but the precision required for crafting arrays was something else entirely. Instructor Fei Ni's arrays were like masterful symphonies, each stroke and symbol an impeccable note in an unseen orchestra. The second-class disciples seemed to weave their qi into arrays with fluid grace, their movements sure and swift. My attempts, however, were more like a toddler's first steps, clumsy and halting.

In today's class, I was determined to master the beginner's array for enhancing the purity of herbs. The process could be replicated by my essence extraction skill, but this was one of the more elementary arrays that I had to learn first. It required a delicate balance of qi, guided by a specific pattern to weave the enhancing matrix. It should have been straightforward. I took a deep breath, steadied my hands over the formation slate, and began to guide my qi into the intricate design.

A ripple of laughter from the corner of the room made my concentration falter. Qi surged unexpectedly, a wild stream breaking from its banks. The result was instantaneous—the array flared a blinding white before emitting a sharp crack, followed by a billow of smoke and a scattering of ash where my carefully placed herbs once lay.

I coughed, fanning away the smoke, my face as red as the firecracker flower, known for its explosive bloom—a comparison I was sure my classmates found amusing in more ways than one. The second-class disciples were already adept at hiding their smiles behind their sleeves, but their amusement was palpable.

"Steady your mind, Kai Liu," Instructor Fei Ni chided, her voice firm yet not unkind. She had thick eyebrows that made her perpetually stern. "An alchemist's greatest tool is his composure. A disrupted mind leads to disrupted qi and thus to disaster."

I nodded, swallowing my embarrassment. I could hear the sympathetic tones of my fellow students whispering that everyone had their first explosion. It was almost a rite of passage in the alchemy pavilion. Nonetheless, it stung. To be skilled in the application of herbs and yet so amateurish in crafting arrays was frustrating. It was clear that alchemy arrays were a profound art, a perfect blend of the scientific and the mystical—and I was far from proficient.

The afternoon dragged on with more attempts, each more cautious than the last. But caution, I learned, was as detrimental as recklessness in Alchemy Array Crafting. Too little qi, and the array wouldn't form. Too much, and, well . . . the evidence of that was still smudged on my robe. Despite the setbacks, my resolve only hardened. I would master this, as I had mastered every other challenge. But this time, I had to admit, the path to mastery would be a steep climb indeed.

My days outside the meticulous demands of class time were comfortably spent in the company of Li Na and Han Wei. They were my equals in the art of learning, not far-flung stars like Feng Wu, whose martial abilities were so advanced that emulating him was like trying to grasp the subtleties of a Go match between seasoned masters—I could see the moves, appreciate their elegance, but the deeper strategy eluded me. Li Na and Han Wei's skills, though superior to mine, were close enough that the bridge between instruction and understanding spanned a shorter divide, allowing me to cross with fewer stumbles.

I was the novel leaf in an ancient tome, an addition, yet not fully part of the narrative.

I took comfort in knowing that Li Na and Han Wei were by my side. Their presence wasn't just for the fellowship; it was a boon for my training. Their expertise wasn't steeped in the alchemical arts but rather in the fluid dance of martial prowess. I gradually learned footwork from observing Li Na and how to incorporate power into my strikes from Han Wei.

They remarked on my ability to utilize techniques, despite my foundation lacking in all aspects. In sparring, the only thing that leveled the playing field was the Rooted Banyan Stance. I was able to stomach Han Wei's blows with it, and prevent myself from getting caught by Li Na's sweeping kicks. It felt like I learned how to utilize the technique's defensive capabilities to the maximum despite its shortcomings.

In the evening, after my mind and body were thoroughly turned into mush, I continued independent study. I spent most of my nights in the sect library, where I continued to learn. Then I'd return to my quarters, meditate, and enter my Memory Palace where I'd take the opportunity to go deeper into the theory of my various disciplines. I followed Feng Wu's advice, and utilized it as a place to refine my mind, rather than just a place to review what I already knew. My mind became a garden where I could contemplate my dao, theorize on new formulas, and plan out what I needed for the next day.

This rhythm of learning framed the tapestry of my week: discipline by daylight, martial tutelage under the veil of dusk, and the nocturne of knowledge until the lantern's glow waned.

Now here I was, resting on a grassy hill and enjoying the fruits of my labor. It was easy to forget the bustle of my usual days. With Tianyi, I found a quiet joy in reading up on alchemy array crafting, a skill I was determined to improve. The sun was kind, the breeze was a gentle audience to my solitude, and the grass felt like a warm embrace.

The alchemy book was thick in my hands, full of complex theories I was itching to understand. It didn't feel like a chore. Learning about alchemy was what I loved, and it showed.

> *Reading has reached level 6.*

The skill alert for Reading popped up unexpectedly. It had already leveled up twice since I arrived here. I suppose reading more educational books rather than fiction helped in that regard. It was a quiet victory, but a victory nonetheless. It was the kind of progress that didn't make a fuss; it was just there, another step closer to where I wanted to be. The next stage, Accelerated Reading, seemed quite interesting. I'd have to see what it gave me once I reached the requirements for the next stage.

When I looked up from my book, I saw Feng Wu standing over me, providing refuge from the sunlight.

"Kai." Feng Wu's voice was an even, welcoming timbre. "I'm glad you've adjusted. You seem to be in high spirits."

I marked my page with a grass blade and stood, grinning widely. "Feng Wu, to what do I owe the honor?" I jested, "Did you come to admire the sect's newest prodigy?"

Feng Wu laughed, a sound that seemed to harmonize naturally with the rustling leaves around us. "Modesty suits you as well as these robes, Kai. But jests aside, I've come to bid you brief farewells."

My eyebrows arched in surprise. "Farewells? You're leaving?"

"Yes, for a time," he said, with the slight nod of one who has already accepted his mission. "As a second-class disciple, the sect looks to us not only for internal endeavors but for maintaining and expanding its reach. You know how a sect like ours operates, Kai. It is a living entity, ever-growing and evolving with the dedicated work of its disciples."

His gaze shifted past the compound walls, to the vast lands that stretched beyond the sect's bordering mountains. "We are but one part of the sect's lifeblood. The first-class disciples and the masters often are cloistered within, delving into higher mysteries and empowering the sect's heart. But we," he continued, turning his eyes back to me, "ensure the sect's limbs are strong and far-reaching."

"The tasks you undertake outside the sect—are they not dangerous?" I inquired, my curiosity piqued.

It seemed in line with what I read in my novels; cultivators going out to exterminate monsters, build the sect's reputation, and collect rewards while gaining experience.

"Often so," he affirmed. "But it is through facing such perils that we temper our spirit and contribute to the sect's prosperity. The errands range from gathering rare materials to establishing alliances, or escorting guests to the sect."

I processed this, letting the structure of our world settle into a clearer picture. The sect was a sovereign power in its own right.

"Think of the sect as a nation," Feng Wu instructed, as if reading my thoughts. "The first-class disciples are like our ministers, managing resources, overseeing operations, and ensuring the internal stability of our sect. The elders, on the other hand, are akin to the Emperor's guard—universally respected, a deterrent for those who would dare challenge us."

The concept of sect politics and dynamics was intricate, fraught with the tension between power and responsibility. It was a game played on a grand scale, and I was only beginning to learn the rules.

Feng Wu stood, preparing to leave. "I trust you'll keep up the progress while I'm away. You seem to have made good friends among the third-class disciples."

"I'll do my best," I assured him, and I meant it. Feng Wu's departure was not just a change in the sect's daily rhythm but a shift in my own.

The sun dipped lower, and I watched Feng Wu's retreating figure, the green of his robe melding with the greens of the forest as he moved toward his undisclosed tasks. I understood then that the tranquility of the sect was a cultivated illusion, preserved by the endeavors of those like Feng Wu.

I turned to Tianyi, who flitted around my head, her wings a blur of iridescent azure. "What do you think, my silent sentinel? Should we continue lazing about?" I posed the question lightly.

Tianyi didn't respond with words—she couldn't, of course. But the fluttering of her wings slowed, and a wave of calm washed over me. I felt a nudge in my mind, a push toward something urgent and unspoken.

I sighed, my joviality faltering. "I know, I know. We're to return. Duty calls." The bond we shared was profound, more so in moments of silence than in any conversation I've had with my human counterparts. Yet today Tianyi's urgency felt different—more pressing, less comforting.

Upon reaching my quarters, the anxiety was a dull thorn in my side. Something was amiss, but I couldn't pinpoint what. The air was the same, the scent of the lingering incense I used for meditation was still faintly there, yet a presence was off. A feeling. It was like entering a room where a painting had been straightened by someone else—not wrong, just different.

I opened the door slowly, and a swirl of emotions from Tianyi flooded me—alarm, confusion, excitement, a cacophony of silent screams. My room appeared untouched, but the Wind Serpent egg's enclosure was shattered, the remains of its once-immaculate shell scattered like a broken dream.

"Who did this?" I whispered.

The Wind Serpent was my charge, my future companion, and an innocent life. It was a loss that could not be measured.

Tianyi circled above, its aura trying to pierce my clouded judgment with some sense of understanding, but the bond we shared was akin to a book with half its pages torn out. Its emotional timbre was frenetic, making my heart race and my mind a tangle of unfocused energy.

There was no way it could've hatched. From what I could tell, it should've been at least three more weeks before it was fully mature.

As my eyes adjusted to the gloom, I searched frantically, my pulse syncing with Tianyi's erratic dance. There was no sign of forced entry, no lingering presence of an intruder. Only me, the remnants of what was, and . . .

A hissing cut through my inner turmoil—a thin, continuous sound that snapped my focus to the corner of the room. There, coiled atop my pile of scattered scrolls, was a snake, pure as the driven snow, its scales catching the last light of the day like shards of broken moonlight.

The hissing ceased as our eyes met. The Wind Serpent, its eggshell nothing more than a memory now, regarded me with a gaze that held the weight of the skies.

CHAPTER FIFTY-THREE

Tofu Mice and Tailor-Made Trouble

The initial commotion within me subsided, only to be replaced by a mix of wonder and questions. Had the serpent hatched by itself?

Tianyi's energy shifted. There was a sense of urging in her actions, a push toward acceptance rather than the pursuit of an answer. It seemed this was what Tianyi was trying to tell me about. Her panicky movements were quite different from other times when she preferred to stay still and wait till the threat went away.

I exhaled slowly, letting go of my confusion and sank to my knees. I decided to observe the Wind Serpent hatchling for a closer look.

As I watched the little serpent, noting its pearl-like scales shimmering with a tinge of blue—the kind that reminded me of those flashy silk robes the rich merchants wore, only these didn't cost a fortune and were a heck of a lot cuter. I found it amusing that something so mystical-looking appeared less like a formidable Wind Serpent and more like a lost cloud trying to find its way back to the sky.

"I bet you hatched early just to meet me," I mused aloud. "Can't blame you, buddy. I'm quite the catch, if I do say so myself."

Wind Serpents were known for their majestic silver and gray, not . . . whatever this fluffy fellow was trying to pull off. Pure white with a lick of ice blue? He was like a winter's day, bright and crisp, with a vibe that screamed, *I'm unique, pamper me.*

"You're definitely not your standard garden-variety snake," I continued, speaking to the hatchling that was now flicking its tongue at me. It was as if the little guy was tasting my soul—hopefully finding it to his liking. "Maybe you just wanted to stand out in the serpent crowd. I can respect that. Always root for the underdog . . . or under-snake, in this case."

I wondered if Tianyi's presence had influenced the qi within the egg. She had an otherworldly luster ever since I healed her using the Moonlit Grace Lily. "Did you juice up the serpent egg, Tianyi?"

How unfair! Why didn't hanging around her turn me blue or majestic? Actually, that wouldn't be as nice as I thought. I'll appreciate the recovery aura surrounding her instead.

The hatchling slithered closer, wrapping its tiny body around my arm with a familiarity that I hadn't earned but was happy to accept. There was something oddly satisfying about being instantly accepted by a creature.

"Okay, let's get you named," I declared with a grin. "How about Fluffyscale? No? Too on the nose?"

It peered up at me, its tiny forked tongue paused mid-air as if considering my suggestion, then resumed its exploration of the world. "Tough crowd." I sighed.

If the early hatching was due to Tianyi's qi-boost, then this serpent was more than just a rare color—it could've been an entirely new breed. A Wind Serpent influenced by the essence of an empowered Azure Moonlight Flutter? The implications were staggering. The thought made me nearly giddy with possibility.

"Now, to figure out what you eat," I pondered. "I hope you like the taste of adventure, because that's all I've got on the menu at the moment."

The hatchling just nudged my palm with its nose—or at least what I assumed was its nose.

"Well, Windy—just a placeholder name, I swear—we've got our work cut out for us. You need to grow up big and strong, and I need to keep you hidden from the sect until I know whether you're safe to reveal. You seem stealthier than Tianyi, at least."

I chuckled, imagining trying to explain to the sect elders about my new serpent-rearing side gig. "We'll have to raise you in secret, huh, Windy?"

Windy seemed to approve, curling up comfortably in the palm of my hand as I sat there, the both of us basking in the possibilities of the future. Who said that a dash of chaos couldn't lead to a groundbreaking discovery? As an alchemist, my favorite ingredient was chaos.

I trod the path to the open fields, my mind a whirlwind of thoughts on the creature I'd left in my room. I was still reeling from the discovery of Windy, who was safely hidden away—for now. The Verdant Lotus Sect was strictly vegetarian, and the little serpent, carnivorous by nature, posed a conundrum.

"My sleeves might work for now," I muttered to myself, only half convinced. "But then again, he could wriggle out and cause a scene during classes." The last thing I needed was for Instructor Xiao-Hu to find a serpent peeking out from under my cuffs after warning me about pets in the classroom.

"Perhaps I can find some small critters on the edge of the sect's grounds," I said, glancing at Tianyi, who was observing me silently. "What do you think, Tianyi? Maybe Windy could dine on pests? It would be . . . natural pest control?"

She stared at me, her wings opening and closing in what I've come to recognize as her own version of a shrug.

"You're not helping," I accused playfully, though her silent counsel often soothed my anxieties.

"Or maybe some tofu? Could mold it to look like a mouse?" I chuckled at the thought, envisioning Windy's baffled face at the first bite. The poor thing expecting a juicy morsel, only to find itself chewing on the sect's favorite imitation dish.

"But what self-respecting Wind Serpent eats tofu mice?" I asked, shaking my head at my own foolishness. "No, it'll have to be the real deal. I'll just have to be sneaky about it."

A tinge of apprehension laced my words. I was, after all, contemplating the sneaking of meat into a taoist sect.

As I walked past the herb gardens, the usual spot for my afternoon exertions, my mind bounced between excitement and anxiety. "Keep it together, Kai. It's just a tiny serpent that could manhandle a group of cultivators as an adult. No biggie."

The afternoon sunlight was warm on my face, a pleasant contrast to the cool shade of the training grounds. I stretched my limbs, preparing for the rigorous physical conditioning I had come to both dread and love.

I was so lost in thought about feeding schedules and stealth techniques that I nearly collided with a third-class disciple. "Sorry!" I exclaimed, sidestepping with an agility that earned me an impressed look. "Gotta keep those reflexes sharp," I said with a wink, as if it was all intentional.

The closer I got to the sect entrance, the more I noticed the buzz of excitement. A crowd had gathered—unusual for this hour. Curiosity piqued, I made a detour, my feet carrying me toward the growing throng of disciples.

The sect entrance was the usual crossroads for news and spectacle, but the throng was denser today, their chatter rising like the hum of swarming locusts. I pushed through, keeping my expression neutral while my heart pounded with the thrill of something amiss.

I noticed Elder Chen, the head of the mission chamber, speaking to someone. He was a quiet man whom I had only seen once at the dining hall. Feng Wu told me that he was a gentle person, but his gaze right now seemed anything but.

A tall man stood in the center, draped in the distinctive cobalt-blue robes. Behind him were familiar silhouettes: a dozen disciples from the Silent Moon Sect. His hair was slicked back into a tail, each strand disciplined into place. Elder Chen's posture was stiff, betraying the tension of their conversation.

I edged closer. The elder from Silent Moon, with his hawk-like eyes, was in the midst of speaking, his voice smooth as silk yet edged with a sharpness that hinted at steel underneath.

"Your disciple showed commendable valor against the Wind Serpents, Elder Chen," he said, his tone almost admiring. "But valor alone does not dictate the rightful claim to the spoils."

Elder Chen's voice was like a taut string, ready to snap. "The Verdant Lotus Sect did not merely 'show valor,' Elder Jun. We acted to preserve lives, not for its reward."

A subtle smirk played on Elder Jun's lips, a smirk that did not reach his eyes. "Indeed, action without benefit is the mark of true cultivators. However . . ." He paused, his gaze sweeping the crowd before locking back onto Elder Ming. "As the sect officially tasked by Qingmu Village, any resources that fell from the Wind Serpents should be considered as Silent Moon's purview. That includes the Wind Serpent's Beast Core."

I grimaced internally, realizing what the deal was about. Instinctively, I gripped the core in my pocket. Elder Jun was sly, and I could almost admire him for it if he weren't angling for what we had earned. He continued, "When one reaps the harvest of another's field, do they owe a debt to the landowner?"

The metaphor drew murmurings from the crowd, a murmur that I could feel the undercurrents of agreement and dissent mingling. For a moment, I saw Elder Chen's eyes flicker from the man before him to me. My heart skipped a beat, thinking for a moment that I'd have to surrender what was given to me. Several thoughts ran through my mind. Hadn't Feng Wu kept my ownership of the Beast Core a secret?

But my anxieties were unfounded. Elder Chen's eyes went back to the man before him. I breathed an internal sigh of relief.

Elder Chen's retort was swift. "By that logic, one could claim the wind and the rain as their own for merely expecting it. We fought, we bled, and the Wind Serpents fell on the village of Qingmu. Should the Qingmu Village residents be the ones to take the resources?"

The conversation was a dance of wits and wills, and I felt a strange kinship with Elder Chen's defiance. Yet the fear that we might be embroiled in conflict with the Silent Moon Sect gnawed at me. They were not only ambitious but aggressive. Elder Zhu's remarks about their attempts at expansion and usurping the Whispering Wind Sect rang in my head.

Elder Jun laughed, a sound that scratched unpleasantly at my ears. "Elder Chen, surely you jest. The wind and rain belong to no one, but the fruits of the earth, when cultivated, surely have a master. As such, your sect's gains in this encounter intersect with our interests."

His manipulation was as blatant as it was smooth, wording his greed as rightful claiming. Elder Jun was a wolf in a philosopher's cloak, his mind as sharp as a blade.

And then, the veiled threat came, "It would be a pity for this to sour relations between our sects. The Silent Moon Sect values harmony, but it is known that imbalance and disrespect can lead to . . . misfortune."

The sect elders were no strangers to these exchanges, but the blunt nature of this threat was a brutal reminder of the stakes at play. I could see it in Elder Chen's eyes, the careful calculation as he weighed his words.

"You speak of respect, Elder Jun, yet it is respect that brings us to share. Our joint endeavor in subduing the serpents was not done for mere profit but for peace," he stated firmly.

The conversation ebbed and flowed around me, the political current drawing in all who listened. I felt like I was witnessing a silent war, where words were the weapons, and the casualties could be counted in lost alliances and tarnished reputations.

I stared at the disciples, none of whom I recognized being in Qingmu Village. They were third-class disciples, but the air around them was different. Much more formidable than the ones lead by Xu Ziqing. And compared to the scholarly disciples present in the crowd, it was no contest to see what would happen if they fought.

Elder Chen's next words were clipped. "The Verdant Lotus Sect will not be coerced into forfeiting what we have earned, nor will we engage in a war of words where action has already spoken."

There was a firm nod from our elder, and some of the gathered disciples cheered, their voices a ragged chorus of support.

Elder Jun's smile never wavered, but his eyes were cold.

His patience seemed to unravel just then, with the subtle play of shadows over his face betraying his next intent. "Then, perhaps, there is another way to resolve this. The Verdant Lotus Sect surely holds numerous treasures that can be used as a substitute for the Wind Serpent Beast Core. Such as . . . the Qinglian Jadeite?"

I balked. I was only beginning my studies in alchemy, but even I knew the worth of the Qinglian Jadeite. It was an item capable of producing the Jade Alchemic Flame, one of the ninety Earthly Flames, for alchemy requiring precision and stability. Unlike other flames, the Jade Flame would not consume or destroy what it touches but instead refines and purifies materials to their utmost quality. They wanted *that* in exchange for the Beast Core?

A grim realization settled over me as I figured out the Silent Moon Sect's true motive.

Using an outstanding debt to obtain something else from the sect. I've seen it before, both in real life and in the stories I read. It was an underhanded trick, and one I didn't appreciate the Silent Moon Sect attempting on my benefactors. Judging by Elder Chen's face, it seemed like he was aware of the ploy at hand. *Outrageous!*

I couldn't let this go.

Before he could finish, I found my own voice, slicing through the tension like a sword through silk. "Elder Jun, the Wind Serpent Beast Core," I said, holding up the shimmering, crystalline object for all to see. I might have looked calm, letting the core roll in my palm like a gambler's coin, but inside, a storm raged, churning with the dual tides of fear and resolve.

"Elder Jun desires it so earnestly that I wonder . . ." I said, my voice firm, betraying none of my inner turmoil, "is the Silent Moon Sect suffering so greatly that they would haggle with a humble gardener over spoils?" I couldn't help but lace my words with a hint of mockery and anger. Elder Jun's brows knitted together, a crack in his facade of unflappable superiority.

Perhaps this wasn't the best idea.

CHAPTER FIFTY-FOUR

A Wager

A ripple of murmurs washed over the crowd as I clutched the Beast Core, its energy pulsating against my skin—a symbol of the intricate play of power, both tangible and political.

"You dare disrespect Elder Jun!" shouted a third-class disciple from the Silent Moon Sect, his voice brimming with contempt. "You tread on death's doorstep with such impudence!"

Yet a simple gesture from Elder Jun halted the disciple's advance. A quiet, yet commanding move that silenced the impending threat.

"Junior, your tongue is as perilous as a thistle's thorn," Elder Jun coldly remarked. "But remember, even a gardener must recognize when to cease pluck-ing, lest he summons a poison far beyond his reckoning." His gaze, heavy and piercing, shifted from the Beast Core to lock with mine, sending a shiver of dread through me.

Beside me, Tianyi was petrified, the crushing weight of Elder Jun's intent pal-pable in the air. In the crowd, Li Na's eyes met mine, her expression a mix of worry and a silent plea for caution. Han Wei, standing beside her, subtly shook his head, his eyes mirroring the same concern. Their silent messages were clear: I was treading dangerously.

I braced myself, recalling the oppressive gaze of the Wind Serpent I had once faced. He was just a man, not some unfathomable beast.

Just then, the Heavenly Interface flickered to life before my eyes, overlaying the scene with a translucent, ethereal screen. Words appeared, floating gently.

> *Elder Jun: Essence Awakening Stage Cultivator,*
> *Known for Strategic Acumen. Suggested Approach:*
> *Diplomacy and Wits over Bravado.*

"Elder Jun, forgive the boy's hasty words. He is under our hospitality, yet unfamiliar with our ways." As Elder Chen's qi enveloped me, easing the suffocating pressure, I felt a mix of gratitude and a sting of being seen as lesser—a mere herbalist in the eyes of cultivators. "He—"

Before Elder Chen could finish, Elder Jun raised his hand, signaling him to stop. His gaze, unyielding and sharp, remained fixed on me. "Enough, Elder Chen. Let the young one speak. It seems he has much to say."

The silence that followed was suffocating. I felt as though I had voluntarily stepped into a spider's web, with Elder Jun the impassive spider at its center, watching my every move. I realized then the precariousness of my position, a guest caught between respect and insubordination, my every word potentially tipping the scales.

Elder Jun's expression remained unreadable, yet there was a glint in his eyes that suggested he found some amusement in this unexpected turn. It was clear he was using my interruption to his advantage, perhaps to test my mettle or to assert his dominance in this delicate dance of power.

I scanned the faces of the Silent Moon disciples, their disdain palpable. The one who had previously threatened me remained silent, yet his hand ominously rested on his sword. Li Na's anxious gaze and Han Wei's disapproving frown were hard to ignore, adding to the weight of the moment. I had made a mistake, running my mouth and letting my emotions get the best of me.

In that moment, I recalled my days as a humble herbalist, dealing with shrewd merchants trying to devalue my goods. Each interaction was a delicate balancing act of tact and assertiveness. Elder Jun's piercing gaze reminded me of those stern customers, and I knew I had to employ the same calm and strategic thinking to navigate this conversation.

"My apologies, Elder Jun," I began, ensuring my voice remained even, masking my inner turmoil. "I never intended to overstep. Yet, given the opportunity to speak, I offer a proposal that respects both our standings."

I swallowed hard, my mind racing. The Interface offered a path, a strategic approach to handle Elder Jun. I didn't know why it chose to activate now, but I could hardly care; it was suggesting diplomacy, a way to engage without direct confrontation. This aligned with my thoughts of proposing a contest, a nonviolent resolution that could appease Elder Jun's pride while safeguarding my interests.

Elder Jun's gaze sharpened. "What just resolution could you possibly offer? The Beast Core belongs to us as its rightful owners."

This was my moment. "While the Beast Core is indeed valuable, I must remind you of the assistance I provided your disciples during the battle. My potions helped restore their vitality, contributing significantly to their victory. Taking this core from a civilian without recompense, especially one who aided your sect, would surely tarnish the Silent Moon Sect's reputation for fairness and honor."

Elder Jun waved his hand dismissively. "Our disciples would have prevailed regardless of your *minor* contributions. But speak your proposition."

As I spoke my proposal, the Interface updated in real time.

> *Proposal Analysis: Alchemy Contest—Strategic value high.*
> *Probable interest from Elder Jun. Balance confidence with humility.*

"My aim was never to stir conflict. I seek to safeguard what I've rightfully earned, as would any of you." The Beast Core's steady hum was a small comfort against my rising anxiety. I spoke slowly, letting my mind absorb the contents of the message before I continued. It felt like I was balancing over the edge of a cliff.

"In exchange," I continued, the suspense hanging in the air, "I propose a just resolution."

The words were a guiding light, reminding me to tread carefully. Each word I chose, every gesture I made, I did so with the Interface's guidance at the back of my mind. It was like having an unseen mentor, providing counsel in this high-stakes exchange.

As I stood there, facing Elder Jun's unwavering gaze, a sense of nostalgia enveloped me. It was like haggling with the toughest of merchants all over again, where every word weighed heavy with consequence. I reminded myself to cool my head, to approach this as I would a tough negotiation—with patience, insight, and a keen understanding of the person I was dealing with.

Elder Jun's penetrating gaze demanded an answer. "Speak your terms," he commanded.

Behind me, Elder Chen's qi was a silent support, but his grip betrayed his apprehension. I could sense his confusion and concern, his uncertainty about my intentions. Even I myself hardly knew what I was going to say next.

The crowd was silent, their eyes a blend of anticipation and eagerness for a misstep. The disciple with his hand on his sword seemed a silent reminder of the potential consequences of my boldness.

"An alchemy contest," I declared, my voice feigning a confidence I didn't feel. "A testament of skill, where I challenge one of your disciples."

Elder Jun's sneer was palpable. "Alchemy? You overreach, boy. We are warriors, not alchemists."

> *Elder Jun: Intrigued yet cautious. Adjust the proposal to include*
> *a martial skill showcase and increase appeal.*

The murmurs around us grew, and I could feel Elder Chen's grip tighten—a mix of support and a plea for caution. I hesitated, searching for an angle that could sway the tide in my favor.

"Then let it be a test of adaptability," I suggested. "A duel of disciplines, where the core is the prize."

Elder Jun, now intrigued, leaned forward. "And what farce do you suggest we indulge in?"

Holding the Beast Core, I gathered my thoughts, speaking with a firmness that belied my inner turmoil. "I propose a dual trial," I began steadily, masking the storm of thoughts within. Perhaps it was the Memory Palace technique enhancing my cognitive abilities, but my mind seemed to race, weaving through numerous ideas. "Firstly, an alchemy challenge: pitting my abilities against your sect's disciples. The victor of this alchemy trial will earn the right to choose the location for the next phase. Should your disciple win, they may select the venue, aligning with your sect's preferences. Then we shift to a combat trial at the chosen location. This challenge will test martial skill, where I must not only defend but also land a single effective strike to claim victory."

The sword-bearing disciple sneered. "Survive? A fitting choice of words for your inevitable defeat."

I met Elder Jun's gaze head-on, clarifying, "Not to endure a beating, but to land a single strike. If I do, the victory is mine."

A hush fell over the crowd as the implications of my proposal sank in. The disciples shifted uneasily, exchanging glances that wavered between skepticism and curiosity. I could see them weighing the proposal, their thoughts churning behind stoic expressions. This wasn't a mere test of skill; it was a spectacle that promised to showcase the strengths and weaknesses of both sects in a way seldom seen. The Beast Core's energy seemed to pulse in sync with the rising tension, a silent chorus to the drama unfolding.

Elder Chen, understanding the stakes, nodded in agreement. "Fair enough. Given Kai's background, a single strike is a reasonable challenge."

The mocking tone in Elder Jun's voice was unmistakable. "You believe a mere *gardener* can stand against one of our warriors?"

I clenched my fists, familiar with the sting of being underestimated. I've faced scorn before, for my humble beginnings and my trade. I gritted my teeth. I was no stranger to being looked down upon. It happened often, especially when I haggled with merchants as a young child. Nobody took me seriously. But I still had my pride as a human being. Being labeled as just a gardener made me clench my fist in anger.

After a moment that stretched as taut as a drawn bowstring, Elder Jun let out another breath, his decision resonating in the sudden quiet that befell the courtyard. He finally acquiesced. "Fine, we'll entertain this wager. In four weeks, we will settle this matter."

Elder Jun's voice, though calm, carried an undercurrent of challenge that rippled through the air. He paused, his gaze lingering on me, as if measuring my worth. "Remember, *boy*," he said, his words deliberate and heavy, "this is not just a test of skill, but a test of honor. In our sect, words are as binding as oaths. Fail to uphold your end, and the consequences will be . . . significant." His tone was not threatening, but the implication was clear.

The Silent Moon Sect members began to withdraw, their movements slow and measured. There was an unspoken tension among them, a mixture of skepticism and anticipation. Their eyes lingered on me, some with undisguised curiosity, others with veiled disdain. As they moved away, the courtyard seemed to exhale, the oppressive atmosphere gradually lifting.

As the sect began to disperse, the disciple with the sword couldn't resist a final taunt. "Enjoy your fleeting peace, herb boy. Your words won't shield you in combat."

Elder Jun, having remained silent through the dispersal of the sect members, finally spoke up, his voice carrying a note of contemplation. "Elder Chen, it seems your guest, this young gardener, has saved your sect from potentially paying a heavy price."

Elder Chen, caught off guard by the remark, could only offer a stiff nod in response. His usual eloquence seemed to falter, replaced by a sense of bewilderment at the turn of events. "Indeed, Elder Jun. Kai has shown a depth unexpected of his years," he managed to say, his words careful and measured.

The Silent Moon Sect elder's eyes lingered on me for a moment longer, as if reassessing his initial impression. Then, with a final nod, he turned and began to walk away, his figure gradually merging with the fading light of the setting sun. The remaining disciples followed, leaving a trail of whispers and murmurs behind them.

Elder Chen turned to me, a grave expression on his face. "That was certainly an unexpected outcome." He paused, as if searching for the right words. "I must bid Elder Jun and his disciples farewell. Please, take a moment to collect yourself. We will need to discuss this further."

As Elder Chen left, I stood there in the now quiet courtyard, the weight of the upcoming challenge heavy on my shoulders. The Beast Core, still pulsating in my hand, felt like a double-edged sword—a prize and a burden.

Oh dear. What have I gotten myself into?

"Kai, you absolute fool!" Li Na's voice snapped me out of my daze as she and Han Wei approached, their expressions a mix of disbelief and frustration.

Han Wei grabbed my shoulders, shaking me slightly. "Do you even realize what you've done? Challenging a Silent Moon Sect disciple in both alchemy and martial arts? Are you trying to get yourself killed?"

I could only manage a weak smile in response, my mind still reeling from the events. "Well, when you put it like that, it does sound a bit . . . ambitious."

"Ambitious? It's madness!" Li Na exclaimed, her voice rising in pitch. "You're an alchemist, Kai, not some invincible warrior!"

Her words stung, but I knew they came from a place of concern. "Hey, I've survived worse. Just testing my inner warrior, is all," I joked weakly, trying to lighten the mood. But the looks on their faces told me they weren't buying it.

Li Na rolled her eyes. "Inner warrior? More like inner fool."

Just then, Tianyi, fluttering around in a frenzy, landed on my shoulder, slapping me with her wings. It was as though she was calling me a fool through our link. But that was crazy. There was no way she would have followed the extent of my conversation with the Silent Moon Sect.

I sighed, patting Tianyi gently. "I know, I know. I may have bitten off more than I can chew this time." The little creature's concern was palpable and, in a strange way, comforting.

Li Na and Han Wei exchanged a glance, then simultaneously sighed. "Well, what's done is done," Li Na said, her tone softening. "We'll have to get you into shape. You're all right for a normal person, but as a cultivator? You're going to need more than luck to survive against one of them."

As they walked away, discussing plans for my training, I took a deep breath, feeling the weight of their expectations—and my own. The Beast Core's energy seemed to pulse in time with my racing heart, a constant reminder of the journey ahead. All I wanted to do was find a way to feed Windy, and this happens?

"All right, Kai," I muttered to myself. "Let's see what you're made of."

CHAPTER FIFTY-FIVE

Brewing Storms

The chamber's door closed with a thud behind Elder Chen as I faced Elder Zhu and Instructor Xiao-Hu, sealing us in with the gravity of the situation. I could feel the weight of my decisions as I stood before them, the Beast Core a heavy presence in my pocket, an unspoken testament to the turmoil I had incited.

Instructor Xiao-Hu stepped in, his voice as direct and unyielding as his disciplined posture. "Kai, your actions today have cast ripples far beyond what you might have intended. The sect's reputation and standing have been put at risk by your gamble," he stated, his dark eyes fixed on me with an intensity that commanded full attention.

Elder Zhu silenced him with a raised hand and fixed me with a gaze that seemed to pierce through to my very soul. "Kai, speak your mind," he prompted in a tone that brokered no evasion.

The words tumbled out of me, a blend of apology and firmness. "I apologize for the trouble I've caused. When I saw the sect's honor threatened, I acted without fully considering the consequences. I-I just couldn't stand to watch the Verdant Lotus Sect be demeaned or manipulated,"

My fears gnawed at me—fears of the repercussions, the upcoming duel, the weight of potential failure—but beneath that surface churned a deep, immovable current of determination. I had made my choice, and I would stand by it.

Elder Zhu listened, his expression unchanging. "Kai, the sect is a refuge, a sanctuary. It is our duty to shield you, to foster your growth. It is not your burden to protect us," he said gently, yet with an undeniable firmness.

Elder Chen, who had been silent until now, stepped forward. His voice, always calm and measured, carried a hint of concern. "Kai, while your intentions were noble, you must understand the complexities of the cultivation world. The Silent

Moon Sect is powerful, and your challenge, though brave, risks escalating this conflict beyond our control."

The room felt colder, the reality of my actions settling in like a dense fog. I shifted uncomfortably, the Beast Core in my pocket suddenly feeling like a stone, heavy with unspoken implications.

Instructor Xiao-Hu's gaze softened slightly. "The Beast Core you possess is a coveted treasure. Its revelation has undoubtedly placed you in the sights of those who would do anything to claim such power."

The Beast Core . . . I had almost forgotten its significance in the heat of the moment. I remembered the pulsating energy it emitted, the way it resonated with my own qi, a beacon of untapped potential. If I were to absorb its contents, I was sure to collect more qi than my Crimson Lotus Purification technique could in months. It was no wonder why a martial sect like the Silent Moon would be reluctant to let such an item stray from themselves.

Feng Wu gave me such an item? And kept it a secret?

"Elder Chen, what about Feng Wu? Will he be in trouble for giving it to me?" I asked, the concern for my friend outweighing my own predicament.

Elder Chen sighed, a rare sign of weariness. "Feng Wu made a choice. He petitioned for you to keep the Beast Core during his mission brief, foregoing the considerable contribution points he would have earned from the mission. His actions were . . . unorthodox, but they speak volumes of his trust in you."

I felt gratitude toward Feng Wu, but it was mixed with guilt. He had risked so much for me, and now I was entangled in a situation that could have repercussions far beyond what I had imagined.

Instructor Xiao-Hu resumed, his tone grave. "Kai, you need to understand the danger you've placed not just yourself in, but also those associated with you. The Silent Moon Sect is known for its retribution. Winning the dual trial might safeguard the Beast Core, but it could invite consequences far more severe."

His words sent a chill down my spine. The thought of bringing harm to my friends, to the sect, was unbearable. My thoughts drifted to Tianyi, always by my side since my earliest days at the sect. The memory of Xu Ziqing's covetous gaze on Tianyi during our last encounter flashed before me. The idea of her being taken, or worse, killed, because of my actions ignited a rage within me, but also a painful realization of the cost of my recklessness.

With a heavy heart, I bowed deeply, deeper than I ever had before. "I understand the gravity of my actions and am prepared to face any punishment. I . . . I am willing to step down from the Grand Alchemy Gauntlet if it means protecting the sect and those I care about."

There was a moment of silence, the weight of my words hanging in the air. Elder Zhu finally spoke, his voice carrying a mixture of sternness and an unexpected warmth. "Kai, your willingness to bear the consequences of your actions speaks to your character. However, we will not remove you from the Grand Alchemy Gauntlet."

I looked up, surprised by his words.

Elder Chen continued, "Your actions, while impulsive, were in defense of the sect's honor. We cannot fault you for that. Instead, we will aid you in preparing for this dual trial. Bravery is a coin of great value in the Jianghu. However, it must be spent wisely. Are you prepared to defend the worth of your actions?"

Instructor Xiao-Hu nodded in agreement. "Your alchemy skills are commendable, but it is in the arena of combat where you will face your greatest challenge. We must ensure you are adequately prepared."

I couldn't hide the relief that washed over me, mingled with a newfound determination. "Thank you, Elders, for your faith in me. I won't let you down. I'll train harder than ever before," I said, my resolve steeling.

The Elders and Instructor Xiao-Hu exchanged a brief, knowing glance before Elder Zhu finally broke the silence. "We will have to discuss with the sect leader about the full ramifications of your actions. For now, you are dismissed."

With a final bow, I turned and left the chamber, the door closing behind me with a finality that echoed my tumultuous thoughts. As I walked through the verdant paths of the sect, I could feel the eyes of fellow disciples and instructors on me, their expressions a mix of curiosity, concern, and in some cases, thinly veiled disdain. The whispers that followed me were like the rustling of leaves in a breeze, a constant reminder of the storm I had unwittingly stirred.

Hastening my steps, I made my way back to the guest quarters, eager to escape the scrutiny and find solace in solitude. As I entered, the familiar sight of Windy greeted me. It coiled playfully around my ankle, its scales shimmering in the dim light.

"Hey there, Windy," I said, trying to muster a smile. "You wouldn't believe the kind of day I've had." The serpent looked up at me, its eyes gleaming with an innocence that felt like a balm to my frayed nerves.

I sank onto a cushion, my thoughts swirling. "I haven't even figured out how to properly feed you yet," I mused aloud, watching as Windy tilted its head as if trying to understand. "And now I've got this whole mess with the Wind Serpent Beast Core to deal with."

The mention of the Beast Core reminded me of its presence in my pocket. I reached in and pulled it out, the pulsating energy causing Windy to perk up immediately. As I held it in my palm, the hatchling slithered closer, its small body circling the core with an unmistakable eagerness.

I frowned, realization dawning on me. "This . . . This is the remnant of your parents, isn't it, Windy?" The thought made my heart clench.

As I moved to put the core away, Windy's reaction surprised me. It nuzzled against the core, wrapping itself around it protectively. "You . . . you want to keep it close?" I asked, my voice softening.

Observing Windy's attachment to the core, a theory began to form in my mind. "Is this why you've been so docile and obedient?" I pondered. "Because I've been handling the Beast Core?"

Windy seemed to hum in agreement, its small form vibrating slightly against the core.

I was a link to its past, a connection to what it had lost.

I knew that death was an inevitable part of life. But being the direct cause of their deaths gave me a sense of obligation to raise Windy. In a way, we bore similar pasts. The only minor, negligible difference is that I'm human and Windy's a magical snake that'll grow up to be the size of a small hut.

I sat there for a long time, Windy curled up beside me, the Beast Core a silent witness to our shared moment. In the quiet of the room, my thoughts turned to the upcoming dual trial. The weight of expectation, the pressure to succeed, the fear of failure—they all loomed over me like an impending storm.

But as I looked down at Windy, its serene presence a contrast to my turbulent thoughts, I felt a sense of calm settle over me. Here was a creature that had lost everything, yet found a way to trust and connect with someone new. If Windy could find the strength to move forward, then so could I.

"I won't let you down, Windy," I whispered, more to myself than to the hatchling. "I'll face this challenge head-on. For both of us."

Tianyi fluttered onto my nose, smacking me with her wings several times.

"Sorry, Tianyi. I meant for all of us."

I summoned the interface into view. There were no changes.

I stared at the screen, my mind racing with questions. The Heavenly Interface had shown itself during my encounter with Elder Jun, guiding my words and actions. But why now? Was it because I was in over my head? Or was it something more, a deeper connection to the interface itself? The lack of information in regard to my Interface Manipulator perk frustrated me. I shrugged off the confusion, deciding there were more pressing matters at hand. It was time to focus on the trial.

"Heavenly Interface, you're a fickle friend," I muttered, shaking my head. "One moment, you're my guiding star, and the next, you're as silent as a mouse."

I leaned back, letting my gaze drift to Tianyi and Windy. "Guys, we've got a big challenge ahead."

Tianyi glowed slightly, fluttering around me as if to offer encouragement. Windy, sensing the change in atmosphere, slithered up to my lap, its scales cool and comforting against my skin.

"All right, let's think this through." I tapped my chin, pondering my options. "A third-class disciple from the Silent Moon Sect . . . They'll be strong, fast, and probably skilled in combat. And here I am, an herbalist with a defensive stance that's barely off the ground."

I chuckled, the absurdity of the situation not lost on me. "Well, at least I won't be bored."

Glancing at my skills, I focused on my strengths. "Okay, Rooted Banyan Stance is all about defense, stability, and endurance. It's not much, but it's something. If I can't outfight them, maybe I can outlast them?"

I contemplated the idea, playing out scenarios in my head. "But endurance alone won't win me this trial. I'd run out of qi and break something important. I need to land a hit, a solid one. And for that, I need an edge."

That's when the idea struck me. "Potions and pills! Why didn't I think of it sooner? If I can't increase my natural abilities, I can at least boost them temporarily. Just like I did against the Wind Serpents."

Tianyi buzzed around my head, as if questioning the feasibility of my plan. "Don't worry, Tianyi, I'm not planning on going overboard. Just a little . . . enhancement."

I sat cross-legged, entering the Memory Palace within my mind filled with notes and sketches of herbs and concoctions.

Let's see . . . Something for strength, agility, maybe a bit of qi enhancement? After a few minutes, I stood up and scribbled down a list of ingredients.

Windy watched with keen eyes, its head tilting from side to side as I scribbled down ideas. They'd need to be the more esoteric ingredients if I wanted something substantial for its effects. "What do you think, Windy? A blend of ginseng and Moonshadow Petal for strength? Oh, and maybe a dash of Starlight Dew for that extra kick."

The serpent seemed to nod in agreement, its small body coiling around my arm.

"All right, it's settled, then." I clapped my hands together, a plan forming in my mind. "I'll split my time between martial arts training and brewing up a storm in the alchemy lab. It's going to be tough, but hey, what's life without a little challenge?"

I stood up, stretching my arms above my head. "First thing tomorrow, training begins. I'll start with class in the morning, and head out to do whatever training the elders set out for me."

Tianyi perched on my shoulder, her presence a constant source of comfort. "Don't worry, Tianyi, I'll be careful. Can't have our resident worrywart fluttering into a frenzy, can we?"

I couldn't help but smile, the daunting task ahead somehow seems a little less intimidating with Tianyi and Windy by my side.

"All right, team," I said, my voice filled with a newfound determination. "Let's show the Silent Moon Sect what a humble herbalist can do. It's not going to be easy, but we're in this together. I'll get a head start and do some training of my own."

With that, I grabbed my iron staff and set out, the sound of Tianyi's wings and Windy's gentle hissing following me into the night. The path ahead was uncertain, filled with challenges and unknowns, but one thing was clear: I wasn't going to face it alone.

The Alchemy Pavilion

I had always been more swift than strong, a whisper of wind in the training yard, where the thud of fists and the clash of steel were the chorus of the day. My fellow disciples towered like sturdy pines while I, a willow, bent and flickered in their shadows. Each day was a test of mettle I seemed destined to fail.

"Disciple Zhu, your strikes must have the force of a tempest, not the tickle of a breeze," Instructor Liang chided, though not unkindly. His eyes held the glint of hope, but I knew better. In the realm of martial prowess, I was a faltering step behind—a second-class disciple in title and in truth.

Yet, amid the symphony of clashing titans, my spirit refused to dim. Each night, as I nursed my bruises, the moon's silver gaze seemed to whisper of hidden strengths, of winds that carved canyons not through force, but persistence. In those quiet moments, I dared to dream of a different path.

The Verdant Lotus Sect valued swiftness and grace, but my body held neither. My strikes, fleet and precise, lacked the finality of power. Our techniques, dancing on the edge of the wind, were lost on me—I could not break a single wooden block in demonstration, while my peers shattered stacks with thunderous roars.

They called me Bamboo Zhu, a joke that poked fun at my swaying frame, thin and hollow as the bamboo that dotted our sect grounds. I knew their mockery bore the sting of truth; I was frail, my pale skin a canvas for blue-green veins, my eyes sunken with the weight of exhaustion no amount of meditation could lift.

Instructor Liang often scolded the others, his voice a crack of lightning across the yard. "Enough! The path of cultivation is unique to each disciple. Mockery is a stone in your own garden, not his," he would say, but the damage, like a bruise on soft fruit, remained.

It was on one such afternoon, after a particularly grueling spar that left me gasping on the ground, my spirit as bruised as my body, that I made my way to the alchemy pavilion. The scent of herbs and the warm hum of brewing potions were a balm to my churning thoughts. Here, perhaps, I could find the tonic to bolster my constitution, a secret brew to infuse my limbs with the strength they so desperately lacked.

The alchemy pavilion stood as a testament to the legacy of the Verdant Lotus Sect, a beacon for those who sought to intertwine their spirit with the elements through the delicate art of potion-making. I had taken beginner classes there as a third-class disciple, learning the basics of herb identification and the rudimentary concoctions that served as the foundation for any budding alchemist. Yet, I never progressed beyond those initial lessons. My interest waned like the moon's crescent—partial, fleeting, never reaching its full glow.

To me, the pavilion had always been a place of quiet introspection, a sanctuary for the mind rather than the spirit. It did not resonate with my yearning for the prestige of a cultivator who could bring the world to heel with his techniques. In the eyes of a young disciple hungry for acclaim, the subtleties of alchemy did not compare to the overt display of martial might.

As I opened the door, my eyes saw past the rows of neatly arranged vials and the meticulously labeled drawers. A voice within me whispered of the pavilion's rich history—the myriad elixirs that had turned the tides of battle, the poultices that had closed wounds which would have otherwise been mortal, and the essences that had bolstered our warriors' qi beyond that of our rivals. Yet these whispers of greatness did not stir my heart as they once might have. The pavilion's contribution to the sect's renown was undoubted, but what use were salves and tinctures to a disciple who wished to be the storm, not the calm after?

The air within the pavilion was thick with the fragrance of rare herbs and the warmth of simmering cauldrons. Crystal vials filled with swirling nebulas of color adorned the walls, their contents glittering under the soft glow of alchemical lamps. The room buzzed with the latent power of creation, as if the very stones and mortar were impregnated with the essence of countless experiments and discoveries.

The pavilion was quiet, save for the gentle clink of glass and the murmur of incantations. First-class disciples, robed in the deep green of the lotus leaf, moved with an alchemist's precision, their hands weaving through the air as if conducting an orchestra of elemental forces.

I hesitated at the threshold, the nickname "Bamboo Zhu" echoing in my ears. What if my weakness was as transparent here as it was in the yard? Shaking off the doubt, I stepped inside, my eyes scanning the shelves lined with jars of starlight dew and moonflower essence. A disciple with hair like raven's wings caught my eye, her fingers deftly coaxing a green flame beneath her pill furnace.

I approached, my voice barely above a whisper, carried away by the draft through the open windows. "Excuse me, I—"

She turned, her gaze locking with mine, and the world stilled. Her beauty was not the delicate kind that withers at the first sign of hardship; it was the bloom of the desert cactus, rare and resilient.

"Can I help you?" she asked, her voice the melody of spring's first thaw.

I swallowed, my prepared speech lost to the wind.

I opened my mouth to ask for the elixir I had envisioned on my weary walk here, the one that would harden my sinews and grant me the might of those sturdier disciples. But in her presence, all my words crumbled to dust.

"An elixir," I started, my voice trailing off as I struggled to encapsulate my needs in a sentence that wouldn't betray the desperation clawing inside. "I mean, I was wondering if . . . um, the properties of . . . That is to say . . . how do the essences blend?"

It was a poor deflection, a question pulled from the thin air that I hoped sounded intelligent enough. Her eyes, a shade reminiscent of the twilight sky, narrowed slightly—not in suspicion, but with a discerning curiosity.

"You're Bamboo Zhu, right?" she inquired, the corners of her lips curling into a smile that could set the horizon ablaze.

I nodded, my cheeks warming under her gaze. It was evident she had heard of me, probably not in the ways one would wish.

"If it's strength you're seeking, there's no potion that can replace the diligence of practice," she said, returning her attention to the beaker. "But if you have an interest in alchemy . . ." She paused, a silent invitation hanging between us.

My eyes followed her hands, those adept fingers moving with a grace I could only aspire to match in my martial forms. "I do," I confessed, a truth I hadn't realized was mine until that moment. "But I'm not sure where to begin."

She placed the beaker down and wiped her hands on her robe, considering my words. "Watch then, if you'd like."

It was then that she shrugged, a gesture that dismissed my failed attempt at discussing tonics and signaled the end of our exchange. With a flick of her wrist, she beckoned me to a nearby bench, laden with vials and alembics, before moving away to attend to her tasks.

Left to my own devices, I felt a mixture of relief and disappointment. I had hoped for some guidance, a direction, perhaps a bit of sympathy. Instead, I found myself alone amid the clinking of glass and the soft glow of enchantments. It was then that I noticed her, Mei, moving with assured steps between the rows of elixirs.

Our meetings grew frequent, woven into the fabric of our daily routines. Mei never spoke much of her past, but the stories she shared were windows into her world—a childhood spent in the outer fringes of Crescent Bay City, where the wilds were an extension of her living canvas, and a family lineage steeped in the ancient dance of elements. She was her own character, strong and sure, with ambitions that stretched beyond the pavilion's walls. Her confidence was infectious, and her presence grounding, reminding me that there was strength in stillness, power in patience.

As weeks turned into months, my visits to the pavilion became my refuge, with Mei's guidance illuminating the once-daunting processes. "This isn't merely a mixture; it's a harmony," Mei explained one day as we examined the subtle reaction of herbs under a gentle flame. "Just like your needlework in combat, Zhu."

Her words wove the fabric of our sessions together, threading my past with my present.

Mei was unlike any in the sect—her stature was not imposing, but her presence was indomitable. As she worked, her hands performed a ballet of exactness and care, coaxing the essence of herbs into potent draughts. Her beauty was a silent force, the kind that did not boast but simply was.

I watched, rapt, as she crushed a petal that bled sunlight into a basin. "You have a fine touch, Mei," I said, the words slipping from me with an ease I did not expect in my nervous state.

Mei glanced over her shoulder, a strand of hair falling across her face. "Observation is the first step in alchemy," she noted. "To see is to begin to understand."

"Is that how you started?" I asked, inching closer, my interest piqued beyond the simple crush I realized was the initial draw.

She nodded, brushing the hair back into place. "That, and the realization that while I may never be the strongest in combat, my strength lies here. In combining them, I found my place in the sect."

Her words struck a chord within me, a resonance of longing and the dawning of possibility. I had spent so long fixating on a strength that was not mine to have, ignoring the potential of what lay at my fingertips.

"I think I'd like to learn, if you would teach me," I said, the declaration setting a new course for my life as surely as a river carving its path through stone.

In the weeks that followed, Mei officially became my mentor. I joined the ranks of the alchemy pavilion as a part-time student. Her patience was a testament to her character, never faltering as I fumbled with measurements and mixed essences with the same cautious precision I used to thread needles for my martial arts training. She taught me that the same focus that guided my hand in a needle's strike could ascertain the delicate balance required in a volatile concoction.

As the seasons changed, so did the nature of our conversations. Mei's tutelage revealed her depth; she was as much a philosopher as she was an alchemist. Her guidance was subtle, a suggestion here, a nudge there, never overt but always present. She shared her insights into the alchemical arts with the same generosity she afforded her knowledge of life's myriad complexities. In her company, I learned the value of silence and the richness of listening—not just to the words spoken but to nature's ceaseless hum that others so easily ignored.

The martial arts I practiced now were of a different nature. The movements were smaller but no less significant—the turn of a vial, the gentle pour of a liquid, the steady hold of a flame. Each gesture was an echo of combat, a fight against the chaos of uncontrolled reactions, a dance of elements at my command.

And so, my days were split between the alchemy pavilion and the training yard, where I still attended to my duties, albeit with a new perspective. My martial artistry improved with my alchemy, the precision of my strikes becoming more lethal as I applied the finesse of my trade to the art of the needle.

I was no longer just Bamboo Zhu. I was Zhu, the alchemist, who wove spells of healing and harm with the same hands that once could not break a wooden block. My pale skin now held a luster from the countless hours spent under the moon, brewing and learning, and my eyes, once sunken, gleamed with the vigor of newfound purpose.

Time passed with the rhythm of a slow drip of an elixir, marking not just the seasons but the unfolding of a destiny once clouded by my own narrow aspirations.

Instructor Liang's words became a distant echo; my hands, once shaky with the weight of a sword too heavy, now held the delicate balance of life and transformation within glass vials. My old nickname, "Bamboo Zhu," shed its derisive skin to become a badge of honor. It wasn't long before I saw the humor in it myself—the bamboo is resilient, bending in the storm but rarely breaking, and so it was with me.

I learned to laugh, a sound I once thought was for those carefree spirits who had not tasted the bitterness of defeat. But as I mixed and melded, as my concoctions began to take on the life I willed them to, the irony wasn't lost on me that the very hands deemed too weak for a warrior's blade were praised for their steady pour and the precise grind of a pestle.

It was in this lighthearted revelation that I began to truly excel. I stopped seeing my past pursuits in martial arts as a quest for fame and realized that the real mastery lay in the joy of the process, not the accolades. I learned that the most profound strength sprang from the well of our own joy and the pursuit of our true calling.

With every sunrise, my mastery over alchemy deepened. My reputation as an alchemist soared as high as the martial banners of the strongest fighters in our sect. Disciples and masters alike sought my advice, not for the breaking of bodies but for the mending of them, for the bolstering of their inner strength, and for the subtle edge in battle.

As I mastered the alchemy under her watchful eye, I saw Mei not just as a mentor or the object of my youthful affection, but as a pillar of the pavilion—a force that drove innovation and excellence. She was respected and admired, her contributions invaluable. And in those quiet moments, when the moon hung low and our laughter mingled with the clinking of glass, I saw the measure of her true impact—on the pavilion, on the sect, and indelibly, on me.

"And that, my students, is the essence of true power," I would tell them, my words a bridge from my experiences to their understanding. Mei would nod, her agreement unspoken but felt, a silent partnership in teaching the next generation of alchemists.

I began to teach, sharing the lessons of the alchemy that had embraced me. Mei, who had become an instructor earlier than I had, helped me refine my lessons, to make it easier to understand. My classes were filled with laughter and carefree challenges that mirrored the very essence of growth that our sect worshipped. The alchemy pavilion, under our care, became a place of wonder, where the intertwining of elements echoed the harmony I had sought all along in martial arts.

Years spun by, marked not by the changing of seasons but by the successes of my students and the evolution of my techniques. I rose through the ranks, from a mere disciple to the head of the alchemy pavilion, not just for my skills but for my ability to inspire.

Alchemy became my solace and the pavilion my sanctuary. As my skill in the art grew, so did my reputation, and with it, the company I kept. Mei was no longer the unreachable star in my night sky but the guiding light in my alchemical studies. We worked side by side, her laughter like chimes in the wind, becoming the rhythm to my day. Our relationship blossomed quietly, like the rarest of lotus flowers that unfurl their petals to the moon, hidden from the prying eyes of day.

It was amid flasks and beakers that I found my identity, the clear purpose that had eluded me in the shadow of stronger martial artists. Mei's tutelage was a testament to patience, each lesson she imparted was a step away from my past insecurities toward a future bright with potential. I no longer saw her through the haze of a lovestruck disciple but as a treasured colleague, an equal in our shared passion for alchemy. Though our hearts may have woven a more intimate tale through the years, it was a story for another time.

Today, standing before a new generation of disciples, I was a testament to the sect's teaching that every path was sacred, every discipline intertwined. The verdant robes I wore were a far cry from the unsure novice who could barely hold his own in the sparring ring. Now they spoke of my journey through the ranks, of the respect I'd earned and the knowledge I'd accrued.

"Understand this," I told the sea of young faces before me. "In the pursuit of mastery, you must let go of the rigid constraints of identity you cling to. The Verdant Lotus teaches us the fluidity of roles, the harmony of nature's elements, and the adaptability of the human spirit."

Some nodded, their eyes gleaming with the fire of ambition, while others shuffled, their gazes still tethered to the ground, unseeing of the broader horizon

I laid before them. To those, I offered a demonstration, a display that might ignite the waning embers of their concentration.

With a fluid motion, I drew from my belt a set of silver needles, their slender forms catching the light of the setting sun streaming through the pavilion's open arches. A hush fell over the courtyard as I took my stance, the wind my silent partner in this dance of precision and control.

I began slowly, each needle twirling between my fingers, an extension of my will. My audience was rapt as the needles flew, not with the wild abandon of a brawler but with the deliberate intent of an alchemist. Each movement was a calculation, the culmination of years spent balancing the scales of ingredients to the exact grain.

I sent a needle spinning into the air, where it caught the light, a glinting star before it found its home in the targeted center of a wooden dummy. Another followed, a whisper of motion that left only the faintest trail of silver, embedding itself with a soft thud into the dummy's outstretched arm.

I finished with a flourish, a needle held between each finger, my arms extended in an embrace of the world's unseen energies. "The alchemist's touch," I said, my voice steady, "is not so different from the martial artist's strike. Both require an understanding of force, flow, and the delicate balance between."

I stepped back, the needles now a constellation of precision on the straw form. The bored expressions had given way to awe, and I saw the shift in their stance, a dawning respect not just for me but for the lesson I embodied.

"Today, I stand before you as Elder Zhu, but once, I was as you are now. A seeker of strength in the wrong places, blind to the versatility of my own gifts. It was through alchemy that I discovered my true strength, and in its practice, I found not only my calling but the full expression of my martial prowess."

I paused, letting my words sink in, allowing them to find root in their youthful minds. "Do not despair if the path you walk takes unexpected turns. Embrace the journey, for it is in the walking that we find our way."

The setting sun cast long shadows over the pavilion, and in this golden hour, I left the disciples with a final thought. "Your path is not a road laid before you but a tapestry you weave with the threads of your talents and desires. Let neither falter, for in their union lies the true art of the Verdant Lotus Sect."

As the class dispersed, a few lingered curiously, their ambitions kindled. They approached, seeking guidance, and I welcomed them, ready to mentor as I was once mentored, for in each of them, I saw reflections of myself, the echo of the past, and the promise of the sect's future. And as the moon rose to kiss the night, I turned my steps back to the pavilion, to the cauldron and the flame, where my life as an alchemist continued to unfold.

Acknowledgments

Blossoming Path was an idea that began in a hotel lobby café, where I decided to sit down and tinker with the idea of combining two genres I enjoyed the most: LitRPG and Xianxia. It was easy enough to think of the first few chapters and the gist of how the story would go, but completing it? That was an entirely different tin of sardines. I experienced a tumult of life-changing experiences during the making of this book, and *Blossoming Path* was the one constant in my life that I began to appreciate. To paraphrase Childish Gambino, writing was my side chick, but now we're moving in together. This hasn't really happened yet, but nevertheless, I strive for the day that I can make it happen.

I'd like to thank everyone who helped me get this far, and all of whom I owe an unimaginable debt to.

To my mom, Ellen, who managed to convince me that being an author was the one-way ticket to wealth and financial stability instead of pursuing a stable office job. Usually it's the other way around.

To my sister and brother-in-law, Alena and Jack, for helping me find my groove and reignite my passion for writing.

To Amanda, for her endless flow of positivity and encouragement, as well as her expertise in Chinese culture so I didn't misrepresent the Xianxia genre.

To Steven, for helping me navigate unfamiliar territory with contracts, negotiations, and general advice.

To Kian and Ben, who taught me about the value of putting your head down and getting work done, as well as health advice to save me from tendonitis and carpal tunnel. I would have the hands of a sixty-year-old that would snap and pop like a Rice Krispie Treat without it.

There are probably a thousand people who I need to thank while I'm at it, but this is all I can remember at this point.

About the Author

Carlos Calma is a Canadian author who has been captivated by LitRPG and progression fantasy since he was young. He began reading these genres as a child and started writing his own stories while in high school. This passion has continued into his adult life. Calma resides in Toronto, Ontario.

Podium

DISCOVER MORE

STORIES UNBOUND

PodiumEntertainment.com

www.ingramcontent.com/pod-product-compliance
Lightning Source LLC
Jackson TN
JSHW022255210325
81251JS00001B/5